"We all have our top ten list of favorite romances. It has been forever since I have read something that enthralled me enough to add to my list. The book must be unique, something that resonates with me on an elemental level; it must have a beautiful storyline, intense passion, and unforgettable characters. *Pippa and the Prince of Secrets* checks all those boxes." -*Reading Rebel Reviews*

"I LOVE a hero that is from the streets like Cull. Gives me Derek Craven vibes." -Nancy, *Goodreads*

"A very hot and perfectly paced page turner, all the way to happily ever after." -*NPR*

"This re-telling of a Beauty and the Beast love story focusing on tender acceptance and loving empowerment is heart-stopping. Mixed in are a dangerous mystery and charismatic secondary characters. The power of the love between the couple isn't something you read every day; this includes the exquisite physicality of the novel. The story stirred my emotions and delighted my imagination." -Jenna, *BookBub*

"Get out the high velocity fan because you will need it while reading this story. It is hotter than hot, I am not kidding. I love a tortured hero and if you do also, then grab this story right away...I love how Grace can pull you into the story of these characters and make you feel as if you are there with them. I was totally enthralled with reading, and I swear I felt as if I was in their dilemma. Astounding storytelling."-Angela, *Goodreads*

"Olivia and Ben are so wonderful together. It is rare to find a match where the H & h share such a deep bond.... This book has it all—lead characters you truly love, fabulous side characters, murder, mystery, action, and a generous helping of steam and romance!" -Nazmin, *Goodreads*

"Despite the age gap, Ben and Livy's friendship is so natural. Their friendship never feels awkward and the transition from friends to lovers is done tastefully (and steamily). Grace Callaway is always reliable when it comes to writing romances that are both romantic and steamy." -*Romance Library*

"An exciting rollercoaster of a love story! This book delivers on a variety of levels. A slow burn, friends to lovers story. The plot is intricate, intimate, and all consuming. The couple's passion burns through the pages." -*Jenna's Historical Romance Blog*

PRAISE FOR OTHER BOOKS BY GRACE

"Readers looking for a good historical mystery/romance or a historical with a little more kink will enjoy *The Duke Who Knew Too Much*." -*Smart Bitches, Trashy Books*

"Grace Callaway writes the way Loretta Chase would if she got kind of dark and VERY naughty." -Nicole, *Goodreads*

"Fairy tale meets Eliza Doolittle. Grace Callaway saves the best Duke book for the end of the series. It was hot, steamy, and warm-hearted." -Stacy, *Goodreads*

"Can a fairytale be sweet, funny, touching, action packed and super hot all at the same time? Yes. This series ender is all that and more. This book is like the fireworks display to end a spectacular series." -Joanne, *Goodreads*

"I have read hundreds and hundreds of different authors over the past five years but actually only have a handful of all time favorites. I have to say Grace Callaway is by far one of those favorites.... Her characters have so much depth and you just feel like you are a part of their story...You can never go wrong by picking up any of her books but be prepared...you will love them so much you will buy every book she has." -Pam, *Goodreads*

"I've now read each of Grace Callaway's books and loved them— which is exceptional. Gabriel and Thea from this book were two of the best characters I read this year. Both had their difficulties and it was charming to see how they overcame them together, even though it wasn't always easy for them. [*M is for Marquess*] is my favorite book of 2015." -*Romantic Historical Reviews*

"Has everything that makes a tale excellent; a headstrong lovely heroine, a damaged too serious hero, a rowdy bunch of loving family members that are living and close and then the amazing adventure to peel back like an onion to find the many layers of the plot. This writer to me is in the leagues of Johanna Lindsey, Lisa Kleypas, Julia Quinn and Amanda Quick." -Kathie, *Amazon*

"Callaway is a talented writer and as skilled at creating a vivid sense of the Regency period as she is at writing some of the best, most sensual love scenes I've read in a long while." -*Night Owl Reviews*

"Grace Callaway is becoming one of my all-time favorite authors. The Kents remind me so much of the Mallory-Anderson saga from Johanna Lindsay or the Spy series from Julie Garwood. I've read those books so many times and now I find myself rereading Grace's books." -Vivian, *Amazon*

Also by Grace Callaway

LADY CHARLOTTE'S SOCIETY OF ANGELS

Olivia and the Masked Duke

Pippa and the Prince of Secrets

Fiona and the Enigmatic Earl

Glory and the Master of Shadows (Spring 2023)

GAME OF DUKES

The Duke Identity

Enter the Duke

Regarding the Duke

The Duke Redemption

The Return of the Duke

Steamy Winter Wishes

HEART OF ENQUIRY (The Kents)

The Widow Vanishes (Prequel Novella)

The Duke Who Knew Too Much

M is for Marquess

The Lady Who Came in from the Cold

The Viscount Always Knocks Twice

Never Say Never to an Earl

The Gentleman Who Loved Me

MAYHEM IN MAYFAIR

Her Husband's Harlot

Her Wanton Wager

Her Protector's Pleasure

Her Prodigal Passion

CHRONICLES OF ABIGAIL

Abigail Jones

Fiona
AND THE
ENIGMATIC EARL

Lady Charlotte's
SOCIETY *of* ANGELS

GRACE CALLAWAY

USA Today Bestselling Author

Cover Art Credit: EDH Graphics

Typography & Book Design: KM Designs

To thine own self be true.

-from *Hamlet* by William Shakespeare

PROLOGUE

LONDON, ENGLAND

It is a truth universally acknowledged that a well-bred debutante should not go skulking around a strange gentleman's bedchamber. Being intelligent and pragmatic, Miss Fiona Garrity was aware of this fact. At nineteen, she had been deemed an "Incomparable" by Society and had a queue of suitors vying for her hand. Yet she yearned for more than social success.

She wanted freedom and adventure. A life lived to its fullest.

Luckily, she'd found an outlet for her independent spirit. Two years ago, she and her bosom friends, Ladies Olivia "Livy" Wodehouse and Glory Cavendish, had joined a secret society. Founded by Lady Charlotte Fayne, the Society of Angels was, on the surface, a genteel charity; the true purpose of the organization, however, was to conduct investigations on behalf of women in need. Although leading a double life was challenging—it was no small feat to pull the wool over her parents' eyes—Fiona adored investigating. It gave her meaning and purpose and fulfilled her craving for excitement.

Hence her presence at Count von Essen's house party this eve. An infamous roué, von Essen was blackmailing the Angels' latest client, Emily Fisher. Mrs. Fisher was a wealthy widow who'd inherited her husband's modest bakeshop and transformed it into Fisher's Fine Foods, a thriving company that produced delicacies enjoyed by London's elite. Mrs. Fisher had been on the cusp of receiving a royal warrant when disaster struck.

"Count von Essen has obtained private letters that I wrote to a former lover, and he is demanding that I pay him for his silence." A handsome blonde in her fifties, Mrs. Fisher's voice had trembled during her interview with Lady Charlotte. *"Not only do these letters contain details of an exceedingly intimate nature, but my lover was an employee and younger than me by some twenty years. If news of this gets out, I, and my company, will be ruined. You are my last hope. Will you help me?"*

The Angels had planned their strategy accordingly. This evening, von Essen was hosting a private masquerade at his town house, and the place was teeming with light-skirts. This allowed Fiona and Livy, her partner for the mission, to infiltrate the count's domain disguised as trollops. Their identities concealed by wigs, heavy paint, and demi-masks, the pair had navigated the party incognito.

At present, Livy was downstairs searching the study while Fi made her way up to von Essen's bedchamber. Dressed as an Ancient Egyptian queen in a tunic that required no unmentionables, Fi moved with easy stealth. Her sandaled feet whispered over the carpeted corridor as she headed for the master suite.

Taking a quick glance around, she tried the knob. Locked...not surprising given the disreputable crowd downstairs and the secrets her host undoubtedly had to hide. Plucking a pair of hairpins from her raven-black wig, she gained swift entry. The bedchamber was dim, the fire in the hearth casting shadows over the ruby damask walls. A large tester bed sat to the left, facing a pair of windows covered by voluminous velvet drapes. To the right, she spotted what she was looking for.

She hurried over to the kidney-shaped desk. The flickering lamp on its surface burnished the walnut burl and the gold frame of the landscape on the wall behind it. Fi jiggled the drawers; they didn't budge.

Crouching, she employed her hairpins again. She rifled through the drawers, finding no letters. She emptied the contents of the deepest drawer, tapping her knuckles against the bottom; the hollow sound verified her suspicions. Running her fingertips along the edges, she found the hidden latch that released the false bottom. Inside the hidden compartment lay a bundle of letters.

With a feeling of triumph, Fi lifted out the stack. There were six letters, just as Mrs. Fisher had described. To verify that they belonged to the client, Fi unfolded the top note.

My darling master,

I have dreamt of you since our last meeting. Never has anyone taken hold of my imagination so completely. In the world's eyes, I am a strong and practical matron; in your arms, I become the weakest of wantons. I long for your dominance, for the sting of your whip upon my naughty bottom, for the discipline of your mighty manhood where I need it most. I yearn to prove my obedience, to worship you upon my knees. I count the days, hours, and minutes until I can service you again.

Your adoring,
 Emily

Sweet heavens. The wickedness made Fi's heartbeat gallop; her cheeks were so hot she feared her face paint might melt off. *No wonder Mrs. Fisher wants these letters back.*

Shoving the bundle into the hidden pocket of her tunic, Fi was about to leave when a faint scraping noise made her freeze. The sound of a window opening? Fi peered over the desk and saw a large male figure emerge from the curtains. Diving into the cove beneath the desk, she pressed her back against the wood, making herself as small as possible.

Her blood rushed in her ears. *Do not panic. Keep your head clear.*

If necessary, Fi could fight her way out of the room, but the last thing she wanted was exposure. She'd secured the client's letters. What she needed now was a clean exit.

She listened for the intruder; whoever he was, he possessed astonishing stealth. She couldn't hear him at all, yet she *sensed* his presence. As if he was silently...waiting. The hairs stirred on her nape, and she strove to quiet her breathing. A pair of large black shoes and long trousered legs materialized in front of her.

Is he going to see me? Quivering, she braced for discovery.

Instead, the man turned and faced the wall behind the desk. From her vantage point, Fi couldn't see what he was doing, but she pictured the landscape painting that hung in his line of vision. Was he trying to steal it? When she heard a click and faint squeal of hinges, it dawned upon her.

There is something concealed behind the painting. An iron box, perhaps?

Her conclusion was corroborated by the unmistakable sounds of a lock being picked. And by no amateur, either; the man knew what he was about. In less than a minute, she heard the release of a locking mechanism, followed by sounds of careful rummaging.

What was the thief—for there was no question that that was the man's occupation—looking for? Jewels, gold, something even more interesting? It took all of Fi's willpower to resist curiosity's pull. To not sneak a peek at the thief at work.

Stay put. He will be done soon. Then you can leave.

It was a pity that she would end her adventure without

seeing the rogue. She had never met a professional burglar before; she wondered what this one looked like. Judging from his lower extremities, he was tall and lean. His dark trousers had a perfect fit, his shoes a buffed-to-perfection shine. She would wager her favorite pair of gloves that his tailoring came from Bond Street—

A quiet thud and muttered oath interrupted her musing. Her eyes widened at the sight of the lock pick that had fallen on the carpet just inches away from her hiding spot. Her heart lurched into her ribs as the thief bent to pick it up.

Dear God, please don't let him look under the desk.

The man turned his head. Framed by a black demi-mask, his gaze met hers. She saw his quicksilver surprise, which vanished the next instant.

"*Bonsoir, mademoiselle,*" he said calmly. "May I offer some assistance?"

His accent was French. Was he a recent *émigré*? Whatever he was, he seemed civilized for a man of his trade. Her training kicking in, she assessed the situation: was it best to finesse, fight, or flee? She decided upon the first option, which was her forte. Her success as a debutante rested in no small part on her ability to brazen her way through anything.

"Why, thank ye, sir." She adopted a cockney accent and a trollop's easy manner. Taking his hand, she rose as gracefully as one could from beneath a desk. "What a gentleman ye are."

He had the look of one, anyway. While the mask and dimness obscured his features, he wore his fine evening wear as if he'd been born to do so, the stark lines immaculately fitted to his virile frame. A thick blond wave swept over his brow. As he swept a gaze of an indeterminable hue over her, she felt an odd shiver.

"Did you find what you were looking for?" he queried.

Dash it all. Does he know my true purpose?

She flashed a smile meant to disarm. "Wot do ye mean, 'andsome?"

"Beneath the desk. That is, I presume, what you were doing there."

Right. Relieved, she improvised. "Silly me, I dropped my earbob, and it fell under the desk. Now that I've retrieved it"—she tapped the gold, boat-shaped earring dangling from her left ear— "I'd best be on me way."

She turned to go; the thief closed a hand around her wrist. His touch was firm yet not forceful. If he had manhandled her or acted brutishly, she would have employed defensive maneuvers. Yet the aim of his hold seemed less to detain her and more to take her measure.

The quivery sensation in her belly grew. She reminded herself to play her role.

She batted her soot-coated lashes at him. "Be ye wanting somefing, sir?"

He swept another glance over her, and she had the alarming thought that he could somehow see through her disguise. Yet that was impossible. Her celebrated flame-red hair was tucked beneath the coarse black wig, her face obscured by her gold mask and layers of paint. In the dimness, no one would look at the scantily clad tart and see Miss Fiona Garrity, virginal heiress.

The thief pulled her closer to him. So close that only a sliver of space separated them. The tiny gap felt charged, like the sky before a storm. An invisible feather teased the curve of her throat, the throbbing tips of her breasts, and lower still. She squeezed her thighs together against a startling pulse of excitement. No man had ever affected her in this way before.

Nonetheless, she kept her head tilted back, maintaining eye contact. Her role was that of a seasoned hussy. She would not be the first to look away.

"What I want to know is this, *mademoiselle.*" He bent his head, his words brushing her lips as tenderly as a kiss. "Are you good at keeping secrets?"

As an Angel, she kept plenty of secrets. Including from her

own family. Leading a double life was, in truth, the biggest challenge of being an agent.

"Keeping secrets is me job," she said honestly.

"*Bien,*" he murmured after a pause. "A woman after my own heart."

Her own organ thumped with a wild and reckless recognition. Her gaze darted to his mouth, the stern yet somehow sensual curve. Was he going to kiss her?

Heavens, do I want him to?

She had a feeling that this stranger's kiss would be nothing like the chaste pecks she'd experienced. Her intuition told her that this man would make love the way he made his living. In a wicked and masterful fashion.

To her surprise, and ever so slight disappointment, he released her.

"You are free to go," he said.

She wetted her lips; her limbs refused to move. What was wrong with her? She felt as giddy as if she'd been imbibing champagne and whirling around the dance floor for hours.

"Unless, *chérie,* you would prefer to stay?"

The dark invitation in his voice snapped her back to her senses.

"Afraid I've a prior engagement, luv." Her regret was not entirely feigned. "A working girl 'as to earn 'er keep."

And a debutante cannot dally with a thief, no matter how dashing he is.

"My loss." He kissed her hand with gallant flair. "*Adieu, mademoiselle.*"

Bemused by her swoony reaction, she turned toward the door...and saw it opening. As she froze, an arm hooked her waist from behind. A heartbeat later, she was lying on her back atop the desk. With one large hand, the thief manacled both of hers above her head. Stretched helplessly beneath him, she felt a shock of heat low in her belly.

His lips found her ear, his command soft and urgent. "Moan like you're about to come."

Simultaneously, she registered that his French accent had slipped a notch and that he was proposing a charade. Although she was a virgin, she was not uninformed and understood what he wanted her to do. She summoned a breathy cry that had a genuine ring. For the thief was kissing her neck, his lips as hot as a brand. As his mouth coursed along the sensitive column, her breasts rubbed against his muscular chest, setting off sparks of pleasure. He roved up to her ear again, suckling the lobe, and she squirmed with irresistible need.

When he wedged a thigh between her legs, another moan broke from her lips. Her private place had grown startlingly wet and rubbing against that sinewy trunk made her even wetter. She couldn't help seeking more of that wicked friction, arching her hips against him. He grunted, and she felt a poker-like object prodding her thigh.

"Ahem," a male voice said. "Are we interrupting anything?"

Dear God. Turning her head on the desk, Fiona saw Count von Essen advancing toward them with a doxy on his arm. Fi had nearly forgotten the reason for the stratagem...that it was a stratagem at all.

The thief straightened. Sneaking a glance at him, Fiona felt a flutter when she saw the substantial bulge at the front of his trousers. He was a splendid actor, evincing flawless surprise as he bowed to the newcomers.

"*Pardon,*" he said. "I did not realize we had company."

Von Essen harrumphed. "As this is my bedchamber, I did not think it necessary to knock."

His black mask accentuating his bloated jowls, the count darted a glance at the painting that hid his secrets. Luckily, the thief was meticulous at his trade, leaving no signs of his tampering.

Nonetheless, von Essen eyed him with suspicion. "How did you get in?"

"Dearie me, I'm to blame, milord." Fi slid off the desk, her tone contrite; she couldn't let her partner do all the work. "Me and my cust—I mean, this lovely gent 'ere wanted to get be'er acquainted. I brought 'im upstairs, and we found this room open—"

"The door was locked," von Essen said.

"It wasn't when we came in," Fi said brightly. "Maybe one o' the servants forgot to lock it?"

Before von Essen could reply, his companion cut in.

"What does it matter, luv?" The tart eyed the thief with a sultry interest that made Fi grind her teeth. "They're 'ere for the same reason we are. Why don't we 'ave our fun together, eh?"

"Alas, *mademoiselle*, I am not a man who shares." The thief nodded to von Essen. "My lord, we will intrude upon your hospitality no longer."

As he led Fi out of the room, she heard the trollop's wistful sigh.

"Come," the thief murmured. "We haven't long."

Trusting her instincts, Fi followed him down the corridor and into another bedchamber. He shut the door, shoving a dresser in front of it. Fi rushed to the balcony, estimating the distance to the garden below.

Seconds later, von Essen's voice boomed through the walls. "I've been robbed! Find those bloody thieves!"

Fi had already stripped the sheets off the bed and was knotting them together. The thief helped her. Within moments, they had a makeshift rope. Carrying it to the balcony, the thief secured it to a balustrade, giving it a testing tug before tossing it over the side. Fists pounded on the door; the dresser legs squealed against the floor.

The thief gestured for Fi to climb onto his back.

She did so, wrapping her arms and legs around him.

"Hang on," he instructed.

He swung them over the balcony. For a terrifying instant, she felt like they were plummeting into nothingness. Then the rope tightened; her fear turned into exhilaration as he expertly navigated their descent against the star-studded sky. She hugged her partner, relishing his rippling strength and coordination. When they touched the ground, she hopped off...and not a moment too soon.

A pair of footmen barreled toward them. The thief dodged the first one's fist, landing a punch that made the other double over. The second footman ignored Fi and lunged at the thief from behind, trapping him in a burly hold. As the thief struggled to free himself, the first footman recovered, marching over with a bloodthirsty expression.

Fi ran full tilt into him, her momentum sending him sprawling.

The footman rose, sneering, "You're going to regret that, bitch."

When he came at her, she evaded his grasp and kneed him in the groin. He went down again, groaning and curling into a fetal position. An instant later, the other footman collapsed beside him, dispatched by the thief's mighty left hook.

"Come, *chérie*."

The thief grabbed Fi's hand. Together, they raced through the dark garden toward the back gate. He gave her a lift, not that she needed it. She scaled the iron fence with ease, landing softly in the lane behind the house.

A moment later, the thief touched down beside her.

There was no time to say goodbye. Beneath his mask, the man's mouth curved, and he reached out, his big hand briefly cupping her cheek. Heart racing, she let her joy show in her smile. Then, without a word, they parted, running in opposite directions. As Fi reached the end of the lane, she saw the Angels' carriage pulling up, Livy opening the door and waving at her. Climbing inside, Fi couldn't resist a glance back.

The lane was empty. Like a figment of a feverish fantasy, her partner in crime had vanished...as if he'd never been there at all.

ONE

TWO WEEKS LATER

The Brambleton ball was a bona fide crush.

Beneath the tiered chandeliers, Fiona performed a lively polka with her partner, Lord William Brambleton. The young viscount's banalities went in one ear and out the next. He could drone on for ages with little encouragement from her. Usually, she managed to hide her boredom, yet tonight a strange restlessness plagued her. She felt like a caged animal on display.

Speculative gazes tracked her and Lord William. As he was young, possessed of all his hair and teeth, and the heir to an earl-dom, he was considered the catch of the Season. The only thing he lacked was money, but that was where Fi came in. She was one of the richest heiresses on the marriage mart, and her beauty and charm had earned her the title of an "Incomparable."

Practically speaking, she and Lord William were a perfect match.

Of course, there were the sticklers who held Fiona's back-ground against her. Her papa was a powerful industrialist with roots in London's underworld, and her mama was a banker's daughter. While her family's wealth had purchased Fi an admission ticket into the upper echelons, getting a good seat was another matter. Because of her middle-class roots, she had dealt with condescension and snobbery all her life.

Indeed, some of her fellow debutantes had dubbed her "Miss Banks" behind her back, a vindictive reference to the source of her familial fortune. Fi did not know what annoyed her more: the moniker's spitefulness or its inaccuracy. As Papa believed in financial diversification, banking institutions accounted for only a small fraction of the Garritys' vast holdings. The blue-blooded twits ought to have called her "Miss Railways," "Miss Factories," or "Miss Large Country Estates."

Some middle-class misses might kowtow to the elitists and accept their lot in life. Not Fiona. Beneath her polished façade burned the fire of rebellion. She was determined to silence the naysayers by proving them wrong. She had made it her mission to conquer Society without a single drop of aristocratic blood in her veins.

She had worked tirelessly at mastering the skills of being a lady. She could play three instruments, sing, and dance. She'd studied fashions until she was not only an expert but a starter of trends. She'd memorized entire volumes on proper comportment—one ought to know the rules, even if one chose not to follow them—and could recite Debrett's from beginning to end.

Fi had also studied the reigning ladies of Society with the avidness of a general preparing for battle. She had followed in the footsteps of the most popular hostesses, learning how to charm, flirt, and maneuver her way to the top. Truth be told, she'd enjoyed the challenge of it. Now she was poised on the precipice of success; to execute her *coup d'état*, all she had to do was make a brilliant matrimonial match.

Which led to a dilemma: finding a suitable husband.

The problem wasn't landing a title. Fi's list of suitors could have been ripped from the society pages. The trouble lay in what happened *after* marriage. For years, Fi had striven to prove she was a lady. She'd done her job so well that she'd fooled everyone...except herself.

She knew who she truly was. Her perfect debutante persona was a sham. The real Fiona Garrity was no demure and genteel lady. Behind her exquisitely groomed façade, she was willful, thrill-seeking, and even a bit ruthless when the situation warranted. Not only had she been leading a double life as an investigator, but she also reveled in the illicit freedom. Delighted in secretly thumbing her nose at the polite world.

In truth, Fi was surprised that she'd managed to hoodwink Society for this long. A part of her had always feared that her scheme would be exposed, and people would see her for the impostor she was. That she would go down in infamy as Miss Banks, Wanton Adventuress. The longer her machinations went unnoticed, the more her anxiety of exposure mounted.

And marriage? That was the scariest proposition of all. For how could she hide her true self from the man she would be living with until death did them part? She could never slip up, never let her guard down. It would be *exhausting*. For any potential union to work, her husband would have to fall into one of two categories: incredibly accepting...or incredibly oblivious.

The latter was definitely a safer bet. In Fiona's experience, acceptance could change. At one time, she'd been the apple of her father's eye and could do no wrong; now Papa questioned her decisions and restricted her freedom. The last thing she wanted was a husband who would do the same. Better to find an unobservant fellow or simpleton to wed...and there was certainly no shortage of those. Yet having an imperceptive or stupid husband wasn't exactly a thrilling prospect.

The dance ended, and Lord William was blathering on about thoroughbreds. By the time he returned her to her mama, Fi felt like her head might explode if she heard one more word about proper conformation.

"I am rather parched, my lord." To soften her interruption of his soliloquy on equine anatomy, she fluttered her eyelashes. "Would you be so kind as to fetch me some lemonade?"

He set off like a knight on a quest. The moment he was out of earshot, she turned to her mother.

"May I be excused to find Livy and Glory?" she asked.

"Must you do so now, my dear?" Mama tilted her head, her red curls tipping to one side. "The viscount will be returning with your beverage. And Lord Sheffield will be claiming his dance shortly."

"Won't you please make excuses for me, Mama?" Fi cajoled.

"All right." Mama bit her lip. "I shall do my best to come up with something."

Fi felt a twinge of guilt at the discomfort in her mother's guileless blue eyes. At times, she wondered why she couldn't have inherited Mama's kind and nice nature along with her looks. Instead, those traits had gone to Fi's younger brother, Maximillian. Fi took after Papa. Driven and focused, she was willing to do what it took to achieve her ambitions.

Scanning the room for reinforcements, Fi spotted Lady Helena, the Marchioness of Harteford. The buxom brunette was one of Mama's friends and a fixture in high society.

"Lady Helena has arrived. Why don't you join her?" Fi suggested. "If anyone comes looking for me, simply tell them that I had an emergency with my slipper laces."

Mama brightened. "What a splendid idea. I've been meaning to catch up with Lady Helena."

After seeing Mama happily settled with the marchioness, Fiona dodged several gentlemen and collected her friends, Ladies Olivia Wodehouse and Glory Cavendish. The trio took refuge in a quiet corner shielded by a row of potted palms.

"Why aren't you dancing, Fi?" A petite brunette, Livy wore a gown of spring-green silk that matched her eyes. Her hair was arranged in chic braided hoops over her ears. "Your card is always full."

Fi glanced at her overflowing dance card. What had once felt like a symbol of achievement now felt like an albatross tied around her wrist.

How did the goal I worked so hard for suddenly become a nightmare?

"I needed a break," she said with a sigh. "I've had to listen to fellows drone on about nothing of consequence all night. My dancing partners have been clods, too, making mincemeat of my toes."

"Poor Fi." Glory's russet-brown ringlets swung as she shook her head dolefully. Slender and athletic, with a dusting of golden freckles on her nose, she had neat features that showed her quarter-Chinese heritage. "Suffering the slings and arrows of outrageous popularity."

"How many proposals has Fi received this week?" Livy inquired. "I have lost count."

"Very amusing." Fiona rolled her eyes as her friends chuckled. "The pair of you ought to set up a stall next to Punch and Judy."

"I could use the pin money," Livy quipped.

Now that *was* laughable. Livy's husband, the Duke of Hadleigh, indulged her shamelessly. And not just for the usual things like clothing and jewels. He supported Livy's passion for investigation.

What would it be like to know such loving acceptance? Fi wondered.

Of course, a girl like Livy deserved true love. She was clever and loyal. She'd pledged her friendship to Hadleigh from the time she was thirteen, those feelings eventually blossoming into a soul-deep love. Fi had no idea what such love felt like. The closest thing she'd felt was a lusty attraction to an anonymous thief.

"Is everything all right, Fi?" Livy asked with her usual acuity.

Although Fi had told her friends about her adventure with the dashing Frenchman, she hadn't divulged what she'd done with him on the desk. Some things were too intimate to share. It would be a secret between her and the thief...who she'd never see again.

Sighing, Fi said, "I don't know what's wrong with me. Usually, I enjoy balls. But tonight, I feel..." She searched for a more delicate word and gave up. "Bored. Out of my wits, actually."

"You are not alone," Glory said with feeling. "I fear that detective work has made everything else seem tedious in comparison."

Perhaps that was the problem. Once upon a time, Fi had dreamed of having a loving marriage like that of her parents. In the two years since her debut, however, she hadn't met a gentleman she found half as exciting as her work. She had become addicted to the freedom of her covert life, and the idea of giving up her independence, of taking on a husband who would tell her what to do, made her entire being tense in denial.

"Not *everything* else is tedious," Livy said with a wink.

"Not all of us have an adoring husband and adorable babe to entertain us," Fiona teased.

Livy snorted. "You have your pick of husbands. You just need to choose one."

"The choices don't feel right," Fi said glumly.

"Well, I hate to be the bearer of bad news." Glory was peering through the palms. "But I think the remainder of your dance card has caught your scent."

Peering through the fronds, Fi saw that a pack of gentlemen was indeed sniffing her out. Panic seized her. She looked for the nearest escape route: the door to a balcony several feet away.

"Go," Livy said. "We'll keep them diverted."

"You are such dears," Fi said gratefully.

Glory's hazel eyes danced. "What are bosom friends for?"

Fiona found the balcony blessedly unoccupied. A cool night breeze stirred the orange blossoms in her long ringlets and brushed over her bare shoulders as she wandered to the balustrade. Here, the streaming moonlight made the paillettes on her white gown glitter like a thousand stars. Leaning her gloved arms on the stone railing, she drew a breath to clear her head.

I'll put off marriage for as long as I can, she decided. *Instead, I'll focus my energies on investigating...and not getting caught.*

Voices interrupted her musings. The door to the balcony was opening... Botheration, had her admirers found her already? Quickly, Fi retreated to the back of the balcony, taking refuge in the shadows.

A gentleman strode out and took her place at the balustrade, the moonlight limning his tall, broad-shouldered frame. He had wavy dark hair, his high forehead and slashing cheekbones giving him an arrogant air. Fi recognized him at once: Lord Thomas Morgan, the Earl of Hawksmoor and eldest son of her parents' friends, the Marquess and Marchioness of Harteford.

As the earl was older than her by a dozen years, their paths had not crossed much. In his thirties, Hawksmoor was an intellectual and inventor whose genius had been compared to Sir Isaac Newton and Mr. Charles Babbage. The earl's wife had passed away three years ago, and he had a reputation for being a staid and cerebral man.

Fi found herself oddly fascinated by Hawksmoor. He was a man in his prime, the faint lines around his eyes and silver threads in his brown hair adding to his austere attractiveness. During their few interactions, he'd been reserved to the point of indifference. While she excelled at reading people, Hawksmoor's eyes, the impenetrable grey of London fog, gave away little. She'd had no idea what was going on in that powerful brain of his. One thing had been for certain: whatever he'd been contemplating, it had naught to do with her.

His disinterest had piqued her curiosity simply because it was unusual. Gentlemen typically fawned over her. Hawksmoor, however? If she danced a jig naked with a lampshade on her head, he would likely yawn and glance at his pocket watch. At balls, he gravitated toward ladies who were her opposite: serious-minded bluestockings who discussed politics and science and disdained frivolous pursuits.

As Fi watched, the earl withdrew something from his pocket. He held the small object up to the light...and her breath hitched in surprise. Suspended from a hoop, the earring consisted of a golden semi-circle the shape of a boat.

It looks like my *earring. The one I lost that night at von Essen's.*

She furrowed her brow. It couldn't be, of course. Why would Hawksmoor have her earring? It must be a strange coincidence. Her earring had been a bit of cheap costume jewelry found in countless shops; the one the earl was holding and looking at so intently just happened to be similar. Perhaps the piece had belonged to his wife...or to his current lover.

As if on cue, the door opened again. Hawksmoor smoothly pocketed the earring, turning to greet the newcomer. A widow known for her high-brow salons, Lady Melinda Ayles typified the sort of female company he preferred. Fi's gaze widened as Lady Melinda wound her arms around the earl's neck and kissed him passionately. He took control of the kiss with a natural dominance that caused an odd quiver in Fi's belly. Behind Hawksmoor's reserved façade apparently lay a rather hot-blooded man. His partner's moan, like that of a cat in heat, caused a wild giggle to tickle Fi's throat. Clamping a hand over her mouth, she willed herself to remain silent.

Hawksmoor set his paramour aside, saying in a deep, firm voice, "Not here, Melinda."

"Why not?" Lady Melinda pouted.

"This is a ball. My parents are in attendance, for Christ's sake."

"You've been ignoring me all night."

"I am practicing discretion," he said calmly. "I suggest you do the same."

"You are not discreet when you look at *her*," Lady Melinda flung back.

A lover's quarrel? Fi could not help but be intrigued. *Who is Lady Melinda accusing Hawksmoor of being interested in? The owner of the earring, perhaps?*

In the moonlight, Hawksmoor's countenance looked carved from granite. "I don't know what you are talking about."

"Don't lie. I saw you staring at that simpering Miss Garrity."

Two thoughts struck Fiona simultaneously.

I do not *simper. And was Hawksmoor truly staring at* me?

"You're being ridiculous," Hawksmoor said shortly.

"I saw you," his lover insisted. "When she was on the dance floor, you could not take your eyes from her."

"That frivolous chit is the last woman I would be interested in."

Frivolous chit? Last woman? Outrage burned in Fi's bosom. *Why, the pompous ass!*

"I'm sorry, darling." Now apologetic, Lady Melinda rubbed against Hawksmoor like a hungry cat. "Of course you're not interested in the daughter of vulgar parvenus. They call her *Miss Banks*, you know."

Her sharp laugh pierced Fi like shards of glass, releasing trickles of humiliation.

"While she is pretty, in a common sort of way, she has nothing of substance to recommend her," Lady Melinda went on. "Unless one counts her dowry, which everyone knows is the real source of her popularity. My jealousy got the better of me. Forgive me, darling?"

A lady would grin and abide, Fi told herself as she balled her hands.

The prudent thing to do would be to wait for the pair to leave.

To pretend none of this had happened. To ignore her hurt and anger and *especially* her urge to retaliate.

"I beg your pardon," Fiona said in a clear, pleasant voice.

She sallied forth into the light, the paillettes on her gown shining like armor. She took grim enjoyment from Lady Melinda's shocked countenance, the way the woman's mouth opened and closed like that of a netted fish.

Hawksmoor's only sign of surprise was the slight elevation of his dark brows.

"Miss Garrity. We did not see you there," he said with cool composure.

Obviously, you blackguard.

"How strange, my lord." Fi bestowed a saccharine smile upon him. "We frivolous chits are usually quite difficult to miss."

"Miss Garrity, if we have, ahem, given you cause for offense," Lady Melinda began.

"Why should I be offended, my lady?" Fi inquired.

"Er...no reason." The lady's face reddened. "But perhaps you misheard—"

"I assure you there is nothing wrong with my hearing. As husbands don't catch themselves, however, I must put my vulgar fortune to work. I will leave the two of you to your rendezvous."

Executing a flawless curtsy, she walked past them, her head held high.

TWO

"Fuck me harder, Hawk." Posed on all fours on the bed, Melinda arched her back, moaning, "*Yes.* Just like that."

Obliging his mistress, Hawk gripped her narrow hips and plowed her with disciplined force. They'd left the Brambleton ball separately, but Melinda had begged him to come by her home afterward. Although he had not been in the mood, he'd relented in the face of her tearful apologies. She'd greeted him at her door wearing a smile and nothing else.

One thing had led to the next.

"Mount my pussy." Melinda tossed her brown curls over her shoulder. "Ram that big cock into me like the stallion you are."

Hawk felt a flash of irritation at the metaphorical commentary and at himself. He regretted giving in to Melinda's advances this eve. When he'd first met her at a gathering of the Society for Scientific Study and Advancement, she'd seemed like the ideal mistress: a self-possessed widow who shared some of his intellectual interests. She'd claimed to want the uncomplicated arrangement he had to offer, and they were compatible in bed.

Six weeks into the affair, however, Melinda had begun to show her true colors. Beneath her composure lurked a volatile, even vindictive streak. The scene she'd caused tonight had been appalling. Not only had she caught him off guard with her disgraceful accusations, but she'd dragged an innocent miss into their private business.

Not that Fiona Garrity was dragged in, precisely, he thought ruefully.

The chit had descended upon them with a goddess's wrath. She'd reminded him of a collection of Norse myths he'd read as a child. An illustration blazed in his mind's eye: Sól, the sun goddess, a red-haired beauty racing a chariot across the sky as she was pursued by snarling wolves. With her fiery hair and celestial blue eyes, her perfect figure clad in a shining gown, Fiona Garrity had been every bit as spectacular as Sól. She'd served him and Melinda her revenge piping hot, and God help him, but her pride and passion had stirred his loins.

When he'd told Melinda that Fiona Garrity was the last woman he would be interested in, he'd been telling the truth. The reason, however, wasn't due to Miss Garrity's lack of attractions but the opposite. She appealed to him far *too* much. From the moment he'd reluctantly re-entered Society, she'd caught his eye... and the eye of every bachelor in London.

He'd avoided her precisely because of the irrational desires she aroused. Depleted by his first marriage, he had no intention of marrying again. He did not have the desire or wherewithal to take care of another wife. Which meant he could not dally with a young virgin, no matter how tantalizing he found her. Moreover, he and Miss Garrity had little in common. She was far too young, spirited, and temperamental for a weary old scholar like him.

Yet he could not deny that Miss Garrity's elemental allure drew him like iron to a lodestone. He was fascinated by the details of her. Her tresses were not auburn or copper, but a pure, flame-red. Not a single freckle marred her creamy skin. He wondered if her skin was that smooth all over. If the curls between her nubile thighs were as fiery as those upon her head. If her virginal cunny was the same lush, coral-pink as her lips—

His rising seed caught him by surprise. Wanting his partner to go first, he held her hips, slamming into her repeatedly. She mewled as she climaxed, and he allowed himself his own release.

Afterward, he dealt with the French letter and began to dress.

Naked, Melinda lounged against the pillows. "Why don't you stay the night, Hawk?"

Her request punctured his brief bubble of relaxation.

A life-long scholar, Hawk had studied topics ranging from mathematics to physics to ancient languages. The pursuit of knowledge was his passion and sanctuary. During his darkest hours, he'd immersed himself in the creation of a calculation engine that, while not as elaborate in scope as Babbage's, proved more practical to build. While Babbage's government-funded project remained unfinished, Hawk had completed and patented his machine. He'd sold several models for tidy sums.

Moreover, Hawk's work had drawn interest from a secret organization. The group, known to a select few as the Quorum, had recruited Hawk, putting his analytical skills to use protecting country and Crown. Given Hawk's expertise in logic and recognizing patterns, he hadn't missed Melinda's habit of trying to alter their agreed-upon terms.

Buttoning his waistcoat, he said, "I told you from the start that I prefer to sleep alone."

"People change." She made a moue. "Why can't you?"

Because I have no wish to change. Or to encourage emotional attachment.

"I have an early appointment," he said.

With a coy smile, she circled her nipple with a fingertip. "I'll get you *up* early."

"Thank you, no." He tied his cravat in an efficient knot.

"Is there something wrong, Hawk?"

Since the scene at the ball, he had known that things were

coming to a natural conclusion. He hadn't banked on cutting ties tonight, however. It would be wiser to have that conversation when they were both rested. And perhaps not immediately after he'd tupped her...which, he acknowledged again, had been a monumentally bad decision on his part.

"I think this is a conversation best had another time," he said.

"I wish to have it *now*." Jerking on a robe, she faced him, her hands planted on her hips. "What about how I feel, Hawk? What I need?"

At times like these, Hawk cursed his animal needs. His wife Caroline had been his first lover. When her illness had struck and their intimate life had dried up, he'd become a master of sublimating his urges. After Caroline's death and his mourning period, he'd gone on his equivalent of a sexual spree...and what, to a rake, was likely an average weekend. Over the space of two years, he'd slept with three women, and the arrangements had all started and ended in the same fashion.

He'd been clear that all he wanted was an exclusive sexual relationship; his partners had said they wanted the same thing. Yet every bloody time, things went south. As a man who valued logic and rationality, he was frustrated by an apparent female inability to stick to the damned plan. He was even more frustrated at himself for repeating the same mistake and expecting a different result. Lust was proving annoyingly illogical.

"When we began our affair, we agreed to a physical relationship with no strings," he said evenly. "Does our arrangement no longer suit you?"

Melinda blinked, her throat rippling. "How could you think that? I care for you, Hawk."

Before he could stop her, she wrapped her arms around his neck, crushing his cravat in a way that was certain to aggravate his valet.

"Don't you care for me too?" she cooed.

When he did not answer, her gaze slitted. She dropped her arms.

"I am not asking for the moon and stars," she said petulantly. "Just simple courtesy from the fellow whose bed I'm sharing."

"I have no wish to hurt you. Nor do I wish to lie." He spoke with care. "We play a specific role in each other's lives, and I am content with that."

"You think of me as your whore," she accused.

"That is untrue. I see us as partners in a situation of mutual benefit."

"Partners," she scoffed. "You don't even trust me. I've told you I cannot conceive, yet you insist on using that blasted French letter."

"Contraception is not the reason I use the letter."

The instant he spoke the words, he regretted them. Not because they were inaccurate but because of the hassle that was about to follow.

She, predictably, pounced. "Why, then?"

Quelling a sigh, he said, "Townsend."

Melinda's pupils widened, yet she clung to the shield of her bravado.

"I don't know what you mean," she said, tossing back her hair.

"I mean that I know you've been fucking Townsend," he clarified.

"That is a *lie*—"

"Last Thursday at noon. I stopped by here and left when I realized that you had company."

Melinda switched tactics with dizzying speed. "It didn't mean anything, darling. I swear—"

"I know it didn't mean anything. Not to me, at any rate. Given the situation, however, I thought it prudent to take certain precautions."

"Are you accusing me of...of..." She sputtered like an overfilled kettle. "Of being *unclean*?"

"I am merely sharing my reasoning. In truth, I had not planned on bringing up the topic. As our expectations are clearly not aligned, however, I think it best that we end our arrangement."

Her face froze with shock. "After everything we have shared, surely you cannot wish to end our affair. I love—"

"I have enjoyed our time together, Melinda." His tone was curt; he had no patience when it came to using love to cover up or justify bad behavior. "Let us part amicably."

"I was warned about you." Her voice shook with sudden anger. "My friends told me that you were an insensitive bastard. I gave you the benefit of the doubt."

"Why would you need to?" He was truly baffled. "I was clear from the start about what I wanted. I never lied."

And I honored our agreement.

"I thought that you would change. That it was your grief over your wife that had made you cold. I thought that I could teach you to love again..."

Hawk flinched at the tear that slid down Melinda's cheek; he had not meant to hurt her. At the same time, the notion of trying to comfort away her tears chilled him. He was done with being a caretaker, wanted no part of it. And he did not speak about his wife—with anyone.

"I did not intend to mislead you," he said. "I apologize if I did."

Her nostrils flaring, Melinda hissed, "Get out, you heartless bounder! You're as unfeeling as one of your blasted machines. I wish I'd never laid eyes on you!"

Back at his town house, Hawk was greeted by his butler.

"How was your evening, my lord?" Weatherby inquired.

"Fine, thank you." Hawk handed over his hat and gloves. To his right, the door to the drawing room was open, revealing the gaping holes in the ceiling and walls. "Why the devil does that look worse than when the renovation started?"

Weatherby gave a long-suffering sigh. "According to the carpenter, the rot from the leak was more extensive than he first believed. He says he will have to rebuild most of the walls and the ceiling. At your convenience, I could schedule a meeting with him—"

"That will be unnecessary." Hawk's temples began to throb; household problems were the bane of his existence. He had neither the patience nor aptitude for dealing with them. "Just talk to him, Weatherby, and make sure he gets the job done."

"Yes, my lord."

As Hawk climbed the steps, he wondered why he could not find a mistress as accommodating as his butler. Weatherby was the soul of discretion and held up his end of the bargain. Of course, Hawk compensated well for the butler's professionalism; the idea of hiring a bedpartner, however, had never appealed to him.

Livingston, his valet, was waiting in his bedchamber. As predicted, the silver-haired fellow grimaced at the state of Hawk's clothing but kept his sartorial opinions to himself as he helped Hawk change.

"Did you enjoy the ball this evening, my lord?" Livingston inquired.

"It fulfilled its purpose." Hawk shrugged into his dressing gown. "Namely that of placating my mama."

As much as he loved his mother, her constant fretting over his happiness drove him slightly mad. Tonight, he'd suffered through dances with several debutantes to appease her. He'd hoped to earn a respite from her visits, during which she dropped hints about the state of his town house and how it needed a "woman's touch." While he knew Mama's intentions were good, he was private by nature. He would rather be put on the rack than discuss his personal affairs. He had the inkling that his papa, whom his mother dragged along to the inquisitions, shared his sentiments.

"It is a mother's job to worry, sir," Livingston said. "Mine still reminds me to eat my peas, even though I have loathed the legume for over half a century."

After Livingston left, Hawk was plagued by restlessness and decided to work in his study. As he left his room, he paused at the next door.

Caroline's bedchamber. He hadn't gone inside for months.

He turned the knob. Good at finding his way in the dark, he went to her dressing table and lit the lamp. The flaring light revealed faded green walls and fragile, spindly-legged furnishings, bringing forth a stream of memories: Caroline's lovely smile. Her cornsilk hair slipping through his fingers. The suffocating weight of her sorrow and pain and despair.

As he stood there, he reflected that Melinda had been wrong about him. He wasn't cold but numb. He doused the lamp, dimming the past. He exited, each step taking him away from the secrets and ghosts. All that he could not change.

In his study, Hawk was greeted by a crackling hearth and the comforting smells of leather and ink. He poured himself a whisky and went to his desk, which was covered in stacks of papers. At the top of one pile was the latest edition of *Philosophical Transactions*. Instead of opening it, he reached into his dressing gown pocket and took out the earring.

He didn't know why he'd taken to carrying the bit of jewelry around. Nor could he explain the instinct that had led him to filch it from the raven-haired light-skirt when they'd parted. He'd just wanted a piece of that moment. Of her boldness and ingenuity and fire. Of the transient yet intense connection that had made him feel...not alone.

While the earbob's weight suggested it was made of tin and the Egyptian-inspired design was far from authentic, the gold felt warm and real in his palm. He wondered if his mystery lady knew that he'd taken it. If she ever thought of him. If she ever fantasized about what they could have done on that desk if they hadn't been interrupted...

Feeling his body stir, he closed his fingers briefly around the earring before pocketing it again. He shifted his attention to work, removing files from a hidden compartment in his desk. With methodical precision, he reviewed documents and began writing his report for the Quorum.

THREE

Two days later, Fi hurried into the private parlor adjacent to Lady Charlotte Fayne's study. Livy and Glory were already there, waiting for Lady Fayne—Charlie to intimates—to bring in the latest client. Through discreet peepholes, the Angels could watch their mentor conduct interviews. Charlie was the face of the covert society. She informed clients that she had "contacts" who could secure information. No one suspected that the agency's work was, in fact, carried out by ladies and debutantes.

Untying the ribbons of her bonnet, Fi said, "Sorry I'm late."

"The client isn't here yet." Livy poured Fi a cup of tea. "All you've missed are some delicious baked goods."

"And there are plenty left to go around," Glory said cheerfully.

She had an assortment of pastries on her plate. Her ferret Ferdinand, nicknamed FF II, sat upon her periwinkle skirts, his furry white paws outstretched for a share of her almond tart.

Perusing the hamper piled with treats, Fi said, "Mrs. Fisher doesn't have to keep sending gifts. She paid us a generous fee and set up a scholarship fund for future clients in need."

"She's grateful," Livy said simply. "And she wants to show it."

Fi recalled Emily Fisher's visit when Charlie had returned her letters. Her back ramrod-straight, the blonde businesswoman had scanned each note before throwing the stack into the fire.

"My former lover told me he'd burned these, and it was my fault for trusting him," Mrs. Fisher had said in a brittle voice. *"You have saved me from scandal and ruin, Lady Fayne, and I cannot thank you enough."*

Knowing that she'd helped Mrs. Fisher, Fi felt a swell of pride.

"What delayed you this morning?" Livy asked.

"Parental troubles." Fi took a fortifying drink of tea. "I'm parched from all the excuses I had to make in order to get here."

Living a secret life had its challenges, especially for the unmarried girls. Livy and Pippa—the fourth Angel who was currently away on a trip with her new husband—could do as they wished now that they were wed and had supportive spouses. Fiona and Glory, however, still had to keep their unorthodox activities hidden from their parents.

Charlie had provided them with a cover: the girls were supposedly doing genteel work for her charity, the Society of Angels. Their parents were told that they spent their time engaged in good works, from delivering baskets to workhouses to writing pamphlets and raising money for various causes. For Fiona, however, the excuse was beginning to get stale.

"You do look a trifle peaked," Livy said.

"It is the stress of dealing with Papa," Fi said with a sigh. "Every time I try to leave the house, he has so many *questions*. Why am I spending so much time here, what are the specifics of what I am doing? I suppose it is my own fault for slipping up...twice."

The first time, her mama had caught her getting dressed after her bath. On a mission the day before, Fiona had scuffled with a brute. She had emerged victorious but not unscathed.

"Oh, my goodness!" Mama had gasped at the large, purpling bruise on Fiona's arm. *"What happened to you, my darling?"*

"I, um, fell." Fi had hurriedly ducked behind her dressing

screen. *"When I was bringing supplies to the women in the work-house. Please don't worry about it, Mama. It looks far worse than it really is, and I have the perfect gown with sleeves to hide it..."*

Of course, Mama had worried *and* told Papa about it. The pair had cautioned her about being overzealous.

"Remember you are a debutante first and a do-gooder second," Papa had admonished in stern tones. *"No cause is more important than your well-being, Fiona."*

That was before Fi's second mistake, which had occurred the night she encountered the thief. She'd given her parents the excuse that she was staying over at Livy's. When she and Livy had arrived home after the mission, Livy's husband, the Duke of Hadleigh, had informed them grimly that Fiona's papa had stopped by, ostensibly to drop off a satchel Fi had forgotten to bring.

Hadleigh had made the best excuse he could—something involving a charity emergency—but Fi knew her father did not buy it. Adam Garrity was nobody's fool. The fact that he had decided to bring the satchel himself, rather than send a footman, was evidence that he sensed something was afoot. In general, Fi was proud of her papa's razor-sharp intellect...except when she needed to keep things under wraps from him.

She understood that her father wanted to protect her; she just wished he could *understand* her as well. Her need for autonomy and freedom. Whenever she tried to follow her passions, all she received were lectures...and, even worse, Papa's disapproval.

"Don't blame yourself, Fi. Keeping our activities secret this long has been no small feat," Glory said with feeling. "Slip-ups are bound to happen from time to time. Do you remember when Mama found the beard that I'd accidentally left in my reticule? I had to convince her that it was for a play we were putting on to raise funds for impoverished widows."

"Your parents are more trusting than mine," Fiona said darkly. "My papa keeps tightening the reins. Meanwhile, Max is allowed to do whatever he wants. If Max wanted to be an investigator, Papa would likely applaud him for his initiative. It isn't fair."

Her friends nodded in empathy. They also had brothers who were permitted more freedoms by virtue of their sex. In Fi's case, however, her father favored Max not only because he was a boy; Papa preferred her brother because he was a better person than she was. Max was not rebellious. He never got into trouble. Instead, he was helpful, considerate, and kind.

In other words, Max was annoyingly good, even to his own detriment. Although Fi bickered with her brother, she was fiercely protective of him. Growing up, she'd had to step in when his so-called friends tried to take advantage of his generosity or bullies his gentle nature. She'd always shrugged off Max's gratitude; someone had to look after his interests. While she would not admit this to anyone, a tiny part of her wished that she could be as well-behaved and well, *nice*, as he was.

Life would be so much simpler, she thought wryly, *if I could follow rules, respect authority, and think the best of everyone.*

"If females had the same rights as males," Glory said indignantly, "then we wouldn't have to waste energy hiding what we do. We could tell our families the truth."

"Unfortunately, I don't think equality between the sexes will happen any time soon." Fi set down her cup with a clink. "Secrecy is the only thing that allows us to carry on our work."

"Marriage to the right husband is an alternative," Livy chimed in.

"And have one more person telling me what to do?" Fiona rolled her eyes. "I need that like I need a run in my stocking. Anyway, I've handled my parents for now. In exchange for coming here, I promised to attend the Hartefords' supper party tonight."

Livy and Glory exchanged grins, for Fi had told them about her encounter with Hawksmoor and his paramour. While her bosom chums had been outraged on her behalf, they'd also found the earl's mysterious immunity to Fi's charms amusing. They'd even given him a nickname.

"Will the Enigmatic Earl be present?" Livy's eyes twinkled.

"Probably," Fiona muttered. "Although the bounder will likely avoid me like the plague."

"That is most unusual behavior for a fellow." A sly smile tucked into Livy's cheeks. "No wonder you are intrigued by him."

"I am not intrigued by a pompous old scholar," Fi scoffed.

Although she might have done a *tiny* bit of digging on Hawksmoor. After all, it was wise to know one's enemy. She'd learned that Hawksmoor was considered a polymath, which apparently meant that he was an expert in not just one boring subject but a bunch of them. The list of his interests included mathematics, physics, philosophy, astronomy, and history...just to name a few. He'd published treatises on everything from hieroglyphics to engineering. He'd even invented a calculation machine for which he held a patent.

Fiona further discovered that the earl had married young. As he'd preferred seclusion for his work, he'd locked himself and his poor wife away at their country seat. The pair had rarely been seen in Society. After his countess's death three years ago, Hawksmoor had gradually re-emerged and showed no interest in remarrying, despite his mama's wishes. Fi's own mother had said that Lady Helena fretted over her eldest's happiness and prayed that he would find a suitable match.

Not that Fi cared, but the *on dit* was that he'd had a few discreet affairs since his wife's death. None had lasted for long. It was whispered that, in bedroom matters, the earl was as emotionless and *tireless* as the machines he designed.

Approaching voices announced the arrival of the latest client. Fi and the others took their places at the squints, which gave them a view of Charlie's study. Charlie entered first; with her honey-blonde ringlets framing her stunning face and her willowy figure clad in a lace-trimmed gown, Charlie was the epitome of a woman thriving in her independence. Her elegant office, with its raspberry silk walls and rosewood furnishings, underscored her status as a lady of power and means.

With her looks and fortune, Charlie could have conquered Society and had any husband she wanted. She chose instead to live by her own rules. She saw widowhood as an opportunity to pursue her ambition of helping other women. To Fiona, Charlie was a role model for feminine independence.

Charlie led the client into the study. From an earlier briefing, Fiona knew the woman was named Geraldine O'Malley, and she was a housekeeper from Yorkshire. Short and thin, she had salt-and-pepper hair and a triangular face stamped by time.

"Why don't you have a seat, Mrs. O'Malley?" Charlie poured out the tea.

Mrs. O'Malley sat, smoothing her plain bombazine skirts.

"It is kind of you to see me, my lady," she said, accepting the offered cup. "My employer, Baroness Markham, said that you were once of great help to her and that you might be able to help me too."

Charlie folded her hands on the desk. "What is the nature of your concerns?"

"I want to find my daughter Lillian." Mrs. O'Malley took a drink of tea; when she replaced the cup, the slight rattle against the saucer betrayed her anxiety. "She is only nineteen, and I fear that something has happened to her."

"When did you last see your daughter?"

"Nine months ago. On my last visit to London." Mrs. O'Malley drew a steadying breath. "A year and a half ago, Baroness Markham moved her household from London to Yorkshire, and I assumed my daughter would come along. The baroness even offered Lillian a position as a lady's maid, but my daughter turned her nose up. Said she was meant for more than a lifetime of service, even though it was a servant's wages that paid for her upbringing. Lillian and I argued—we have a habit of locking horns—but there was nothing I could do to sway her. She stayed in London to pursue her dream of being an actress."

Her expression sympathetic, Charlie said, "Tell me more about your contacts with your daughter. And why you fear that something may have befallen her."

"When I saw Lillian nine months ago, she seemed her usual self. Headstrong, determined to make a go of being an actress." Mrs. O'Malley shook her head. "My husband died when Lillian was a babe, and I brought her up on my own as best I could. But she was always a handful...always so much work to manage."

Fiona's heart clenched. As a girl, she'd overheard her father saying the same thing about her.

"We must curb Fiona's willfulness," Papa had said to Mama. *"She is a handful. While that may be charming now, when she is older such pertinacity will lead to trouble. She will run roughshod over others. When she is of age to marry, men will be afraid to take her on."*

Fi shut out the painful memory, which was further associated with a terrifying incident that she did not like to think about. Instead, she focused on Lillian, the empathy she felt for this girl who marched to the beat of her own drum.

"I tried to keep in touch with Lillian through letters. Since she was always sporadic about responding, I didn't think much of it when I didn't hear back from her. Then I had the chance to visit London this week, and so I came, hoping to surprise her. I went to her boarding house on Golden Lane; to my shock, Mrs. Bridges, the proprietress, told me Lillian had left six months ago. She'd kept the letters I sent in case Lillian came back for them. But she never did, and Mrs. Bridges has no idea where she went."

Charlie was discreetly jotting into a notebook with a silver pen. "Have you spoken to anyone else who knows Lillian?"

"My daughter never had many friends. Growing up, she did not fit in with her peers; she was too independent and ambitious for her own good. The other girls made fun of her, calling her 'Miss Siddons' because Lillian dreamed of being as successful as the legendary actress Sarah Siddons." Mrs. O'Malley dabbed at her eyes with a worn handkerchief. "It is my fault for overindulging Lillian. For not curbing her wildness."

Glancing at Livy and Glory, Fiona saw the empathy on their faces. Back in their schoolgirl days, the three of them had been dubbed "the Willflowers" by their peers because of their unconventional ways. At least they'd had each other to count on; Lillian, it seemed, had no one.

"Do you have the letters Lillian sent you?" Charlie inquired. "They might contain clues to her current whereabouts. A likeness of her would also aid our search."

"I have both." Mrs. O'Malley withdrew some letters and a small frame from her satchel, sliding them across the desk. "The baroness paid to have a daguerreotype taken of Lillian so that I could take it with me to Yorkshire."

Charlie studied the image. "Your daughter is beautiful, Mrs. O'Malley."

"She is, and it adds to my worries." Mrs. O'Malley gripped her bag tightly. "Lillian exudes charm and confidence, which makes her a magnet for ne'er-do-wells. Before I moved to Yorkshire, I kept a strict eye on her and kept her away from bad influences. My daughter is innocent in the ways of the world; her heart is far too idealistic and trusting. My fear is that she got involved with the wrong man"—the housekeeper's voice hitched—"and she is avoiding me out of shame. But nothing she has done could change the love of a mother for her only child."

"I understand," Charlie said quietly.

"Will you please find Lillian for me, Lady Fayne? When I went to the police, the inspector said that since Lillian is an adult and there is no sign of foul play, they could not waste resources looking for her. Then I went to a private investigator. He said Lillian was just a 'silly girl' who would likely return on her own. He said he would look for her, but his retainer fee alone was beyond my means." Leaning forward, Mrs. O'Malley said, "I don't have much, but I will gladly give you all my savings—"

"Money is not an issue. We will look into the matter for you, Mrs. O'Malley."

"Oh, *thank you*. My prayers have been answered." The housekeeper clasped her hands to her bosom. "God bless you, my lady."

After Charlie finished conducting the interview, Fi and the other Angels trooped into the study.

Charlie tossed her pen into a filigree tray. "Well, Angels? What do you think?"

"We must help Mrs. O'Malley," Livy said determinedly.

"And Lillian," Fi said.

She studied the daguerreotype on the desk. Lillian was indeed beautiful, with dark hair and expressive eyes. She had a waifish figure, her features bordering on ethereal.

"If the poor girl did get entangled with the wrong sort of man, she will need our help," Glory agreed.

After the encounter with the thief, Fi understood the temptations posed by a debonair rogue. Luckily, she was sensible enough to know the difference between fantasy and reality and had the protection of friends and family. Alone in the world, Lillian might easily fall prey to a bad decision.

Charlie steepled her fingers. "It is possible that Lillian does not want our help. Or her mother's interference."

"But what if Mrs. O'Malley is right?" Glory argued. "What if something terrible has befallen Lillian?"

"We cannot stand by and do nothing," Fi insisted.

Charlie smiled, as if she'd been expecting their responses. "Then what is your plan, Angels?"

"We can start by talking to the others at Lillian's boarding house," Livy suggested. "Perhaps someone there knows something."

Fi glanced at the clock on Charlie's desk. Squeezing in a bit of sleuthing before the Harteford party would make the evening more tolerable.

"A splendid idea," she said. "Shall we go now?"

Four

"Thomas, my dear. You are not leaving, are you?"

Caught in the act of doing precisely that, Hawk stifled an oath. He turned around to face his mother. Seeing the resolute glint in her hazel eyes, he knew the jig was up.

"Thank you for the hospitality, Mama," he began. "It is getting late—"

"Nonsense. It is not yet ten o'clock." She took him by the arm, leading him back into the ballroom that he had almost escaped. "The night is young, dear boy. You must enjoy yourself."

He had been planning on doing that. By leaving the bloody party. His vision of enjoying a glass of whisky by the fire while perusing a scientific periodical vanished as his mama drew him back into the throng. Even in the glittering crowd, one couple stood out from the rest.

Fiona Garrity was dancing with Lord Sheffield, the youthful pair so dazzling that others made way for them. While Sheffield was light-footed, it was undoubtedly his partner who elevated him. Miss Garrity's beauty lit up everything around her. Her red curls gleaming, she moved with effortless grace while chatting with her partner. Her yellow satin gown was embroidered with rosebuds and showed off her lissome figure. The bodice bared the smooth slope of her shoulders, molding to her full breasts and narrow waist. As she spun, Hawk caught flashes of her trim ankles beneath her fluffy skirts.

She was Sól come to life. Her vibrant femininity blended sensuality and innocence, and men responded like wolves. When the dance ended, they surrounded her, rabid for her attention. Watching her bestow a smile as polished as a golden apple upon each of her admirers, Hawk felt a primal burst of heat in his loins. He had the irrational urge to beat back her suitors and claim her radiance for himself.

Deliberately, he turned his back to the dance floor and away from temptation. For him, logic trumped lust. He and Miss Garrity could not be more ill-suited. More to the point, after their last encounter, she likely wanted nothing to do with him, and he didn't blame her. He had no desire to irritate her or embarrass himself further.

"Do you see anyone you would like to ask to dance, Thomas?" his mother asked.

"No," he said.

"Surely there must be someone." Mama's encouraging smile reminded him of the one she'd worn the day she and Papa had dropped him and his twin brother Jeremiah off at Eton.

"Try to make friends, my dear," she'd told him. *"Do not get too lost in your studies."*

"There is not." Hawk searched for a diversion. "Have you seen Jeremiah?"

"He's probably dancing with Effie." A content smile tucked into Mama's rounded cheeks. "You know how the two of them are."

Hawk did know, at least intellectually. Wed for seven years, Jeremiah and his wife, Euphemia, still acted like newlyweds. His brother took after their parents in that way. Hawk, himself, had never experienced that sort of giddy emotion. His and Caroline's love had been more reserved in nature. He had been awkward and shy, she quiet and bookish. In each other, they'd found an intellectual match which had led him to propose to her at the age of one-and-twenty.

Neither of them had been prepared for her illness, how swiftly it had transformed her quietness into despair and her reserve into an inability to be around others. They'd consulted numerous physicians whose "cures" had ranged from ineffective to harmful. The most common prescriptions —bed rest and laudanum—had done little for Caroline's melancholia. Weeping and ashamed, she had begged him to keep her affliction a secret. Not knowing what else to do, he'd agreed.

He'd taken her to the country seat and given her the solitude she needed. He'd never spoken of her moods to anyone. He'd done this out of love, and it was only after her death that he realized the cost. To protect Caroline, he'd cut himself off from those who loved him. His years of absence had strained the bonds with his family.

He'd done a shoddy job of keeping up with Jeremiah, Effie, and his two young nieces. He hadn't been there as his younger brothers, George and Henry, had grown into manhood. He'd missed birthdays, anniversaries, and holidays. The worst of it was that his family did not hold any of it against him, welcoming him back with open arms.

Hawk, however, held himself responsible. Yet he didn't know how to bridge the chasm he'd caused. How to make up for everything he'd missed.

Papa arrived, bending to kiss Mama's cheek. "There you are, Helena, my love."

"Have you seen Jeremiah and Effie, darling?" Mama asked.

"I saw them escape onto a balcony not too long ago."

"How romantic." Mama sighed. "Remember when we used to sneak away from balls?"

Papa's grey eyes flashed with amusement. "You mean last week?"

Blushing, Mama said, "Well, at least that is one son accounted for." She slid an unsubtle look in Hawk's direction. "Perhaps you can talk some sense into another."

"What has Hawk done now?" Jeremiah drawled.

Hawk's fraternal twin sauntered over. While their height and looks identified them as brothers, their personalities were as different as night and day. Mama liked to jokingly claim that she had planned their birth order. According to her, she'd known that Hawk's analytical nature would make him the ideal heir to manage the lands and holdings of the marquessate whereas Jeremiah's outgoing charm would make him the perfect successor to Fines, Morgan & Co., the family shipping business.

"Hawk refuses to dance," Mama said. "Even though many ladies present would give their eyeteeth to take a turn with him."

"You might as well give up on your plot, Mama," Jeremiah advised. "By now, you must know that one cannot make Hawk do something he does not wish to do."

"Very well." Expelling an exasperated breath, Mama asked, "Where is Effie?"

"She is, er, freshening up."

At Jeremiah's satisfied smile, Hawk felt a tug in his chest. It wasn't envy, for he didn't begrudge his brother's happiness. What he felt was curiosity: what was it like to have a passionate marriage? To have a partner whose desires matched one's own?

Mama waved at someone behind Hawk. "Mr. and Mrs. Garrity! How lovely to see you."

Greetings were exchanged with the newcomers. With prickling embarrassment, Hawk wondered if Miss Garrity had mentioned the Brambleton ball incident to her parents. Seeing no sign of animosity from the Garritys, he concluded that she had not. In addition to her looks, he now had her discretion to admire.

"Thank you for inviting us, Lord and Lady Harteford."

Gabriella Garrity's blue eyes exuded sincerity. "We are enjoying ourselves ever so much."

To Hawk, she seemed like a softer version of her daughter. She was shorter, curvier, with pleasantly rounded features. She was a warm hearth to her daughter's blazing fire.

"I am pleased to hear it." Mama beamed. "As usual, your lovely Fiona is making quite the splash. She has been surrounded by a legion of admirers, and I have not seen her sit out a single dance."

"Fiona is not one to sit still, my lady." Garrity's dark gaze glittered with amusement and unmistakable pride.

While Miss Garrity had inherited her coloring from her mama, Hawk gathered her confidence and spirit had a strong paternal influence. With inky hair touched by silver at the temples and hawkish features, Adam Garrity had the aura of a man used to being in command.

"I wish Hawksmoor, here, would take a page out of her book," Mama said brightly. "I was just encouraging him to ask a lady to dance."

Gazes turned upon Hawk.

"Do you enjoy dancing, my lord?" Mrs. Garrity asked.

About as much as he enjoyed being the center of attention.

"Not really, ma'am," he said politely.

"My brother just hasn't found the right partner, but his luck may be about to change." With a devilish grin, Jeremiah directed his gaze to a spot behind Hawk's shoulder. "Good evening, Miss Garrity. You are in exceptional looks tonight."

Pivoting, Hawk found himself face to face with Fiona Garrity. Although it defied logic, she affected him like the sun affected the earth. She exerted an invisible force upon him; her mere proximity pumped his heart and pulled blood into his loins. As if he were a damned greenling instead of a widower of one-and-thirty.

It took all his willpower not to get hard. To maintain a façade of indifference.

Not that she would notice. She did not spare him a glance.

Bestowing a dazzling smile upon his brother, she said, "How kind of you to say, my lord."

Her curtsy was a work of art, the dimple in her right cheek a bloody masterpiece.

Even Jeremiah looked a bit dazzled.

"I am merely trying to do justice to this splendid occasion." Miss Garrity's coral-pink lips formed a demure curve. "As usual, Lord and Lady Harteford, your party is an absolute crush."

She waved her fan gracefully, wafting her scent in Hawk's direction.

She smelled like peaches. He wanted to eat her.

"I am glad you are enjoying yourself," Mama said warmly.

Miss Garrity's eyes sparkled. "I do adore dancing."

"How fortunate," Jeremiah said. "Because my brother here is in search of a partner."

Hawk tensed.

After a pause, Miss Garrity arched her brows. "Is he indeed?"

"What a brilliant idea," Mama enthused. "Hawksmoor, you must ask Miss Garrity to dance."

He saw no polite way to extricate himself. It was one thing to avoid her, another to show her public disrespect. As torturous as it was going to be to hold temptation in his arms, he would have to grit his teeth and bear it.

"Would you do me the honor, Miss Garrity?" he asked.

His tone was terser than he intended. And perhaps he'd waited a second too long before asking. Flames of anger leapt in Miss Garrity's eyes before she banked them.

"The honor is mine, my lord," she said in a dulcet voice.

He cleared his throat and held out his arm; she placed her gloved fingertips upon his sleeve as if it were the carcass of a diseased animal. As he led her to the floor where the orchestra had started up again, he heard Mrs. Garrity say merrily, "Oh, this waltz is one of my favorites..."

Bloody perfect.

I cannot believe I am stuck with this boor, Fiona silently fumed. *And for a waltz, too!*

Noticing the glances aimed their way, she kept her smile fixed in place as she and Hawksmoor took their place on the dance floor. He, of course, did not bother to smile or convey the slightest pleasure at being her partner. His arrogant features looked carved from stone, his mouth forming a taut line. He said not a word as he positioned a hand on the small of her back.

Two can play at this game, she vowed. *If he isn't going to talk, then neither am I.*

She reached up, placing one gloved hand upon his broad shoulder. She slid her other hand into his waiting one, poised in the air. His large hand engulfed her fingers entirely. They began to move. Neither of them said a thing.

Fi kept her gaze focused on a spot just above his shoulder. Used to carrying on a conversation while she danced, she found herself with a surfeit of mental energy. Yet she refused to be the first to speak, to lose this battle of wills. She concentrated on the physical movement of dancing instead. To her surprise and irritation, Hawksmoor was a superb dancer.

He moved with the confidence and grace of a man in his prime. Fi had waltzed with countless gentlemen and was used to keeping herself in check so that her partner could keep up. While it was the male's role to lead, Fi usually controlled the dance. Her chief accomplishment was that she managed to do so without her partner realizing it.

Yet Hawksmoor did not need to be led; he was in complete command. He executed the patterns with clean precision, his turns and change steps flawless. Moreover, his male vigor sped up Fi's pulse, challenging her to match him step for step. Many ladies would swoon at the pace he was setting; Fi found it exhilarating.

It was as if their silent warfare had morphed into a contest of who could keep up with whom. If there was anything Fi loved, it was competition. When he swung her into a reverse turn, she lifted her rib cage, stretching her spine over his supportive arm, adding momentum and grace to their spin. He did not falter. Instead, he tightened his hold on her, his large hand covering the small of her back as they glided, then twirled in the opposite direction.

The dynamism of the dance overtook Fi. She lost herself in the music and the moment, stepping and spinning without holding back. Her blood rushed with pleasure as Hawksmoor swung her in a powerful spin, then pulled her close again. The chandelier blazed above them, picking out the strands of silver in his thick, mahogany hair.

She became aware of the heat between their bodies, the firm grip of his hand on hers. His masculine scent, clean and woodsy, infiltrated her senses. They spun again, the turn even more daring than the last, rustling a laugh from her throat. His hand slid upward on her back, his fingertips brushing the bare skin above her dress.

The sensation jolted her. Startled her into looking Hawksmoor in the face. The silver flash in his eyes sent a sizzling charge through her. She couldn't read what he was thinking or feeling, yet her skin prickled, the tips of her breasts tingling against her bodice. She felt dizzy as they slowed to a stop. Bemused by the sound of applause, she saw that she and the earl had garnered an appreciative audience.

"Thank you for the dance," Hawksmoor said tonelessly.

He offered her his arm. Given the eyes on them, she had no choice but to take it.

"We frivolous chits serve our purposes," she said tartly.

"About that." Instead of escorting her back to her parents, he steered her on a promenade around the dance floor. "You misunderstood a private conversation."

"Beg pardon. I didn't realize that a conversation held on a public balcony was private."

He drew his brows together. "The discussion was not meant for your ears."

"Obviously."

"Are you always this difficult?" A hint of impatience entered his voice.

"Only with condescending prigs." Her smile was for their audience, her words for his ears only. "As it happens, my lord, our feelings are mutual. For you are the last gentleman *I* would wish to wed."

"That is, indeed, a relief."

His detached tone irked her. Made her want to get a rise out of him.

"I find emotionless scholars boring," she said rashly.

"And I find temperamental flirts exhausting."

"Oh, I can imagine the sort of wife *you* are looking for."

His quirked brow heightened his aura of arrogance. "Enlighten me."

"An obedient, demure creature," she said scornfully. "Who lives to do your bidding."

His smile was humorless. "If I were looking for a wife, I would settle for one who helps me fulfill my duty."

"A broodmare. How lovely for her."

"As this conversation is degenerating," he said coldly, "shall I return you to your parents?"

"I would not dream of inconveniencing you," she retorted. "I can find my own escort."

To prove her point, she donned a come-hither smile and cast her glance around. Several gentlemen took the bait, wading through the crowd toward her.

"Don't let me keep you, my lord," she said sweetly.

Hawksmoor clenched his jaw.

Deliberately, she turned her back on him to greet the new arrivals.

FIVE

Hawk arrived at Garland's Curiosities and Collectibles before noon. Located on a busy street in Holborn, the shop had a striped green awning and an unassuming air. As Hawk entered, a tiny bell tinkled overhead. Inside, cabinets lined the border of the shop, filled with everything a collector's heart could desire: snuff boxes, coins and stamps, and antiquities from around the world.

Hawk headed to the counter where the proprietress was waiting. A handsome widow, Anne Garland had a robust figure and silver hair worn in a habitual chignon. Although Hawk had known her for years, she greeted him like he was a new customer.

"Good afternoon, sir," she said. "May I help you with anything in particular?"

"I am interested in specimens of Roman glass," Hawk replied with equal formality.

"You have come to the right place, for we have a new shipment in. Please follow me."

She led the way to a door at the back of the shop. Unlocking it, she ushered Hawk through.

A twinkle in her eye, she said in a hushed voice, "You know where to go from here, my lord."

He nodded. "Thank you, Mrs. Garland."

He continued down the corridor to the first room on his right. The chamber was used as a storage area and filled with boxes and crates. As Hawk passed one straw-filled container, he glimpsed a granodiorite tablet carved with hieroglyphics; he resisted the urge to examine it.

Until Fiona Garrity, Hawk had had no problems resisting urges. He prided himself on being a rational fellow, not one prone to foolish impulses. The troublesome Miss Garrity, however, tested his self-discipline. Last night, their waltz had felt more like foreplay than a dance. Her sensual vitality had ignited his basest instincts: he'd wanted to toss her over his shoulder, find the nearest bedchamber, and do unspeakably carnal things to her. No sooner had he gotten his lustful impulses in check than she had provoked him into an argument.

Devil take it, she was a little minx.

He'd never been comfortable around vivacious coquettes, and Miss Garrity was a case in point. Her assumption that she knew what he wanted in a wife was maddening, especially since he had no intention of remarrying. His brothers could provide an heir to the title. All he wanted was some bloody peace...which was clearly not something to be found around Fiona Garrity.

All the more reason to stay away from her, his voice of reason said.

Striding to the door nearly hidden behind a stack of boxes, he inserted a key. The space inside was the size of a water closet, with a flickering lamp mounted on the wall. He closed the door and pulled on the arm of the lamp, activating a hidden mechanism. As the room began to descend, Hawk was pleased to note the smoothness of the ride. He'd designed the elevator using a system of counterweights and belt-driven mechanics.

When the elevator came to a stop, he exited into a large room.

Upon the walls hung assorted maps of London, England, and the Continent. Several desks and filing cabinets sat at one end of the room while an oak table took center stage.

The five men at the table rose at Hawk's entry.

"Right on time," the man at the head seat said.

The Quorum was a covert organization created before the Napoleonic Wars; its sole purpose was to maintain the interests of the Crown and country. The man speaking was the leader of the group, spymaster Charles Swinburne. With steel-grey hair and sideburns, Sir Swinburne had a militaristic bearing from his years in the army.

"Good afternoon, sir." Hawk took the unoccupied seat to the spymaster's right. "Gentlemen."

Greetings were returned from around the table. The members of the Quorum all brought specific strengths to bear. Next to Hawk was Oliver Trent. The former dockworker had the pulse of the working class. With his craggy face and salt-of-the-earth manner, he had the ability to pass as the everyman.

The opposite could be said of Francis Devlin, the copper-haired Adonis seated across from Hawk. The son of an earl, Devlin's old bloodline and rakish charm gave him entrée into the highest circles. Hawk had known Devlin since their Eton days; back then, he and the popular rogue had not been friends, and the trend continued. Beside Devlin was strapping and beetle-browed Kenneth Pearson, a former prizefighter and champion of several infamous carriage races.

Finally, Inspector Rodney Sterling of the Metropolitan Police had the end seat. The Quorum had been recently called upon to assist the police in a case involving national security. For over six months now, a gang of criminals had been wreaking havoc in London's streets, holding up carriages of the wealthy and stealing fortunes in jewelry and gold.

The thieves cheekily called themselves the Merry Sherwood Band. The leader, according to victim accounts, was a charismatic

Robin Hood-type figure. Masked and dashing, he apparently requested "donations" from his rich targets to feed the poor—never mind that this was done at gunpoint. Gossip had spread like wildfire about ordinary folk finding bags of gold on their doorsteps. Trent, who'd tracked the rumors, said every working-class fellow had a friend of a friend who'd experienced the Sherwood Band's largesse.

The rumors, however, appeared to be grossly exaggerated. After weeks of searching, the Quorum had found only one man, an honest blacksmith, who'd come forward with his share of the bounty: not a bag of gold, but a small pouch half-filled with coins. The Sherwood Band's modus operandi had become clear. Their crimes were not motivated by an altruistic desire to help the poor but regular, old-fashioned greed. Their public image had been cleverly constructed to earn the goodwill and protection of ordinary folk.

And it worked. The thieves' popularity soared; no one would rat on them. The police could not find eyewitnesses or information that would lead to the gang's capture. The robberies encouraged anarchy, tearing at the fabric of lawful order in the city. Copycat crimes and destructive mobs were on the rise. The government, already on high alert from the revolutionary fervor across the channel and the threats of the recently suppressed Chartist movement, viewed the Sherwood Band as the match that could light the powder keg that was London.

That was where the Quorum had come in. Their mission was to assist the police in capturing the thieves. Given the nature of their organization, their role was to be a covert one; Inspector Sterling served as their police liaison.

"I have gathered all of you to discuss a new development," Swinburne said in brisk tones. "Inspector Sterling, if you would be so kind as to brief the group?"

Sterling rose. He was a gangly fellow in his late thirties, with sand-brown hair and habitually rumpled clothes.

"On behalf of the police, I would like to begin by extending sincere thanks," Sterling said in his genial way. "Lady Ingersoll was most grateful for the return of her ruby-and-pearl brooch, which, as you know, was stolen during a Sherwood Band heist. The fact that Hawksmoor retrieved the item from Count von Essen's safe allowed us to bring the count in for questioning. Confronted by the facts, von Essen broke down and admitted that he had been pawning the Sherwood Band's nicked goods to his contacts abroad."

"Well done, Hawksmoor," Swinburne said.

Hawk inclined his head in acknowledgment. When the spymaster had recruited him five years ago, he'd been surprised. He'd seen himself as a scholar, not a spy.

"We need men of all talents," the spymaster had said. *"According to my sources, you have an extraordinary aptitude for analyzing information. Your nation could use your help in protecting its interests."*

Prompted by a sense of duty, Hawk had joined the team. As the Quorum required secrecy from its members, he had never told Caroline about his spy work. She hadn't had the wherewithal to question his activities, although she had depended upon him to stay at the country seat with her—had dissolved into tears at the thought of being "abandoned" by him. Thus, he'd worked mainly from home, identifying patterns in information, deciphering codes, and deconstructing foreign technology to learn its applications. The work had been engrossing and, truthfully, a welcome distraction from the stresses of his domestic life.

After mourning Caroline, he'd grown interested in expanding his skills beyond the desk. He'd discovered a latent craving inside him. An unexplored need for excitement.

"Beginner's luck," Devlin drawled.

Once a bully, always a bully. Hawk clenched his jaw. Devlin had not changed since their Eton days. Even then, he had needed to prove his superiority, usually at the expense of others. As a scrawny and awkward lad who knew all the answers in class, Hawk had been a ripe target for Devlin and his cronies.

"It was not luck." Swinburne lowered his brows. "Hawksmoor spent weeks analyzing the financial records that we obtained of suspected pawns. It was through this process that he discovered a series of unexplained deposits made by von Essen a few weeks after each of the thefts."

"I would have investigated von Essen personally," Devlin snarled. "Hawksmoor should have consulted with me; he had no business going into the field himself. That is *my* job. And Trent and Pearson's."

"Leave me out of this," Pearson said in his rumbling voice.

"I would have consulted you, Devlin." Hawk kept his voice even. "At the time, however, you were otherwise occupied at, ahem, a house party. As I could not risk von Essen moving the goods, I had to act quickly on my own."

Devlin turned red, as well he should. The "house party" Hawk referenced was a euphemism for a week-long countryside bacchanal that was notorious for offering every sort of vice. Even if Hawk had contacted Devlin, the latter would have been in no shape for a mission.

Devlin gripped the table. "You were bloody lucky that von Essen did not see through your disguise. You could have compromised our mission and our group."

Hawk bristled at the other's condescension. "I wore a mask and wig and put on a French accent. Even if I had not taken those precautions, I still would have been more fit than you were."

"That is enough." Swinburne spoke with the authority of a commanding officer. "While Hawksmoor acted for the greater good, in the future he will run any plans by me before acting upon them. Is that clear?"

"Yes, sir," Hawk muttered.

"As for you." Swinburne directed a stern glance at Devlin. "While you have rendered great service to our country, you must not forget that every man at this table has done the same. There is a place for everyone. It is not our individual successes that matter but what we are able to accomplish as a team."

"Fine." Devlin folded his arms over his chest. "If you wish to allow Hawksmoor to run amok in the field like a bull in a china shop, that is your prerogative. Just don't expect me to clean up the mess."

"I don't need you or anyone cleaning up after me," Hawk said flatly. "Because of my visit to von Essen, we are one step closer to apprehending the Sherwood Band."

"As to that." Sterling cleared his throat. "When we questioned von Essen, he didn't tell us much about the gang. Claimed that he never met the leader or any Sherwood member. He said that they corresponded through letters which, of course, he burned."

Trent frowned. "Sure, are you, that von Essen is telling you the truth?"

"I cannot be certain, but he provided some leads," Sterling said. "The count confessed to taking part in four transactions. Each time, he was directed to a specific location where a street urchin delivered a bag of stolen goods to him. After the sale of the goods, he returned to the same location with the gang's cut, which was picked up by another waif. His descriptions of the messengers —small, dirty, and young—were not helpful."

"But he revealed where the exchanges took place?" Hawk asked.

"He gave the names of four public houses scattered across town," Sterling replied.

Swinburne drew his gaze around the table. "Since there are four of you, I propose that you each take a pub and search for clues to the Sherwood Band. What do you say, gentlemen?"

At Devlin's glower, Hawk felt a rush of satisfaction.

"Ready and willing, sir," Hawk said.

Six

"Fiona, Mama and I wish to speak to you before the Hadleighs arrive," Papa said from the bottom of the stairwell.

Botheration. That tone never bodes well.

Fi continued descending the steps in a swish of flounced, salmon-pink skirts.

Putting on a quizzical smile, she asked, "What about, Papa?"

"We'll discuss it in private."

With growing fear of an ambush, Fi followed her father into the drawing room. Her suspicions were confirmed at the sight of Mama, who was perched on a chaise like a bird ready to take flight. Confrontations always made Mama nervous.

Drat. Fi stifled a sigh. *I hope this lecture does not make me late for tonight's assignment.*

The Angels had visited Lillian's boarding house the day before. Mrs. Bridges, the landlady, did not have new information to add. However, the Angels found a cheery milliner's assistant named Eloise, who'd had a passing acquaintance with Lillian. According to Eloise, Lillian was ambitious, hard-working, and always on the search for something "better." While Eloise couldn't say where

Lillian had worked or whether she'd had a suitor, she did know that Lillian had frequented a tavern called the Royal Arms.

As it happened, the Royal Arms was located a stone's throw away from the Theatre Royal on Drury Lane. Which had presented Fiona with an ideal cover for her mission this eve.

If I can get out of the dashed house.

Papa stood by Mama's chaise; Fi decided to remain standing as well.

Facing her parents, she said brightly, "I hope this discussion doesn't take too long. The Hadleighs will arrive any moment, and I don't want to make us late for *Hamlet*."

As luck would have it, the bard's longest play was being performed tonight. Fi and Livy planned to sneak out after the lights were dimmed, check out the Royal Arms, and return by intermission. Livy's husband would make any necessary excuses for them.

Her parents exchanged a look. Mama took a breath before speaking.

"We are ever so glad you are going to the theatre tonight, Fiona dear. A young lady ought to enjoy appropriate entertainments. Rather than, um, less appropriate ones." After a pause, Mama said in a rush, "What I mean to say is that while your charitable efforts with Lady Fayne are to be commended, Papa and I are concerned that you might be overdoing things. You've seemed, well, a bit tired lately."

"I feel perfectly fine. I am doing something worthwhile," Fi parried, "and my Season has been a smashing success. I assure you there is naught to be concerned about."

Mama's brow pleated. "I suppose all that is true."

Fi pushed her advantage. "If success can be measured by proposals, I've received more than any other debutante for two years running. Moreover, it is every lady's responsibility to assist those less fortunate than herself. Not only is volunteerism the Christian thing to do, but it is also the *right* thing."

"There are many ways to help others, Fiona," Papa cut in.

While her mama was bendable like a birch, her father was an unyielding oak.

"Ways that do not include coming home with bruises or wandering about God knows where in the middle of the night." Papa's gaze was sharper than a blade. "What, precisely, was that 'charity emergency' you and Lady Olivia were attending to a few weeks ago?"

Botheration. I knew he was suspicious.

"I told you." Fi flashed her winningest smile. "There was an urgent situation at the poorhouse. We were helping women in need."

"Helping them or helping yourself?" Papa's question was clearly rhetorical. "Are you certain this charity of yours is not just an excuse to have adventures?"

When one cannot defend, she thought determinedly, *then one must attack.*

"That is not fair." She raised her chin. "Other parents would be overjoyed if their daughters were having the Season that I am having. Why am I being called to task for doing everything right? Furthermore, you never question what Max does."

Max's voice cut in. "What did I do?"

Pivoting, Fiona saw her brother enter the room. At seventeen, Max had sprouted up like a tree. Overnight, it seemed, he had lost his youthful pudginess. Beneath waves of unruly coffee-black hair, his face was now lean and taut. His eyes, though, were still the same: brown and hopelessly earnest.

"You shouldn't sneak up on people, Max," Fi retorted.

"I didn't mean to, but I heard my name," he said. "What are you talking about?"

"We are having a family discussion, dear," Mama said.

"About me?" Max tilted his head. "Have I done something wrong?"

What an apple-polisher, Fi thought in exasperation. To her knowledge, her brother's worst trespass was nabbing an extra piece of cake from the kitchen. Which he would gladly share if one asked, due to his good and generous heart.

"Of course not, darling," Mama said quickly. "No one has done anything wrong. We were just having a chat about Fiona's, um, schedule."

At least Max was providing a useful distraction. By Fi's calculations, Livy should be arriving at any moment, putting an end to the parental inquisition.

"Mama and I were reminding Fiona to pay attention to her future," Papa said.

"I *am* paying attention."

Fi fought to keep the frustration out of her voice. Her parents had *no idea* how many balls she was keeping in the air, playing the parts of a successful debutante and secret agent. She could outperform the dashed jugglers at Astley's Amphitheatre. The truth was she did feel a bit frayed at the edges...not that she would admit it.

I can handle everything. I always have.

"Then why haven't you settled on a husband?" Papa raised his brows. "God knows you have a long enough list to choose from."

"No one possesses all the qualities I seek in a husband. And you," she said pointedly, "taught me never to settle."

Papa's gaze thinned. "Be that as it may, popularity is a fickle thing, my dear; you must not rely on it to last forever. Take too long closing the deal, and you may regret it."

Hoping the lecture was over, she bit her tongue.

"Don't be cross, Fiona," Mama said. "We love you and wish to keep you safe."

Whereas Papa's sermon had fanned Fi's defiance, Mama's genuine concern dumped ashes on the flames. Truth be told, Fi felt guilty. She knew her parents wanted to protect her; she just wished they accepted her as well.

"I know," she muttered.

The lines eased around Mama's eyes. "With crime on the rise, it simply isn't safe for you to be traipsing about London. Why, this morning the papers said there was another attack by the Sherwood Band. Lord and Lady Easton were held up in their carriage at *gunpoint.*"

"Until those criminals are captured," Papa said, "Mama and I have decided that you must take a pair of footmen with you when you visit Lady Fayne's."

The decree felt like a noose tightening around Fi's neck. To date, she'd gotten away with bringing along her lady's maid Brigitte. She'd hired Brigitte on Charlie's recommendation; her mentor had praised the maid's skills, which included loyalty and discretion. While Brigitte could be depended upon to keep Fi's secrets, footmen were another matter.

"I am perfectly safe at Charlie's," she protested. "Please trust me on this."

"It is not about trust but safety," Papa said firmly.

"Glory, Livy, and Pippa don't have to bring footmen with them—"

"What those ladies' husbands and parents permit is inconsequential. You are my daughter, and I am saying you will bring footmen. Or you will not go at all."

Angry heat pushed behind Fi's eyes. "That is dashed unfair!"

"Regardless, the choice is yours," Papa said flatly.

Before Fiona could respond, the doorbell rang. The Hadleighs had arrived.

Her breath hitching and hands balled at her sides, Fi strove to calm herself. There was no point in arguing with Papa once he made up his mind. She would simply have to figure out some way to manage the latest Draconian requirement.

"Fine," she said tightly. "Is there anything else?"

Papa sighed. "You know we only want the best for you, don't you, Fiona?"

With a pang, she remembered a time when she'd been the apple of her father's eye. When he had given her everything and anything her heart desired. Then, when she was nine, Papa had been shot. Even now, the memory of that terrifying time chilled her. She recalled how still and waxen he'd looked, how devastated Mama had been despite her efforts to hide it. Most nights, Fiona had cried herself to sleep, only to be jolted awake by horrible dreams of loss.

Luckily, Papa had made a full recovery. Since his injury, however, he'd changed. Max had become his favorite whilst with Fiona, he'd become stricter and less indulgent. It was as if his brush with death had made him see her more clearly...and he didn't like what he saw. She'd tried to impress him with all her genteel accomplishments, her popularity.

While achievements are important, he would say, *do not let ambition rule you. Never lose sight of what is important, Fiona: the people you love and who love you in return.*

He seemed to see through her machinations, straight to her flaws. The willful and defiant nature she couldn't change, even if she wanted to. Helpless frustration knotted her insides. It seemed like her fate was to be judged wanting by others. By the snobs, her father...even that blasted Hawksmoor, who thought she was "frivolous" and a "temperamental flirt" even though he hardly knew her.

Who cares what anyone thinks? What I need is to secure my freedom—and soon. If I have to, I'll marry an oblivious fool to gain my independence.

Tamping down her ache, she brightened her smile. "Of course, Papa. Now may I be excused? I do not wish to keep my friends waiting."

Fiona and the Hadleighs arrived at the Theatre Royal awhile later, and visitors immediately swarmed the Hadleighs' private box. Once a wild rake with a tarnished reputation, Livy's handsome, dark-haired husband was living proof of the adage about reformed rakes. The duke had become a new man since his marriage. Seeing the loving glow in Hadleigh's midnight-blue eyes when he looked at Livy, Fiona was very glad for her friend.

For her part, Fi worked at being her charming best. Her presence tonight functioned as an alibi, and she wanted to make sure her parents heard about her impeccable behavior. It still stung that her father did not trust her judgement and insisted that she take footmen to Charlie's...but she would worry about that bridge when she crossed it.

For now, she would focus on the night's plan.

Anticipation simmered in Fiona as the lights finally dimmed in the theatre, dispersing the visitors from the Hadleighs' box. A few minutes later, the velvet curtains parted to reveal the ramparts of Elsinore Castle. As the watchmen came onto the stage, Fiona saw Hadleigh bend his head toward his wife.

"Are you certain you do not need my escort, little queen?" he said softly.

"You must hold the fort until Fi and I get back." Livy brushed her lips against his lean cheek. "We won't be long, darling."

Fi and Livy exited the box, hurrying down the empty corridor and stairwell to one of the back exits. Hawker, Charlie's butler and one of the Angels' teachers, was waiting for them. Sitting on the driver's perch of an unmarked carriage, he resembled a brawny pirate with his black eye-patch, short, bristly hair, and fierce scowl. Fi suspected that he used his rough exterior to cloak his gentle heart.

"'Urry up," he grumbled. "You've got an hour and a 'alf before the sweet prince sticks a blade in old Polonius and intermission begins."

"Well, don't ruin the plot for us," Fi teased as she climbed in.

Hawker snorted. "If you don't know the bard's masterpiece by now, there's no 'ope for you."

Inside the carriage, the curtains were already drawn. While the tavern was a stone's throw away, Fi and Livy needed a place to change into their disguises. Thanks to the genius of the Angels' modiste, Mrs. Quinton, the transformation from lady to light-skirt took place in a blink.

The expert tailoring of their evening gowns hid the fact that all pieces were detachable. Delicate tiered skirts were unhooked, thin sateen layers attached in their place. Elegant off-the-shoulder bodices were replaced with gaudy low-cut ones, and their ringlets were covered with heavy wigs. Face paint concealed their features. When the carriage pulled up to the Royal Arms several minutes later, a pair of blonde tarts emerged.

Entering the rowdy public house, Fi assessed the dimly lit space. A carved wooden bar took up one side of the room, behind which the barkeep was filling glasses and palavering with patrons balanced on rickety stools. The area next to the bar was packed with tables, barmaids weaving through the throng, delivering refreshments and dodging groping hands. At the back of the pub, three steps led up to another seating area, the packed booths shrouded by the smoky haze of the hearth.

Fi noted the mix of people present in the front room. From bricklayers who wore the dust of their labor to aristocrats looking to cure their ennui, the Royal Arms opened its doors to all. She saw the way some patrons eyed one another: like predators judging the worthiness of prey. Despite the pub's cozy ambiance, Fi did not doubt that it was a hunting ground where vice and danger lurked.

Did Lillian fall prey to a predator? she wondered with a shiver.

In an undertone, Livy said, "Shall we talk to the barmaids first?"

"Let's start with the auburn-haired one." Fi gave a subtle nod in the woman's direction.

The barmaid greeted her patrons by name. Her weathered face and shrewd eyes suggested that she'd seen her share of comings and goings and missed little that happened around her.

When a group of aristocratic gentlemen drunkenly abandoned their table, she collected her tips, scowling at the paltry coins in her palm.

Fi and Livy secured a table in her section, next to the steps that led to the upper seating area. The serving maid came over, with a tray tucked under her arm and a smile that didn't reach her close-set eyes.

"Good evenin', luvs. Ain't see you in 'ere before," she said.

"Being working women, me friend and I don't 'ave many nights off." Thanks to the Angels' training, Livy's cockney accent was quite creditable.

"Know what that's like, don't I," the barmaid said. "My idea o' a good time is putting me feet up in front o' a fire. Name's Ruby, by the by."

"I'm Annie," Livy said, "and this is me friend, Rosalind, but everyone calls 'er Roz. We're seamstresses o'er in Spitalfields."

"Seamstresses, eh? 'Ard way to make a living."

"Wages ain't much," Livy agreed. "We 'ave to work nights to make ends meet, if you know what I mean."

"A woman's got to do wot a woman's got to do," Ruby said philosophically.

"Ain't that a fact." Livy heaved a sigh, obviously getting into the part.

While Fi admired her friend's performance, she was aware that the clock was ticking. They had about an hour left; time to get the ball rolling.

"We've been meaning to come by," Fi said in a friendly tone. "E'er since a friend o' ours told us 'ow much she fancied this place."

Ruby lifted her straight brows. "Did she now?"

Fi nodded. "She said it was the genuine article and not like other pubs that are catering more and more to the 'igh-kick crowd. Said the barmaids 'ere were salt-o'-the-earth."

Fi knew she'd chosen the right approach when Ruby preened.

"We pride ourselves on being welcoming to folk from all walks o' life," the barmaid said. "Who's your friend wot recommended us?"

"'Er name's Lillian. Lillian O'Malley. Maybe you remember 'er?"

Ruby scrunched her forehead. "Waifish thing wif black 'air and blue eyes? Real looker with a will-o'-the-wisp manner about 'er?"

"That's our Lillian." Hiding her excitement, Fi said ruefully, "Always wif 'er 'ead in the clouds, that one. Actually, we were 'oping to run into 'er tonight. You 'aven't seen 'er, 'ave you?"

"Sorry to say I ain't seen 'er for, oh, five months at least. Before that, she was a regular. Seemed like a nice young woman." Ruby pursed her lips. "Any particular reason you're looking for 'er?"

"We're worried," Fi said honestly. "She seems to 'ave vanished into thin air. The last time we saw 'er she was trying to make a go o' it as an actress."

"Lillian did speak o' that," Ruby said. "Said she 'ad to settle for working at third-rate theatres and music halls since she couldn't land any good parts."

"Do you know the names o' any of those places?" Livy asked.

Ruby shook her head. "Sorry. Wish I could 'elp."

"Was Lillian ever 'ere wif anyone?" Fi asked. "A fellow, maybe?"

Ruby hesitated, then leaned closer. "One o' the last times I saw Lillian, she was wif some cove. Reason I noticed is because she usually swatted men away like flies. She knew wot she wanted, and it weren't an old pot and pan and brace of brats 'anging onto 'er apron strings."

An old pot and pan, Fi knew, was rhyming slang for "husband."

"But she seemed different with this cull," Ruby went on. "Clinging to 'is every word, acting as if 'e walked on water."

"Can you describe 'im?" Livy asked.

"'E was in 'is thirties, fine-looking fellow. Medium height, wif golden-brown 'air and light-colored eyes...green, maybe? It was 'ard to tell in this light. Anyway, 'e 'ad a way about 'im...I can't describe it exactly. But it was like one o' those mesmeric shows. You know, where the performer puts people in a trance, and they dance and sing at 'is command?"

A shiver crossed Fi's nape. "Do you know his name?"

"Didn't catch it. 'E and Lillian were only 'ere together once. They were real lovey-dovey...but I didn't trust 'im."

Fi tilted her head. "Why not?"

"'E 'ad a roving eye," Ruby said flatly. "When Lillian went to use the necessary, 'e chatted wif every female that passed by 'is table."

She was interrupted by patrons shouting for drinks.

Pivoting, she yelled back, "'Old your bleeding 'orses! I'm wif paying customers." Turning back to Fi and Livy, she said, "I'd best take your orders and get on."

"Two ales," Livy said. "And our thanks for your 'elp."

"We females 'ave to stick together." With a nod, Ruby hurried off.

When the barmaid was out of earshot, Fi whispered, "So Lillian *was* involved with a man. And he sounds like a shady character—"

She cut herself off as a group of men stumbled down from the upper seating area and past the table. She sat up straighter, staring at their backs as they headed for a side door. Two stocky brutes supported a well-dressed man between them. By the way he was being dragged, the man appeared to be three sheets to the wind. Two other rough-looking fellows took up the front and rear of the procession.

The men could be helping a drunken companion get some air. Or they could be planning something nefarious. Which was none of Fiona's business, except...

"What is it?" Livy asked alertly.

"The man being led to the door." Pulse racing, Fi craned her neck. "I can't get a view of his face, but could it be Hawksmoor?"

"Hard to say from behind. But, yes"—Livy's voice crested in surprise—"it *does* look like him."

As the brutes hauled the man outside, Fi could not ignore her intuition.

"If that is Hawksmoor, he's no match for those ruffians. He's a stodgy, bookish fellow, for heaven's sake." She shot to her feet. "We have to help him."

SEVEN

"Easy does it, guv," a voice said. "We're almost there."

Hawk felt himself being dragged along.

"Where are we going?" His voice was slurred, his vision blurry.

"You need some air, guv. You 'ad too much to drink."

Did I drink too much? Hawk shook his head, trying to clear it. *Why can't I think?*

A moment of clarity surfaced between disorienting waves. *The mission.*

"Play the part of the jaded lord looking for a diversion," Swinburne had instructed. *"Your job is to observe. To collect information about the Sherwood Band."*

Hawk had been listening to the ebb and flow of conversation in the pub. The Sherwood Band had come up more than once... mostly the object of admiration, although a few patrons had voiced their condemnation of the group's methods. Hawk had taken note of all that he'd heard. Then four men had asked to sit at his table. Porters, they'd claimed to be, and seemed friendly enough. Thinking that the men added to the veracity of his cover, he'd bought them a round. One of the coves had gone to fetch the drinks...

The realization burst through the fog in Hawk's brain.

Devil take it...I've been drugged.

He was hauled through a door and into an alleyway silvered by moonlight. Brick walls seemed to stretch upward and curve over his head. He struggled, the effort making his head spin.

"It'll go be'er for you if you don't fight us, guv," a sneering voice said.

Hawk's back was slammed against brick. Dark waves of oblivion rose around him.

"Anyfin' we find on the nob, we get to keep. Ain't that right, Big Jim?" another voice replied.

"That's right. If 'e gives you any trouble, bash 'is bleedin' noggin in."

The pawing hands jolted Hawk. He flashed to moments in his life when he'd been preyed upon. The bullies at Eton beating him for being scrawny and studious. He hadn't stood down then; he wasn't about to now.

Rage pushed back his drugged haze.

He swung out with his fists, felt a satisfying crack. A bastard howled in pain, grabbing his broken nose. Hawk punched again and caused another man to double over. When a third man came at him, he feinted left and used the blackguard's momentum to send him crashing into the brick wall. Another attacker plowed into Hawk, knocking him to the ground.

Hawk grappled with his foe. Even as his vision began to blur, he managed to get the upper hand, plowing his fists into the other's face. Two men grabbed him by the arms, dragging him back, and he fought them with everything he had.

"For a stodgy, bookish fellow, Hawksmoor certainly holds his own." Livy's tone was dry. "Are you certain he needs our help?"

Watching the men brawling at the far end of the alleyway, Fiona saw with some shock that Hawksmoor knew how to put his fists to use. In fact, she thought with an appreciative tingle, he fought as well as he danced. If he hadn't been drugged—she guessed that had to be the reason for his unsteady stance—he could have taken the four blighters on his own.

He battled like a warrior. Like a dashing hero.

Excitement shivered through her. *Like my thief.*

Fi tucked away her speculation for now. Waving a hand at the scuffling men, she said indignantly, "Not only is Hawksmoor outnumbered, but he's obviously been drugged. We must assist him."

"I thought he annoyed you."

"He does. But I cannot allow him to get pummeled."

"All right. Just remember we're due back at the theatre soon." Livy raised her brows. "And you'll have to explain to Hawksmoor what we're doing here dressed like this."

"I'll come up with something." Fi removed the small pistol hidden in her skirts. "This won't take long."

Raising her arm, she let off a shot. The sharp crack echoed through the alleyway and interrupted the fighting. The men whipped their heads in Fi's direction.

"Leave the toff alone," she said. "And no one gets hurt."

"Mind your own business, wench," a brute spat.

"Leave the ladies to me." A bearded man with a low-domed hat leered at Fiona. "You fellas take care o' the nob; I've a mind for a quick upright."

"Don't come any closer," Fi warned.

He advanced.

Taking aim, she fired.

"Bleeding 'ell!" He grabbed at the empty space above his head.

Twisting, he looked at the ground behind him where his hat now rested, sporting a large new hole. "That was me favorite 'at!"

"It'll be your favorite *heart* next." Fi took out her dagger, letting the moonlight glint off its honed blade. "You and your gang 'ad better leave now."

The bastard charged...because bastards always did.

She let her dagger fly. She aimed for his upper arm, a flesh wound to deter rather than do permanent damage. Not that one would know it from the way the brute screamed and slumped against the wall. Unfortunately, the sound spurred the other blackguards into action. Two came charging at Fi and Livy, while another grappled with Hawksmoor. The Angels adopted the fighting stances that Mrs. Peabody, their combat instructor, had taught them.

Mrs. Peabody's advice played in Fi's head. *Your opponent will be larger, stronger. Therefore, you must be smarter.*

Fi waited until the last possible moment to dodge her attacker, sticking her foot out as she did so. He tripped and went flying. When he rose, he was angrier than a hornet.

He swiped a hand at his bleeding nose. "You're going to pay for that, you bleedin' whore."

Keeping light on her feet, Fi evaded him while sizing up his fighting style: slow, heavy, and predictable. Dodging one ham-sized fist, she went in on his weak side, landing two blows to his gut before stomping on his foot. As he gasped, she kneed him in the groin.

He crumpled to the ground, whimpering.

"Watch out!"

At Livy's warning, Fi spun around. A brute came at her, his fist aimed at her head. When she ducked, his hand caught on her wig; pain shot through her scalp as he yanked it off. He shoved her into a wall, her cheek smacking against brick. On instinct, she dropped into a crouch and grabbed her second dagger, slashing it upward as she came up. Her opponent screamed as the steel sliced through flesh. Grabbing his bleeding arm, he ran from the alley.

Livy was beside her in an instant. "Are you—?"

"I'm fine," Fi panted. "The blighters—"

"They're done for tonight." Livy had her pistol out, aiming it at their remaining foe.

Bloodied and beaten, the men limped past them.

Fi's gaze flew to the other end of the alley. Hawksmoor's shoulders-back posture was that of a warrior who'd defended his keep, his fierce scowl promising retribution to any enemy who dared to return. His gaze remained trained on the ruffians as they scurried off into the shadows. Only then did he let down his guard, bracing one hand against the wall.

Livy picked Fi's wig up from the ground; it looked like a trampled animal.

"This won't be of much use," Livy muttered.

"Hawksmoor's drugged," Fi said. "Perhaps he won't recognize me."

"Good luck. While you tend to him, I'll get a hackney to take him home."

As her friend rushed off, Fiona went to the earl.

Using her best trollop's voice, she said, "'Ow are you, guv?"

Hawksmoor stared at her. "Miss...Miss Garrity? What're you doing here?"

So much for him not recognizing me.

Despite his dilated pupils and slurred speech, Hawksmoor apparently retained his intellectual powers. That he'd stayed on his feet and given a splendid accounting of himself against four brutes was a miracle. His eyes were glazed, closing; he was unlikely to remember much come tomorrow. Which was a good thing, where Fiona was concerned. Before he gave into oblivion, however, she had to assess the damage.

"Are you hurt?" she said. "Is anything broken?"

His eyelids shut, his legs giving out. He slumped, unconscious, his back against the wall.

Crouching next to him, she checked for injuries. As her palms brushed over hard, bulging muscles, she felt a warm flutter. Clearly, Hawksmoor did not spend all his time behind a desk. She continued her inspection, finding no critical wounds. When she saw the state of his damaged knuckles, however, she blew out a breath.

"We'll need something to bind your hands," she murmured.

She unwound his cravat.

"Are you undressing me, Miss Garrity?"

She jerked her gaze up to his. Although his words were slurred, he was watching her with a smoldering intensity that quickened her breath.

"I need your cravat to bind your hands," she said. "You're bleeding all over the place."

"Like you...undressing me." His gaze grew unfocused again. "Wish you'd do it more often."

She felt her cheeks flame. Was Hawksmoor *flirting* with her? After he'd made his disinterest in her abundantly clear?

He's drugged, she reminded herself. *He doesn't know what he's saying.*

"As I recall, I am the *last woman* you'd be interested in." She tore the cloth into makeshift bandages. "It must be the drink talking."

"Not the drink. Truth." His eyes closed, he mumbled, "You're a...bloody goddess. My Sól. Can't stop thinking...about you..."

Stunned, she asked, "Then why did you insult me?"

"Didn't mean to." He lifted his lashes, gazing blearily at her. "Doesn't matter. Bad idea...you and me..."

Fi wrapped the bandages around his large hands, trying to fathom his startling words. He *was* interested in her? Thought she was a goddess? His *soul*? What on earth did that mean?

Hawksmoor's snore broke her reverie.

Torn between amusement and exasperation, she said loudly in his ear, "Get up, my lord. We have to get you home and into bed."

He popped open one eye. "Are you joining me?"

She chuckled at his drunkenly hopeful tone. "Who knew you were such an outrageous flirt?"

"Don't know how to flirt," he said solemnly.

Amused, she asked, "Do you know how to stand up?"

"Think so." Furrows deepened on his forehead. "Maybe not. Legs aren't working."

"Here, lean on me, and I'll help you."

Placing his arm over her shoulder, she managed to get them both to their feet. He leaned heavily on her, what felt like fourteen stone of pure muscle. By the time they got to the mouth of the alley, she was panting.

"We'll wait here for your ride," she said.

"You're not coming with me?" He gave her a crestfallen look.

"All proprieties are lost on you at the moment, aren't they?" Shaking her head, she said with a rueful smile, "I rather like you this way."

"You like me?"

Her belly flip-flopped at Hawksmoor's hungry intensity. The male longing that flooded his gaze with sudden lucidity. Her lips parted in surprise as he pressed her against the wall; Hawksmoor loomed over her, his palms planting on either side of her head. His chiseled features taut, he stared at her as if she were the only thing he cared to see.

"I like you, too," he said thickly. "My bold, bloody-minded little minx."

Her pulse fluttered wildly as he bent his head. She could have stopped him, but she didn't want to. From the moment they met, a part of her had been curious about his kiss.

Hawksmoor's lips were firm, molding to hers with masterful precision. Her head whirled as he deepened the pressure, coaxing her lips open with sensual sweeps of his tongue. She quivered at the taste of him, hot and male and tinged with spirits. The memory of her other passionate encounter wisped through her head.

Like the thief, Hawksmoor doesn't make love like a gentleman.

Hawksmoor continued the hot onslaught on her senses. When his tongue stroked hers, she moaned and wound her arms around his neck. Liquid heat poured through her veins, vaporizing her inhibitions. This was what she wanted, what she craved. This feeling of excitement, of being passionately *alive*. Only one man had affected her this way before.

The fire inside her grew as he devoured her mouth. She burned with desires she couldn't hold back. Flames licked over her skin as he pressed her harder into the wall. Trapped against his muscular chest, her breasts heaved, their tips stiff and tingling. Needing more, she speared her fingers in his hair, tugging him closer.

He growled in approval and thrust his tongue nearly down her throat. At the same time, he clamped his hands on her bottom and wedged his thigh between her legs. Shocking pleasure blazed through her. The thin skirts of her disguise offered little protection against his sinewy masculinity, the firm ridges rubbing against her most private place. She ignited with bliss and need and utter desperation. She was hot everywhere: her swollen lips, her throbbing nipples, and her woman's place where wetness suddenly gushed. She squirmed against his muscular thigh, wanting more of the sensations. More of him.

"Christ, yes," he groaned against her lips. "Ride me, you wicked chit."

He called her "wicked" as if it were a good thing. His praise was tinder to her fire. She rubbed herself against him, faster and faster, their kiss raging out of control...

"Ahem."

Livy's voice pierced Fi's fog of desire. She opened her eyes; with a gasp, she shoved Hawksmoor away. He stumbled, catching himself against the opposite wall.

"What in blazes?" he muttered.

He looked disoriented and disheveled. Like a man who'd been drugged.

What's my *excuse?*

Fi wetted her lips and tried to calm her unfulfilled shivers. She saw the waiting hackney. Wordlessly, Fi crossed to Hawksmoor, who stared at her with glazed eyes.

"Time to get you home," she said.

She ducked under his arm, helping him into the hackney, where he sprawled onto the bench. She barely got his address from him before his eyelids slid shut. Furtively, she searched his pockets; in an inner compartment of his coat, she found what she was looking for.

She pulled out the earring. Pocketed it.

In Hawksmoor's current state, the austere lines of his face were softened, giving him an almost boyish quality. She brushed a stray lock from his brow before closing the door. She gave the driver extra coin to get him home safely.

As the hackney bumped off, Livy cleared her throat. "What was it that you once called Hawksmoor? A 'pompous old scholar'?"

Cheeks flaming, Fi muttered, "I don't want to talk about it."

EIGHT

Fi floated into wakefulness as if surfacing through warmed honey. She opened her eyes and blinked dazedly at the ruffled ivory canopy of her bed. She wasn't used to sleeping so deeply. Her busy mind usually woke her up early with to-do lists: required steps to keep her status as an Incomparable, essential subterfuges to maintain so that she could continue being an investigator. She often jolted awake, already in a panic that she'd forgotten to do something.

This morning, however, her mind felt pleasantly groggy. As if she had nothing to do, nowhere to be but where she was, in her cozy featherbed. She snuggled deeper under her coverlet, savoring the feeling of languor. She'd had the most marvelous dream. She tried to recall the details, what had made her feel so warm and tingly...

Her eyes flew open as the events of last evening came rushing back.

Heavens, Hawksmoor kissed me...and it was splendid.

Memories of their torrid embrace awakened her fully. His masculine intensity had overwhelmed her senses. Beneath his buttoned-up exterior lay a man of deep passions...and one who was not afraid of a woman whose desires matched his. Recalling how he'd told her to ride him and how wantonly she'd obeyed, she felt a flutter in her private cove.

The earl was a surprise...in every way.

Sitting up, she opened the drawer of her bedside table and removed the pair of earrings she'd placed there last night. She held one in each hand: the golden semi-circles were a perfect match. Either it was an unbelievable coincidence or...

The Earl of Hawksmoor is my dashing French thief.

Her heart hiccupped. The way she'd responded to Hawksmoor confirmed her intuition; only he and the thief had inspired such wanton feelings in her. Furthermore, the two were of a similar height, build, and the eyes behind the mask which had intrigued her for weeks now appeared a stormy grey in her mind. Both men could also hold their own in combat. Considering the evidence, she was left with a question: what on earth had the reputedly staid and proper earl been doing disguised as a Frenchman in von Essen's study?

She didn't think Hawksmoor was a professional burglar. From all accounts, he was as rich as Croesus; why would he risk his honor for money he did not need? A likelier explanation was that the dodgy count had had in his possession something of Hawksmoor's...something that Hawksmoor had wanted back. Or the earl, like Fi herself, could have been helping someone else. Perhaps von Essen was blackmailing a friend of his.

The possibilities were as numerous as they were fascinating. Yet one thing was for certain: Hawksmoor was no stodgy scholar. Like her, he had secrets.

Perhaps they were more alike than she realized. Recalling the longing in his eyes when he'd asked her if she liked him, she felt an odd spasm.

"I like you, too," he'd said.

While she'd been showered with compliments since her debut, she could not recall a single man who'd told her that he *liked* her. And not for the superficial trappings of her looks and wealth. He had singled out her boldness and bloody-minded nature, traits she didn't think any man would admire. The same qualities, in fact, that had earned her father's disapproval.

Hawksmoor's rationale for resisting his attraction to her was an enticing mystery. As was his presence at both von Essen's and an establishment like the Royal Arms. Frowning, Fi wondered about his purpose last eve. He didn't seem like a louche aristocrat out to relieve his ennui.

She knew that helping him had come with risks; Charlie would likely chastise her for compromising the mission. Thankfully, the earl was unlikely to remember much of what happened. In his drugged state, he hadn't even registered that Fi had been dressed like a trollop.

She told herself it was for the best that Hawksmoor was unlikely to remember much of last night, including their kiss. Drugged, his inhibitions had been loosened; sober, he was bound to feel differently about her. In fact, he would probably revert to his old proper and disapproving self.

The thought was rather deflating.

Stop being a ninny, she lectured herself. *Between pulling the wool over Mama and Papa's eyes, conducting investigations, and dazzling Society, you have enough on your plate. You don't have time to worry about whether an enigmatic earl likes you.*

The reminder of all that had to be done got her out of bed. She went to the washstand to splash water on her face...and gasped in horror at her reflection. A bruise had unfurled like an exotic purple bloom on her right cheek. The swelling had spread beneath her eye, giving her a shocking shiner.

"Dash it all," Fi breathed. "I'm doomed."

The bruise hadn't looked bad last night. During the carriage ride back to the theatre, Livy had expertly applied concealing face paint, and Fi had pulled her ringlets forward to hide the area. During intermission, Fi had been careful to stay in the shadowed area of the Hadleighs' box; no one had seemed to notice anything different about her.

Now, however, the bruise shone like a dashed beacon; it might take days to fade. She shot a desperate glance at the gold shepherdess ormolu clock on her dressing table. The clock face next to the beaming country lass showed that it was already eleven in the morning.

"What do you have to be so cheerful about?" Fi moaned to the innocent shepherdess. "If I don't figure something out, I am going to land in hot water for certain. How am I going to show my face to my family...and to the visitors who will undoubtedly call this afternoon?"

She'd been lucky her parents had been abed when she arrived home last night. But she couldn't hide in her bedchamber all day. She rang for Brigitte, praying that her maid could work a miracle. In the meantime, she sat at her dressing table, frantically dabbing on concealing paint.

The knock on her door filled her with relief. "Come in, Brigitte—"

"Fiona, dearest, it is Mama. Papa and I wish to speak with you."

Her mother's gentle voice acted like a spring, catapulting Fi from her chair. Shoving the cosmetics into a drawer with shaking hands, she called out, "I am still in my nightgown, Mama, and not presentable."

"Are you all right?" Mama's worry filtered through the wood. "It is almost noon. You are never abed this late."

"I'm fine." Fi whirled around her room. *What can I use to hide my face?*

"Fiona, this is Papa. Open the door now."

Dash it all.

"Um...I can't. I can't find my dressing robe," Fi lied.

"You have at least a half-dozen hanging in your wardrobe," Mama said helpfully.

"I need time to change. If you'll just wait for me in the drawing room—"

"Unlock this door, young lady." Papa's tone brooked no refusal. "Or I will."

Fiona backed away from the door. Wildly, she looked for a place to hide...and ducked behind the dressing screen in the corner. And not a moment too soon. She heard the click of the lock, and her parents entered.

"I...I'm just getting changed." Her heart thundered in her ears; her voice tremored.

"I'll help you, dear," Mama said.

"No, truly, it is not necessary—"

It was too late. Mama stood at the opening of the dressing screen. Her blue eyes rounded with heart-wrenching dismay.

"Oh, my heavens!" she cried. "What happened to your face?"

"It was just an accident, Mama. It looks much worse than it is—"

Then Papa was there, looming next to Mama. He roved a pitch-black gaze over Fiona. Seeing the white lines slashed around his mouth, Fi knew she was done for.

"Come out this instant," he snapped.

She did as she was told. Shoulders hunching, she faced the firing squad.

"I can explain," she began.

"The time for explanations is over, young lady," Papa bit out. "We know what you have been up to."

Fi's breath jammed in her throat. *Oh, no. How did they find out about my investigating?*

"We forbid you from further participation in Lady Fayne's group." Papa's expression was foreboding. "Your charity work stops now."

Charity work. That's what they think I've been up to. They don't yet know the truth.

Fi's relief was halted by her father's continuing lecture.

"In case you plan to participate behind our backs, I will be paying Lady Fayne a visit and making my wishes clear." Menace threaded Papa's voice. "Her reputation may be spotless, but my instincts tell me that woman is hiding something. If she chooses to involve you in her schemes any further, she will answer to me."

"You cannot threaten Charlie," Fiona said, aghast.

"Watch me."

Hands balling at her sides, Fi narrowed her gaze; Papa did the same. Neither backed down.

"Now, my dears. There is no need to get overworked." Mama got in between them in a rustle of rose-colored silk. "Let us discuss the situation like reasonable adults."

"That would require that you *treat* me like an adult," Fi blazed.

"Act like one, and we will," Papa clipped out. "What in blazes do you think you're doing, Fiona? You look like a prizefighter, for God's sake. You are a debutante, not a bloody daredevil. I don't care how important your so-called charitable cause is: I will not have you getting hurt and ruining your reputation over it. And that is final."

"That is dashed unfair!" Fi fought back tears of frustration. "For once in my life, I am doing something meaningful—something I *want* to do. Why can't you support me? Why are you always so disapproving?"

"Because you are too stubborn and reckless for your own good," Papa fired back.

His censure felt like a blow. Yet pride kept Fi's chin up.

Mama wrung her hands. "We love you, Fiona. We want you to be happy but *safe* as well."

"If you loved me, then you would understand how important the Society of Angels is to me," Fi said bitterly. "Livy, Pippa, and

Glory get to participate without being interrogated by their families."

"Livy and Pippa are married," Mama said with infinite patience. "You know that married ladies have more freedoms. They can do what they wish, if their husbands agree. As for Glory, well, every family has its own rules..."

Despite Fi's turmoil, a lightning flash went off in her head.

Married ladies have more freedoms. They can do what they wish...

She blinked as the solution to her problems flared in her head. She couldn't believe she hadn't thought of this sooner. While she had considered marriage as a way of gaining her freedom, she'd balked at the idea of tying herself to an imperceptive fool. Now she realized she had another option.

What if she found a *convenient* husband?

A gentleman who would agree to lead separate lives. Who had his own hobbies and interests to keep him out of her hair. Who would not question her activities...because he had his own secrets to keep.

"Why do you have that look on your face?" Papa's gaze was narrowed.

"What look?" Her tone was innocent, her mind performing calculations.

Hawksmoor could use a wife to fulfill his duty, couldn't he? Especially a wife who would look the other way when it comes to his unorthodox pursuits. I, myself, need a husband to give me freedom. And there is the undeniable attraction between us...

"The look that says you are up to something. Whatever is in your head, get it out," Papa ordered. "I bear the blame for being too lax with you. You need guidance, and as your father, it is my duty to ensure that your future is a happy one. You will trust me on this."

"Yes, Papa," Fi said.

She needed guidance like she needed her shiner. Now that a

plan was forming in her head, however, she kept her expression guileless. She didn't know if her stratagem would bear fruit...if Hawksmoor would be open to her proposition. Botheration, she had dozens of suitors; why was the fellow best suited to her purposes the one she was least certain of?

If only I had a sign that my proposal would be welcomed.

A rapping sounded on the door.

"What is it?" Papa said.

The butler entered. "My apologies for interrupting, sir. A visitor has arrived."

Mama pinched her brows together. "Who would call at this unfashionable hour?"

"The Earl of Hawksmoor, ma'am."

Hawk had once been summoned to deactivate an explosive device. Another time, he'd had mere hours to crack an enemy code with the lives of fellow countrymen at stake. He'd also disguised himself and broken into a man's home to retrieve a priceless stolen brooch. Yet he had never felt as ill at ease as he did at this moment sitting in the Garritys' drawing room.

The longcase clock in the corner counted out the silence tick by tick. Hawk was seated adjacent to the settee occupied by Miss Garrity and her mama. Adam Garrity occupied a wingchair, his fingers drumming against the arm, his obsidian gaze hard and assessing. The tension in the room was thicker than the clotted cream that accompanied the scones on the pastry tray.

As Mrs. Garrity gamely started a conversation about the weather, Hawk knew that he'd committed a faux pas in calling at this early hour. Yet he'd been driven here by a burning question.

What the hell had happened last night?

This morning, he had awakened with a pounding megrim and equally pounding cockstand. While his memories of the previous evening were nebulous, he knew that Fiona Garrity had something to do with both conditions. The ill-concealed bruise on her cheek confirmed his worse suspicions and made his hands clench with protective rage.

Who had hurt her? Why had she been in that alleyway?

What in the devil happened between her and me?

What Hawk did remember was this: while on his mission, he'd been duped and drugged by a gang of ruffians. From there, his memories turned dark and fuzzy. Trying to recall what happened was like peering through a soot-covered window: he could only catch glimpses. He'd fought the brutes, and during the battle, Miss Garrity had somehow shown up and come to his aid.

But how had a debutante scared off a gang of brutes? Had she called for help? What in blazes had she been doing in that disreputable area in the first place?

The fact that she'd intervened on his behalf—that she'd stuck her swan-like neck out for him—filled him with wonder and rage. She was so feminine and delicate, and he wanted to tear whoever had hurt her from limb to limb. For the sake of his honor, he had to find out exactly what had happened, during the brawl...and after.

He'd come to in his own bed this morning, sweating and hard from an erotic dream. One in which Miss Garrity had played a starring role. Her red hair and celestial eyes had teased his mind's eye, made his hand travel over the rigid furrows of his stomach to his raging erection. He hadn't known if it was reality or fantasy he was reliving as he pressed her against a wall, plundering her mouth and making her ride his leg until she came. Feeling her hot, virginal pussy creaming against his thigh, he'd used a pillow to smother his groan as he spent with her taste on his tongue.

He could not have imagined her sweetness. The heat of her kiss. Something *had* happened between them...not that one would know by perusing the object of his fantasy.

Miss Garrity appeared utterly at ease. Her demure pink frock brought out the fire of her hair. Even her bruise highlighted her exquisiteness, the delicacy of her bone structure. She gave a dainty nibble on a cucumber sandwich as if she hadn't a care in the world. When she licked a crumb from her lush bottom lip, his balls drew up taut.

"...this time of year, don't you, my lord?"

Hawk swung his gaze at Mrs. Garrity, who regarded him with a quizzical expression. He had completely lost track of what she was saying.

"I beg your pardon, ma'am?" he inquired.

"I was asking if you had a preference for outdoor activities this time of year, my lord."

After a stilted pause, he said, "I enjoy riding."

"You and Fiona have that in common." Mrs. Garrity's smile was warm and unaffected. "She also has an excellent seat on a horse."

"Miss Garrity excels at anything she does," he murmured.

At the surprised pleasure that flashed through Miss Garrity's eyes, he felt a jolt of satisfaction. It was akin to the feeling he had when watching a machine of his design come to life for the first time. When it came to females, he did not have the gift of charm, yet he was not unobservant. Miss Garrity had a dazzling array of accomplishments, from dancing to conversational skills to personal style. Everything she did was of the highest caliber.

He understood ambition and respected achievement.

"That is kind of you to say, my lord," Miss Garrity said.

"It is the truth."

"In addition to riding, sir, do you also enjoy flora and fauna?"

The communication in her gaze was more complex than the scheme for an analytic engine. While he knew she was a project beyond his scope of understanding, he was utterly and inexorably captivated. She was like an idea that he knew would require too much of him and yet could not relinquish.

"I do," he said.

The mysteries of the universe rested in her smile, which he wanted to lick from her coral-pink lips.

"Then perhaps I might interest you in a tour of my mama's prized roses." She turned to her parents, the very picture of decorum. "May I have permission to show Lord Hawksmoor the garden?"

NINE

As Fiona led Hawksmoor into the garden, she was aware of two things. First, her parents were keeping close watch from the window of Papa's study, and they would not allow her to be alone with the earl for long. Second, this was her opportunity to take destiny into her own hands. Before she committed to her plan, however, she needed to ascertain how much Hawksmoor remembered of last night. His presence conveyed that he recalled something; the nature and extent of his memories would dictate her next moves.

As Fi led Hawksmoor down the pebbled path lined by manicured hedges, she was acutely aware of his robust virility. Unlike her, he looked none the worse for the wear. His navy frock coat was superbly fitted to his wide shoulders, his buff-colored trousers tailored to his long, muscular limbs. Black leather gloves hid his battle-worn knuckles. In the sunlight, his hair gleamed like a rich pelt.

It was his expression, however, that stirred a deep, feminine awareness. He looked as stern and austere as a schoolmaster, yet she knew what lay beneath his buttoned-up exterior. She'd felt the rough-silk slide of his hair between her fingers, the hot plunge of his tongue inside her mouth…

Don't get distracted by desire. Stay focused on your goal of determining whether Hawksmoor is the answer to your problems.

She took the bull by the horns. "Why did you come today, my lord?"

"I am not entirely certain." His gaze held a hint of storms roiling behind the placid surface. "May I be frank, Miss Garrity?"

"I would prefer it, my lord."

"Last night…you were there, weren't you?"

She was not about to incriminate herself any more than necessary.

"Where, exactly?" she asked politely.

"Devil take it, you know where." Frustration etched lines on his forehead. "At the Royal Arms. You witnessed my altercation with a gang of ruffians. As I had, ahem, overindulged, my memory is regrettably lacking in detail. But I would wager my estates on the fact that you were there. That you somehow came to my aid."

From their prior interactions, she knew him to be a proud, self-contained fellow. One in complete command of himself. The fact that he couldn't recall most of last night must be driving him mad. What he did remember made it necessary for her to provide a creditable reason for her presence.

"I was there," she admitted.

"I *knew* it." Relief blazed in his eyes. "But what were you doing there?"

"I might ask you the same thing," she said sweetly.

He looked discomfited. *Interesting.*

"I was in search of a diversion." After a pause, he raised his brows. "And you?"

Charlie had taught the Angels that the best excuse was often the simplest and closest to the truth. Fiona had discovered this for herself ages ago. She'd been a Willflower before she was an Angel; a girl with a taste for adventure had to master the art of providing plausible explanations for her behavior.

"I believe you are acquainted with the Hadleighs?" At his nod, she went on glibly, "The duchess is my dear friend, and we were on our way to the theatre. Our carriage happened to stop by the alleyway. I saw you being attacked and went to help."

He shot her an incredulous look. "You left the safety of your carriage, in Covent Garden at night, and dashed into an alleyway to help me?"

"And how fortunate for you that I did." She gave him an innocent smile. "And I was not alone; Lady Olivia was there with me. The brutes scattered when we raised the alarm."

His gaze locked on her bruised cheek. "How did that happen?"

Flushing at his intense scrutiny, she said, "As one of the blackguards was fleeing, he knocked me into a wall. I know I must look a fright, but it's just temporary."

"Nothing could detract from your beauty."

His stark words caused a flutter in her chest.

"Yet you took a great risk coming to my aid. I do not know whether I ought to thank you or lecture you."

She beamed at him. "Your thanks will do. And you're welcome."

Hawksmoor's bluntness and grumpy attitude combined for a rather charming effect.

He lowered his brows like a professor whose student has missed the point completely. "While I am in your debt, it is unacceptable for you to put yourself in harm's way. For any reason."

"Nothing happened," she said blithely. "I am perfectly well—"

"Are you certain nothing happened?" he interrupted.

"Like I said, the bruise will soon fade—"

"I'm not talking about your injury but about...us." Squaring his shoulders, he said, "To wit, have I done anything I need to apologize for, Miss Garrity?"

That depends. How sorry are you that you kissed me senseless? That you touched me, told me to ride you, and made me feel such deliciously improper things?

"No," she said honestly.

His eyes measured her. "No, I don't need to apologize...or no, nothing happened?"

She couldn't fight her rising blush. Maybe she didn't want to.

"Something did happen." His countenance darkened. "I *knew* it."

She cleared her throat. "Pray do not concern yourself over it, my lord—"

"If it is not my concern, then whose is it?" He lengthened his stride along the pebbled path, forcing her to keep up. "First you are hurt because of me. Then I bloody *compromised* you."

Casting a backward glance at the window where her parents were watching, Fi said urgently, "Will you please slow down? We will look suspicious otherwise."

"I am sorry, Miss Garrity. Sorrier than I can say for the harm I have caused you." He halted, clearly fighting to compose himself. "My behavior last night was inexcusable."

"The blame does not lie entirely at your door, my lord," she said candidly. "And I have come to no serious harm."

"Will you allow me to rectify the situation by marrying me?"

A connoisseur of proposals, Fi had to give Hawksmoor points for originality. His stark, unpolished offer stood out from the rest. Her own response was also unusual. She'd been proposed to by song and sonnet, yet she'd never felt this stirring excitement, this sensation of wild wings beating in her chest.

At the same time, she refused to take advantage of his honor. Her pride would not allow her to net a husband out of obligation. If they were to wed, she wanted it to be for the right reason: namely, that the match would bear advantages for both parties involved.

Hawksmoor and I each have secrets to hide. Families who want to see us settled. And we share a passionate connection. A marriage of convenience could be just the ticket for both of us.

"You honor me, my lord." She kept her gaze steady. "Before I accept your proposal, however, I have a few stipulations to make."

The fact that Miss Garrity didn't reject him out of hand stunned Hawk.

He felt almost giddy. Quite unlike his rational, level-headed self.

Then the voice of reason took over. *First, find out what her "stipulations" are. Fiona Garrity has her pick of husbands. Why does she want you—an older scholar with a temperament so different from her own?*

Logic cooled his euphoria. Reminded him of his own misgivings. Even though his honor had prompted him to make her an offer, he was far from certain that they would be a good match. While he was undeniably attracted to her, their personalities were too different. He'd avoided her initially because she was too young and unpredictable, and those qualities had not changed. Hell, this was the longest civil conversation they'd managed to have.

He eyed her. "What are your stipulations?"

"First, you should know that I value my independence," she said in crisp, businesslike tones. "I am a free-thinking woman. As such, I seek a modern sort of marriage."

As he hadn't been born yesterday, he asked warily, "What does a modern marriage entail?"

"Freedom, first and foremost. I am not a lady who would enjoy living in someone else's pocket," she said with candor. "I have my own interests and hobbies and would not welcome a husband's interference."

Hawk wondered if other men knew that Miss Garrity's delicate femininity hid a will of steel. He rather liked her forthrightness. Even as her words caused a boulder to sink in his gut.

You knew there was a catch, he told himself.

He matched her bluntness. "Would those interests and hobbies involve other men?"

"Heavens, no." Twin lines appeared between her brows. "Why would you think that?"

Her surprise seemed genuine...thank Christ.

He gave her a wry look. "What else would 'freedom' in marriage mean?"

"Oh...I see. Perhaps I did not express myself well." Her cheeks turned the color of peaches, heightening the vivid sincerity in her eyes. "I believe fidelity is a requirement of marriage, my lord."

"On that, we agree," he said firmly.

"Not only will I be faithful to my vows, but I would also expect the same from my husband."

He understood her message. It was, after all, as subtle as a dagger point.

"I was faithful during my first marriage." Recalling the scene she'd witnessed between him and his former mistress, he cleared his throat. "And I have ended any arrangements I've been privy to since then."

"Good." Miss Garrity's expression was adorably prim. "You might as well know that I am quite selfish and do not like to share. Anything."

"Nor would I expect you to," he said gravely. "This freedom you wish for then..."

"Pertains to my hobbies. I know you think I am a frivolous creature—"

"I do not think that."

Her gaze was shrewd. "Don't you?"

"That time you overheard me, I misspoke," he admitted. "I

think you are young, popular, and vivacious...in short, the opposite of me. Yet you also strike me as a lady who knows her own mind and acts according to her own code of honor. Your character is anything but frivolous."

She came to an abrupt halt. "My lord."

Hawk cocked his head. "Did I say something wrong?"

"On the contrary." Her eyes shone. "I do believe that is the nicest thing anyone has ever said to me."

He couldn't believe that to be true. Not when men had supposedly composed odes to her many graces. Yet there the chit was, staring at him in wonder.

"I meant every word," he said gruffly.

She gave him a tremulous smile, then continued strolling. "The truth is that I am a lady with ambitions beyond marriage. No offense."

"Why should I be offended?" Shrugging, he decided to be direct. "Marriage is not my sole purpose in life either. In fact, I had thought myself quite done with the institution."

She canted her head. "Why is that?"

Because my first experience made me doubt my ability to be a good husband. Made me wonder if I am capable of giving a wife what she needs...and if I even want to.

"What is your view on love?" He flinched slightly; he had not meant to sound abrupt or dismissive.

Yet Miss Garrity seemed unfazed by his question.

"I am glad you brought up the subject," she said earnestly. "For me, love is not a prerequisite for marriage. In fact, I think it may unduly complicate a relationship. It can lead to overprotectiveness and disappointment, two things I would rather do without. To my mind, an ideal marriage would be a partnership built on mutual respect. One in which a husband and wife would enjoy one another's company and work toward shared goals, but also retain their privacy and freedom to pursue their own interests."

Bloody hell...I could not have said it better myself.

He was astonished that she was proposing the exact kind of relationship he wanted. One in which he would have the benefits of marriage with none of the drawbacks. After Caroline's death, his attempts to seek companionship had been abysmal failures. His partners had all wanted what he did not have left to give: love.

But Miss Garrity did not want his love. The things she desired —freedom, companionship, and respect—*were* his to offer. Along with a title.

"Has my candor shocked you, my lord?" Miss Garrity bit her lip.

"The opposite is true," he hastened to say. "We are of one mind. The last thing I want is a complicated relationship. If possible, I would prefer to avoid emotional outbursts, unnecessary sentiments, and messy attachments altogether. I am not a romantic, by nature or inclination."

"Neither am I."

Her dimple peeped out, torturing him with hot, uncivil impulses.

Yet he had to make sure she understood. "As a widower and older man, I am unlike your dashing young suitors. I am not promising you the moon and the stars. To be a storybook prince or everything you need. What I offer, and what I seek, is a peaceful and easy partnership. To be frank, I do not have the capacity for more."

Caroline's weeping filled his head. His failed attempts to comfort her, to soothe away her pain. He saw her empty space at the supper table and the closed door between their chambers.

"You need not worry on my account, my lord." Miss Garrity's sunny confidence dispelled the shadows of his past. "As I've said, I value my independence above all. The last thing *I* want is a prince telling me what to do. I am a self-possessed creature who can take care of herself."

"So I am beginning to gather," he said with dawning hope.

"Our expectations are well aligned." Her optimism was infectious. "And we share a lot in common. As a polymath, you have many interests that keep you occupied. From your work with hieroglyphics to analytic machines—"

He felt a pleasant jolt of surprise. "You know about my work?"

"Your genius is well-known, my lord," she said smoothly. "My point is that we both have driving passions. My charity work is of the utmost importance to me. In fact, it is the reason why I would like to wed without delay. By special license, if possible."

"Why does your charity work necessitate haste?"

He asked out of curiosity. While he'd count himself lucky to skip the rigamarole of a wedding, he thought ladies lived for this sort of thing.

She set her jaw. "My parents believe that my involvement with the Society of Angels is unsuitable for an unwed lady. Yet participating in the charity means the world to me: it gives me a sense of purpose and satisfaction to know that I am helping others. And I will not give it up, even temporarily, for anyone."

Hawk understood her fervor; he felt the same way about the Quorum.

"I will not interfere with your work," he said. "You have my word."

"Thank you." Her smile was brighter than the sunrise. "In return, you have my promise to be a good wife. To make you and our families proud. At the risk of sounding immodest, I can claim a few accomplishments, all of which will be at your disposal. You may rest assured that I will fulfill my duties as your countess with the utmost diligence..."

As she listed her contributions, he tried to pay attention. But he was too aware of her nearness. Her peachy, mouth-watering scent. Caroline had been his first lover; in retrospect, he knew that their relations had not been particularly inspired. With the mistresses he'd had since, he had discovered more about his own sexual appetites and wanted a wife who enjoyed coupling as much as he did. Who wanted more than a perfunctory, once-a-month bedding. Who would be open to exploring their mutual carnal desires.

He tipped up Miss Garrity's chin with a gloved fingertip. Testing her and himself.

"Will you be a good wife to me?" he asked huskily. "In bed?"

Her lips parted, yet no words came out.

Good. It was nice to know that he could have the upper hand occasionally.

"My lord." Her voice was breathy. "That is wicked of you."

"It is best for you to know the kind of husband you will be getting."

Awareness deepened the blue of her eyes, the pulse at her throat fluttering. With other females, he would fear that he'd offended their sensibilities. But not with this bold little chit, praise God.

"I already know, my lord." She peered at him through her lashes. "I had a sampling last night."

His groin heating, he asked in a low voice, "What happened last night? Tell me the exact details."

"Ladies do not discuss such matters. If you want to know, you'll have to try to remember."

"Believe me, I *am* trying."

Her throaty laugh pulled on his cock.

"Try harder."

"Christ, you're a little minx," he growled.

"Are you certain you wish to marry me, my lord?"

He'd never been more certain of anything. His desire for her was like alchemy: it defied logic and yet even learned men could not resist its lure.

"I'm certain," he said. "By the by, you may call me Hawk. Or Thomas, if you prefer."

"Hawk." She blushed, looking sensual and innocent at once. "Then I am Fiona."

"My dear Fiona." Saying her name expanded his chest with proprietary pride. "Shall I speak to your father?"

Her face was radiant with promise. "Yes, please."

TEN

"It's almost time." Smoothing her white satin skirts, Fi checked the looking glass in a guest suite of the Hartefords' town house. "How do I look?"

Her maids of honor were Livy, Glory, and Pippa, the fourth Angel who'd just returned from a country sojourn with her husband Timothy Cullen. The trio smiled in unison, looking fetching in gowns of peach-colored silk, matching blossoms in their hair.

"Like a thousand hearts breaking," Glory declared. "Hawksmoor will be the envy of men."

The last week had passed in a blink. After Fi and Hawk's discussion in the garden, Hawk had spoken to her papa. The men had spent a long time locked in the study, ratcheting up Fi's anxiety.

After the earl's departure, Papa had asked her, *"Are you certain Hawksmoor is the husband you want, Fiona?"*

It was a bittersweet irony that her father was finally trusting her to make her own decisions.

She'd affirmed her choice.

With a grave nod, Papa had clasped her shoulder. *"Then I*

believe you have made a good choice, my dear. Hawksmoor strikes me as a steady and honorable fellow. Moreover, his prospects are excellent and not merely because of his title. The fellow understands the value of diversifying one's portfolio."

From her father, this was lavish praise indeed. Mama and Max, who both tended to like everyone, took a special liking to Hawk. From Lady Helena, Mama learned Hawk's teatime favorites and had them prepared for his visits. Hawk and Max hit it off, talking about their favorite museums, and Hawk even promised to show Max his computation machine.

Hawk's family had welcomed Fiona with equal warmth. Lady Helena was as kind-hearted as Fi's own mama, and the Marquess of Harteford's austerity reminded Fi of Hawk. Hawk's younger brothers, George and Henry, were a merry duo whose antics made Fi laugh. Hawk's twin Jeremiah was charming as always, and Fi had enjoyed a cozy chat with his pretty blonde wife Effie.

Effie had admired Fi's gown, bemoaning the fact that, after her second child, she felt like a sausage being squeezed into the latest styles. Fi shared her philosophy that fashion should flatter the wearer and not the other way around. She was certain that Mrs. Quinton—Mrs. Q to intimates—could show Effie's lovely curves to advantage, and Effie had been over the moon when Fi offered to secure her an appointment with the exclusive modiste.

While their families had questioned their decision to marry by special license, Fi and Hawk had held firm to their plan. Relenting, the families had put the full force of their social power behind the marriage. The Hartefords had offered their house for the intimate ceremony. Fi's mama and Lady Helena had worked together to cover the haste of the wedding with the gloss of romantic impetuosity.

The mamas' plan appeared to be working. Gossip raged about the unexpected love match, with several wags claiming they had predicted it after Fi and Hawk's passionate waltz. The engagement was being compared to a faerie tale. The small and exclusive wedding, to which only family and close friends had been invited, was hailed as the event of the Season. Indeed, footmen had to shoo away curious onlookers hoping to get a glimpse of the bride and groom.

Everything is going according to plan, Fi thought with satisfaction.

"Your dress is breathtaking." Pippa, a sunny blonde, bent to straighten the train. "I cannot believe Mrs. Q created it in less than a week."

Gazing at her reflection, Fi had to agree. While she'd wanted a quick wedding, her vanity had demanded that she look her best. Fortunately, her bruise had healed, and her bridal gown was a testament to Mrs. Quinton's genius.

Constructed of ivory satin, the off-the-shoulder dress had a fitted, elongated bodice and a deep flounce of priceless Belgian lace on the frothy skirts. The same lace trimmed the short train and bodice. Fi's hair had been dressed in a coronet studded with diamond pins and garnished with fresh orange blossoms.

She'd kept her jewelry simple. The engagement ring Hawk had given her—a large oval sapphire framed by diamonds—sparkled on her finger. In keeping with tradition, she also wore a pearl bracelet borrowed from her mama and a sapphire brooch gifted by Lady Harteford.

"Since Mrs. Q has created weapon-proof corsets for us," Livy said with a grin, "I'm certain designing a wedding dress poses little challenge. Unless the dress has special features that we are not aware of?"

"According to Mrs. Q, this dress has the most special feature of all," Fi said impishly.

"Is it waterproof? Fireproof?" Glory guessed.

"Does it have detachable skirts?" Pippa chimed in.

"This dress's secret power is..." Fi paused for effect before winking. "Its ability to bring a husband to his knees."

Livy rolled her eyes. "You hardly need a dress for that."

"In fact," Pippa said, a sly curve to her cheek, "the *lack* of a dress might accomplish that feat better."

Pippa and Livy exchanged knowing looks and giggled.

With a disgruntled sigh, Glory crossed her gloved arms. "Now that Fiona is getting married too, I shall be the only unwed Angel left. You have all gone and joined a club to which I don't belong."

Fi reached out and squeezed her friend's hand. "You will always belong, dear."

"*Sisters first will see us through.*" Livy and Pippa quoted the Angels' creed in unison.

"Besides, nothing is going to change after I'm married," Fi said. "I will carry on precisely as I've always done."

Silence greeted her statement. Livy and Pippa shared another glance.

"What?" Fi tilted her head. "Hawk and I have the perfect arrangement. He is not going to interfere with my work, nor I with his."

She hadn't told her friends about her suspicion that Hawk was, in fact, the raffish French thief. The secret did not feel like hers to share. Besides, she had decided that she would not speculate about her fiancé's hobbies. It seemed only fair that she should afford him the same privacy that he was giving her.

"Being married may change your perception of things," Pippa said gently.

"I am not letting marriage interfere with being an Angel." Fi's wave was dismissive. "Besides, you and Livy haven't stopped investigating."

"That is true," Livy acknowledged. "Yet there is more to balance as well. I must consider Hadleigh's wishes and he mine. Moreover, we have our daughter Esme to think about. Marriage simultaneously gives one more and less freedom; it is about compromise."

"Love changes everything." Pippa's azure eyes turned dreamy.

Fiona felt a strange thrill of panic...bridal jitters, she told herself.

"As Hawk and I have agreed to a partnership based on convenience, not love," she said doggedly, "I don't see why anything has to change."

"If you say so," Livy murmured.

Fi had an uneasy feeling that her friends, who'd married for love, did not believe that she had made a different choice. Being driven and self-possessed, she would choose the freedom to determine her own destiny over love any day. She would be perfectly content with a marriage built on respect and passion.

"I do say so. And Hawk agrees with me," Fi said firmly.

"Since I have known Hawksmoor all my life," Pippa said, "I would say that you are more than a convenience to him, dearest. I've never seen him look at a lady the way he looks at you."

As Pippa's parents had a close connection to the Hartefords, she'd grown up around Hawksmoor. She'd been delighted to hear of Fi's engagement to him, saying she believed their match to be ideal. Her present observation stirred Fi's curiosity. During their whirlwind engagement, Fi hadn't had a chance to be alone with Hawk, and she realized that there was much she didn't know about him.

Fi cleared her throat. "Is it different from the way he looked at his first wife?"

"Hawksmoor married when he was barely of age. From what I recall, Caroline was a lovely, intellectual lady," Pippa said thoughtfully. "He was very fond of her. Yet as the years passed, I did not see much of them. They lived year-round at their country estate since Hawksmoor preferred the seclusion for his work. Apparently, the pair did not welcome visitors. His mama often complained to mine about how infrequently she saw them."

Fi made a mental note to schedule regular visits with her mama-in-law. As she'd told Hawk, she was committed to being a good wife to him. To her mind, her role included maintaining good relations with his family and taking charge of the domestic sphere. Her pride demanded that she fulfill her new duties with excellence. She would never give Hawk cause to regret choosing her to be his countess.

"After Caroline's passing, Aunt Helena wanted Hawksmoor to remarry, but he wasn't paying her much mind...until he met you." Pippa beamed. "I think you are just what he needs, Fiona."

The idea of being needed struck a wistful chord in Fi. Yet she told herself that Pippa, being a romantic, was likely exaggerating.

"Hawk and I want the same things from marriage: respect and privacy," she said in pragmatic tones. "And he is holding up his end of the bargain splendidly. Two days ago, he invited me for a drive during the time I'd planned to canvass theatres for clues to Lillian. When I told him I was otherwise engaged, he was perfectly understanding. He didn't raise a fuss or question what I was doing. I didn't even have to make an excuse."

"That is wonderful, dear..." Pippa began.

"What is more, he listens to me. When I requested that we postpone our wedding trip—I don't want to go anywhere until we find Lillian—he replied that I should let him know when and where I wanted to go. How agreeable is that?"

A knock interrupted Fiona. Charlie entered, looking effortlessly chic in a gown of bronze moiré silk. Her honey-gold hair was tucked beneath a headdress of lace.

"I thought I would see how the bride was faring." Gliding over, Charlie kissed the air by Fi's cheeks. "You are stunning, my dear."

Fi was relieved by her mentor's genuine warmth. When she'd first told Charlie about her nuptial plans, the other had expressed some skepticism...which was no surprise. Although Charlie rarely spoke about her past, the little she'd said implied that marriage was not an institution she held in high regard. Nonetheless, Charlie's belief that every woman had the right to determine her own destiny took precedence over her personal feelings. She had respected Fi's decision to wed, even if she questioned whether marriage would lead to freedom.

"Have the guests arrived?" Fi asked.

"They are assembling in the drawing room," Charlie replied. "Your parents will come to fetch you soon. Before they do, however, I have a small gift for you."

Taking the velvet pouch Charlie proffered, Fi untied the drawstring ribbon. She took out the brass disc, brushing her fingertips over the filigreed cover before flipping it open.

"A compass," she breathed. "How beautiful."

The directions were elegantly engraved on the face of the compass, with north being represented by a single, sparkling diamond. On the back of the piece was an inscription: *May you never lose your true north.*

"I won't." Meeting her mentor's gaze, Fi said fiercely, "From now on, I will be able to dedicate myself to the Angels more than ever. You'll see. And I won't betray the oath I took; Hawksmoor need never know about my investigating."

"We shall see what the future holds." A distant look came into Charlie's eyes before she blinked it away and patted Fi on the cheek. "For now, my dear, enjoy your special day."

Soon after Charlie's departure, Fi's parents came in.

Mama looked stunning in a belted blue gown that complemented her curvy figure. She clutched a handkerchief in her gloved hands, her eyes already reddened from crying. Papa had an arm around her waist and was murmuring something in her ear. He was elegantly garbed for the occasion in black and white, a peach-colored bloom in his boutonniere.

The other Angels went to wait outside, giving the family a few moments of privacy.

"Oh, my dear, you are so...so b-beautiful." Mama's voice hitched. "I cannot believe it is your w-wedding day. That you'll be l-leaving us..."

Fiona went over and hugged her mother, who returned the

embrace fiercely. Mama's comforting arms and the familiar scent of her perfume brought unexpected heat to Fi's eyes. Despite her struggles with her parents, she knew they loved her. On the cusp of gaining her hard-won independence, she felt a sudden spike of fear...like a child who has strayed from the safety of home and finds herself lost.

"I won't be going far, Mama," she whispered. "And I shall visit all the time, I promise."

"Our girl is all grown up." Papa's voice had a gravelly edge. "Are you ready to walk down the aisle, my dear?"

Fi quelled her doubts. "I am always ready for an adventure, Papa. You know that."

"Marriage certainly is an adventure." Glancing at Mama, Papa smiled faintly. "Full of unexpected surprises."

"Adam," Mama protested with a blush.

Papa kissed Mama's hand. Their gazes held; some secret message passed between them. Witnessing her parents' private yet undeniable devotion, Fi felt a lump rise in her throat.

The price of love is freedom, she reminded herself. *I don't want that. I want to investigate and do as I please.*

Papa turned back to her, saying quietly, "I hope Hawksmoor knows what a lucky fellow he is."

She felt a sharp pang. "I'll make certain that he does."

"And he had better make you happy."

Her father's unmistakable threat made her want to laugh and cry at the same time.

"As a Garrity, I would not settle for anything less," she managed.

"That's my girl." Papa placed a kiss on her forehead before studying her. "I only want the best for you. You know that, don't you?"

I know. And I'm sorry I've disappointed you. I will try to make you proud.

Her throat tight, she nodded.

"Er, hello." Max poked his head in. "Am I allowed to come in? Or is this a private meeting?"

"Come in, you dolt," Fi said with exasperated affection.

"You look beautiful," Max said. "I am going to miss you."

Her heart full, she hugged him, whispering, "I am going to miss you too, dear. Try not to be *too* good in my absence."

"You're just in time, Max," Papa said. "You and I can share the honor of escorting the most beautiful ladies in London."

Max bowed to Mama with unexpected grace. "May I take you in?"

"Of course, dearest," Mama replied, beaming.

"Ready, my dear?" Papa held out his arm to Fiona.

Inhaling, she placed her fingers on his sleeve and straightened her shoulders.

"I'm ready," she declared.

ELEVEN

I am a married man.

The thought sent a surge of elation through Hawk. When it came to his studies and espionage, this was not a foreign emotion; it had been a long time, however, since he'd experienced this sense of heady triumph in his personal affairs. Yet what man wouldn't feel this way after laying claim to a goddess?

Not that I've claimed Fiona fully. That is still to come.

With simmering anticipation, he eyed the door that connected his bedchamber to hers. He wondered how much time he ought to allow his bride to get ready. They had arrived at his town house an hour ago, after the intimate ceremony and reception at his parents' home. He'd introduced Fiona to the staff and given her a tour of the house.

Seeing the place through her eyes, he'd had to hide a cringe at its shabbiness; the drawing room was in utter shambles. His neglect of domestic matters showed. Luckily, his new bride seemed unperturbed by the state of her new home.

Instead, she'd charmed all the servants by learning their names. Weatherby and the housekeeper, Mrs. Lawson, had been gratified by their new mistress's interest. Encouraged by Fiona's attentiveness, the typically taciturn butler had been downright chatty. All in all, the introductions had lasted longer than Hawk anticipated, which meant Fiona had had less than thirty minutes to prepare for bed.

A gentleman should give his young virginal wife at least an hour, he decided. *He should not pounce on her like some ravenous beast.*

It would take self-discipline to make love to her with the courtesy she deserved. He was damned randy for her; he couldn't recall any woman who'd heated his blood to this degree. It didn't help that Fiona had flirted with him all day. After the reverend had pronounced them man and wife, Hawk had intended to give her a chaste kiss appropriate for the occasion. When their lips met, however, hers had parted on the softest of sighs. Her sweetness had lured him to make the kiss longer—and, frankly, deeper—than it ought to have been.

Only the clearing of men's throats and muffled giggles from the ladies had brought Hawk to his senses. His father's stoic amusement and his mama's beaming delight had been more than a little embarrassing, especially for a man of his years. Yet Fiona had a way of making him feel like an unschooled lad.

As eager as Hawk was to explore the delights of his marital bed, doubts also niggled at him. Not about Fiona, but himself. About his ability to be a good husband to her. He couldn't stem the memories of Caroline's anguish and his powerlessness to help her.

Why does life hurt so much? she'd wept. *Help me, Thomas. Make it stop.*

He curled his hands. While he'd failed Caroline, he would not fail Fiona. He and Fiona had gone into this with proper expectations. She did not need him to take care of her emotionally; she'd told him that she was a self-possessed and independent female. They were to be partners who enjoyed each other's company in bed.

Hawk was determined to start their physical relationship off on the right foot. To show husbandly restraint and take things slowly. Despite Fiona's spirited nature, lovemaking would be new to her; everyone knew that virgins tended to be nervous. Caroline had had a fit of the vapors the first time he'd disrobed.

Grimacing at the memory, he reminded himself to dim the lights and give his new bride adequate time to prepare herself. He wondered idly how much Fiona knew about the marital act. Contemplating her carnal knowledge did not help his own lust. To distract himself, he poured a whisky and drank it by the fire.

A soft knock interrupted his brooding vigil.

Setting down his glass, he went to the door that adjoined the master suites. Opening it, he found his new wife standing on the other side, and his mouth went dry.

By Jove, she's stunning.

At their wedding, Fiona had looked like a princess in her ivory gown, and he'd thought with pride that no woman could be more beautiful. He'd been wrong; in dishabille, his wife was even more glorious. Her hair was a loose, shining curtain of fire that fell to her waist. Instead of the voluminous wrapper he associated with well-bred virgins, she wore a sensual and tasteful dressing gown of yellow silk trimmed with orange ribbon.

She was Sól, the sun goddess, come to life.

And he was the ravenous wolf in pursuit.

Down, boy, he lectured himself sternly.

"I hope you don't mind, but I got tired of waiting," she said lightly. "Are you ready?"

Hell, yes.

Enchanted by her initiative, he responded by entering her chamber, closing the door behind him. Being in the room caused a brief twinge of unease. While he'd had Caroline's belongings removed, the space still bore her fingerprint in the muted palette and fragile furnishings.

He cleared his throat. "Are you comfortable in here? Feel free to make any changes you wish."

"Thank you. I shall." She tilted her head. "Speaking of which, do I have leave to make adjustments to the rest of the house as well?"

Wry amusement filled him. *Give the chit an inch.*

He liked her exuberant feminine energy. He'd wanted an equal partner, and that was clearly what he was getting. The opportunity to hand off pesky domestic concerns to his better half was, in truth, a dream come true.

"Change anything you want," he said with satisfaction. "This is your home now."

"Carte blanche is a splendid way to start our marriage."

Unable to resist her teasing, he caught her chin, gazing into her vivid eyes.

"The fun is yet to begin," he murmured. "Do you know how exquisite you are?"

"If I say yes, will you think me immodest?"

He smiled slowly, enjoying their banter. "I happen to value honesty over modesty." He trailed a finger along her shoulder and felt her shiver. "Nervous, my dear?"

With a charming blush, she nodded. "But I find myself equally...well..."

"Yes?"

"Curious." Her eyes shone with sensual innocence.

Christ, this woman was made for him. He could not have designed a wife more perfectly suited to his desires. Excitement dissolved the rest of his tension.

Everything will be all right. Fiona and I both want a convenient marriage. We both want...this.

He slid his fingers into her luxuriant hair, savoring the silken texture and her vibrant interest.

"Then allow me to assuage your curiosity," he said.

Bending his head, he kissed her.

Hawk's kiss was glorious. It sparked the tinder of Fiona's desire, heat sweeping through her. Everything about him felt right: his taste of whisky and male, the way he cradled her head for his kiss, the bold and proprietary sweep of his tongue.

My husband. He's mine, she thought with possessive wonder.

Alone in her new bedchamber, she'd felt torn between nerves and anticipation; the latter had won out. For better or worse, she'd pledged herself to Hawk, and tonight they would embark on their first adventure in the marital bower.

She had a good idea of what to expect on her wedding night. As an Angel, she'd witnessed considerably more of life than the average debutante. Mama had also sat her down and blushingly explained married love, using phrases such as "surrendering to crashing waves of fulfilment" and "souls becoming one on an ecstatic plane" until Fi had begged her to stop.

In the end, it was the advice of Fi's friends that had stuck with her.

"Trust your instincts," Livy had said. *"Do what feels right in the moment."*

"Whatever feels good for you," Pippa had added, *"is likely to feel good for him."*

Following her instincts now, Fiona reached up and wove her fingers through Hawk's hair, enjoying the feel of the thick waves. He deepened the kiss, and the fire in her leapt higher. She kissed him back with equal fervor. He made a low sound in his throat, the demanding thrust of his tongue weakening her knees. When she stumbled, he swept her into his arms.

"Am I too heavy?" she asked breathlessly.

"You're not as heavy as a computation engine."

She laughed. "You do know how to flatter, my lord."

"And you seem to have a low opinion of my physical abilities, my lady." He lay her on the canopied bed, his eyes gleaming down at her. "You have conveyed your surprise at my prowess on several occasions."

She took in the way his black dressing gown molded to his broad shoulders and lean hips.

"I do not doubt your physical prowess one bit," she breathed.

"I plan to make certain of that tonight." He nuzzled her ear. "Shall I dim the lights, my sweet?"

"And make me miss everything?" She furrowed her brow. "No, thank you."

His eyes crinkled at the corners. His lips curved in a slow, approving smile that made her heart thump with furious longing.

"I should have known we would be of one mind on this," he murmured. "As we are with everything else."

Then he was kissing her again. Slowly, deeply until she was gasping. Desperate for air and even more desperate for him. His lips meandered along her throat, and she clutched the coverlet, overwhelmed by the sensations he roused in her. How good he made her feel. How much more she needed. When he strung a necklace of kisses over her collarbones, she arched her back with a whimper.

He tugged on the belt of her robe, pushing it off her shoulders. Fi trembled as he raked a smoky gaze over her. In Mrs. Q's dressing room, she had felt sophisticated trying on the long, sleeveless gown, graced with high slits on each side. Now, doubt assailed her as Hawk went completely still.

"Do you, um, like it?" she dared to ask. "I thought it was more interesting than the usual nightgown."

"Interesting is one word for it," he said thickly. "Christ, one look at you could set a man afire."

Her confidence returned. Teasingly, she said, "I take it that is a good thing?"

"A very good thing."

He traced a long finger along the vee of the negligee, which was filled with a triangle of golden lace. Her respiration quickened as his blunt fingertip neared the swell of her right breast.

"Did I ever tell you that you remind me of Sól?"

She had to force herself to focus. To pull her awareness away from his fingertip lazily circling toward the tip of her breast. The stiff bud was visible, jutting against the silk.

Recalling he'd mentioned something about a soul in the alleyway, she asked, "Whose soul?"

"Not soul—Sól. The name of a beautiful goddess from Norse mythology. She rides a chariot, pulling the sun across the sky and lighting up the heavens. At the same time, she is pursued by snarling wolves, which she manages to outrun."

Flattered, Fi said, "She sounds very brave and bold."

"Very bold," he agreed.

Her breath stuck in her throat as his touch spiraled closer and closer to her throbbing peak. Her lower belly tightened; when he finally brushed his thumb over the aching point, the shock of bliss pushed a breath from her lips.

"Do you like that, Fiona? Like me touching you here?"

She bit her lip against a moan as he gently rolled her sensitive bud between finger and thumb. She wasn't certain how to respond to the direct question. Would he think her brazen if she told him the truth? While Hawk had made it clear that he wanted a passionate marriage, she wasn't sure exactly *how* passionate she was supposed to be.

"It feels very...very nice," she managed.

"I think I can do better than nice."

He settled next to her on the bed; bending his head, he licked her through her nightgown. Surprise gave way to pleasure as his mouth enveloped her in heat. His tongue teased her ripe bud through the damp silk, swirling and flicking. His long fingers strummed the aching tip of her other breast. The sensations shot to her core. She squeezed her thighs together, whimpering.

"You're so sensitive," he murmured.

He had no idea. Or perhaps he did, for he redoubled his efforts until pleasure and need became one, and she couldn't tell which was which. Only that she needed *more*.

"Hawk," she panted. "Please. I need...I need..."

"Do you want to come for me, my sweet?"

Gone was the aloof intellectual; Hawk was once again her thief, his gaze molten silver and hot with lust.

"Would you like to spend while I lick your delectable breasts?"

His wickedness brought her to a crazed edge. She didn't know what was happening. Only the certainty of her answer.

"Yes, please," she whispered.

Triumph blazed on his face. Then his mouth was on her again, the sucking pressure seeming to pull at her core, drawing a gush of wetness between her thighs. Suddenly, he pinched her other nipple, the pleasure-pain catapulting her over the edge. Spasms shook her, and she flew into ecstasy with a startled cry.

I made my wife come whilst she was still clothed. Without even touching her pussy.

Astonished lust pounded in Hawk's veins. He knew, without a doubt, that this marriage was the best decision he'd made in a long time. Maybe ever.

"Oh, Hawk." Sighing, Fiona stretched like a languid kitten. "That was lovely."

The dazed pleasure in her eyes burgeoned his chest. And his cock. Then again, he'd been rock-hard since he'd made her come by sucking her tits. He'd never been with a woman as responsive as his new bride. Never felt as intense a physical connection.

"You're lovely," he said hoarsely. "I would like to see more of you, if I may."

At her dreamy nod, he hid a smile. Apparently, a climax made his wife agreeable; it was something to bear in mind for the future. Kneeling beside her on the bed, he pulled the lacy straps of her negligee down her shoulders. He felt like he was unwrapping a present.

Her skin was petal-soft beneath his fingertips, her scent of peaches heady. He drew the silk over her bosom, the material snagging on her taut nipples before sliding down to reveal utter perfection. The full, creamy mounds of her breasts were topped with buds the color of ripe strawberries. His mouth watered for another taste, this time without the barrier of fabric. Although a blush suffused her cheeks, she made no move to cover herself. Instead, she studied him as he looked his fill, her brazen curiosity fanning his lust.

He dragged the nightgown past her delicate rib cage and narrow waist, over the lush curve of her hips. When he removed it completely, his heart punched his ribs. He felt the way he did whilst working on an engrossing project: the world fell away, and he was utterly absorbed by what was before him.

"By Jove." He was awestruck. "You could not be more captivating."

She fluttered her lashes. "Am I as captivating as, say, the Rosetta Stone?"

He didn't know what aroused him more: her body or her wit.

"If you were found side by side with the Rosetta Stone and the excavators could only take one item," he said gravely, "hieroglyphics would remain unsolved to this day."

Her appreciative giggle warmed his chest and swelled his balls. When he placed a hand on her delicate ankle, she quieted, her eyes growing wide. Reverently, he caressed her satiny leg up to her pretty knees, which were pressed tightly together.

"Part your legs for me, sweeting," he murmured.

Letting out a soft breath, she obeyed.

He positioned himself between her slender limbs, touching her sleek inner thigh, feeling her quiver as he regarded the flame-red nest that guarded her feminine secrets. He ran a finger along her slit, and his blood rushed.

"Devil and damn, you're wet," he said in hoarse wonder.

She was dripping, her dew coating his finger.

She bit her lip, looking worried. "Is that, um, normal?"

"It is bloody marvelous." He parted her with his thumbs, his cock jerking at the piquant combination of her red curls and dewy pink flesh. Imagining being buried in her lushness, he shuddered with desire. "The wetter you are, the easier it will be for me to get inside you. Here, in your sweet pussy."

Seeing her flicker of excitement at the naughty word, he thanked his lucky stars once again. Damn, but he was going to enjoy playing with his lusty little wife. He circled her opening, sliding the tip of his index finger inside. Feeling her untried muscles clench around him, he stifled a groan. With his other hand, he found the tiny bud hidden in her thatch, and she jolted, letting out a soft moan.

"Do you like that, sweeting? Like me rubbing your pearl?"

"It makes me feel so...so *awash*."

"What about this?" He diddled her harder.

She whimpered, her honey flowing into his palm. He'd never had a woman respond to him with such utter abandon, and it made his head spin. As he stroked her little love-knot, he eased a finger into her channel—*God*, she was snug.

Luckily, she was also very wet, and she showed no signs of discomfort as he pushed all the way in. Her sheath squeezed his finger, wringing an anticipatory drop from his iron-hard cock. As her muscles relaxed, he added another finger, stirring gently. When her thighs tightened around his hand, he frigged her faster.

"Come for me again," he commanded.

She bit her lip, her eyes closing, a gorgeous flush rising over her face. Watching her go over again shredded the last of his control. He tore off his robe and nightshirt, needing to get inside his wife.

TWELVE

Floating on waves of pleasure, Fiona watched her husband disrobe.

He is magnificent, she thought dreamily.

He had the taut, masculine grace of a Greek sculpture. His shoulders and arms were sleekly bulging, and his chest was a masterpiece of carved muscle covered in wiry, dark hair. The hair narrowed to a trail between his ridged abdomen, leading past his narrow hips to...

Sweet heavens. She blinked, staring. *His manhood is enormous.*

On the sculptures she'd seen, this part of the man's anatomy had been far more modest. Nothing like what hung between her husband's hair-dusted thighs. Her gaze widened as he took hold of himself, his long fingers barely encircling the thick shaft. His phallus stood upright, the length girded with veins, the purplish head stretching to his navel.

Why didn't I listen more carefully to Mama's wedding night advice?

Fi recalled her mother saying any discomfort would be minimal and pass quickly. But what if Hawk's proportions were abnormal? How was she supposed to accommodate his excessive size?

Even his finger felt stretching. Her alarm built. *He is going to skewer me with that thing...*

He came atop her, and she fought her rising panic. Although he kept his weight off her, his sinewy length caged her against the bed. She tried to relax, telling herself that this was part of the bargain she'd made. When she felt his blunt tip push against her opening, she sucked in a breath and braced.

Hovering over her, Hawk stilled. "What is the matter, sweeting?"

She was a lady who took pride in being bold and in control. She wasn't used to admitting her fears. Yet the concerned warmth in Hawk's eyes, the way he was holding himself in check despite his advanced state of desire, undid her.

"It has come to my attention that you are, um, rather over-sized," she said in a rush.

He drew his brows together. "Oversized?"

"Your man's part. Is it unusually large? Not that I mean to imply that you're abnormal. In a way, I suppose it goes with the rest of the territory, for you are robust in general—"

He halted her babbling by placing a finger on her lips.

"Fiona, it's all right to be frightened," he said softly. "It is your first time."

"I'm not frightened," she countered. "Merely a trifle...apprehensive."

A smile lurked in his eyes. "Will it ease your apprehension if I promise to be gentle?"

"I know you will be." As soon as she said it, she knew it to be true.

Thus far, Hawk had been patient and considerate, introducing her to pleasure beyond her wildest imaginings. She wanted to give him the same in return. Even if it meant a bit of discomfort.

"Trust me to take care of you," he said.

She released a breath. "I do."

His gaze felt as warm as summer rain. "Then kiss me."

She tipped her lips up to his, the melding perfect and sweet. She sighed as he settled atop her. She loved the feel of his skin against hers. Their bodies fitted naturally, every part of him seemingly designed to delight her. His chest hair abraded her tingling nipples, the ridges of his torso pressing deliciously against her belly. Then he moved his hips, dragging the heavy length of his manhood against her feminine mound, sparking pleasure in his wake.

"Doesn't this feel good?" he murmured.

"So good," she breathed.

"It will feel even better if you move with me." He trailed persuasive kisses along her throat. "I won't go inside your pussy unless you ask me to."

Unable to resist, she followed his suggestion, and heavens, he was right. This *was* better. Holding onto his shoulders, she arched her hips tentatively, then with growing confidence. She matched the rhythm of his slow thrusting...it was like dancing, she realized. A sensual, horizontal waltz. The weighted slide of his shaft against her sensitive peak set off quivers in her woman's part...her pussy, he'd called it. Just thinking the word made her feel hot. Heightened the fluttering ache of emptiness.

"Perhaps you could try going inside?" she whispered. "Just a little?"

"Like this, sweetheart?"

She felt his wide head notch against her damp flesh. He moved slowly, his gaze intent upon her as if she were an enthralling experiment. Sweat glazed his brow; his features were stark with concentration. Warmth curled in her chest as she recognized the self-restraint he was exercising...that he'd been exercising all night.

He'll take care of me. Her anxiety ebbed. *The way I'll take care of him.*

She touched a hand to his taut jaw. "Come inside, Hawk."

"Are you certain?" he said hoarsely.

She nodded. "I want to know what it is like to be your wife."

"Fiona, sweeting..." With a groan, he pushed inside.

Her breath caught at the sudden fullness, the pinch of pain. Yet the discomfort soon faded to a throbbing, stretched sensation. She squirmed and gasped as he slid even deeper.

"Are you all the way in?" she asked with a squeak.

"I'm mostly in."

"Define mostly," she protested.

His eyes had a devilish silver glint. "I'd rather do this."

He kissed her breast, suckling her nipple. At the same time, he slid a hand between them, seeking out her pearl. His tongue and fingers made her blood churn with pleasure. When he began to move, all she felt was an exciting fullness. A needy pulsing at her core.

"See how well we fit?" he rasped. "You're like a hot, tight glove around my cock."

Her pussy clenched at his wicked words. Grunting, he drove inside her, and only then did she realize how much he'd been holding back. Now what he was doing felt good, better than good, and she didn't want him to stop.

"More, Hawk," she pleaded.

"Are you certain you want more, sweetheart?" His smoldering intensity riveted her, thrilled her. "Certain you can take me deeper inside your snug little pussy?"

"Yes, please," she moaned.

With a satisfied smile, he said, "Since you asked so nicely."

His incursions grew more forceful, his lunging hips billowing her fire. Clutching his bulging biceps for purchase, she instinctively moved with him. Even though she was a novice, her husband was an expert leader, and they found an exhilarating cadence. She met his thrusts, pleasure streaking outward from her center to her limbs.

"That's it, sweeting," he growled. "Let me all the way in where I want to be."

His tempo became pounding, unrelenting. Their bodies rose and fell together, skin slick against skin. The world spun as pleasure raged out of control. Everything in her suddenly seized...then bliss erupted from her core.

"*Devil and damn*, I can feel you coming."

His eyes lightning-bright, he plunged inside her again and again, then threw his head back on a guttural shout. He flooded her insides with hot, vigorous blasts that prolonged her tremors and added to her feeling of completion.

Afterward, Hawk hung over her, breathing harshly. The air was humid, rich with the scent of their lovemaking. Their bodies still connected, they gazed at one another. As if they were seeing each other for the first time.

Fiona took in the details of her husband: the softened lines of his face, the sated glow that mellowed his gaze. Upon his forehead, a dark, silver-threaded lock hung like an upside-down question mark, and she brushed it away with trembling tenderness.

Her throat suddenly thickened. *I've never been this close to anyone before.*

Hawk grazed his knuckles against her cheek. "How are you feeling?"

Knowing what he was asking, she regained her self-composure. Reminded herself that he did not like unnecessary sentimentality. Besides, she was no watering pot; she was a woman in command of herself.

She managed a smile. "I feel like a wife."

"You may be sore in the morning," he said gently.

"It was worth it." Overcome with sudden shyness, she said, "I...I enjoyed being with you."

His gaze soft as smoke, he rubbed a thumb over her bottom lip. "I enjoyed being with you, too, my sweet wife."

THIRTEEN

Fiona woke up alone in her bed the next morning. The lingering trace of Hawk's woodsy male scent made her feel giddy.

She hugged a pillow to herself. *I am truly Hawk's wife.*

She felt an unaccustomed twinge between her thighs. After their lovemaking, Hawk had taken tender care of her. He'd soothed her aching flesh with a warm towel and coaxed her into taking a dose of willow bark. Then he'd tucked her into bed, giving her a lingering kiss before returning to his own suite. Alone, she'd experienced a brief longing to feel his arms around her, but she'd soon slipped into a sated slumber.

Unused to sleeping so deeply, she felt refreshed and full of energy. She sat up, glancing at the closed door between their chambers. She wondered if Hawk was awake...if he would come into her room to bid her good day. She realized that she did not know the protocol for the morning after one's wedding night. Nor had she and Hawk discussed their respective schedules. Given that she'd delayed their wedding trip, he might be carrying on with his usual routine.

Getting out of bed, she rang for Brigitte. The maid told her that the earl had departed for an early appointment. The note he'd left snuffed Fi's flicker of disappointment.

Dear Fiona,

I have engagements today, but we could sup at home this eve if it suits your schedule. Leave word with Weatherby. I shall be home by six.

Your servant,
   Hawk

Reading her husband's boldly penned lines, Fi had a swoony feeling. Others might think his message was brusque; to her, it was better than any love letter because he'd acknowledged her autonomy. He did not assume that she would be at his beck and call. He'd invited her to spend the evening with him, yet the choice was hers.

Could my marriage be any more perfect?

Inordinately pleased, she met with the cook to design a romantic menu for supper *à deux.*

She spent the next few hours getting the house in order. She began by meeting with the staff. Mr. Weatherby and Mrs. Lawson seemed overjoyed at her willingness to take charge of domestic matters. She did not blame them; the state of the house made it obvious that Hawk's varied interests did not include household management. Luckily, he had her now. Consulting the servants, she made a list of concerns and prioritized them.

The most urgent problem was the drawing room; with holes in the ceiling and walls, the space was a bona fide disaster. Mr. Weatherby confided that the problem had begun with a leak and rapidly spun out of control. Fi asked him to summon the carpenter. It took Fiona five minutes with the shady fellow, a Mr. Sheeve, to figure out why.

She dismissed Sheeve on the spot. Then she sent for the carpenter and plasterer patronized by her family and, indeed, many fashionable members of society. Mr. Weatherby nearly jumped for joy when both arrived that same afternoon to assess the problem. Fi also set up appointments with various tradesmen, from furniture makers to drapers. She was not about to waste the carte blanche Hawk had given her.

Having made significant inroads into her wifely duties, Fiona set off for Charlie's.

There, she found Pippa already in a male disguise. Over the last week, the Angels had methodically searched theatres and music halls for clues to Lillian's whereabouts. Pippa was about to head off to the next venue on the list; after a quick costume change, Fi went with her.

As the carriage jostled off, Pippa asked, "Are you certain you wish to accompany me, dear?"

"Of course," Fi replied.

"But you were married yesterday—"

"Which is why I am free to investigate," Fi said brightly. "Henceforth, I can do whatever I wish."

"While that is all well and good, you are a newlywed." Beneath her top hat, Pippa's blue eyes were knowing. "You ought to enjoy being one."

"I *am* enjoying it. Right now, however, there is nothing else I'd rather do than work on the case."

Pippa lifted her brows. "*Nothing* else?"

"Really, Pippa." Fi's cheeks flamed. "That is most indelicate."

"As your friend, your happiness is more important to me than delicacy." Lacing her gloved hands atop her trousered lap, Pippa said, "I have always felt like an older sister to you and the other Angels, and I want you to know that you can discuss anything with me. Even things that might seem, well, uncomfortable."

Fi squirmed on the velvet squabs. "There is nothing to discuss, I assure you."

"During my first marriage, I had disappointments that I kept to myself. That I was too embarrassed to talk about with anyone," Pippa went on. "And I don't want you to suffer that same fate."

Knowing what she did of her friend's first marriage, Fiona felt a rush of sympathy. "That is kind of you, Pippa, but—"

"Whatever happened, or didn't happen, on your wedding night, you can talk to me about it without fear of judgement. I am here for you, Fiona."

"That is kind—"

"While physical love between husband and wife can be a beautiful thing, it can also take practice. Ladies, especially, may not experience the same satisfaction as men do without certain, ahem, preliminary activities." Her cheeks rosy, Pippa plowed on. "Communication is key, and as you and Hawksmoor haven't known one another for long, it might be understandably difficult to discuss certain sensitive topics. But you can ask me any question you like or share your feelings whatever they may be—"

"Being with Hawksmoor is wonderful." The truth seemed the best way to allay her friend's concern. "Better than I imagined it would be. And I had rather high expectations."

"*Oh.*" Pippa's smile lit up her face. "Dearest, I am *so* glad to hear it. But why then are you not..."

"Not what?"

"Why are you not with your husband? When Cull and I were first married, we didn't leave the bed for days." Pippa's eyes twinkled. "We're still that way."

Fiona gave an exaggerated sigh. "Knowing that, how am I supposed to look Mr. Cullen in the eyes when I see him next?"

"There is naught to be ashamed about when it comes to love and passion," Pippa declared. "I learned this the hard way and don't want you to bottle things up the way I did. If there is anything you ever wish to speak about, I am here to listen."

Fi flashed to the closed door between her and Hawk's chambers. Her desire to see him this morning. Perhaps to feel his arms around her while she slept.

Don't be a ninny, she chided herself. *Your arrangement with Hawk is perfect.*

Her marriage was based on different principles than Pippa's. While Pippa wanted intimacy, Fiona needed privacy to carry on as she pleased. Why complicate her marriage with excessive closeness? Why risk exposing parts of herself that Hawk might find problematical—or, worse yet, demand her to change? As she'd once told him, the last thing she wanted was to invite overprotectiveness and disappointment into their relationship.

Stick to the terms of your marriage, and you won't get hurt.

"Thank you for the offer," Fi said. "If I ever have questions, I know who to come to."

Fiona and Pippa's destination was crammed between a pawn shop and tea purveyor. Dubiously named "Pandora's Box of Wonders," the music hall consisted of a large room with a stage framed by tattered red curtains. Waitstaff were setting places at the long tables scattered throughout. The smells of ale and roasting meat permeated the air.

"'Ow can I 'elp you gents?" one of the serving maids asked.

Fi pitched her voice to a masculine register. "We are looking for the manager."

"You'll be wanting Mr. Hutchings. 'Is office is the last room behind the stage."

Behind the stage, Fi and Pippa found a series of small rooms. Each contained threadbare furnishings and, oddly, a wooden pole that ran from floor to ceiling. At the end of the hall was a closed door. When no one answered her knock, Fi tried the knob. The door opened to reveal a man asleep at a cluttered desk.

"Mr. Hutchings?" she said loudly.

The man jerked awake; spittle clung to the corner of his mouth. Blinking his bloodshot eyes, he grumbled, "Who are you?"

"Jones and Courier, solicitors," Pippa said crisply. "One of our firm's clients recently departed and left a large bequest. We are looking for her beneficiary, a Miss Lillian O'Malley. We were told that she worked here."

Licking his thick lips, Hutchings sat up fully. The movement pulled his shirt out of his waistband, revealing an overhang of hairy flesh.

"'Ow large is the bequest?"

"That is a matter for us to discuss with Miss O'Malley, sir," Fi said. "There may, however, be a reward for anyone who helps us to locate her."

"As much as I'd like to 'elp, I don't know any Lillian O'Malley." Hutchings's regret seemed genuine, likely stemming from self-interest rather than a desire to assist.

"Miss O'Malley might have used a different name." Pippa removed Lillian's daguerreotype from her satchel, placing it on the desk. "Here is a likeness of her."

Hutchings studied the image with glinting avarice. "Oh, 'er I do know. She was one o' my performers. But she went by the name o' Sarah Mallery."

Like me, Lillian thumbed her nose at her detractors. Empathy swelled in Fi. *Her peers mocked her dreams by comparing her to Sarah Siddons, but she took on that identity with pride, combining it with a variation of her own surname.*

Hutchings waved Fi and Pippa to the pair of rickety chairs on the other side of the desk. Opening a drawer, he withdrew a flask and some grimy glasses. "Care for a libation while we talk things o'er?"

"No, thank you," Pippa said. "About Miss Mallery, then. Do you know her address?"

"Not exactly. But I get paid if I 'elp you find 'er?"

"If the information you provide assists us in locating her, you will be rewarded," Fi promised.

"Well, it's been a while since Sarah worked 'ere..."

"How long?" Fi persisted.

"Seven months, maybe eight, I reckon."

Although the trail was colder than Fi hoped, it was better than nothing.

"She worked 'ere for maybe six months. Popular with the gents, if you know what I mean." Hutchings waggled his brows. "Couldn't sing in key to save 'er life, but she could dance. Always got a standing ovation when she did one o' those 'igh kicks that showed off 'er legs."

Slimy bounder. Fi forced herself to stay in her role. "Why did she leave?"

"She said she was 'eading off for greener pastures." Hutchings's gaze shifted. "You know 'ow these young girls are. Always thinking they're be'er than they are and ne'er satisfied wif the job they're fortunate to 'ave."

"What did Miss Mallery's job here entail, precisely?" Fiona narrowed her gaze. "Beyond showing off her legs, that is."

"Now see 'ere," Hutchings huffed. "Ain't none o' my girls forced to do anything they ain't signed up for. But if some o' them want to give private performances to earn extra coin, it ain't my business."

Fi recalled the rooms she'd passed. "You mean you turn a blind eye and take a cut."

"I give 'em a safe place to conduct their business and take a small fee for the trouble." Hutchings spoke with a righteousness that Fi associated with pimps and proselytizers.

"Did Miss Mallery take part in any of these transactions?" Pippa asked quietly.

"Only once. A gent wanted an introduction after a show. 'E must 'ave made an offer she couldn't refuse because she went into a room wif 'im. Ne'er did that in all the weeks before. And ne'er did it again because she left soon thereafter. Without a word, and I ain't seen 'er again."

"Can you describe this gent?" Fi asked.

"Good-looking cove, as I recall. Brown 'air with blond mixed in, light-green eyes. In his thirties, maybe."

That matches the description of the man with Lillian at the Royal Arms. Did she first meet him at this music hall? Was he a "customer" who became something more?

"Did you get his name?" Fi pressed.

"Sure. 'E said it were John Smith." Hutchings snorted. "Or maybe it was Jones."

Fiona removed a coin purse, dangling it to jog the pimp's memory. "You don't recall anything else about this man?"

"No...but I know someone who might."

"Who?"

Hutchings held out a beefy palm.

"The name first, if you please," Fi said.

He grunted. "While Sarah mostly kept to 'erself, she was friendly wif one o' the other dancers. Vera Engle."

"May we speak to her?" Pippa asked.

"Thing is, Vera left for Derbyshire last week. Said she 'ad to take care o' a sick uncle...who knows, maybe she 'as an inheritance too. Wouldn't that be somefin?" Hutchings slapped the desk. "Two o' my girls, heiresses."

Fi held onto her patience. "When will Miss Engle be back?"

"Got the schedule 'ere somewhere." He fumbled through a pile of papers on the desk. "Ah, 'ere it is. Vera's slated for the Sirens o' the Sea revue a week from today. I can tell 'er to expect you when she returns."

Rising, Fi tossed the coin bag onto his desk. "Thank you for your time."

Fourteen

Hawk savored dessert, a confection of silky custard and fluffy meringue, with a sense of satisfaction. There was something gratifying about dining at home with one's wife. In recent years, he'd become accustomed to taking supper on a tray in his study. While he did not mind solitude, he far preferred Fiona's charming company, especially after a long day filled with Quorum business.

After von Essen's information had led to dead ends all around, Hawk and his colleagues had been at a standstill. Then Trent had picked up a rumor that the Sherwood Band had distributed more money, and the team had split up to chase down leads on supposed recipients of the gang's largesse. They hadn't turned up any new clues yet, and the surveillance would continue on the morrow.

Hawk let the dark business fade to the back of his mind. It wasn't difficult; the meal, which had included sole meunière, duck with fig sauce, and buttered asparagus, was a delicious diversion and his companion even more delectable. Fiona was a vision in a gown of pale-blue taffeta that showed off her creamy *décolletage*, rounded bosom, and narrow waist. She'd pinned a corsage of cornflowers between her breasts. Her bright hair was draped in long, sensual curls over her right shoulder, more flowers blooming behind her ear.

She was fire and ice, and he burned just looking at her. Burned remembering the feeling of being inside her, the decadent squeeze of her pussy around his cock. In truth, memories of their coupling had distracted him throughout the day—even during his mission, which was irregular to say the least. He was a man known for his intellectual prowess and focus. In the past, after he'd satisfied his sexual appetite, he'd quickly returned to his normal, cool-headed state.

His wedding night had had a different effect. Instead of satiating him, fucking his bride had made him hungrier for her. It brought to mind Shakespeare's description of Cleopatra: *other women cloy the appetites they feed, but she makes hungry where she most satisfies.* Consequently, Hawk had been battling a cockstand throughout supper and not just because of Fiona's physical attractions. Her charming playfulness, quick wit, and merry laughter quickened his blood with longing.

Although chitchat had never been his forte, Hawk found his new countess easy to talk to. Fiona had asked about his day, and since he could not speak of Quorum business, he'd told her about his other hobbies. The genuine interest in her eyes had prompted him to describe his calculation machine. In his experience, his research tended to bore glamorous young ladies to tears, yet Fiona had seemed engaged. She'd asked intelligent questions that sparked several intriguing ideas. Her attention energized him, made him feel less stodgy and old.

When he'd asked about her day, he'd been amazed by all the domestic projects she already had underway. Her indignant recounting of her meeting with the "shady Mr. Sheeve" had made his lips twitch. He wondered if she knew how adorable she was with her spitfire personality and take-charge attitude. With wry amusement, he decided that she probably did.

He liked that Fiona did not pretend to be modest about her appeal. Her honesty was as rare as her ambition and drive. While she could have relied on her looks to get by in life, she clearly did not. Her many accomplishments—from dancing to alleyway rescues to household management—showed an exuberant and achievement-oriented spirit. Case in point: after setting their house in order, she'd apparently pranced off to do some genteel volunteering with her friends.

He couldn't help but notice the contrast between his past and present. Suppers with Caroline had been steeped in silent, unrelenting tension. Drained by her illness, she had found social interactions exhausting and triggering of her megrims. She had gradually started taking meals in her bedchamber. He was ashamed to admit that he'd been relieved.

Fiona, however, sparkled. There was no better word to describe her luminescent poise. No wonder she'd conquered Society. Her enchanting company reassured him that this union would be different from his last. He did not need to be on guard for emotional volatility. Did not have to be braced to deal with sudden tears, stony silences, or suffocating despair. Fiona could take care of herself and did not need things from him that he could not give.

She did, however, inspire specific needs in him. As he watched, she gave her dessert spoon a delicate lick that made an image blaze in his head: her pink tongue trailing up the length of his cock. It wasn't the sort of thing a man could expect of his wife, yet he couldn't help but wonder if Fiona would be open to exploring oral pleasures. If she would let him gamahuche her...if she might be bold enough to return the favor.

Beneath the table, his napkin tented.

Easy, fellow. This is supper, not foreplay.

Despite his rampaging lust, he had decided against visiting Fiona's bed this eve. First and foremost, she was likely sore from last night and needed time to recover. Recalling the traces of blood on the towel he'd used to tend to her, he felt a surge of possessiveness. She was his now, for better or worse, and he would take care of her as best he could.

Which led to his second reason: he ought to show some husbandly restraint. A gentleman did not foist his attentions upon his lady every single night. The last thing he wished to do was wear out his welcome. He would wait a few days before visiting Fiona's bedchamber again; if her delightful response last night was any indication, she ought to be open to a weekly bedding.

Or even twice weekly, he thought wistfully.

Thus, he planned to bid her good night with a peck on the cheek and go tinker on a project in his study. Afterward, he would go to bed alone. And resist the urge to frig himself like a randy greenling while fantasizing about his wife.

As the last course was cleared away and the footmen left the room, Hawk said, "Thank you for arranging such an enjoyable supper."

"You're welcome," Fiona said demurely. "I wanted to do something special for our first evening home together."

He could think of several special things he wanted to do with her.

He got himself in check. "You must be ready for bed..." *No, don't go there.* "After everything you accomplished today, you must be tired."

"Not really."

The sultry invitation in her eyes mesmerized him.

"Are you tired?" she asked. "You put in a hard day's work as well."

She had no idea how hard he was.

Stick to your plan; self-discipline is key.

"Actually, I was going to continue working in my study."

"Oh." Disappointment flickered on her face.

"Unless you would..." He cleared his throat. "Would you care to join me there for a nightcap?"

One drink won't hurt.

Her smile dazzled him. "I would love to."

As Fi followed her husband into his study, she shivered with excitement.

During supper, she'd had a humming awareness of Hawk. Her senses had never been this attuned to anyone before. Her husband's thick, silver-threaded hair gleamed from a wash, the somber yet elegant cut of his clothing accentuating his lean virility. When he wrapped his hand around his wine glass, her skin tingled with the memory of his skillful touch. As he ate, she remembered that hard, sensual mouth plundering hers. By the time dessert arrived, her insides had felt as quivery as the meringue clouds floating on the pool of custard.

She wondered if Hawk was as aware of her as she was of him. Throughout supper, they'd had an engaging conversation. He'd been polite and affable, yet so different from the smoldering lover of last night. It was as if there were two Hawks: the rational, reserved scholar and the wickedly passionate man. She found the contrast intriguing and, frankly, a bit of a challenge.

What would it take to summon my sensual lover?

"What would you like to drink?" Hawk asked.

"Whatever you are having will do," she said offhandedly.

"I am having whisky."

Whisky was considered too potent for a miss...but she was married now. *And married ladies,* she thought with a touch of smugness, *have more freedoms.*

Feeling quite daring, she said, "Whisky sounds lovely."

Although Hawk's brows elevated slightly, he strode to the spirits cabinet without comment.

Surveying her husband's inner sanctum, she saw that, like the rest of the house, it needed refurbishment. His desk was a master-piece of clutter, piled with papers and odds and ends. Yet the space had an ambiance of masculine comfort, with its dark wood paneling and leather furnishings. She wandered over to the glass-fronted cabinets that lined one wall, studying the objects inside. In particular, she was intrigued by a metal block that took up an entire shelf. Composed of multiple vertical rods strung with gears, the contraption was connected to a roll of paper and what looked like a tiny printing press.

Sensing Hawk behind her, she asked, "Is this one of your computation engines?"

"It is a prototype." He handed her a glass. "The actual machine is much larger."

She sampled the whisky, approving the smooth burn. "You didn't say what inspired you to create this machine."

"Truthfully?"

She nodded.

"I had nothing better to do."

She blinked at him. "Boredom motivated you to invent and patent new technology?"

He shrugged. "I don't like to be bored."

Come to think of it, neither do I.

Perhaps that explained her wicked craving for excitement. Why she couldn't be more conventional. Why she had to pretend to be a lady.

"I like to keep busy as well," she said.

"I can tell." His lips twitched. "Were you always this way?"

"I was a handful as a child." Squelching a pang, she asked, "What were you like?"

"Serious and intellectual." He tossed back the rest of his whisky. "Shall we sit by the fire?"

She followed him to the cozy seating area by the hearth. He went to get himself another drink, and she took the opportunity to make herself as alluring as possible. Arranging herself on the studded leather sofa, she unpinned the corsage that had shielded her cleavage, shoving it between the cushions. Unbuckling her shoes, she curled her legs beneath her, making sure that her stockinged feet and ankles peeped artfully from beneath her skirts.

When Hawk returned, she gave him a coquettish smile and patted the seat next to her.

"Tell me more about your childhood," she said.

He sat beside her, slanting a glance at her silk-covered feet.

"What do you wish to know?" he asked.

She wound one of her curls around her finger, hiding a smile at the interested gleam in his eyes. She enjoyed flirtation in general and with Hawksmoor in particular. There was something infinitely delicious about tempting her older, brilliant, and self-disciplined husband. Perhaps it was the rebel in her that enjoyed getting through his wall of control.

His gaze strayed from her twirling finger to the dip in her neck-line. Her respiration quickened, her nipples tingling against her corset. She had to gather herself before speaking.

"What was it like growing up in your family?"

"Noisy and full of mayhem." He quirked an eyebrow. "You have met my brothers."

She nodded with amusement. His younger siblings were rowdy rogues. At the wedding reception, George and Henry had flirted shamelessly with her in an obvious attempt to get under Hawk's skin.

"You are different from them," she observed.

"I take after my father." Hawk's mouth formed a faint curve. "My brothers take after Mama."

"But the marchioness is a most refined lady," she said in surprise.

"Don't let Mama's perfect manners fool you. She is a tigress when it comes to the family." He paused. "One time, when I was at Eton, she came to see the headmaster. A fearsome fellow by the name of Mr. Stratton who struck terror in the hearts of all his pupils. He emerged from Mama's visit as a shell of his former formidable self; he was never the same again."

Fi canted her head. "What prompted her visit?"

"As I mentioned, I was a serious and intellectual lad. This did not endear me to my peers." Hawk drank more whisky. "One of the popular boys targeted me for bullying. He and his cronies would wait until I was alone, then pounce. When I showed up at Michaelmas break with a pair of shiners, Mama demanded to know what had happened."

"And well she should have," Fi said indignantly. "I hope those bullies got what they deserved."

"I refused to tell her their names. And I swore Jeremiah to secrecy. That was why Mama was so furious at Stratton, you see; he couldn't punish the bullies because he did not know who they were."

She gaped at him. "Why would you protect those dreadful boys?"

"Because the only way to deal with a bully is by facing them yourself," Hawk said bluntly. "Knowing Mama, she would have had the boys expelled, and trust me, that would not have helped my standing with my peers. Papa understood. That was when he took me into the sparring ring and taught me how to solve my own problems."

She thought of Hawk's prowess in the alleyway scuffle. Her heart melted as she realized that his skill had come from a need to defend himself. She knew what it was like to have to protect oneself from the rejection of peers. While her weapons hadn't been fists, she'd honed her wit, charm, and cunning to be equally lethal.

"Your papa taught you to fight?" she asked softly.

He nodded. "Papa did not inherit the title until later in life. He grew up in the streets and made his own way in the world. He taught me to fight like a gentleman but also to survive. To give a good accounting of myself, no matter the circumstances."

Fiona knew of the Marquess of Harteford's unusual rags-toriches story. She thought it was one of the reasons why he and her own father got along.

"My papa is a self-made man as well," she said proudly. "I learned from him never to settle. To always go after what I desire."

"Is that what you are doing at the moment? Going after what you desire?"

At the amused glint in Hawk's eyes, her cheeks grew hot. Most gentlemen enjoyed her attention; certainly, no one had ever called her out for being a flirt. Flustered, she brought her glass to her lips and finished her drink instead of replying.

"Are you done?" Hawk inquired.

She wetted her lips, noticing how his gaze followed the path of her tongue.

"I don't think I should have more whisky," she said.

"I am not referring to the whisky." He took the glass from her and set it aside. Then he cupped her jaw, his firm touch sending tremors through her. "I'm talking about your attempt to seduce me, little minx."

She squirmed with embarrassment. It was on the tip of her tongue to deny it, yet her husband's keen expression told her it was pointless. He knew what she was up to, and besides, she was no shrinking violet. She was Fiona Garrity Morgan, the Countess of Hawksmoor, and she would go after what she wanted.

She fluttered her lashes at him. "Is it working?"

Rare delight flashed in his eyes. An instant later, smoky intensity took its place.

"Are you sore, sweeting?"

His blunt inquiry caused her blush to deepen. "Only, um, a bit."

He rubbed his thumb over her bottom lip. "As much as I want to make love to you again, I don't want to make your poor pussy ache any more than it already does."

The part in question spasmed, as did her heart. Even though

theirs was a marriage of convenience, Hawk took such care with her. Made her feel...safe.

"I don't mind," she said tremulously.

"But I do."

His heated gaze turned her insides to honey.

"Luckily," he said, "there are some alternative ways of exploring our desires."

FIFTEEN

"Heavens." Fiona's fingers clenched in his hair. "Are you certain you should be kissing me *there*?"

Placing a kiss above his wife's garter, Hawk looked up and was treated to a cock-hardening view. Fiona was naked... save for the beribboned blue garters and white silk stockings he'd left on. Reclined on the sofa, she was a glowing vision against the dark studded leather. Her cheeks were flushed, her breasts heaving from the recent climax he'd given her. He'd suckled her nipples and frigged her pearl for less than a minute before she'd gone off like a Roman candle.

By Jove, I'm a fortunate man.

Now he was kneeling on the carpet between her spread legs, the scent of her feminine arousal making his head spin. Her gorgeous pussy was drenched with dew. He'd only gamahuched one other female, a mistress who'd taught him what she liked, and his mouth watered at the prospect of Fiona allowing him such a treat.

"You can always tell me to stop," he murmured. "But I think you'll like it."

He leaned in, swiping his tongue up her delicate pink gash.

Christ, she tasted sublime. His erection strained against his trousers as he feasted. Her shocked gasps melted into breathy moans as he ate her cunny, licking his way to her peak, teasing that little jewel with the tip of his tongue. Her bucking hips told him she liked that. He experimented with flicking, laving, sucking.

"Hawk. *Hawk.*" She chanted his name.

"Do you like that, sweeting? Like having my mouth on you here?"

Her dazed, heavy-lidded eyes met his. "It feels so *good*."

Her honest sensuality called forth his darkest fantasies. Desires he'd never fully explored because he'd never had the right partner to do it with. A woman who made his blood run this hot and who wanted him back with equal abandon. Although Fiona was nearly a virgin, he trusted her to know her mind and desires. To be his partner as they invented their own brand of passion. He wanted to experiment with all the ways they could find pleasure together.

"Ask for more of it, then," he said.

At his command, her thighs tensed against his palms. She blinked at him, surprised but also aroused. He saw it in her dilated pupils, the fresh wash of dew glazing her womanly petals.

"Ask for it?" she whispered.

"Ask me to lick you," he coaxed. "To eat your pussy."

Would his bride utter such naughty words? Was she brazen enough to demand her pleasure?

She gave him a bashful look. "Will you please eat my pussy?"

Her request, filthy and polite, squeezed a drop of seed from his cock. Her dimple told him that she knew her effect on him...and was enjoying the game.

Devil and damn. She was his perfect match.

"With pleasure, little vixen," he growled.

He used his fingers and mouth: teasing, licking, sucking her until she was moaning. Her back arched against the leather, her fingers tugging at his hair. He circled her pearl with his thumb as he found her tight entrance and licked inside.

"Does my tongue make you sore, sweeting?" he murmured.

Her glorious hair rippled against the cushions as she shook her head, pressing her cunny against his mouth. A perfect answer. Stiffening his tongue, he fucked her steadily with it, groaning at the greedy clutch of her sheath. She spent with a wild cry, so juicy and hot that he nearly came himself.

Breathing heavily, he swiped the back of his hand across his mouth, shuddering when it came away wet. He concentrated on not spending in his pants like an untried lad. The sight of his wife, splayed like a satiated goddess before him, didn't help his roaring lust. When she stretched her arms above her head, her full tits bobbing over her narrow rib cage and one silk-clad leg bending wantonly at the knee, his vision darkened.

She was his fantasy come alive. And he couldn't hold back any longer.

Even drunk with pleasure, Fiona saw Hawk undressing, and she didn't want to miss a thing.

She watched with avid interest as he shed his outer layers. His utilitarian movements didn't take away from the splendor of what he revealed. As he unbuttoned his shirt, she ran a covetous gaze over his chest, the lightly furred and hard-packed blocks of muscle. Then he unfastened his fall, and her breath caught as his manhood sprang free. Memory had not diminished the size of his mighty shaft, which bobbed heavily as he finished undressing. He wrapped his hand around the thick pole, grimacing slightly.

Sitting up, she asked, "Do you, um, want help with that?"

Raw lust blazed across his austere countenance.

"Next time." His voice was guttural as he stroked his erect flesh. "Licking your cunny made me so hard I shan't last long. When I teach you to frig me, I am going to take my time and do it properly."

Her intimate muscles clenched at the mention of her future lessons. At the notion of being tutored in naughtiness by her husband. She couldn't look away from his pumping fist, the way it moved the supple skin along his shaft. Her insides fluttered as he wrung a pearly drop from the purplish tip.

"Do you like to watch?" he asked.

With blushing mortification, she realized that she did. She'd never seen anything as potent as her husband handling himself. She chewed on her bottom lip, debating whether she could admit her depraved enjoyment aloud. Hawk came closer, his large feet bracketing her stockinged ones on the carpet. With him standing and her sitting, his cock was at her eye level; she could see the prominent veins along his member as he stroked himself in a slow, disciplined rhythm.

"There's no need to be shy."

He curled a finger beneath her chin, tipping her gaze up to his. The fact that he continued to fist his cock while he touched her sent a sizzle up her spine.

"I am your husband; you've had my cock inside you." Never had facts sounded so wicked and seductive. "Why shouldn't you take a good look at it?"

Hmm. He does have a point.

"It is rather stimulating." She bit her lip. "Watching you...um, you know."

"I'm frigging myself, sweet. Say it. And tell me how it makes you feel to watch me."

His intensity was mesmeric.

She took a breath. "When you, um, frig yourself"—heavens, just saying the word made her feel naughty—"I feel fluttery."

"Where?"

She couldn't resist his smoldering challenge.

"Between my legs," she whispered.

"You know the proper word, sweetheart."

She did. Because he'd taught it to her. "In my...my pussy."

"There's my bold girl." His nostrils quivered, his fist taking on a rougher, faster cadence. "Is your pussy wet again?"

She pressed her thighs together, feeling the slickness. "Yes and no."

He arched a brow. "Explain."

"Well, it is, um, wet, but not exactly *again*, per se. I think I've been this way, um, continuously?"

Her honesty was rewarded by a ragged groan.

"Show me," he rasped. "Christ, let me see that pretty, soaked cunny of yours."

His thief's eyes burned into her, incinerating her inhibitions. His desire fed her sense of power. Never in her life had she felt this wanted. This needed. The back-and-forth game of seduction she played with her husband was as fun as flirting...as thrilling as a mission.

With coursing excitement, she leaned back against the sofa, arching her back to show her bosoms to their best advantage. Hawk watched like a starved wolf as she trailed her fingertips over her right breast. When she circled the pouting peak with her index finger, he grunted, massaging another droplet from his cock. His features were harsh with hunger as she brought her hand down the valley of her belly...and rested it lightly on her clamped-together legs.

"Don't stop now," he bit out.

"Aren't you forgetting the rules?" She tapped her chin. "One has to ask nicely."

At her turning of the tables on him, something like joy blazed in his eyes.

"Please, Fiona," he said thickly. "Be a good wife and show me your pussy."

Obediently, she widened her knees. Trembled beneath his greedy, possessive gaze.

"Show me more."

With a shaky hand, she parted herself for him.

"Christ, you're beautiful." His tone was reverent, as desperate as the grip he had on his enormous shaft. "Pink and plump, dripping with dew..."

She grew even slicker as he pumped himself harder, faster. His biceps bunched as he frigged himself, the muscles of his torso flexing. With his other hand, he cupped the dusky sac that hung between his bulging thighs. She saw pleasure overtaking him, the grooves on his hips tautening, the cords in his neck standing out in stark relief.

His wild, wolfish gaze locked on her.

"Do you want to watch me come?" he gritted out.

She gave a breathless nod.

He clenched his jaw, wrenching his fist once, twice, a growl tearing from his throat. An instant later, a milky stream erupted from his cock, landing with a faint splatter on the rug. Grunting, he shot his seed again and again; her heart pounded at his copious virility. She loved witnessing this primal act. Loved the way her husband's cold control transformed into raw, animal desire.

Afterward, Hawk collapsed onto the sofa next to her, cuddling her close.

"Poor wife," he murmured. "Subjected to such a dirty show."

Since he radiated satisfaction, she didn't think he was all that sorry. She wasn't either. Call her depraved, but she liked their adventurous lovemaking. Liked how free she felt in his arms. Liked how they could make one another wild with desire.

"I enjoyed it," she said shyly.

His eyes crinkled at the corners. Then he brushed his lips over her forehead.

"Let's get you dressed," he said.

He assisted her, his movements as efficient and methodical as Brigitte's. His manner turned brooding. The energy in the room shifted, and Fi didn't know what to make of it. Uncertainty crept over her.

Was I too wanton? Did I encourage him too much, participate too eagerly?

"Hawk?" she blurted.

"Yes, sweeting?" He was behind her, working on her corset laces.

She twisted around. "What are you, um, thinking?"

Lines deepened on his forehead, his silence ramping up her anxiety.

"I did not realize how good a marriage of convenience could be," he said quietly. "That is what I was thinking."

"Oh," she breathed with giddy pleasure.

His lips twitched. Leaning forward, he kissed her softly on the mouth. "Now, curious minx, let us finish getting you dressed and up to bed."

SIXTEEN

A week later, Fiona welcomed Mrs. Lawson into her newly refurbished sitting room.

"How bright and cheery everything looks," the housekeeper exclaimed. "You've worked wonders in a short time, my lady."

"I am rather fond of the changes," Fi said, smiling.

Fi had switched the palette of her suite from pastel green to a vibrant shade of blue. For the accent colors, she had gone with ivory, buttercup-yellow, and gold. She had donated the old furnishings and replaced them with pieces fashioned from gleaming rosewood.

Settling at the table with Mrs. Lawson, Fi said, "Fill me in on everything."

Fi liked the housekeeper, not only because the latter had thoughtfully brought a pot of tea and a plate of fresh biscuits. Mrs. Lawson had been an invaluable ally during Fi's transition into her role as lady of the house. Together, they'd tackled everything from household accounts to the acquisition of new linens and staff uniforms. Mrs. Lawson was excellent at taking direction, and her capability freed up time for Fi to investigate.

At the same time, the housekeeper was humble and non-assuming. She performed her role seamlessly; the stitches of her competence were so neat that one could overlook them, even though they held the fabric of the household together. Her hair secured in a practical twist, the housekeeper now crossed another item off her list.

"Thank you for approving Mary's leave, my lady," she said. "She will appreciate the time off to attend her father's funeral."

"Of course." Fiona sipped her tea. "Is there anything else we can do for her?"

Hesitating, Mrs. Lawson said, "Mary hasn't been with us long, and I think her circumstances are rather, well, strained. The cost of the train fare to the funeral…"

"Cover whatever she needs. If she balks out of pride, tell her it is a customary practice in this household. Which, if it was not the practice before," Fi added, "it is now."

"That is most generous, my lady," Mrs. Lawson murmured. "I also wanted to convey the staff's compliments for their new uniforms. Everyone below stairs is walking a bit taller these days."

"I am glad to hear it," Fi said.

Mama's philosophy was that happy servants made for a happy household, a fact borne out by the longevity of the Garrity staff. Fiona wanted to foster the same loyal, thriving relationships in her new home. She had her work cut out for her, however. According to Mrs. Lawson, the retention of staff had been a long-standing problem.

Though the housekeeper's professionalism prevented her from gossiping, Fi had the sense that her predecessor hadn't taken much interest in domestic matters. The dilapidated state of the house, which clearly predated the countess's death, as well as the servants' tattered livery and discontent, spoke volumes. Perhaps Caroline Morgan had neglected the town house because she spent most of her time in the country. Fi couldn't help but wonder about Hawk's previous wife and marriage.

It was the strangest thing. A week after her wedding, Fiona felt like she knew her husband both more and less. On the one hand, they'd spent every night together, exploring physical intimacies. No one knew her body better than Hawk, and she was learning what made him shudder and growl with pleasure. When they were not making love, they shared easy conversation, yet certain topics remained forbidden.

One night over supper, Fi's growing curiosity had prompted her to ask Hawk how he'd met his first wife. The warmth had fled Hawk's gaze; something in him had shut like an iron gate. He'd answered curtly that he met Caroline in the usual manner at a ball and said no more. The tension that followed had been a marked change from their earlier banter.

It had been a palpable reminder of the terms of their arrangement. They were partners, not soul mates. Hawk had a right to privacy. If she did not want him prying into her secrets, then it was best that she return the favor.

Other topics were not off-limits, however. Last evening, Fi had brought up the subject of the staff's wages to her husband. He'd given her a lazy smile and agreed to her suggestion of a fifteen percent increase across the board. The fact that he'd just climaxed, and she was sitting atop him—a new position she adored and showed her appreciation for by coming twice—probably influenced his amenability.

"It wasn't enough that you've had your way with me." His eyes had glinted up at her. *"Now you wish to get your way too."*

Hawk wasn't wrong, she thought with a touch of smugness.

"Is there anything else, my lady?"

Fi yanked her thoughts back into the realm of appropriateness.

"There is, actually," she said. "The earl will be discussing the details with Mr. Weatherby, but I wanted to let you know that the staff can expect an increase in wages. With a special bonus to you and Mr. Weatherby for your excellent service."

"Oh, my lady. I...I don't know what to say. Thank you."

Fi had never seen the stalwart housekeeper flustered before.

"It is my pleasure. Between you and me, I am aware of who has kept things afloat around here." Fi smiled warmly. "Now, would you mind passing those delectable biscuits?"

Fi arrived at Charlie's early that afternoon. From Hawker, she learned that Livy, Pippa, and Glory were finishing up sparring practice with Mrs. Peabody.

"Give that woman a chance, and she'll wear you down to a nub," the butler growled...somewhat nonsensically, in Fi's opinion. "She never knows when to stop."

Fi raised her brows but said nothing as the butler stomped off. She knew who Hawker was referring to. Mrs. Peabody and Hawker sniped at each other constantly, looking for fault where none was to be found. Indeed, Fi thought they fought like a pair of small children...or disgruntled lovers.

Fi went to the drawing room to wait for her friends. She and Pippa would be paying a second visit to Pandora's Box this afternoon. Today marked Vera Engle's return, and they planned to catch her before her Sirens of the Sea performance. To prepare for the interview, Fi decided to re-read Lillian's letters to her mama.

Removing the letters from a drawer, she went to the sideboard and helped herself to tea from the silver samovar and a finger of shortbread, courtesy of Fisher's Fine Foods. Curling up on the settee, she nibbled on the buttery treat as she rifled through the letters; the last two had been written around the time Lillian had been employed at the music hall.

The first one was dated eight months ago.

Dear Mama,

Thank you for your letter. I am well and wish you would not fret. Although I have not yet achieved my ultimate ambitions, I remain steadfast in my choices and pursuit of my dreams. I am optimistic that opportunities will present themselves. Until then, I am making do as you taught me.

On an encouraging note, I have received positive reviews for my performances. I believe they will soon lead to better roles that display my true talent. You did not raise me to be a quitter, and I hope to have even better news to share in my next letter.

Your loving daughter,
   Lillian

Reading between the lines, Fiona felt Lillian's conflict. She knew how hard it was to stay the course of one's dreams when they did not fit the conventional mold. Lillian wanted to allay her mother's fears, which meant she couldn't share her true feelings: the disappointment and despair she must have felt working at a place like Pandora's Box. She'd wanted to be Sarah Siddons and instead found herself doing lewd dances for strangers in a seedy revue.

The next letter, written a month later, had a markedly different tone.

Dear Mama,

I hope this letter finds you in excellent health. Sometimes life can take an unexpected turn, and that is what has happened to me. These days, I am thriving in London and have a newfound conviction in the path that I've chosen. While some may look down upon me, I now appreciate my own worth. It is the worth that every man, woman, and child has by right—that we, as citizens of a free and just society, must fight for and claim for ourselves.

I hope you will be happy, Mama, because I am happy. Truly. You needn't fret about me any longer. I am safe and secure, and my dreams are coming to fruition in ways that surpass my grandest dreams.

Your loving daughter,
  Lillian

"What gave you such hope, Lillian?" Fi murmured. "What changed in your life?"

Footsteps and voices interrupted her musing. She looked up to see the other Angels troop into the drawing room.

"How did the training with Mrs. Peabody go?" she asked.

"Badly for us, as usual." Glory stopped at the sideboard to get herself tea and shortbread. As she plopped into an adjacent chair, her ferret clambered onto her lap and made himself at home on her dotted skirts. "We did a practice round, and Mrs. Peabody beat all three of us. *At the same time.*"

"Something lit the fire in her," Livy agreed.

"I think it wasn't something but rather *someone*." Pippa shared Fiona's settee, her blue eyes bright with humor. "And his name rhymes with 'gawker.'"

"He was in quite the mood when I arrived." Fi arched her brows. "Anyone care to wager on how long it will take for them to get together?"

"Not another wager," Glory grumbled. "I always lose."

Nonetheless, she made her bet along with the others.

"I see you're re-reading Lillian's letters." Pippa glanced at the notes on the seat cushion. "Any new discoveries?"

"No, but I was wondering what happened to change Lillian's perspective during this period."

Fi showed the others Lillian's oddly optimistic letter.

Glory furrowed her brow. "Perhaps Lillian landed an excellent role?"

"Maybe that was why she left Pandora's Box soon thereafter. A better opportunity came along," Livy mused.

"One hopes it was a better opportunity. The timing of this letter also coincides with when Lillian met that fellow Hutchings mentioned. Perhaps her new beau was responsible for her change of heart." Pippa frowned. "Something seems amiss in this letter. The part about 'citizens of a free and just society' doesn't sound at all like Lillian's previous writing."

"I agree," Fi said. "I hope Vera Engle will be able to shed some light on the matter."

"We don't need to leave for a while yet." Pippa's smile was impish. "Which gives us time to catch up...and ask you how married life is going."

Faced with her friends' inquisitive gazes, Fi felt her cheeks warm.

"You're blushing." Pippa chuckled. "Things *must* be going well."

"My married life is as it should be," Fi said with great dignity.

"I am glad to hear it, dear." Livy's eyes sparkled above the rim of her cup. "Is there anything you'd care to discuss with us married ladies?"

Fi gnawed on her bottom lip. "Actually, there is one thing."

"Here we go." Rolling her eyes, Glory stretched and rose. "I think this is where FF II and I will take our leave."

"You don't have to go," Fi protested.

"I promised I'd spend the afternoon with my brothers anyway. But I shall see you at the ball tomorrow night?"

The annual ball, hosted by Livy's parents, the Duke and Duchess of Strathaven, was a *crème de la crème* affair and would mark Fiona's first public appearance as a married lady. While newlyweds were afforded privacy, staying out of the public eye too long could lead to gossip. Truth be told, Fi looked forward to stepping out on Hawk's arm. And yes, that wicked, rebellious part of her also wanted to show her critics that she'd succeeded where they told her she could not: Miss Banks was now the happily married Countess of Hawksmoor.

Fi had ordered a new gown from Mrs. Q and consulted with Hawk's valet, Livingston, to coordinate Hawk's finery with her own. When Hawk had teased her about her labors for a mere ball, she'd told him, *"A title is like a superb figure. If you have one, you might as well show it off."* While Hawk had seemed amused, she knew he didn't fully understand her need to cement her new position. How could he when he'd been a titled blue blood his entire life?

"Hawk and I will be there," Fi promised.

After Glory left, Livy tilted her head. "Now, what is your question?"

Fi blurted, "What are your, um, sleeping arrangements?"

Pippa's brow pleated. "I'm not sure I follow, dear."

"I mean, how long does your husband stay? After, you know... Before returning to his own chamber, I mean."

"Oh, I see. Cull doesn't return to his room," Pippa replied. "We spend the night together."

"As do Hadleigh and I," Livy said, nodding.

Fiona blinked. "Even after you-know-what?"

"Actually, we sleep together even when we don't make love," Pippa said.

Again, Livy bobbed her head in agreement.

"Really?" Fi's eyes widened.

A few times after she and Hawk made love, he'd stayed until she'd fallen asleep. In truth, his presence made it easier for her to drift off; she liked snuggling with him, the feeling of being surrounded by his warm strength. At some point during the night, however, he always returned to his own room. She'd concluded that she wasn't fond of waking up alone. Which was why she'd asked her friends for advice.

"It is not that unusual." Pippa gave her a curious look. "When you were little, didn't you ever accidentally find your parents in bed together in the morning?"

Fi shook her head. Her parents were private people. Although their devotion was unquestionable, what happened in their marital life was a mystery—and she preferred it that way.

"Mama and Papa kept their doors locked," she said. "And Papa was very strict with Max and me about knocking before entering."

"There was probably a reason for that," Livy pointed out.

Fi immediately blocked out the image. "*Eww.*"

"It's a fact of life, dearest, and the reason for your very existence." Lips quivering, Pippa said, "Back to your question. I take it Hawksmoor does not spend the night?"

"He and I spend time together every night. But we don't sleep together."

"Would you like him to stay?"

At the thought of waking up next to her husband, Fi felt a flutter of yearning. Yet unease slithered through her as well. What if she drooled in her sleep? Snored or mumbled things? And Lord knew her hair could resemble a bird's nest in the mornings. She wasn't sure she was ready for her husband to see all her imperfections.

If they spent more time together, would Hawk also grow curious about her activities? Would he want to know what she was doing with the Angels? The closer they got, the more opportunities she would have to slip up...the way she had with her parents. What if *Hawk* started to interrogate her, put limits on her, disapprove of her? Her newfound longing for intimacy could lead to dangerous consequences.

"Perhaps?" she ventured.

Pippa raised her brows. "When you decide what you want, you should let him know."

"Are you certain sleeping together is normal? And we do have an agreement—"

"Agreements can be renegotiated," Pippa said firmly. "And

there is no right and wrong in marriage: you and your husband get to make the rules. The important thing is that you communicate your desires."

Fi chewed on her lip. "What if he doesn't want the same thing?"

"I doubt that very much," Pippa said.

She and Livy exchanged knowing smiles.

"If your husband is anything like mine, I think he will enjoy the benefits of sharing your bed all night." Livy took a sip of tea, her lips curving. "And waking there in the morning."

Seventeen

"So you're the gents Hutchings mentioned," Vera Engle said in a sultry voice. "The solicitors wanting information on Sarah. Now, me, I've a liking for professional fellows."

Subjected to Miss Engle's openly interested gaze, Fiona willed herself not to blush. The voluptuous, raven-haired actress had taken her and Pippa, once again disguised as solicitors, into one of the "performance rooms" to talk. A tattered chair, sofa, and tiny platform with a wooden pole took up the cramped space.

Leaning against the pole, Miss Engle struck a pose that thrust her ample bosom forward and hiked up the hem of her short sea-green robe. She was in her thirties, with sharp features more arresting than beautiful. Her masterful use of face paint and intricate coiffure of curls and looping braids gave her a glamorous air.

"'Ave a seat, sirs," she purred. "Maybe you'd care for a private show before we chat?"

"Thank you, Miss Engle, we'll stand," Pippa said gruffly. "We at Jones and Courier do not believe in mixing business with pleasure."

"Pity." With a good-natured shrug, Miss Engle sauntered off

the platform and sat on the sofa. She crossed her long, bare legs. "Let's get on to business then."

"We are trying to locate Miss Mallery on behalf of our client and understand you knew her well," Fiona said.

"I knew Sarah as well as anyone 'ere did, which ain't saying much. I'm not sure I can 'elp you. I 'aven't seen 'er in o'er six months. The last time was soon after she quit this place. I went to check up on 'er at Mrs. Bridges's on Golden Lane."

"Miss Mallery has since vacated that boarding house. Do you have any idea where she might have gone?" Fi asked.

"Like I said, Sarah and I 'aven't kept in touch."

Pippa cocked her head. "Do you know why she left?"

Miss Engle leveled a hard stare at them. "I'll answer that if you tell me what this is really about."

Fi coughed in her fist. "As we told Mr. Hutchings, our client has left a bequest—"

"Oh, I know the cock and bull tale you told Hutchings. Unlike 'im, I ain't stupid." The actress cast her gaze heavenward. "What I want to know is why two ladies would dress up as solicitors looking for a girl who I consider a friend."

Fi looked at Pippa, who gave a shrug. Since the jig was up, there was no point in keeping up the pretense. Vera Engle struck Fi as a shrewd individual who suffered no fools. Miss Engle also seemed loyal and protective of Lillian. The truth might get them answers that subterfuge had not.

"How did you know?" Fi asked casually.

"Don't get me wrong, your disguises are first-rate. Could've fooled most folks, I reckon. But costumes are me bread and butter." Miss Engle jerked her chin at Pippa. "Your eyebrows are too light for your wig, and you're too light-footed for a cove. Try putting weights in your shoes. And you," she said to Fiona. "You need more than a mustache to cover that peaches-and-cream complexion. Darker-toned face paint, or better yet a beard, would do the trick."

Impressed, Fi said, "Thank you for the tips."

The actress preened, taking her due. "Now what do you want with Sarah?"

"We're investigators," Fi said. "Sarah's real name is Lillian O'Malley. Her mama hired us to look for her."

"Female investigators, eh?" Miss Engle's soot-thickened lashes fanned upward. "Thought I'd 'eard o' everything, but this is a first."

"Our agency works on behalf of female clients who cannot find remedy elsewhere," Pippa explained. "Mrs. O'Malley hasn't heard from Lillian for months and is concerned that her daughter might have gotten mixed up in bad business."

"I've a daughter myself." Miss Engle's expression turned fierce. "If my Gretchen disappeared, I would move 'eaven and earth to find 'er."

"Then you'll help us?" Fi said.

"I'll do wot I can. Like I said, I don't know where Sarah... Lillian, I mean, is."

Fi took the chair closest to the actress. "Do you know why she left?"

"Lillian weren't 'appy 'ere." Miss Engle's painted mouth twisted. "Who is? It weren't my dream either to dance 'alf-naked in front o' randy bastards, give said bastards private 'performances,' then 'ave to hand o'er a cut to a bleeding pimp. But I've accepted my lot for now because I'll do whate'er it takes to give my Gretchen a better life. Now Lillian, being 'eadstrong and young—reminded me o' myself at 'er age—she 'adn't reached that point yet. She couldn't give up 'er dreams o' being the next Sarah Siddons. Which meant she was frustrated, angry, and despairing. For 'er, working 'ere was torture. Every dance she did made 'er feel like more o' a failure."

"That is why she left?" Pippa asked. "Because working here reminded her of her broken dreams?"

Miss Engle shook her head. "Lillian was a dreamer, but she 'ad bills to pay like everyone else. She left because she found another way to survive. But I 'ope to God she didn't jump out o' the frying pan and into the fire."

Unease prickled Fi's nape. "What do you mean?"

"She met a cove 'ere. 'Is name was Martin, apparently—that was the only thing she'd tell me about 'im, other than the fact that 'e was a 'noble prince.'" Miss Engle snorted. "'E filled 'er 'ead with nonsense that sounded like the old Chartist chatter about equality for all men, and we all know wot that got us. A whole lot o' nothing. I thought the infatuation would fade. Instead, it got worse. Weren't long before all Lillian could talk about was 'er rights as a free citizen...ne'er mind that the Chartists were as quiet as the grave when it came to rights for women. Mostly, though, it chilled me because this Martin controlled 'er voice and thoughts like 'e were a bloody puppeteer and she a wooden dummy on strings."

This explains the changes in Lillian's letters to her mother. As far as Fi knew, the Chartist movement had dissolved after a petition for equal rights was delivered to the government and failed to bring about any changes. Was Lillian's disappearance linked to an offshoot of the political movement? Was this Martin some sort of radical?

"Being no stranger to 'princes,' the last one being Gretchen's sire who left while she was still a bun in my oven, I tried to warn Lillian," Miss Engle went on. "Tried to tell 'er that this cove was trouble and that the only one she could count on was 'erself. But the stars in 'er eyes blinded 'er to the truth. She quit this place soon after."

"And you have no idea what she did next?" Pippa pressed.

"Like I mentioned, I went by 'er lodgings a few weeks later to see 'ow she was faring."

A chill spread through Fi at Miss Engle's grim tone. "Did you speak to Lillian?"

"Aye, but she didn't say much," the actress said tersely. "She didn't 'ave to. The bruise on 'er face spoke volumes."

Fi swallowed. "She was being abused?"

"She denied it, o' course. Got angry when I told 'er she needed to leave the bastard. Defended 'im, said 'e were an important man under a lot o' pressure...as if that justified 'im using 'er like a punching bag." Miss Engle expelled a breath. "There was nothing I could do. When I went back a few days later, she was gone. I haven't seen or 'eard from 'er since."

Hearing Miss Engle's resignation, Fi said quietly, "You did your best."

"Aye, but it weren't good enough." Miss Engle straightened. "Do you think you'll be able to find Lillian?"

"We will do everything in our power," Fi promised.

"Is there anything else you can remember, no matter how trivial it may seem, that might help us find Lillian or this Martin fellow?" Pippa asked.

"I think Lillian's cove was flush in the pocket," Miss Engle said after a moment. "That last time I saw her, her room was piled with packages. I remember 'er pointing at 'em, saying 'ow well Martin took care o' 'er. As if gifts proved anything. Plenty o' bastards throw their blunt *and* their fists around." She shook her head. "But I recall the presents were finely wrapped like they'd come from an expensive shop."

A possible lead. Eagerly, Fi asked, "Do you know which one?"

"The name o' the establishment weren't on the packages. But the boxes were wrapped with ivory damask paper and tied with black satin bows. And tucked in each bow was a black swan's feather, which was unique enough to catch my eye."

And hopefully unique enough for us to track down the shop.

"If you find Lillian," Miss Engle said, "will you tell 'er to call on me?"

"We will," Pippa promised.

"If there's nothing else, I'd best be getting ready." The actress's briskness didn't hide her lack of enthusiasm. "Got a show to do and performances lined up afterward."

Fi glanced at Pippa, who dipped her chin in agreement.

"Before you go." Fi handed Miss Engle a calling card.

The actress took it. "The *Society of Angels*." She looked up. "Why are you giving me this?"

"Because we could use a woman with your talents," Fi said.

EIGHTEEN

At ten o'clock that evening, Hawk found himself in a carriage in the East End. He was accompanied by Devlin, Pearson, and Trent. Earlier this week, the Sherwood Band had struck again, robbing the carriage of a rich merchant and his mistress. The gang had set up detours that forced their unsuspecting victims into an alleyway and a waiting ambush. The criminals had made away with a fortune in jewelry.

This time, however, they might have left a trail. Trent had caught wind of gossip: a woman named Lizzie Farley had been bragging that she'd witnessed the attack and met the gang's leader. The Quorum's goal this eve was to talk to Miss Farley and discover whether she had any useful information.

"When we're inside, let me do the talking." Devlin peered out the carriage window.

"As if a cove could get a word in edgewise," Pearson said beneath his breath.

Hawk agreed with his bearded colleague. Devlin had been issuing orders as if he were in charge and the rest of them were his lackeys. While Hawk found it irritating, he wanted to get the job done so that he could go home to his wife. The thought of Fiona sent a pulse of warmth through him. Last night, when he'd told her he had plans this evening, she hadn't raised a fuss. The fact that he'd just plowed her and made her spend thrice probably accounted for some of her amenability. Nonetheless, he marveled at the easiness of their relationship.

He hadn't lied when he told her he never expected marriage to be this good. It wasn't just the physical aspect...although God knew the fucking was sublime. With her, he was insatiable; the time they spent together made him crave her more. But not just her nubile body. He wanted more of her playful teasing. Her clever wit and lively spirit. He found her more fascinating, more absorbing than even his work.

In her presence, his numbness dissipated, and he felt engaged...alive.

He had not wanted to miss out on time with his wife tonight. Yet he would return too late to make love to her. He toyed with the idea of visiting her this eve, of not waking her but just sleeping beside her. Would Fiona want him in her bed if they weren't making love?

Caroline hadn't. In fact, she'd wanted privacy immediately after coupling. He'd become accustomed to sleeping alone, a policy he'd continued with his mistresses. With Fiona, however, he was reconsidering things. Several times, he'd come so hard that he'd almost fallen asleep while still inside her. He wondered what it would be like to hold her through the night. To wake up with her in the morning...

The carriage door opened, revealing Trent's rugged mien. With his ability to blend in, Trent had gone into the public house to do some initial reconnaissance. He took the seat next to Devlin.

"Well?" Devlin demanded.

"Do you want the good news or bad news first?" Trent returned.

"Bad," Hawk and his colleagues said as one.

At least we agree on something.

"The bad news is that the rumors I heard about Lizzie Farley appear to be true. She's a sot. On her third tankard, and the only thing that's stopping her from drinking more is lack of coin. No wonder people question her credibility. She's an unreliable eyewitness, to say the least."

Hawk lifted his brows. "What is the good news?"

Trent shrugged. "She's here. And the only lead we've got."

"Let's go in," Devlin said decisively. "I'll take the lead with Lizzie Farley; Hawksmoor will be my second. Trent and Pearson can go in separately and keep watch for trouble."

"What is our plan if things go awry?" Since they were about to enter a tavern that was barely a step above a flash-house, Hawk's question was not unreasonable.

"Shoot first, ask questions later," Pearson suggested.

"There'll be no need for that." Devlin straightened the lapels of his impeccably tailored jacket. Beneath the carriage lamp, his copper hair gleamed in fashionable waves. "It never takes me long to extract information from a female subject. I'll be in and out."

"That's what he tells the ladies," Pearson said.

Pearson and Trent both guffawed.

"If you're quite done with the schoolboy humor," Devlin said in frosty accents, "perhaps we can carry on with the mission?"

Trent grinned. "Whatever you say, guv."

As the team headed to the tavern, Hawk hung back with Trent for a moment.

"Any progress on the favor I asked of you?" he said in an undertone.

"Still looking," was Trent's reply.

The inside of the tavern was dim and smoky, packed with local denizens swilling away their troubles. Hawk and Devlin made their way to the bar where Lizzie Farley sat at one end. Pretending to wait for a drink, Hawk studied her beneath his lashes. She appeared to be in her thirties and had a grubby appearance. Her low-cut bodice was stained, as was the mob cap sitting askew upon her greasy hair. As she glanced blearily his way, he noted the dirty smudges on her puffy cheeks.

"Lovely evening, isn't it, miss?" Devlin appeared on her other side.

She turned her head to Devlin. "You talkin' to me?"

Devlin flashed a charming white smile. "With whom do I have the honor of speaking?"

"Name's Lizzie Farley." She took a drink from her tankard, then twisted her head to look at Hawk. "You two coves together?"

Hawk nodded. Before he could say anything, Devlin cut in.

"I say, you're not *the* Lizzie Farley I've been hearing about, are you?"

Lizzie belched. "Depends on what it is you've 'eard."

Devlin lowered his voice to a conspiratorial tone. "Some friends of mine were talking about a Lizzie Farley who met the leader of the Sherwood Band."

"That's me, all right." Lizzie gulped the rest of her beverage.

"Aren't you a fascinating one," Devlin purred.

"You're the only one who thinks so. No one else in 'ere believes me." She waved drunkenly at the room. "But I ain't making the story up...I saw the bugger wif me own eyes. Spoke wif 'im too."

"Do tell us more, love." Devlin aimed the full force of his charm on Miss Farley.

Oddly, she turned from him to look at Hawk. "Can't talk wif a dry throat, can I, 'andsome? Need to wet me whistle."

Hawk ordered another tankard for her.

She took a long swig, licking the foam from her lips.

"As I was saying, three nights ago, I was working in the scullery at the chop 'ouse o'er on King Street. I was taking me break in the back lane, just minding me own business, when a carriage comes through. Only it don't go through on account o' the lane being a dead end. Next thing I know, another carriage pulls up and blocks the other end, and these coves wearin' masks leap out. Knowing trouble when I see it, I 'ide behind a stack o' crates. Now the newcomers, they surround the first carriage, and I can tell they mean business because not only did they say so, but they were also waving pistols like bleedin' flags."

"How many masked men were there?" Devlin asked.

"I ain't sure...five or six, maybe? I was too busy fearin' for my life to be counting. But one o' the men was clearly the leader. 'E 'ad a deep, raspy voice that carried, and I could tell 'e were a good-lookin' cove, even wif a mask on. 'E were real polite, not wot you'd expect from a 'ighwayman, and 'e cut a fine figure. But he weren't as tall and strapping as you, eh?"

At Lizzie's suggestive wink, Hawk felt his neck heat.

"What happened next?" Devlin's words were filtered through his teeth.

"Well, the leader gets the driver to lie on the ground. Then 'e tells the 'igh-kick couple in the carriage—a toff and 'is ladybird—that no one'll get 'urt if they do what 'e says. 'E tells 'em to hand o'er their jewels and furs to 'is associates. After the pair gives up the goods, the leader thanks 'em, real elegant-like, for their"—she mimicked a man's voice— *"donation to the welfare o' their fellow men.* Then 'e bows like an actor in a play."

The hairs tingled on Hawk's nape. Miss Farley's description of the leader—his appearance, theatrics, and modus operandi—matched the accounts of the victims. Her story seemed legitimate.

"Can you tell us anything else about the leader?" Hawk asked. "Or his gang?"

"Another round might jog me memory," Miss Farley said.

After downing half of a fresh tankard, she continued her story.

"The transaction being finished, the leader turned to go when all o' the sudden I lost me balance and fell, knocking o'er one of the crates. The cove whipped around, 'is gaze locking on me while I cowered there on the ground. Before I could open my mouth to scream, 'e were looming o'er me. I thought I were done for.

"Instead, the leader lays a finger to 'is lips. Like 'im and me, we're sharing a secret. Then 'e gives me 'is hand, covered in soft leather, and 'e 'elps me to me feet like I'm a bleeding princess. And I'm lookin' straight into his eyes and they're the finest eyes I e'er saw. Pale...like moonlight. 'E says to me, *I'll give you a trinket, pretty lady, if you keep this a secret, hmm?*"

As Miss Farley sighed dramatically and took another long gulp, Devlin snorted. Hawk shot the other a warning glance. Now was not the time to upset the eyewitness. Miss Farley, with her ale-loosened lips and lack of discretion, was a godsend.

"When I nod," she went on, "the cove reaches into the pocket o' 'is greatcoat. I freeze, thinking 'e was about to pull out a knife and slit me bloody throat. Instead, 'e gives me this."

She lifted her fingers to her neck, tugging on a thin silver chain to dislodge an object from the deep crevice of her bosom.

"Go on, take a closer look." Smirking, she leaned toward Hawk, giving him an unwanted eyeful of her jiggling flesh.

Focusing on the jewelry, he saw that it was a vinaigrette. The oval piece looked to be crafted from silver plate, with holes along the perimeter to disperse the perfume stored inside. The front bore the stamp of a feather, with a distinctive curl at the end. Hawk knew fine craftsmanship when he saw it, and the scent that wafted toward his nostrils was an expensive mix of spice and musk.

Miss Farley batted her eyelashes at him. "You can touch it if you like, 'andsome."

"As a matter of fact, I would like to." Hawk withdrew a coin purse, seeing her eyes widen at the heavy jingle. "How much for the vinaigrette, Miss Farley?"

NINETEEN

"Heavens," his wife cried. "*Hawk.*"

"Do you like it like this, my sweet?" he growled. "Like being tupped against the wall?"

If Fiona's moan wasn't answer enough, then the lush constriction of her pussy certainly was. She'd already come, the gush of dew anointing his driving prick and making his neck arch with bliss. There was no better feeling than this. Not just being buried in his wife's hot, tight cunny but knowing that he wasn't alone in his insatiable hunger. She wanted him as badly as he wanted her.

He'd come into her bedchamber to give her a gift to wear at the ball tonight. He'd found her half-dressed in her corset, stockings, and garters. The electric look that passed between them had sent her lady's maid scurrying out of the room. Hawk had backed his wife into the nearest wall. Her arms had circled his neck as their lips melded in a scorching kiss. It had taken the work of a moment to undo his fall, release his rearing erection, and order, "Hop on, sweeting."

She'd done so with a sensual grace that stopped his breath. While his wife appeared delicate, she had the lithe athleticism of a ballerina. Perhaps dancing lessons had given her such supple feminine strength. Whatever the case, he thanked his lucky stars that she had no trouble wrapping her legs around his hips and holding onto his shoulders as he plowed her against the wall.

"Oh, *heavens*," Fiona gasped.

He stared at her passion-flushed face and thought he would be content to look at naught else for the rest of his days. Yet her other charms also drew his gaze: the curves of her tits bouncing above her corset, the hourglass perfection of her waist. Lewd delight shuddered through him as he watched their joining. The way his cock speared her pretty cunny, her pink petals spreading to accommodate his veined girth. When he withdrew, his shaft glistened with her pearly dew.

Seeing their fucking as well as feeling it nearly took him over the edge.

"Hold on," he bit out.

When he released his hold on her hip, she clung on, crossing her ankles behind him, her hands clenching his hair. He used his free hand to delve between them. Searching out her bold little love-knot, he frigged her in rhythm to his thrusting. The effect was instantaneous. Her silk-covered heels dug into his flexing arse, her thighs clamping his hips. Her sheath pulsed around him, the voluptuous massage too much to resist. Bliss erupted like a geyser, jetting from his prick, and he swooped his head down, drinking in her cries, then pouring his own groans down her throat.

When he regained his wits, he withdrew, shuddering at the wet rush of their mingled pleasure. Gently, he set his wife on her stockinged feet and touched his forehead to hers. They said nothing, breathing in unison, the soft, ragged sounds filling the chamber.

"I take it you missed me last night?"

Fiona's teasing wrestled a chuckle from his throat. Since the interview with Miss Farley had lasted until the wee hours, he'd decided not to disturb his wife. He raised his head to look into Fiona's bluer-than-heaven eyes.

"I did," he affirmed. "Did you miss me?"

When she nodded, his chest expanded.

"I'm glad you came to say hello before the ball." She blew at a stray curl that dangled over her eyes, managing to look both adorable and thoroughly debauched. "Luckily, there is sufficient time for Brigitte to fix my coiffure. If I can coax her back in here after our scandalous behavior, that is." She giggled. "You did not even remove your trousers, my lord. Or your shoes."

Bemused, he realized that she was right. He'd never been this impetuous before, this unbridled in his desire. And it made him feel...free.

After he rearranged his clothing, he raked a glance over his countess. Took in the erotic details of her, locking them away in the vault of his fantasies. Her red, kiss-swollen lips. Her heaving bosom. The glossy trail that leaked from her pussy, wending down her thigh to seep into her stocking. He felt lust, yes...and something else. Something deep and proprietary.

Something that whispered, *She's mine.*

Taking out a handkerchief, he wiped his seed from her thigh, savoring her tremble of awareness. He tucked the linen back into his pocket and looked into her heavy-lidded eyes.

"I'm going to keep this handkerchief with me tonight," he murmured. "As a token of what you gave to me just now. I want you to remember that when you are dancing with all those namby-pambies who will no doubt be vying for your attention."

She blinked. Roses bloomed in her cheeks.

"How could I have *ever* thought you dull and proper?" she breathed.

He barked out a laugh. "You must be a bad influence, minx. Speaking of which, you distracted me from my purpose. I came in here to give you this."

Removing the jeweler's box from his coat pocket, he handed it to her. "For your first public appearance as the Countess of Hawksmoor."

She dimpled, opening the flat velvet box. "How thoughtful of...*oh my goodness.*"

Her gasp justified the extravagant purchase. Knowing the importance she placed on tonight's event, he'd wanted to give her an accoutrement worthy of a countess. The string of sapphires and diamonds from Rundell, Bridge & Co. had fit the bill.

"To match your engagement ring. Do you like it?" he asked.

"Like it? I absolutely *adore* it!" she squealed. "Help me put it on, will you?"

He hid a smile at Fiona's unabashed excitement. He liked that she enjoyed gifts—liked being able to please her in this fashion. As he removed the necklace from its bed of satin, she turned around, and he almost dropped the costly piece at the sight of her corseted backside. Devil and damn, his wife was temptation from every angle.

He fastened the necklace and led her to the cheval glass by her dressing screen. Their combined reflection filled him with pride: his wife was without equal, and every glowing inch of her belonged to him. She touched the strand around her neck, her eyes outshining the jewels.

"It suits you," he said huskily.

She faced him. "Thank you, Hawk. For the gift and your thoughtfulness. I'm so lucky to be your wife, and I vow I'll make you proud tonight."

His throat cinched at her heartfelt declaration. At the glowing sincerity in her eyes.

"I am proud," he managed. "Very proud to be your husband."

He bent his head and kissed her.

Everything is going as planned, Fiona thought happily.

Her first public appearance as the Countess of Hawksmoor was a smashing success. As she'd descended into the ballroom on

Hawk's arm, wearing an elegant gown of cerulean taffeta and her spectacular new necklace, she saw a mix of admiration and envy on the faces around her. Her hard work had paid off: she had secured her place in Society. In truth, she was happier than she could ever remember being. All because of Hawk.

Their waltz had been the highlight of her evening. Dancing was definitely her second favorite activity to do with her husband. Yet even when they were apart, she felt his presence. Several times, she and Hawk had locked gazes across the crowded ballroom. The proud approval in his eyes made the rest of the room—nay the *world*—seem to fade. Their connection filled her with exhilarating confidence.

For the first time, she wasn't just playing the role of a dazzling lady, she was living it.

Maybe I am not an impostor after all, she thought with wonder. *Maybe I've found a place where I truly belong...by Hawk's side.*

"You are absolutely glowing this eve, Fiona."

The Duchess of Strathaven's voice dispelled Fi's reverie. Her Grace was a lovely brunette with a warm smile. She was accompanied by Fi's mama-in-law.

Fi curtsied to both ladies. "Thank you, Your Grace."

"Your dress is divine." The duchess's eyes had a lively acuity that she'd passed on to her daughter Livy. "And is that a new necklace?"

"It was a gift from Hawksmoor," Fi said with pride.

"He has very fine taste." The duchess shared a conspiratorial look with Lady Helena. "In jewelry as well as in his choice of a bride."

The ladies laughed while Fi blushed.

"I am glad my son is showing his appreciation, my dear," Lady Helena said. "I have heard through the grapevine that you've done wonders with the town house. I'm all agog to see the changes."

"Would you like to come over for tea?" Fi asked.

"How about Wednesday?"

Fi hid a grin at her mama-in-law's prompt reply. "That would be lovely."

After chatting a while longer, Fi excused herself to use the necessary. On her way, she spotted Hawk talking with his brother Jeremiah, the twins a virile pair in their stark evening clothes. While Jeremiah seemed to be doing most of the talking, the faint curve of Hawk's lips conveyed that he was enjoying the brotherly bonding. Fi made note to invite Jeremiah and his wife Effie over for supper soon.

Passing the checkered marble dance floor, Fi saw Livy whirling around with Hadleigh. The pair was laughing at some private joke. Fi's parents were also dancing, gazing into each other's eyes as they moved as one. For the first time, Fi had an inkling of what the couples were feeling.

I feel that same connection...with Hawk.

Giddy with that insight, Fiona entered the plush retiring room. In addition to the dressing tables and carpeted seating areas, there were two modern water closets. She had just shut herself in the nearest one when she heard newcomers enter.

Familiar accents filtered through the walls of the closet. "I cannot take another moment of that ill-bred hussy flaunting herself!"

Her nape chilling, Fi recognized the voice of Lady Melinda Ayles, Hawk's ex-lover.

"She is no better than she ought to be," a woman with nasal accents agreed. "Marrying a title doesn't erase the fact that her family came from the gutter."

"And we all know why Hawksmoor married her." The third female had an affected lisp. "Her dowry would tempt Croesus himself."

"Money is not the only reason, my dears."

Melinda's nasty tone caused Fi to brace.

"You are forgetting the bride and groom's hasty wedding.

While their families have tried to make it look like an impetuous love match, I know the truth. Hawksmoor does not believe in love or emotional entanglements; he told me so when we were together. In fact, he never had the courtesy to stay the night—*that* is how cold and insensitive he is."

Fi's heart pounded. Her emotions were as jumbled as her knitting bag. Anger, humiliation, jealousy...she couldn't untangle the skeins of what she was feeling.

What gives Lady Ayles the right to be so malicious? How could Hawk have been involved with that wretched woman? Does he treat me the same way he treated her?

Fi was forced to confront the fact that Hawk left her bed in the same perfunctory manner that he'd apparently left his mistress's. She hated how the knowledge cheapened what transpired in her marriage. Was their lovemaking nothing special to Hawk? Was *she* nothing special?

Nasal Lady tittered. "Are you saying that Hawksmoor married her out of, ahem, necessity?"

"She's a brazen tart masquerading as a lady," Melinda said flatly. "I would be surprised if he was the only one who'd had her before the marriage."

How dare she impugn my honor. I cannot allow her to slander me.

Trembling with indignation, Fiona reached for the door handle of the closet.

"But Hawksmoor is a gentleman," the third lady said. "Surely his honor would not allow him to dally with a virgin..."

"He may be a gentleman, but he likes bed sport. In fact, he was such a glutton for it that I had to end the affair. A true lady has limits."

Melinda's words slammed like a stake through Fiona's heart, making her jerk her hand back.

"But some females will do *anything* for a title."

Fi tried to stanch her pain and humiliation. *Don't listen. Ignore them...*

"You have the most *delicious* gossip, Melinda," Nasal Lady said excitedly.

"*Everyone* is talking about it, my dear. In fact, there are wagers going on about when the babe will be born. I have twenty pounds that says seven months hence..."

Laughing, the women left.

Alone, Fiona tried to stop shaking.

TWENTY

Something is wrong with Fiona. Hawk felt it in his bones.

When she'd wanted to leave the Strathavens' ball early, he'd sensed something was amiss. She had claimed to have a megrim and looked a trifle pale. With gnawing worry, he'd made their excuses and summoned the carriage. His concern had grown when he'd put an arm around her shoulders, intending to comfort her during the ride home. He'd expected her to lay her head on his shoulder; instead, she'd held him off.

Then she'd moved to the opposite bench.

"If you don't mind, I would like space," she'd said. *"For my head."*

He had minded because her behavior was unusual. Usually, she welcomed his affectionate gestures. Then he remembered Caroline's megrims, and a chill entered his blood. His first wife's moods had begun with a headache too. From there, they'd spread into fatigue and weeping and despair. Excuses, empty seats, and closed doors.

Closed doors...like the one currently between him and Fiona. The one he was staring at as if he could decipher the secrets of the universe in the grain of the wood.

What the hell am I doing? he thought starkly. *I have no talent for this. I could not help Caroline then, and I cannot help Fiona now. Besides, Fiona and I agreed that there would be no emotional complications. I am under no obligation to find out what is bothering her. She expressly told me that she can take care of herself.*

Shoving his hands into the pockets of his dressing gown, he retreated from the door and downed a whisky. When that didn't help, he had another.

Even twenty-year-old Scotch couldn't thaw the block of ice in his gut. He was surprised to realize that he could name what he was feeling: fear. Since marrying Fiona, his numbness receded. Her presence—in his bed, at his table, just bloody hovering in his mind—had reawakened him to feeling. To desire and happiness and hope.

Hope...the most dangerous feeling of all.

Yet he couldn't stop himself from thinking about Fiona as she'd danced with him at the ball. As usual, she'd been a magnet for male attention, but she'd had eyes for only him. Feeling the envious stares of other men, he'd known that he was the luckiest bastard alive...especially with that handkerchief tucked in his pocket. The reminder of just how thoroughly his wife belonged to him.

By Jove, she'd let him take her against the wall in one of the hottest experiences of his life. What could have changed between then and now? Bewildered frustration filled him, outweighing the fear. There had to be a *reason*, something that had transpired... maybe something he had or had not done? This was Fiona, he reminded himself. While vivacious, she was also forthright and even-keeled, not prone to fluctuating moods.

The more he thought about it, the more convinced he became that he ought to try to ask her again what was wrong. Maybe she wouldn't tell him. Maybe history was repeating itself, and there was no rhyme or reason to his wife's change of disposition. Maybe he was like Sisyphus, destined to push the same bloody boulder uphill again and again, only to get flattened each time.

Because this was Fiona, however, he had to try.

He went to the closed door. The light seeping from underneath told him she was still awake. Inhaling, he rapped on the wood.

He heard rustling sounds, and Fiona's voice filtered through the barrier.

"Yes?"

She sounded distant. As if she were miles instead of mere inches away.

"I...I..." He cursed his own ineptness. "I wanted to see if you needed anything."

"No, thank you."

He curled his hands at his sides. "May I come in?"

"It's rather late."

"Why are you avoiding me?" His anger took him by surprise. "Has something happened?"

Silence greeted him. Too late, he remembered that his frustration helped nothing. Confrontations had only resulted in more withdrawal, more weeping and silence. Bloody hell, he almost wanted the numbness to return. Feeling nothing was better than this gut-wrenching helplessness. This cataclysmic sense of failure...

The door clicked open, revealing Fiona. Her reddened eyes and the tear tracks on her cheeks struck him like a physical blow. She wasn't wearing one of her usual bedtime ensembles, those sensual scraps that made his hands itch to tear them off. Instead, she was bundled up in a worn chintz wrapper, her bare toes peeping out from beneath the voluminous folds. Her hair hung over one shoulder in an untidy plait.

Because of Fiona's poise, he sometimes forgot that she was only nineteen. Right now, she looked her age—looked achingly young and vulnerable. Every instinct in him clamored to hold her, protect her, soothe away her pain. He just didn't know if he was capable of giving her what she needed.

"Are you...is everything all right?" he asked.

"No. Everything is *not* all right." When her bottom lip quivered, she bit it in an obvious attempt to control whatever she was feeling. "That is why I wanted to be left alone."

Retreat, a voice in his head warned. *She wants to be left alone. You can do nothing.*

He crossed the threshold; she retreated a few steps.

"Tell me what is wrong," he said.

"Not *what*. Who." She hugged her arms around herself. "How *could* you, Hawk?"

"How could I what?" he asked warily.

"Sleep with that horrid Melinda Ayles," she burst out.

It took him a moment to register what she was saying. To recognize that Fiona wasn't caught in the throes of despair that had no apparent cause. No, she was *jealous*...over a past lover of his.

Relief flooded him, rocking him to the core. Guessing that she must have seen Melinda at the ball, he could understand her feelings. After all, he'd burned with possessiveness whenever Fiona had danced with another man. If he'd had to interact with a former paramour of hers, he'd probably be fit to kill. Not only did he comprehend Fiona's reaction, but he also knew what to do about it. As a young bride, Fiona undoubtedly needed husbandly reassurances—reassurances that he was happy to give.

"I ended my affair with Lady Ayles before we were married. It was a brief arrangement," he said. "There is no need to be jealous."

His complacency vanished at the flash of ire in Fiona's eyes.

"You think I am jealous of Lady Ayles?"

He sensed a trap. "Er, aren't you?"

"No, Hawk, I am not jealous. I am furious," she declared.

She gave a huff of rage that he probably should not have found endearing. She began pacing, her braid bouncing over her shoulders.

"There I was, having a splendid evening. Then, out of nowhere, I am ambushed by that vindictive woman and her friends."

Hawk's amusement faded. He would not tolerate anyone mistreating his wife.

"Lady Ayles ambushed you?" he asked, frowning. "At the ball?"

"Not publicly."

Fiona shot him a look that he wasn't used to receiving. The kind that implied that he might not be very bright.

"Her sort never says what they think to your face. She and her conspirators were gossiping behind my back in the retiring room. They didn't know I was in the water closet, and they...they *slandered* me, Hawk."

He clenched his jaw. "Tell me what they said."

"They called me an ill-bred hussy. Said that I trapped you into marriage by doing things that...well, that no lady would do." Fiona's cheeks reddened. "Lady Ayles said that you were a glutton for bed sport, and she ended her affair with you because of it. Then she said that I used your lustful appetites to get myself in an unfortunate way and trapped you into marriage. She said there are wagers going on about when our babe will be born!"

"I see." Hawk kept a firm leash on his anger. "Did she say anything else?"

"She said I'd probably had other lovers before marriage."

"I will take care of her," he said grimly. "Leave it to me."

"What can you do about it?" Fiona threw up her hands. "The gossip she is spreading is insidious. You cannot fight it. The more you try, the more tongues wag. Do you know how often I've been called *Miss Banks* behind my back? Trust me, I have dealt with this brand of condescension and snobbery my entire life. The fact of the matter is, I would have dealt with her then and there, but..."

"But what?"

"But you *slept* with her. Shared intimacies with her," Fiona wailed. "How could I put her in her place knowing that you treated her the same way you treat me?"

Then she burst into tears.

Fiona felt Hawk's arms close around her. He lifted her as if she weighed less than a feather, carrying her to her sitting room. He settled her firmly on his thighs and wiped her wet cheeks with a handkerchief. She didn't have the wherewithal to stop any of it. She was overwhelmed—distraught, angry, heartsick...she couldn't name everything she'd kept bottled up inside.

At the ball, she'd thought about finding Livy and Glory and telling them what she'd overheard. Yet the idea of sharing Hawk's intimate dealings had made her feel nauseous. She didn't even want to think about him with Melinda Ayles, let alone tell her bosom friends that the other woman had turned him away for being a "glutton."

Fiona felt humiliated and crushed. While she knew her marriage was one of convenience, she'd believed that her physical connection with Hawk was...unique. That they were building something special. Yet, apparently, he was randy and intense with all women. Although she tried to tell herself that what went on before their marriage didn't matter, she couldn't stop despair from spreading.

Hawk thought you were a frivolous and temperamental flirt, a voice inside her whispered. *He only proposed because you leapt into that alleyway, and he feels responsible for compromising you. And you willfully used the situation to maneuver him into a marriage of convenience. If not for his honor, Hawk would never have married you. He has no emotional attachment to you. You are just a convenient bed partner and a way for him to fulfill his duty.*

Self-doubt attacked like a pack of ravening wolves. She

couldn't defend herself from her spiraling thoughts. She felt desperate and out of control, and she didn't like it.

She pushed him away, burying her face in her hands. "Just leave me alone."

"I will not. Not until you clarify what you just said."

"You said you didn't like emotional outbursts." She lowered her hands to glower at him. "In case you haven't noticed, I am having one now."

"Carry on," he said.

His calmness annoyed her. How could he be so dashed controlled when she was coming apart at the seams?

"There will be weeping, raging, and likely name-calling involved," she warned.

He raised his brows. "Will you be calling *me* names?"

"Quite possibly."

"Noted. Now, you were claiming that I treated you and Lady Ayles in the same fashion," he said with equanimity.

He wants the truth? she thought darkly. *I'll give it to him.*

"Lady Ayles said that you do not believe in love," she stated. "That you told her you were not interested in emotional entanglements. Which is the same thing you told me when you proposed."

"Go on."

"Then she said that after the two of you made love, you never stayed the night. Also a habit of yours that I am familiar with."

Hawk cocked his head. "Do you want me to?"

"Want you to what?"

"Stay the night."

Caught off guard, she said stiffly, "That is hardly the point."

"On the contrary. You are angry because you believe I treated you and my ex-mistress in the same fashion. The logical conclusion would be that you wish to be treated differently. Ergo, you want me to sleep with you."

Devil take the man and his superior reasoning.

She took refuge in indignation. "I am your wife. I deserve respect."

"Some ladies prefer privacy after coupling. My first wife was one of them. I did not stay the night with her out of respect for her wishes."

The flatness of his tone gave Fi pause. "Truly?"

He gave a curt nod. "I wanted to show you the same respect."

She bit her lip. "And that is also why you never stayed with Lady Ayles?"

"No. I never stayed with Lady Ayles because I had no desire to wake up next to her," Hawk said bluntly. "I had no wish to extend my time with her beyond our specific arrangement which, by the by, was about slaking a need and not making love."

Although Fi was cheered by the statement, she recalled what Hawk's mistress had said about his appetite. "But she said that... that you couldn't get enough of her." She had to unclench her jaw to get the words out. "That she ended things because of it."

"As a gentleman does not call a lady a liar, I can only say that Lady Ayles is a stranger to the truth," Hawk said coolly.

Relief rolled through Fi. "I just cannot bear the thought of you and that...that woman."

A corner of his mouth lifted. "Is that your best attempt at name-calling?"

"I don't wish to stoop to her level," she said primly.

"How magnanimous of you. But you could never, you know."

"Never what?"

"Be at her level. Or rather, she could never be at yours." Hawk cupped her cheek, his gaze as warm as his touch. "You are special to me, Fiona. Not only because you are my wife. I have never wanted anyone the way I want you."

"Truly?" she whispered.

"Truly. And I cannot tell you how good it feels to be on the receiving end of your sweet, generous passion."

His eyes were so intense that a part of her wanted to look away; the other part wanted to drown in those silver-grey depths.

"But I like being with you in more than just the Biblical sense, Fiona. I like talking and having supper and doing everyday things with you. I like how committed you are to your charity and your friends. I like that you want to know about my interests and that you ask intelligent questions. I like what you've done with the house and even how readily you spend my money."

Her eyes threatened to overflow again. Her heart, too. No one had seen her this way before. No one had made her feel this wanted, this special, this...this *valued* for who she was.

Overwhelmed, she tried to pull herself together. To lighten the mood.

"It is my money too." She adopted a cheeky tone. "I didn't come to you a pauper."

"No, you didn't." There was a tender look in his eyes, as if he knew what she was up to. "Just so you know, however, I have no need of your dowry. That money will go to the children I hope we will one day be blessed with. Sons and daughters with their mama's incomparable spirit."

Botheration. She couldn't stop the tears from spilling down her cheeks.

"I p-promise I'm not a w-watering pot," she sniffled.

"I don't care if you are." He dashed away a tear.

"But you don't like unnecessary s-sentiments. You told me so when you proposed."

"I have changed my mind."

She pinched her brows together. "When did that happen?"

"Right now. I have never seen anything as charming," he said solemnly, "as you at this moment."

Awareness jolted her. *Heavens.* She'd been so caught up in her emotional maelstrom that she'd forgotten about her appearance.

She clapped her hands to her cheeks. "I must look like a fright—"

"You are beautiful exactly as you are." He pried her hands from her face, kissing the palms. "And you are mine, Fiona."

"You're mine too," she felt compelled to say.

"I would not have it any other way."

She slid him a considering glance. "Does this mean that our relationship might get, um, complicated?"

"I think," he said dryly, "we are rather past the point of 'might.'"

"Oh." Her heart stuttered. "I suppose you're right."

"I usually am." A smile lurked in his eyes. "You still haven't answered my question."

She had to think back. "You mean...about staying the night?"

He dipped his chin, his gaze watchful.

Suddenly, she flashed back to their daring escape from von Essen's balcony. That dizzying fear she'd felt when looking down... but also the soaring exhilaration. Back then, she'd trusted him enough to take the leap—and her instincts hadn't changed.

"The answer is yes," she said breathlessly. "Please stay the night with me."

TWENTY-ONE

Hawk surfaced on a disorienting wave of pleasure. He kept his eyes shut, wanting the erotic dream to last. Nothing in real life could feel this good. When he was awake, his companions were loneliness and exhaustion. Or work... he could always bury himself in his inventions. But he would rather bury himself in this fantasy lover. Bloody hell, she felt fine. He groaned, breathing in the scent of peaches and woman, thrusting his cock against giving flesh...

"Well, good morning to you too."

The teasing voice lured him into wakefulness. Opening his eyes, he saw a flash of red...red hair. *Fiona's* hair. Relief and fierce gladness surged over him as he returned to the present. He and his wife were in bed together, lying on their sides like a pair of spoons. His morning erection was cradled against her lush derriere, his hand filled with her soft, firm breast.

Last night, they'd had what qualified as their first marital disagreement, and a part of him couldn't believe how well they'd managed the conflict. Not only had they addressed the problem head-on, but they had also resolved it openly and directly. They had made their way through a jungle of emotions without getting

trapped in tar pits of hopelessness or despair. For him, it was a reve-
latory experience, and it made attachments, in general, seem less
daunting.

Afterward, he and Fiona had cuddled in bed, talking until
sleep had claimed them. Even though they hadn't made love, he'd
liked having her close. Sleeping with Fiona, waking up next to her
felt...right.

Everything with her did.

He swept aside her braid to nuzzle her ear. Savoring her shiver,
he murmured, "Good morning, sweetheart."

"Do you always wake up this way?" There was a catch of
laughter in her voice.

"Aroused, you mean?" He plumped her breast, searching out
the needy tip beneath her night rail. He pinched lightly, smiling
when her breath hitched. "I'm afraid it is a common morning
condition. Luckily for me, you are the cure. Now be a love and
pull up your nightgown."

Giggling, she worked the fabric up past her hips. Her
delightful wriggling made him harder than a steel pike. He ran a
proprietary hand down her front and between her trembling
thighs. His blood rushed to find her pussy slick with dew.

"Do *you* always wake up this way?" he asked huskily. "This wet
and wanting?"

"Um...sometimes." She squirmed.

Christ, this woman. Her honesty undid him every time.

He delved deeper, relishing her moans as he rubbed her needy
little love-knot.

"If I wasn't here," he said into her ear, "what would you do
about it?"

She stilled, and he could see the embarrassed blush spreading
over her cheek. He didn't let her withdraw, keeping his hand firmly
on her cunny. With his free hand, he yanked his nightshirt out of
the way. He ground his bare cock against her ass, and she
whimpered.

"Would you touch yourself here?" He circled her pearl with his middle finger. "Have you ever made yourself spend, little minx?"

"Hawk..."

The pleading way she said his name lured a drop of pre-seed from his cock. His slow, slick thrusting against her rear crevice caused them both to pant.

"Yes or no," he coaxed.

A heartbeat passed.

"Yes."

At her shy admission, satisfaction raged through him.

"I've frigged myself thinking about you." He suckled her earlobe, glorying in the way she worked her pussy against his fingers. In the desperate, wet friction they were creating together. "Yesterday morning, as a matter of fact, I lay in bed thinking of you on the other side of the door. I fucked my own hand, imagining that you were there with me. That you were begging me to eat your pussy in that delightfully wanton way of yours."

She stiffened, coming with a loud cry that the servants could probably hear.

He didn't give a damn. In his hot, blinding lust, he wanted the world to know how thoroughly his wife belonged to him. Hunger took over, and he sat up, jerking off his nightshirt and Fiona's. Then he rolled onto his back, pulling her over him.

She smiled her siren's smile, undoubtedly believing that she was about to ride him. The chit did love being on top. He loved it too, but he had a hankering for a different sort of treat this morning. He glimpsed her startled expression as he yanked her upward, positioning her cunny over his face.

"Hawk?" she breathed.

"Hold onto the headboard, sweetheart," he growled. "Time for a new kind of ride."

It was depraved. Dirty. *Delightful.*

Gripping the wood, Fiona moaned as she rode her husband's mouth. A part of her wondered if she should do something this outrageous. The larger part of her melted into the experience, into the hot, swirling persuasion of Hawk's tongue.

"Christ, you're delicious."

The fact that his deep voice was muffled by *her* made her squirm with embarrassed arousal.

"Give me more of your sweet cream."

She rocked against his ravening mouth. Even though she controlled the movements, he controlled her pleasure. His hot licking incinerated her inhibitions, and when she felt his tongue stab inside her, she whimpered, grinding against him. She felt starved for even that small, wicked penetration. Hawk freed her of care. Of anything but her desire to please and be pleased.

As if he knew what she needed, he slid two thick fingers into her aching sheath.

"Move this naughty pussy, Fiona," he growled. "Fuck yourself on my fingers until you come."

As if trained to his command, her hips moved, pushing back on his impaling touch. Desperate sounds crowded up her throat as he screwed his long digits into her, held her against his furnace-hot mouth. His lips latched onto her pearl, the suction pulling bliss from her core. Her release gushed from her in torrents that made her tremble and Hawk grunt with approval.

Hawk rolled her over, entering her in a swift thrust. His big cock pushed out whatever breath remained in her lungs, her spent nerves trying to adjust to more sensation. She didn't know how much more pleasure she could take.

"Relax, darling," Hawk murmured. "You did so well. Let me take care of you now."

Mesmerized by the smoky pleasure in his eyes, she obeyed, surrendering to his loving. To the deep strokes of his cock and the heated possession of his touch. Their sweat-slickened bodies heaved as one. When he leaned down to kiss her, however, she suddenly remembered and turned her face to the side.

Hawk caught her chin, making her face him. "What is it, sweetheart?"

"I...I haven't done my morning ablutions," she blurted.

His dark brows collided. "So?"

"I haven't brushed my teeth. My breath..." She trailed off when his broad shoulders began to shake. "Are you laughing at me?"

His roar of mirth confirmed this.

Annoyed, she slapped at his chest. "I fail to see what you find amusing."

"You, that's what." Bending down, he gently nipped her ear. "Worrying about your breath when I've just feasted on your pussy."

When the part in question clenched, he gave her a rather smug look.

She huffed out a breath. "That is beside the point..."

"No, it *is* the point. There isn't a part of you I don't find delectable. To me, you will always be perfect as you are."

His eyes blazed with tenderness and lust, calling forth her deepest longings. Her greatest fears.

Swallowing, she said, "Even if my eyes are red from crying?"

"Even then."

"And my hair looks like a bird's nest?"

"Tousled suits you."

"What if my cheeks are blotchy?"

Amused lines fanned from his eyes. "Are you going to fish for compliments all day, or allow me to finish making love to you?"

"You may finish..."

Her breath stuttered when he plunged to the hilt, stirring deep inside her.

"I won't be the only one finishing, will I?" he asked huskily.

He kissed her then, open-mouthed, deep-tongued, his growl of enjoyment dissolving her worries. She ran her fingers through his thick hair, pulling him closer. Everywhere they touched, pleasure ignited. His firm, hairy chest teased her nipples, his rippled abdomen grinding against her belly. The forceful drives of his cock and the heavy slap of his stones stoked her desire.

"Christ, I can't get enough of you," he bit out.

"I can't get enough of you either," she panted.

A wicked glint entered his eyes. He grabbed her legs, hooking them over his shoulders one by one. She gasped at the new angle, the deepness of the penetration.

"Here is more for you, sweetheart," he rasped. "Can you take me this way?"

"Oh, Hawk." She clung to his bulging biceps, feeling his controlled power as he pushed into her core. "That's so...so *deep*."

"It bloody well is." His voice slurred. "I love how flexible you are."

He slammed his hips, each heavy thrust grazing her pearl and hitting a deep, ecstatic place inside. She went up in flames, and he followed her with a shout, blasting her again and again with his heat. Afterward, he settled atop her, blanketing her with his strength, burying his face in her neck. She stroked the sculpted lines of his back as they floated in bliss together.

"I am glad you stayed with me," she whispered.

He raised his head, his gaze sated and soft as summer rain. "I am glad you asked me to."

Twenty-Two

That afternoon, Hawk arrived just in time for the meeting at Garland's Curiosities. Devlin slunk in behind him. The rake looked like he'd slept in his clothes.

"Rough night?" Hawk inquired.

Devlin grunted, going to the sideboard to slosh coffee into a cup before heading for the table where the rest of the team was assembled. Swinburne called the meeting to order. He began by reviewing the report Hawk had written on Miss Farley.

"And this Miss Farley is a creditable witness?" the spymaster asked with a frown.

"She is *a* witness." Looking surly, Devlin took out a flask, adding a shot of its contents to his cup. "Might have a problem with her eyesight, if you ask me."

"We're tracing the vinaigrette," Hawk said. "I brought it to a jeweler, who gave me a list of places he believes might stock such an item. Apparently, the feather design on the piece is unique, which will make identification easier."

"A lead, excellent." Inspector Sterling's face was rueful. As usual, he looked rumpled, his sandy hair sticking up at the back, his wrinkled frockcoat hanging loosely on his rangy form. "My superiors are breathing down my neck. Apparently, the most recent victim of the Sherwood Band is threatening to post a reward for their capture. And we all know how that will go."

He received grim nods from around the table. Rewards often hindered more than they helped, leading to bloodshed and loss of life as cutthroats hunted for their bounty. In this instance, the risk was even greater since the gang had cultivated the reputation that it represented the people. Vigilante efforts to capture them would undoubtedly lead to resistance and fan the flames of anarchy.

"Actually, we have more leads." Hawk cleared his throat. "When I was drugged at the Royal Arms, the attack seemed too organized and targeted to be a random crime. Thus, I asked Trent to try to locate the ruffians involved. And he has discovered some information."

With a nod, Trent took up where he left off.

"Hawksmoor didn't give me a lot to go on. Just that there were four assailants, one by the name of Big Jim. I managed to pin down the bastard yesterday. He didn't want to talk at first, but I persuaded him to chat."

The glint in Trent's eyes conveyed the nature of the "chat."

"Jim confessed that he and his friends had been hired to make trouble for a nobleman who was showing up at the pub that night. According to Jim, he was given Hawksmoor's description and a powder to put in his drink. He was instructed to give the target a beating and make it look like a robbery."

"Good God." Inspector Sterling's throat bobbed above his lopsided cravat.

"By whom?" Swinburne demanded.

"Jim says a footman found him in the pub, made him the offer, and gave him the money." Trent paused. "The footman didn't say who his employer was. Jim, however, snuck out after him and heard him say, *'It's done, my lord'* as he entered an unmarked carriage. Jim claims he never saw who was inside."

Devlin spoke into the tense silence. "Who do we think was in the carriage?"

"My guess is von Essen," Hawk said broodingly. "He saw me the night I retrieved Lady Ingersoll's brooch from his safe. True, I was in disguise, but he might have seen through it. He knows the brooch was used to prove his involvement with the Sherwood Band, *and* he was the one who pointed us to the Royal Arms."

"For what purpose would he target you?" Swinburne asked.

"Retribution, perhaps. Or to create a diversion."

"Thus far, von Essen has sent us on a wild-goose chase." Trent ran a hand through his shaggy hair. "His information has led us nowhere. He's not telling us the truth, despite the police interrogation...no offense, Sterling."

"None taken," the inspector assured him. "We've allowed the count to remain free in hopes that the Sherwood Band might contact him again. Perhaps it is time to reel in the bait."

Swinburne gave a decisive nod. "It's high time the Quorum paid von Essen a visit."

Hawk's next stop was the monthly meeting of the Society for Scientific Study and Advancement, held at the residence of noted inventor Harry Kent. Upon Hawk's arrival, several of the senior members flocked to him to offer felicitations. The crusty old intellectuals insisted on toasting Hawk; apparently, they considered his securing of the Season's Incomparable not only a coup for himself but for the scholarly community at large.

More than a few fellows observed that marriage appeared to agree with Hawk. As he was not one to wear his emotions on his sleeve, Hawk was surprised that his contentment seemed obvious to all and sundry. He soon stopped worrying about it. There were worse things than others knowing that one was happy.

And he was happy. Bloody over the moon, to be exact. Having

Fiona in his life made him feel alive again. He'd been wandering through a thick fog for years, realizing it only now when he'd suddenly stumbled into the light.

For all the brightness Fiona brought into his life, he was discovering that she harbored her own shadows. How strange that a woman with her beauty and talents could have insecurities, yet he now knew that his wife had a deep streak of vulnerability, one she hid behind her dazzling confidence and wit. Her admission about being bullied because of her family's origins roused all his protective instincts.

From here on in, no one was going to slander his wife.

Thus, although Hawk had pressing Quorum business, he'd stopped at the present gathering first. He wandered through the displays, which included models of analytic engines inspired by the designs of Babbage, various steam-driven mechanisms, and even a few hybridization experiments involving plants. As intriguing as some of the exhibitions were, Hawk was not here for the science today.

"Hawksmoor, well met."

Turning, Hawk saw his host approach. Harry Kent was tall and built like an athlete, yet his unruly dark hair and spectacles gave him an intellectual air. Oddly enough, he was in his shirtsleeves, with something strapped to his chest. The contraption consisted of a fabric pouch, with leather straps extending over Kent's broad shoulders and circling his hips. In the pouch was a sleeping infant, the tiny dark-whorled head nestled beneath Kent's cravat.

"One of your creations?" Hawk asked in a low, amused voice.

"They both are," Kent said with a grin. "Although Mrs. Kent did most of the work where little Tobias is concerned. As for the carrier, necessity is the master of invention." His bespectacled gaze turned rueful. "The nursemaids were at their wits' end trying to get Tobias to sleep. After careful observation, I realized that he likes to snooze when there is noise and movement. The sling, which Mrs. Kent has dubbed 'the Sanity Saver,' allows him to be carried while keeping one's hands free. I'm thinking of patenting it."

"It will be a smashing success, no doubt."

Kent gave him a sly look. "Perhaps you would care to be put on the waitlist?"

Hawk's face heated. At the same time, the image of Fiona ripe with his child sent a primal rush through him. He did not know when duty had become desire, when he'd begun to have that old dream again. Of having a home full of life and love like the one he had grown up in.

"Perhaps," he said thoughtfully.

"Nothing would please Garrity more. And God knows we at Great London National Railway prefer him in a happy state," Kent said with feeling.

Kent happened to be business partners with Hawk's new papa-in-law, operating one of the most successful railway companies in England.

"I shall keep it in mind." Hawk cleared his throat. "If you'll pardon me, I came to speak with an acquaintance."

"By all means." Kent bounced the Sanity Saver, which had begun to wriggle. "Since Tobias is awakening, I'd better set up the rock blasting demonstration. That will put him out like a light."

They parted ways, and Hawk went through the rooms, looking for his target. He spotted her in the library; she'd been cornered by Lord Tumley, a well-meaning but droning fellow whose sagging jowls put one in mind of a bullfrog.

Hawk bowed to them both. "Good afternoon."

"Hawksmoor," Tumley said cordially. "I'm surprised to see you here. If I had a lovely young bride such as yours, wild horses couldn't drag me away, sirrah."

Melinda had a pinched, annoyed mien. The lines that creased her narrow features betrayed a history of malcontent. Hawk wondered what he'd ever seen in her.

He inclined his head. "As my lady volunteers for philanthropic causes, I had some free time."

"Charitable and charming." Tumley sighed. "You're a lucky chap, old boy."

"Indeed. What man wouldn't wish to be married to a saint?" Melinda said snidely.

Hawk kept his tone pleasant. "Lady Ayles, I was hoping for a few moments of your company. Given your expertise in botany, I thought you might help me identify some of the rare plants on display."

Melinda's sulky expression vanished. Triumph flared in her eyes.

"I would be glad to assist, my lord," she nearly purred.

He offered her his arm, hiding his distaste when her fingers dug possessively into his sleeve. Her countenance turned positively gloating when he led her into the secluded orangery.

She aimed a coy look at him. "Why have you arranged for us to be all alone, I wonder?"

"I wished to have a word in private," he said.

At the word "private," she smirked. "Bored already? I knew you would tire of that chit."

"The opposite is true. I have never been more content," he said coolly.

Her eyes slitted. "Then why in blazes did you seek me out?"

"To deliver a message. You will desist your slander of my wife and my marriage. If you see her, you will treat her with the respect she deserves. To her face and behind her back."

"How *dare* you tell me what to do," she seethed.

"You will find that there is little I won't do when it comes to protecting my wife."

Melinda's eyes bulged in their sockets. "Are you threatening me, you bastard?"

"Merely reminding you that one sows what one reaps. Your lies pale in comparison to what I have at my disposal."

"And what would that be?" she spat.

"The truth. Of every affair, every man you've shared your bed with." He paused. "Including the husbands of several of your friends."

Melinda's face whitened with rage. "That is blackmail, damn you."

"Think of it as an exchange. You stop spreading lies, and I keep the truth to myself." He held her gaze. "An arrangement that benefits all parties."

"For months, I did everything I could to please you," Melinda choked out. "To make you care."

He knew that he'd been a challenge for her, a trophy she'd wanted for vanity's sake. She collected lovers the way a numismatist did coins. But if she wanted to adopt the stance of an injured party, he would let her for expediency's sake.

"Yet despite my efforts, you were not moved to even stay the night. Now you've been married for a few weeks, and you're willing to do whatever it takes to protect that simpering chit?" Rage melted through Melinda's mask of martyrdom. "What is so bloody special about her?"

To Hawk, the answer was obvious.

"Everything," he said.

Twenty-Three

No matter how busy the Angels were, they never missed their weekly session with Mrs. Peabody. The training took place in a building behind Charlie's courtyard. Mrs. Peabody, a petite half-Chinese, half-English woman, worked for Charlie as a housekeeper and combat instructor. Dressed in the training uniform of tunic and trousers, her brown hair scraped back in a bun, Mrs. Peabody looked delicate but could take down opponents twice her size.

This morning, Mrs. Peabody showed no mercy with her drills. She ran the Angels through exercises designed to improve strength, endurance, and flexibility. She honed their fighting techniques by having them spar with one another in the practice rings.

Assess your opponent. Find their weakness. Strike when they least expect it.

Beneath her tunic, Fi was perspiring quite profusely when Mrs. Peabody announced it was time for dagger practice.

"Face your targets, Angels." Mrs. Peabody waved at the line of wooden dressmaker's forms. "Ready, aim...release."

One by one, Fiona let her daggers fly. Beside her, Glory and Livy did the same. The thunks of metal sinking into wood echoed through the chamber. When the Angels were finished, Mrs. Peabody surveyed the dummies.

"Very good, Glory." Mrs. Peabody gave a crisp nod of approval. "One hit to the arm, one to the lower leg. No permanent damage done, but enough to deter an attacker and prevent him from escaping. Efficient and effective."

Glory glowed at the praise. "Thank you, Mrs. Peabody."

"Livy. One hit...and one miss."

"Sorry, Mrs. Peabody." Livy tried to stifle a yawn. "I did not get much sleep last night."

"That is no excuse for sloppiness," Mrs. Peabody said, frowning. "You must learn to focus, no matter the circumstance. What if you were on a mission and your life or those of your fellow Angels depended upon your accuracy?"

"I promise to do better," Livy said contritely.

"Remember the technique I taught you. Picture the target in your mind and see your dagger hitting the desired spot. That will help you focus."

As Mrs. Peabody moved on, Fi said under her breath, "I thought you said you left the ball early last night. Did Esme keep you up?"

"No," Livy whispered back. "It was Hadleigh."

Seeing her friend's rosy cheeks, Fiona needed no further explanation. Being married had affected her rest as well. At the same time, with Hawk holding her through the night, she'd experienced the deepest, most refreshing sleep of her life. Her marriage of convenience wasn't so convenient anymore, and she was glad. Glad for their growing closeness, which had allowed her to talk about the incident with Lady Ayles. Hawk's understanding had made Fi feel safe in a way she'd never felt before. As had sleeping and waking in his arms.

"Fiona." Mrs. Peabody's voice snapped her back.

"Um, yes?"

Brows raised, the instructor directed a look first at Fi, then at

Fi's target. "A direct hit between the eyes and in the heart. Feeling bloodthirsty, are we?"

"I was, um, imagining that I was in mortal danger," Fi said.

"Did you use the visualization technique?"

Fi had mentally affixed Lady Ayles's smirking visage onto the dummy's head. Just because Fi felt secure in Hawk's affections didn't mean she forgave his ex-mistress for slandering her.

"Yes, Mrs. Peabody," she said truthfully. "It was very effective."

Pippa and Charlie entered the room. Their bonnets and redingotes indicated that they'd just returned from an outing.

"We've identified the shop that Lillian's packages came from," Pippa announced. "A plumassier I spoke to sells black swan feathers in bulk to a shop in Soho called Swann's. The shop uses the feathers to embellish its parcels."

"Are we off to Swann's then?" Fiona asked.

"It is not quite that simple." Pippa exchanged a look with Charlie.

"Swann's, as it turns out, is a unique establishment," Charlie said. "The discretion of the proprietress, Susanna Swann, is such that I had to do some digging to find out more about her."

"What did you discover?" Glory wanted to know.

"Mrs. Swann bills herself as a purveyor of sexual fulfillment," Charlie said matter-of-factly. "From what I can tell, she is not a bawd and does not employ prostitutes. Instead, she facilitates the exploration of desires. Most of her patrons are couples, and her shop provides a place and tools for them to carry out their fantasies."

Charlie was not one to mince words. Her philosophy was that ignorance made women vulnerable, and empowerment lay in having access to accurate information.

"Oh." Glory's lashes waved rapidly over her large hazel eyes. "Well."

"If this Susanna Swann is as discreet as you say, do you think that she will talk to us?" Livy asked. "Tell us what she knows about Lillian?"

"I am not certain." Charlie folded her arms over her forest-green redingote, her gaze contemplative. "Mrs. Swann is reputed to be as tight-lipped as a clam, which has earned her an elite and loyal clientele."

"Then we will need to go in disguise," Livy surmised.

"Mrs. Swann is said to be very shrewd," Charlie said. "Which, given her entrepreneurial success, comes as no surprise. I do not think it will be easy to pull the wool over her eyes. We will have one shot to gain her cooperation. If we trigger her distrust, we will learn nothing. We must select our strategy with the utmost care."

"Perhaps we can appeal to her empathy." Fi chewed on her bottom lip. "A woman who has risen on her own merits might be inclined to feel compassion for another who is struggling to achieve her dream."

"You are suggesting that we tell Mrs. Swann the truth?" Charlie asked.

Fi nodded. "Lillian is an ambitious young woman who is flying in the face of convention to follow her heart. Who could understand better than an owner of an, ahem, unusual business?"

"An excellent point," Livy said, her looped braids swinging.

"Moreover, a girl's welfare is at risk," Fi went on. "If we tell Mrs. Swann that Lillian has fallen prey to an abusive man, perhaps she might want to help. We've seen time and again that there is honor among women, especially ones who have fought for their survival."

"We have also seen the opposite." Charlie narrowed her eyes. "Survival can strip one of compassion, leaving only the skeleton of self-interest. The question is what kind of woman is Susanna Swann?"

"I could find out," Fi offered. "If I meet with Mrs. Swann, I can follow my instincts and adjust my strategy—truth or subterfuge—accordingly."

"When it comes to managing people, Fi is the best of us," Glory piped up.

Fi's cheeks warmed. Among her brilliant and capable friends, she was a trifle embarrassed to have her paltry talent highlighted.

"It is not much of a skill," she averred.

"There's no need to be modest, Fi," Livy said. "You have gotten us out of more than one corner by reading people correctly."

"As a recent example, you adroitly handled the situation with Vera Engle," Pippa added.

"It was nothing—" Fi began.

"Why is it difficult to accept your due, my dear?" Charlie asked abruptly.

Because I do not deserve praise. I am not as talented as my friends. I just work hard.

Under Charlie's scrutiny, Fi felt like a butterfly trapped beneath glass.

"It's, um, not," she said awkwardly. "I am glad to contribute where I can."

Charlie's gaze lingered a moment longer. "Good. For you have my vote of confidence as well, Fiona. I have learned that Mrs. Swann interviews prospective clients on Tuesday evenings—which happens to be tomorrow night. Shall I procure you an appointment?"

Fi nodded. "Yes. You may count on me."

She would have to miss supper with Hawk, but she was certain he would understand. After all, he had his own engagement— some scientific gathering—tonight. In truth, they were both so busy that she ought to create a combined social calendar for them. She liked the idea of coordinating their schedules. Of them being accountable to one another, even when they were off on their separate endeavors. Of her and Hawk sharing more and more.

Maybe someday, came the unbidden thought, *you might even tell him about the Angels.*

Trepidation shivered through her. What would her husband have to say about that?

"Bloody hell." Hawk expelled a breath. "How did this happen?"

He was standing at a dark corner with Trent and Devlin. His colleagues had tracked down von Essen at his club on St. James's Street, and Hawk had just arrived to meet them. Instead of collecting their target for a chat, however, they were staring at his unmoving form lying across the street. The sickly glow of a gas lamp revealed von Essen's trampled state, his innards a gory bouquet above his shredded waistcoat. He attracted a milling crowd that the constables were trying to disperse to make way for the approaching mortuary cart.

"It happened minutes before we arrived," Trent said in a low voice. "I heard eyewitnesses talking to the constables. They said a carriage came out of nowhere, plowing into von Essen as he was leaving his club. The driver made no attempt to stop, and he wore a dark neckerchief over his face."

"Not an accident, then," Hawk said grimly.

"Christ." Devlin looked queasy as two men grabbed hold of von Essen's arms and legs, tossing him into the cart like a side of beef. "Do you think his murder is related to our case?"

"He had his fingers in a lot of unsavory pies," Trent muttered. "Pawning, stealing, blackmailing...the list goes on. But the timing of his death, just as we were closing in on him, feels like too much of a coincidence."

"A coincidence is often a pattern that hasn't been recognized." Hawk lowered the brim of his hat as the cart drove off, and the onlookers began to scatter. "My gut tells me the Sherwood bastards are behind this."

"Von Essen knew too much," Trent agreed. "And they got rid of him...and our best lead."

"As to that." Devlin had a cat-that-got-the-cream look on his face. "I tracked down the origin of the vinaigrette. To a rather special kind of shop."

"What's so special about it?" Trent furrowed his brow.

Devlin smirked. "Oh, you're going to love this."

TWENTY-FOUR

"I am not certain you should undertake this mission alone," Charlie said pensively.

Fi's mentor did not often show ambivalence. They were standing in the antechamber of Charlie's home, and Fi was about to embark on her night's mission.

"I can manage Mrs. Swann." Fi donned her gloves. "Bringing others will only rouse suspicion. Trust me."

"I do trust you, my dear." Charlie sighed. "But this von Essen business has me on edge."

The count's death had come as a shock. According to the papers, he'd been mowed down by an anonymous carriage last evening. Charlie suspected this was no accident; with von Essen's shady dealings, he could have had any number of enemies.

Grimacing, Charlie said, "To think, I sent you into that man's lair just a few weeks ago."

The night I met Hawk while he was disguised as a thief.

With a twinge of unease, Fi wondered if Hawk knew about von Essen's death. She couldn't stop her thoughts from straying: what had Hawk been doing in the count's study that night?

Should she have told Charlie and her friends about her husband's secret? To do so now felt like a betrayal.

If you don't want Hawk nosing around in your business, then don't nose around in his.

Yet the rules of their marriage were changing, shifting in ways that felt exhilarating and scary at once. She adored the life she was building with Hawk: their bantering, sharing, and soul-searing lovemaking. At the same time, the closer they got, the more anxious she felt.

She told herself to focus on the business at hand. "I accomplished the objective then, and I'll do so tonight."

"All right," Charlie relented. "Don't forget to send word after you're done."

Hawker dropped Fi off at Swann's. The shop was situated on a quiet lane in Soho, a neighborhood that was squeezed like a middle child between haughty Mayfair and saucy Covent Garden. Fi concealed her face with the hood of her cape as she headed to the entrance. Given Mrs. Swann's reputation for astuteness, Fi's instincts had told her to forgo an elaborate disguise. The one precaution Charlie had taken was to book the appointment under an alias, a common practice amongst the clientele and unlikely to rouse suspicion.

At first glance, the two-story shop was unprepossessing. Curtains were drawn over the windows, revealing nothing of what was inside. The tidy brick front and beige awning blended with neighboring buildings, making the place easy to miss unless one was looking for it.

Which, Fiona supposed, was rather the point.

A hanging lantern illuminated the brass plate on the door.

By appointment only. Ring bell for assistance.

Fi rung. The door opened to reveal a woman in a black gown, her hair secured in a severe bun. She greeted Fiona with a deferential dip of the knees.

"Good evening. I have an eight o'clock appointment," Fiona said.

"Mrs. Swann is expecting you, ma'am. Please come in."

Fiona was led into the establishment. The front room looked like a typical shop with polished wood counters and cabinets. The merchandise on display seemed innocuous: gloves, stockings, and assorted accessories. A glass case showed off a selection of vinaigrettes and accompanying sachets of perfume. The only thing that hinted at anything out of the ordinary was the lighting: the crimson glass shades of the fixtures bathed the room in a sensual glow. The assistant unlocked a door behind the counter, revealing a corridor flickering with that same, carnal light.

"Right this way, ma'am," she said.

Pulse quickening, Fi followed. She was directed into a room, which she saw with some relief was a regular sitting room. Two black damask chairs sat by a cozy fire, refreshments waiting on a small round table. A bookcase stood against one of the burgundy walls.

"Mrs. Swann will be with you shortly." The assistant closed the door behind her.

Too nervous to sit, Fi wandered to the bookcase, tilting her head to read the titles. *Miss Fanny and the House of Flagellation, The Lust of the Footman, The Secrets of an Amorous Maid...*

"See anything of interest, Mrs. Smith?"

Fi jerked upright, her cheeks aflame. The lady who stood in the doorway was younger than she expected...in her mid-twenties perhaps. Blue-black ringlets framed the woman's oval face, her blue eyes unnervingly bright against her pale tawny skin. Clad in a high-necked gown, she moved with uncommon stealth, her plum-colored skirts barely rustling despite their fashionable fullness.

"Beg pardon, I did not mean to startle you," she said in a throaty voice. "I am Susanna Swann."

Fi regained her wits. "Pleased to meet you, Mrs. Swann."

"The pleasure is mine. Hopefully, it will be yours as well." Mrs.

Swann's red lips curled. "Shall we make ourselves comfortable and discuss the purpose of your visit?"

Mrs. Swann waved Fi to a wingchair while she poured small glasses of port. Accepting the drink from her hostess, Fi knew she'd been right to leave off the disguise. Susanna Swann possessed a disquietingly perceptive air. She reposed in the opposite chair, her manner that of a cat watching a mouse.

Here goes.

"I am here on behalf of a friend," Fi began.

"How original." Mrs. Swann's expression turned ironic. "Come now, Mrs. Smith, there is no need for dissembling. If you know about my business, then you also know that I am known for my discretion. Here at Swann's, you are free to explore your heart's desires." She took a sip of the ruby-red beverage. "Of course, getting to those desires may take getting through fear."

The words sent a shiver through Fi. She thought of Hawk, the excuses she'd told him about her whereabouts tonight. She'd stayed as close to the truth as possible, saying that she was delivering assistance to a woman in need. He'd interpreted this to mean that she was bringing food baskets to the poor. The fact that she hadn't corrected him—that she was willfully misleading him—made her feel annoyingly guilty.

Reminding herself that he had his own secrets didn't help. It made her wish that they could, well, be more honest with one another. If she revealed her true activities, however, would he try to stop her? Change her? Swallowing, she couldn't imagine that he would approve of her present undertaking.

"It is not easy to speak from the heart, is it?" Mrs. Swann's smile held potent understanding. "But that is why you've come to me: to uncover the secrets of your desires. And that can only be discovered if you're willing to delve past your fears."

Concentrate on the assignment Charlie trusted you with. Don't let Lillian down.

Fi squared her shoulders. "I am here for a friend. Her name is Lillian O'Malley. I believe she is a client of yours."

Was that a flicker of recognition in Mrs. Swann's gaze?

"Even if this Lillian O'Malley were a client, I would not discuss her." The proprietress's expression was cool. "I make it a rule not to meddle in the affairs of others. For any price."

Fi heard the steel in Mrs. Swann's voice. In truth, she admired the other's strict code. It spoke of honor...which she could leverage to her advantage.

Thinking quickly, Fi asked, "Is everything I say during this meeting under strict confidence?"

Mrs. Swann waved a slender hand. "As I've said, you may speak freely."

"I am part of a society that specializes in helping women in trouble. We were hired by Mrs. O'Malley to find her daughter Lillian, who has gone missing. Our investigation thus far points to Lillian falling under the influence of a man who has been control- ling and abusing her. One who, around six months ago, made a large purchase at your shop."

Mrs. Swann wasn't the only one good at reading people. Fi noted the businesswoman's dilated eyes, the rapid surges of the cameo brooch pinned upon her breast. Her hand flitted to her neck, a movement that seemed unconscious. Protective, perhaps.

I've struck a nerve. She knows something.

"I need your help, Mrs. Swann," Fi pressed on. "Lillian's well- being depends upon it."

The proprietress's eyes had a cynical glint. "Why should I believe what you say? Your story is outlandish. Who has heard of a female investigator? And clearly a well-bred one at that."

"What I've told you is true. Every word of it."

"Is it, *Mrs. Smith*?" Mrs. Swann arched her brows. "How can I trust you when I do not even know who you are or anything about you?"

Taking a breath, Fi went with her instincts. "If I tell you what you wish to know, will you return the favor?"

"An exchange. Now that *is* intriguing." Propping her elbow on the arm of her chair, Mrs. Swann rested her chin in her hand, her gaze penetrating. "If you answer my questions truthfully—and trust me, I will know if you are lying—then I may help you find what you seek. If you lie to me, our interview ends, and you will not be welcomed back. Agreed?"

Fi's heart thumped like a rabbit's foot. "Agreed."

The assistant's voice filtered through the door. "I am sorry to interrupt. Your next appointment has arrived early, Mrs. Swann."

"I shall be right back." The proprietress rose in that mysteriously silent way of hers. "Take the time to prepare yourself."

For what? Fi's chest knotted. *Dash it all, what have I gotten myself into?*

The clock on the mantel claimed Mrs. Swann was gone for mere minutes. To Fi, who'd been marinating in anxiety, contemplating the things she most feared exposing, it felt like hours. Her palms were clammy as the other took the opposite seat again.

"We'll start with the basics," Mrs. Swann said. "What is your name?"

In for a penny.

"Fiona Morgan."

The proprietress's gaze hooded. "Are you married?"

"Recently," Fi said cautiously.

"Do you enjoy relations with your husband?"

The swift detour into intimate territory caused Fi's cheeks to flame.

She swallowed. "Yes."

"Good. How often?"

Heavens. "Um, almost every night."

"*Very* good." Mrs. Swann's mouth curved. "Tell me more about your husband."

It was a tricky balance to tell the truth while keeping as much back as possible. Luckily, Fi had had a lot of practice.

"Well, he's tall. An attractive man in his prime. Highly intelligent."

"What do you find most attractive about him?"

Everything. Yet Fi knew Mrs. Swann would not be satisfied by vague replies. She sensed that the woman was cataloging her responses, in a manner that seemed...professional. It reminded Fi of how she'd studied the reigning hostesses to learn how to become a social success. Perhaps this was Mrs. Swann's way of learning more about her chosen trade of desire.

"He makes me feel wanted," Fi said honestly.

"Forgive me, Mrs. Morgan. You strike me as a lady who does not suffer from a lack of male attention."

"Wanted for who I am," Fi amended. "Not just the outer trappings."

"Ah." Mrs. Swann's eyes lit up with genuine interest. Had she a pen and paper handy, she would likely be jotting down notes. "How does he make you spend?"

"P-pardon?" A mortified breath puffed from Fi's lips.

Mrs. Swann's gaze slitted. "You do know what that is, don't you?"

"Um, yes." Her heart raced; she felt utterly exposed.

"That is a relief. Now, then, how does he make you come?"

Heavens. "He accomplishes it in the, um, usual manner, I suppose?"

"If by 'usual' you mean penetration, that is not the primary way most ladies achieve satisfaction." Mrs. Swann sounded like a schoolmistress giving a lesson. "Has he diddled you, played with your pearl?"

Squirming, Fi dipped her chin.

"Does he also pleasure you with his mouth?"

"Yes," she whispered.

"Have you returned the favor?"

The room felt sweltering; perspiration misted Fi's brow. "N-no."

"You ought to try it. I think you will find the sense of power gratifying." Mrs. Swann drummed her fingers on the arm of her chair. "Given that you are a lady used to being in control, I would also suggest experimenting with restraints."

"R-restraints?" Fi could hardly breathe.

"Ropes or manacles, perhaps. Of course, some ladies prefer the feeling of velvet ties against their skin."

Fi could think of no reply.

"That is your desire, my lovely, is it not? You are a strong woman, used to controlling everything, including your fears. Wouldn't it feel nice to surrender for a time?" Mrs. Swann's voice was cajoling, seductive. "To show your lover who you truly are?"

Hot memories flooded Fiona. Of how thoroughly she had given herself over to Hawk's lovemaking. How he'd coaxed out her most wanton impulses, teaching her naughty words and even naughtier deeds, and how much she'd loved all of it. The surrender and trust and relief that came from not having to hide.

With Hawk, she showed more of herself than she ever had. And his response—his hot masculine approval—made her want to expose even more of herself. To risk not just her body but her...heart.

Blinking, she said hoarsely, "You are right."

"I will help you achieve your desires." Mrs. Swann rose.

Her head spinning, Fi followed suit. "You will, um, help me find Lillian?"

"Come with me."

Mrs. Swann was already exiting the room, and Fi scrambled after her.

"Where are you taking me?" Fi asked.

"You will see."

At the end of the hallway, Mrs. Swann led Fi down a flight of steps. The lower corridor was decorated with thick carpeting and scented with an exotic potpourri of roses, cinnamon, and patchouli. The doors along the corridor were tightly sealed. Fi's pulse beat a mad staccato as Mrs. Swann stopped at the first door.

"The truth you seek is inside." Mrs. Swann inclined her head. "If you are ready to look."

Before Fi could ask questions, the proprietress was gone.

Fi stared at the closed door. *What is inside? Does it have to do with Lillian?*

Stiffening her resolve, she reached for the knob, the metal turning in her clammy hand. Inside, the room was dim and cavernous. Cabinets along the walls were filled with an assortment of objects that teased goose pimples over her skin.

Blindfolds, birches, and beads...oh my.

She passed three closed doors before turning the corner. A blazing hearth limned the figure of a tall, broad-shouldered man, bringing her to a breathless halt. He turned, and she saw her own shock reflected in her husband's face.

TWENTY-FIVE

"Fiona?" Hawk said stupidly. "What the devil are you doing here?"

He was a man known for his intellect, yet he couldn't get his brain to function. To comprehend the sudden and inexplicable collision of two separate spheres of his life.

What in blazes is my wife doing at a bawdy house?

Shock gave way to a burst of disquieting clarity. The fact was that he knew little of how Fiona spent her time outside their home. Of what she did when they were not together. While he knew she devoted considerable energy to her charity, she was vague on the details of the actual activities. Mostly she talked about meeting the needs of underserved women and children.

He'd been so enchanted by her passion and dedication that he hadn't pushed her on the specifics. Come to think of it, when he did ask questions, Fiona had a way of diverting him...with a charming story or even more charming kisses. The result was that he'd assumed she and her friends spent their days at Lady Fayne's, writing pamphlets or organizing benefits to raise funds for the less fortunate.

Certainly, she has never mentioned visiting a club catering to carnal fantasies. He clenched his jaw. *I would have remembered that.*

Fiona narrowed her eyes at him. "I could ask you the same thing."

Too late, he remembered the glass panels of the house he was presently standing in. He had sworn an oath of secrecy to the Quorum; he could not betray his Crown and country. Especially to a woman whose trustworthiness he now had cause to doubt.

The thought plowed into him like a fist.

You always knew this was too good to be true, a voice inside his head said. *Did you actually believe that a stunning young woman like Fiona would want you? Did you buy her asinine excuse that she wanted a marriage of convenience so that she could do* charity work? *What kind of a fool are you?*

His hands balled. When the rug had been ripped from beneath him during his first marriage, he'd been young and inexperienced; no one could have predicted Caroline's illness. This time around, he had no excuses. He'd known from the start that Fiona was a flirt and a handful, that their temperaments were night and day...and he had married her anyway.

He should have known better than to be seduced by her and the dream of happiness. Logic dictated that the best predictor of the future was the past. He'd never had success with females; why should things go his way now?

"You will answer me first," he said in peremptory tones.

She crossed her arms. "Fine. I am here on business."

"What sort of business?" The words escaped through his teeth.

"Society of Angels business."

"Do not bloody lie to me."

"I am *not* lying," she retorted. "A young woman served by my charity has gone missing. We've been worried about her. I heard that she might have come here before her disappearance, so I came to make inquiries."

"You expect me to believe," he bit out, "that you came to a

goddamned brothel in the middle of the night to question a bawd about a missing woman?"

"That is a gross misrepresentation. This is not a brothel, nor is Mrs. Swann a bawd. Actually, I don't know quite how to categorize her." Fiona cocked her head, as if contemplating how the madam fit into the order of the universe. "At any rate, I did not question her; we had a conversation."

"Do not try to distract me," Hawk said with lethal calm. "You claim that you are here in the spirit of volunteerism?"

"It is the truth." She lifted her chin to a mutinous angle. "Now why don't you enlighten me as to the purpose of your visit, my lord?"

Hawk studied his wife, buying time for his temper to cool. He was a level-headed man, yet Fiona had a way of getting past his rationality to his rawest instincts and urges. She did this even when they were getting along, which, he had to admit, was most of the time. Her presence aroused and bothered him...reminded him that he was alive.

With a stark flash, he realized that he *did* believe her. As farfetched as her story was, it was precisely the sort of bold and reckless thing Fiona would do. She had once charged into an alleyway to save him from cutthroats, for Christ's sake. His wife was loyal and brave to a fault.

Grudgingly, he had to admire her character and strength of will even as he wanted to shake some sense into her. What was she doing, risking her reputation in such a manner? Now that he was thinking clearly again, he saw that Fiona was dressed in a conservative cloak and walking dress. Hardly the type of outfit one would wear to a tryst. She was dressed for a practical purpose...such as a search for a missing woman.

He realized that his anger had been fed by an irrational fear that, once again, his marriage was headed for disaster. That he and Fiona couldn't possibly be as happy as they were. Yet they *were* happy; in his gut, he knew that whatever Fiona was doing here, it wasn't to play him false. She had too much honor for that. And, from a logical point of view, the frequency of their lovemaking ought to satisfy even the most wanton of appetites. Hell, his gorgeous young wife wore *him* out...and he'd had years of pent-up needs.

"I am waiting, Hawksmoor," she said.

He had not known that a scowl could be adorable. Trust Fiona to make one so. Christ, she was a rare jewel, and she was his. All bloody his. Yet his relief was tempered by a deepening awareness of his husbandly responsibility. He had been too lax with his young countess. From here on in, he had to look out for her, protect her from her own worst impulses.

I failed Caroline; I will not fail Fiona.

Knowing that his wife needed an answer, he focused on his present, which presented a host of intriguing possibilities. With her hair glowing like embers, Fiona was the hot-blooded goddess of his fantasies. And they were in a club that catered to couples interested in exploring forbidden desires.

Hawk knew all about Swann's since Devlin had filled him in and volunteered him for the assignment. As a newlywed groom, Hawk had a credible pretense for visiting the shop. His story was that he was in the market for equipment to enhance his marital relations. His plan had been to get his foot in the door, then question Mrs. Swann about the man who'd purchased Miss Farley's vinaigrette. He'd only exchanged brief introductions with Mrs. Swann before she departed with a promise to return. Then Fiona had shown up instead.

Now Hawk realized that his cover might provide an adequate explanation for Fiona. A rationale that, as he contemplated the possibilities that Swann's offered to him and his nubile bride, was growing more convincing by the moment.

"I am here because of you," he said.

"Me?" Fiona's gaze was steady, assessing. "Explain."

His wife was no fool. In truth, her intelligence aroused him as much as her delectable body. He prowled toward her, his blood thrumming at the feminine recognition in her eyes. Heat that had naught to do with the blazing hearth swirled between them.

"An acquaintance of mine mentioned Swann's," he said. "I thought I might find things here to augment our bedroom activities."

"Augment?" She wetted her lips. "How do you mean?"

"The shop caters to sexual fantasy and sells merchandise that enhances pleasure. I thought I would do some shopping for us. I would not wish for you to grow bored of my lovemaking."

The last part, he realized with a prick of discomfort, was no lie.

A part of him still couldn't believe that a woman as magnificent as Fiona was his. That she desired him as much as he desired her. He knew what it was like to be loved and depended upon as a husband. To be a lover used to scratch a sexual itch. But to be wanted for being a man—for being *himself*—was new and exhilarating.

With Fiona, sex wasn't a duty or even a pleasant pastime. It was an expression of something deeper, of wants and desires he'd never felt comfortable exploring before. Perhaps because he'd never found a woman who was his match the way Fiona was. She roused his inner beast; with her, he could unleash his darkest yearnings because she was strong enough to bear his desires. To answer them with her own.

It was Fiona's turn to study him. Whatever she saw caused her fury to ebb. With a pleasant jolt, he realized that she'd been feeling jealous too. While he didn't want her to suffer unnecessarily, it was good to know that he was not alone in his possessiveness.

"Bored of your lovemaking?" She rolled her eyes. "That hardly seems possible."

Her response puffed up his chest. His cock as well.

"I am relieved to hear it, my sweet wife. Yet variety is the spice of life." He tipped her chin up, feeling her shiver in his balls. "Since you and I are both here, why don't we browse together?"

Fi couldn't resist the seductive challenge in Hawk's eyes. She adored this wicked side of her husband, so at odds with the aloof scholar the rest of the world saw. While she knew he'd had other lovers—how could she forget the spiteful Lady Ayles—he belonged to *her* now. Every moment they spent together strengthened their bond. His explanation that he'd come to Swann's to enhance their marital pleasure seemed genuine...although the coincidence of them both being here *was* uncanny.

Clearly, Mrs. Swann had figured out the relationship between Fi and Hawk. Yet the proprietress was known to be discreet. What harm would a little tryst do?

"I would never wish to make you uncomfortable, sweetheart." Hawk's gaze was keen. "If you wish to go home, I will escort you now."

This is why I trust him. His care for my comfort above all.

Hawk might not think of himself as a sentimental man, but she felt his care for her in everything he did. And it made her long to have another adventure with him, this time without disguises. To be his partner in this game of passion.

"Nonsense. You know shopping is my favorite sport." She gave him a flirty smile. "Do I have carte blanche?"

The lines around his eyes relaxed; the grey orbs took on a wolfish gleam. "Haven't I always given you what you want?"

"Why change a winning strategy?"

His lips curving, he took her hand, his long fingers engulfing hers.

"Then why don't we see what tickles your fancy," he murmured. "Mrs. Swann said there are three 'playrooms' to explore in here."

Hawk led Fi to the row of doors she'd passed earlier. He opened the first one, and with tingling anticipation, she entered with him. The first thing she saw was a large wooden cross upon a dais; the rough wood and dangling manacles made her tense. Her apprehension increased when Hawk opened the cabinet next to the cross, revealing a collection of whips, chains, and birches.

"No?" Hawk tipped her chin up, staring into her eyes before confirming quietly, "No. We'll move on."

"Do you find this, um, merchandise intriguing?"

"I am only interested in what intrigues you, sweetheart."

"But do whips interest *you*?"

"I have no particular interest in inflicting pain." He trailed his fingertips along her jaw. "Nor would I wish to mark your beautiful skin. Not with a whip, at any rate."

Hot curiosity filled her. "How else would you, um, mark me?"

Instead of answering, Hawk kissed her. Long and slow and deep. Until she was clutching his lapels for support, ready to go on the cross, to try anything with him.

"Come, my sweet." He wrapped a steadying arm around her waist. "Let us see what else Mrs. Swann has in store."

The next playroom was decorated in the style of the Near East. The *trompe de l'oeil* mural on the walls depicted windows looking out to an azure sea. Next to it was a round mattress covered in emerald silk and tasseled pillows. Fiona wandered over to the white cupboard decorated with arabesque fretwork. Opening the door, she let out a startled giggle.

The shelves were lined with replicas of the male member. They were made of wood, ivory, and India rubber, some with a leather sac attached at the base. The fake cocks, available in a variety of flesh tones, were neatly organized by size, from small to eye-poppingly large.

Hawk quirked a brow at her.

Hiding a grin, she said demurely, "I prefer the real thing."

They entered the final room, and awareness shot through her. The walls had been stuccoed and painted to resemble a rocky cave, flickering wall sconces bathing the space in a primordial glow. In the middle of the cave was an altar built of black marble, glossy and veined, a bearskin rug on the ground beside it.

Fiona flashed to an image of herself laid upon that hard, paganistic rock. Of being offered like a carnal sacrifice. Of being helpless to her husband's darkest demands. Her cheeks throbbed with heat; her pussy clenched against a moist rush.

Hawk's eyes gleamed as if he could glean her fantasies. As if her every wicked thought fed his ravening hunger. He closed the door, sealing them inside.

Fi felt trapped...and, simultaneously, free.

"My sweet Sól," he said huskily. "I believe the wolf has caught up with you at last."

Twenty-Six

Excitement swept through Fiona. She couldn't resist the game they were playing. She remembered what Hawk had told her of Sól, the brave, bold goddess of the sun, and a fantasy ignited in her head. Of being captured and made to submit to her husband's desires.

Although she would not yield easily; the chase was too much fun.

"What does the wolf want with me now that he has me?" she asked with playful defiance.

"Such impudence from my prisoner."

The feral glitter in Hawk's eyes weakened her knees.

"Turn and place your hands on the altar."

Shivering, she did. The stone was cool beneath her palms as Hawk undressed her. Her buttons and laces were no match for his inventor's hands. He stripped her layer by layer until she was left trembling and bare. When he pulled the pins from her hair, the freed strands curled against the small of her back.

"Now face me."

Goodness, she adored his firm voice. It made her want to do

anything he asked. When she turned, his proprietary gaze made her feel even more exposed.

"Aren't you going to undress as well?" she asked.

"You cannot resist giving orders, can you? Even though you are my captive," he said sternly.

She slanted a coy look at the bulging placket of his trousers.

"Who is in control of whom, I wonder?" she asked in dulcet tones.

Amusement flitted through his eyes, but his expression remained implacable.

"I'll have to find a better use for that saucy mouth of yours. On your knees, goddess."

She knelt gracefully onto the bearskin rug. The fur was a sensual brush against her calves. She watched avidly as Hawk released the fall of his trousers, his erect member springing free. He pumped the huge, veined shaft, a bestial contrast to his elegant tailoring. Each slow and thoughtful stroke of his fist twisted her insides with excitement.

Until now, he'd focused on pleasuring her during their love-making. She'd loved it, of course...but now she wanted more. She wanted to touch him. To taste him. To be taught all the ways he liked to be pleasured.

"You may touch my cock," he said.

She wasted no time, wrapping a hand around his shaft. He pulsed with hot vitality. She stroked him with care, mimicking what she'd seen him do, marveling at how his supple skin moved over the rigid core.

"You frig me so well," he said in a guttural voice. "Now try doing it harder."

"Like this?" She firmed her caress.

"Yes." He inhaled sharply. "Now squeeze when you get to the tip...*devil and damn.* Exactly like that."

Pride burgeoned in her as she saw the arousal staining Hawk's cheekbones. She wanted to please her husband better than all his past lovers. Wanted to obliterate his memory of anyone else. Wanted to be his every fantasy—to be everything to him.

His cock throbbed against the confines of her grip, a bead of milky dew clinging to the engorged head. She looked up at Hawk. Holding his smoldering gaze, she leaned forward and caught the drop on her tongue.

Christ, this woman. She was going to be the death of him.

And I am going to die a very happy man.

"Did I say you could lick my cock?"

With that admonishment, Hawk took his prick away from her. He frigged himself slowly, deliberately, drawing out their game.

"I suppose not." Although Fiona looked abashed, her twinkling eyes gave her away. "You don't mind, do you?"

"Cheeky chit. Just because you are a goddess does not mean you get to disregard the rules."

"There are, um, rules?"

She sounded distracted. Her eyes were on his leisurely pumping fist. Knowing that he was giving his curious young bride a depraved show made him stiffer than a poker.

"You are my prisoner," he said sternly. "You do as I say."

"All right," she breathed.

Her eager acquiescence made his lips twitch. Even when submitting, his lusty girl liked to be in control. He didn't mind; he adored her spirit. As delightful as it was to have her kneeling at his feet, his true fantasy lay in unleashing her passion. In discovering how hot his wife could burn before they both went up in flames.

"Take my cock again," he ordered. "Bring it to your lips."

"Like this?"

Only Fiona could manage to sound prim while holding his turgid prick mere inches from her face. Her breath caressed his moist head, making him shudder.

"Kiss the tip," he said huskily.

She brushed the softest, sweetest kiss on his burgeoned dome. The ladylike offering lured more seed from his slit.

"You get wet too," she said.

Her coquettish observation made him hot all over. Made him want to give her a taste of his wetness. The forbidden notion of spilling in his bride's mouth shot an arrow of heat up his spine. He'd never done that before and wouldn't expect a lady to allow such a thing.

"Open your mouth now," he instructed. "I want to feel those pretty lips around me. Just remember to keep your jaw loose, breathe through your nose, and watch your teeth, all right?"

In reply, she parted her lips, and he pushed inside.

Sheer, hot *bliss*. Watching her delicate lips stretch around his veined girth added to his bank of fantasies. He took care not to push too deep; for now, it was enough to feel her soft, wet mouth surrounding his head. She sucked on him like he was a boiled sweet while she continued to frig him.

"Look at me, goddess," he commanded. "Do you like your first taste of cock?"

Her gaze was glazed with divine lust. "Mm-hmm."

He trailed his knuckles along her jaw. "Do you want to take me deeper?"

Without stopping her delightful ministrations, she bobbed her head.

"Place your hands on my thighs then. Relax your jaw and let me have you."

She obeyed, resting her palms on his bulging thighs.

He stared at his wife with her angelic eyes and cock-stuffed mouth, and recognition flooded him.

"Such a good, wicked girl," he said hoarsely. "Everything I've ever wanted."

Her gaze widened, shimmering. Her sound of joy was distorted by his plunging prick. Weaving his fingers in her hair, he held her steady while he thrust into her mouth. While he lost himself in her pure, honest fire.

He'd never had a woman who was his equal in every way. Who took everything he had while her eyes begged for more. He groaned as he availed himself of her sweet generosity. As he plumbed the depths of her kiss. Swamped with pleasure, he buried himself to the hilt and jerked when her throat cinched around his tip.

"Christ, I'm sorry." He pulled out, gasping. "Are you all right, love?"

Her lips red and swollen, she looked at him with a goddess's eyes.

"Give me more," she said in a throaty whisper. "Give me everything."

Devil and damn. I think I could fall in love with my wife.

His chest seizing, he thrust himself back into bliss. He held her steady for his plundering, fucking her mouth like he had her other sweet hole. She moaned, her knees splaying, putting her pussy in contact with the fur rug. She squirmed against the soft tufts with needful abandon. The beast in him roared in recognition of its mate. Her tongue flicked at his invading head, and he bared his teeth, feeling the hot pulsing of his stones.

He pulled out an instant before he lost his mind. Fisting his cock, he gave in to his primal urge to mark her. He aimed at her beautiful tits, her belly, her cunny, roaring as he lashed her with frothy streams of pleasure. He came and came, shuddering as Fiona moaned, rubbing his seed over her nipples and skin with her elegant fingertips.

Everything. An agony of joy gripped him. *She's everything I've ever wanted.*

He was still hard. Still wanting.

Fiona gasped when he scooped her up in his arms and lay her on the altar.

"Now it's my turn to worship," he rasped.

"Sweetheart, we need to talk."

Sitting on her husband's lap in their carriage, Fiona snuggled against his broad chest and said languidly, "Talk away."

"Tupping really does make you agreeable." Amusement threaded his deep voice.

"It behooves you not to forget it, my lord."

His chuckle rumbled beneath her ear, filling her cup of contentment to overflowing. And not just because Hawk had worn her out with pleasure. After she'd sucked his cock and he'd marked her in that thrillingly depraved manner, he had laid her on the altar. Burying his head between her thighs, he'd eaten her pussy, using his fingers and tongue to make her spend so many times that she'd lost count.

Then he positioned her hands above her head, his large hand manacling her wrists as he'd stretched over her like a voracious beast.

My beautiful goddess, he'd growled. *All mine.*

He'd claimed her with a savage thrust that caused her spine to bow off the marble. He'd continued drilling into her, pushing deep into her core until she clenched helplessly around his huge cock. They'd come together, sweaty and panting and tangled.

"Such a naughty girl." He tightened his arm around her waist. "Good thing I like your cheek in bed."

"We weren't in a bed."

"Cheeky, as I said." He tipped her head back, giving her a tender kiss that curled her toes. "Now stop distracting me from the lecture I'm about to give."

"Lecture?" Dismay punctured her bubble of serenity.

"You did not think you could visit a bawdy house without repercussions, did you?"

His serious tone dispelled her good mood. She shoved herself off his lap. Sitting on the cushions beside him, she faced him with a scowl.

"What I do as part of my charity work is none of your affair. We established those terms before our marriage. You have your work," she said pointedly, "and I have mine."

"Terms can be renegotiated." His voice was calm and irritatingly rational. "And should be, if they endanger your welfare."

"I am perfectly capable of taking care of myself!"

"You are a lady. You had no business being at Swann's. Even if one ignores the physical perils of you being alone in such a place, think of the scandal if you were to be seen there. You are a lady, Fiona. A countess, my *wife*," he said with emphasis. "I would be remiss in my duty if I let you come to harm."

Panic surged as she saw Hawk's resolute gaze. She felt trapped, and this time not in a good way. All her life, she'd hated being dictated to—hated feeling fenced in by unfair restrictions.

This is exactly what you were trying to avoid, her inner voice warned. *Your husband had a mere glimpse of what you've been up to, and already he's bringing down the guillotine on your freedom. You cannot let him stifle you or try to change who you are.*

She strove to remain composed. "Do I question your activities? Where you go at night, what you do, and with whom?"

"That is..."

He cut himself off—a testament to his intelligence or self-preservation, she didn't know which.

"Things change," he said finally. "Things *have* changed between us. We began this marriage with both of us wanting a marriage of convenience. Now look at where we are."

"Where are we, exactly?" She didn't know if she was angry or hopeful.

"You matter to me, Fiona, and I will not let anything happen to you. With you, I feel things that I did not think I could feel again. That I haven't felt since..." He broke off, frowning.

She hazarded a guess. "Since your wife died?"

He rarely spoke of his first marriage; because of their agreement, she had never pushed him. Yet her intuition told her that his past was important. It would help her to understand him and navigate the growing complexity of their marriage.

Hawk gave a terse nod. "Losing Caroline was…it was difficult."

Because you loved her?

Snuffing the flicker of possessiveness, Fi asked, "What was Caroline like?"

Lines deepened on Hawk's forehead. "She was quiet and gentle, a well-mannered lady. An intellectual who preferred the company of books over people."

In other words, Caroline was the opposite of Fiona. A perfect lady who wasn't just masquerading as one. Heart sinking, Fi berated herself: she knew it was silly and immature to compete with a ghost. Yet learning that Caroline's personality matched so well with Hawk's made her sick with jealousy.

Fi drew a breath. "Since Caroline and I are so different, there is no reason for you to fear that we will come to the same end, is there?"

Hawk drew his brows together. "That is hardly the point."

"That is precisely the point. Because you lost your first wife, you fear that something might happen to me. But, as you are fond of pointing out, that smacks of bad logic."

"Caroline has nothing to do with this," he said tightly. "We are discussing you and your reckless behavior. Do not try to deflect."

"And do not presume to lecture me," she retorted. "We have our terms, and we are sticking to them. I will not bow down to your high-handedness, Hawksmoor. You cannot tell me what to do."

She saw the moment she pushed him too far. When his temper broke through his control.

"For your own bloody good, you will do as I say," he growled.

"Or what?" she flung back. "What will you do if I am not the perfect wife that Caroline was?"

The lightning-filled tempest in his eyes halted her breath.

Hawk still grieves Caroline, still loves her...when I want his heart to belong to me. The realization shook her. *Botheration, do I truly want his love, knowing that it will come with restrictions? With disapproval, rejection, and pain?*

"You are overwrought." Hawk straightened his lapels, speaking in the detached manner that she hated. "This is a conversation better had in the morning when we are both rested."

The carriage was slowing to a stop. They were home. Only she felt terrifyingly unmoored...as if the ground were crumbling beneath her feet. She might be losing her heart. Might be falling in love with her husband, who not only harbored feelings for his dead wife but showed an inability to accept Fi for who she was.

If he cannot handle my explanation that I was helping a friend tonight, Fi thought in despair, *how will he ever accept that I am an investigator?*

Needing to steady herself, she grabbed the handle of the door. "When we have this conversation matters not. If you cannot accept me as I am, then our marriage is over."

Opening the door, she descended on her own and dashed into the house.

TWENTY-SEVEN

The following afternoon, the Marquess and Marchioness of Harteford came to visit. They brought along their other daughter-in-law Effie. After Fi gave a tour of the house, Hawk and his papa retreated to his study while Fi entertained the ladies in the drawing room.

"What lovely changes you've implemented, Fiona," Lady Helena said. "You've breathed new life into the place."

Effie's blonde ringlets bounced as she surveyed the drawing room.

"Your décor is ever so fashionable," she enthused.

The refurbishment had turned out well. The faded beige walls had been repainted a vibrant forest green. The new rosewood furnishings gleamed with polish, and the fringed pillows matched the rich hues of the freshly cleaned Aubusson.

"I am glad you both approve." Fi distributed gilt-rimmed cups of tea. "My mama's decorator, Mr. Stiles, did most of the work."

"You are far too modest, my dear. Mr. Stiles's work always reflects the taste of his clients. You have your own distinct style, and heaven knows this place needed your touch." Lady Helena's hazel eyes had a conspiratorial glint. "Do tell: when you decided to refurbish the place, did Thomas put up much of a fight?"

Not about that, Fi thought darkly.

Oh, her husband was quite happy to let her take charge of the pesky details of domestic life. It was only when she wanted to pursue her own ambitions that he issued his Draconian edicts. Hurt and anger smoldered beneath her breastbone. They'd slept apart last night, and when she saw him just before the arrival of his family, she had given him the cold shoulder. He hadn't been overly friendly either, his manner cool and guarded.

Isn't it perfect that we're fighting during his family's first visit? Fiona fumed. *Here I am trying to play the role of a good wife, and Hawk goes and ruins everything with his boorish behavior.*

She summoned a smile for her guests.

"Quite the opposite," she replied. "Hawk gave me carte blanche for the renovation. With the caveat that I stay out of his study."

"Like father, like son." Lady Helena wrinkled her nose, giving her ruffled maroon skirts a flick. "After the maid and I go through his study, Nicholas always grouses that he cannot find anything. As if he could find anything in the first place beneath those towering stacks of papers."

At her mama-in-law's wifely exasperation, Fi had to smile.

Effie's eyes danced. "I wonder if the men's ears are burning."

It was just as well that Lord Nicholas and Hawk were locked in the study. Fiona didn't want her new family to see her staring daggers at her husband.

"If their ears are burning, wouldn't ours be as well?" she said lightly.

"Not likely." Lady Helena gave a delicate snort. "Nicholas and Thomas are stoic peas in a pod. Knowing those two, they are puttering over one of Thomas's inventions. They could happily tinker with gears and whatnots and not exchange a single word for hours."

"Hawk's inventions are remarkable," Fi said grudgingly.

Even if the man himself is an emotional clod. Frustration gnawed at her. *Given his own passions, why can't he understand mine?*

"Thomas always was clever. It is wonderful to see him happy as well."

Faced with her mama-in-law's gratitude, Fi fidgeted in her seat. Once again, she felt like a fraud. She wasn't any better a wife than she was a lady. A good wife would be more forgiving of her husband's flaws. She probably wouldn't be stewing and storing up rebuttals for later use.

Lady Helena excused herself to freshen up, leaving Fi with her sister-in-law.

"I wanted to thank you for introducing me to Mrs. Quinton," Effie said.

"You're welcome," Fi said brightly. "How did your fitting go?"

"The styles Mrs. Quinton chose for me made me feel confident and, well, *pretty* again. I cannot wait for the gowns to arrive."

"You *are* pretty. Clothes have naught to do with it."

"You shall be the first person I show my new wardrobe to. After Jerry, of course." Blushing, Effie confided, "Mrs. Quinton is designing some additional items which are rather scandalous, but which she insists husbands enjoy."

"As usual, Mrs. Q is right." Fi couldn't resist adding, "And if you like the items, I would advise ordering spares. That way, you have extras on hand should your husband's enjoyment prove to be a trifle, well, enthusiastic."

In his haste, Hawk had ripped several of her negligee sets.

Not that he deserves such treats, she thought indignantly. *From now on, he is getting starchy, bulky nightgowns fit for a nun.*

Laughing, Effie reached out to squeeze her hand. "Oh, this is so lovely. I have always wanted a sister."

Fi returned the squeeze. "I have as well."

"You really are perfect for Hawk, you know. Jerry says he's never seen his brother so content."

Faced with Effie's boundless goodwill, Fi couldn't keep up the pretense any longer.

"I am far from perfect. In fact," she said with a sigh, "Hawk and I are in the middle of a row."

"Welcome to married life, my dear." Effie lifted her brows. "May I ask who started it?"

"Hawk did, of course." Fi scowled. "He can be quite overbearing."

"That is a husband for you. And Morgan men are notorious for being stubborn." Effie smiled over the rim of her teacup. "Just ask Mama."

"In all fairness, I can be a bit hotheaded myself." A glum thought struck Fi. "Hawk probably never fought with his first wife."

"Come to think of it, I don't think I did see Hawk and Caroline disagree." Effie pursed her lips. "Not that I saw them very often. They rusticated at their estate in Bedfordshire and didn't encourage visitors."

"Why not?"

"Hawk said he needed solitude to work." Effie hesitated. "May I say something in confidence?"

Fi nodded.

"Jerry and I suspected that Hawk wasn't the one who wanted seclusion."

"You mean Caroline...?"

"She was lovely, but she did not seem to care for our company. I always had the feeling she would rather be on her own. She was a noted bluestocking; perhaps she enjoyed the company of books more than people? Anyway, I think Hawk wanted her to be happy, so he made excuses and took the blame for their absence."

That sort of noble gesture did sound like Hawk.

"After Caroline died, Hawk wasn't the same. Jerry said he seemed half-alive."

Fi's heart ached for her husband.

Wistfully, she said, "He must have loved Caroline very much."

"Devotion is another Morgan trait. Yet I think it was more than that." Effie leaned closer. "Hawk and Caroline were rather too much alike. They both lived in their heads and reinforced each other's solitary tendencies. After Caroline's passing, Hawk was awkward around us, as if he'd forgotten how to be a part of a family. But now that he has found you, he is different."

"By different, do you mean annoyed?" Fi asked dryly.

"He is *alive*. No longer sleepwalking through life. Jerry says that at the Strathaven ball, he and Hawk had the best chat they'd had in ages. True, they *were* bonding over their wives' excessive spending habits." Effie winked. "But my husband is grateful to have Hawk back; we all are. And we owe it to you."

Her sister-in-law's words warmed Fi. *Do I really have that effect on Hawk? Is it possible that I, with all my flaws, am what he needs?*

Fi gave Effie a hopeful look. "Do you have advice on resolving rows with one's husband?"

"Compromise is usually the best solution." Effie smiled demurely. "If that fails, you could always do what I do."

"What is that, pray tell?"

"Pretend to let him win."

Papa examined the sketches for a new analytic machine on Hawk's desk.

"How is the project coming along, son?"

"It needs work," Hawk said.

Like so many things in my life at present.

A knot tightened in his chest. He didn't know how he and Fiona had ended up in the present state of warfare. One minute, she was performing exquisite fellatio on him in a pleasure house, the next she was dashing out of their carriage declaring that their marriage was over if he did not accept her.

Her volatile behavior was enough to drive a fellow mad.

You should have stuck to the rules, he thought grimly. *Attachments always lead to trouble.*

"Do you need a hand, Thomas? With the machine or, er, anything else?"

He glanced at his father and saw the discomfort on the other's rugged features. Like him, Papa preferred to leave well enough alone. Hawk's inner turmoil must have shown in order for his father to intervene. He recalled the time he'd been beaten by bullies at Eton. Even then, Papa hadn't said much; he'd taken Hawk to the sparring room, handed him a pair of gloves, and said, *"This is how one deals with bullies, lad."*

Hawk raised his brows. "Did Mama put you up to this?"

Papa's lips twitched. "Not this time. She and Effie are too busy recruiting Fiona for their team."

"What team?"

"Wives versus husbands." Humor flitted through Papa's eyes. "Sorry, son, but you're not on the winning side."

He doesn't know the half of it.

Hesitating, Hawk said, "Shall we have a drink?"

"If it's the Tobermory, I won't say no."

Drinks in hand, Hawk joined his father in the wingchairs by the fire. They sat, sipping the aged whisky in meditative silence.

"Marriage isn't logical," Hawk said.

Papa choked on his drink. "Er, what made you arrive at that conclusion?"

Hawk angled forward, resting his elbows on his knees. "I cannot seem to make sense of it, even when the terms are laid out clearly."

"Terms, son?"

Hawk shifted a look at his father. "Can this discussion stay between us?"

"What is discussed in the study stays in the study. Rule of gentlemen."

"When Fiona and I wed, she wanted the freedom to continue doing her charity work. I saw no problem with it, so I agreed. Now I am regretting my decision."

"Why?"

"Because she is too reckless and bold by far," Hawk said savagely. "To help a 'friend,' she pranced into a...a shady part of town. If I hadn't been there, who knows what might have happened? I forbade her from taking further risks for her own good."

"Ah. How did that go over?"

"Like a bloody bag of bricks. She accused me of being overbearing"—Hawk raked a hand through his hair—"when I am just trying to keep her safe."

I cannot lose her, he thought fiercely.

"I understand, son. Better than you know." Papa took a drink of whisky as if to fortify himself. "Like you and Fiona, Mama and I did not know each other well when we wed. It led to a rocky start."

Hawk's surprise must have shown for Papa gave a rueful chuckle.

"Things weren't always a bed of roses for your mama and me. Now, I always knew she was the woman for me; I just didn't comprehend all of the woman that she is."

"I don't follow."

"The biggest mistake I made in my marriage was underestimating your mother. She may be a delicate lady, but she has a spine of steel." Papa raised his brows. "Your bride strikes me as being cut from a similar cloth."

"Fiona is headstrong," Hawk said grimly. "I have to protect her from herself."

"Who are you protecting, her or you?"

"What the devil does that mean?"

"You know I hate interfering. You are your own man, and I respect your judgement." Papa cleared his throat, rolling the empty glass between his palms. "However, you have not been yourself since Caroline's passing."

Hawk's gut clenched. *You don't know how I failed Caroline. Failed to protect her.*

"But you've remarried," Papa said. "To a lovely bride who will make you happy...if you let her. Opening your heart and risking the pain that comes with it isn't easy. But it was also the best decision I have made in my life."

Hawk absorbed his father's words. "You are saying that I should let Fiona do as she pleases, even if it means endangering her well-being?"

"Bloody hell, no. But I am saying that you should talk to her about it. Try to understand her perspective while sharing yours."

"What if we cannot come to an agreement?" Hawk asked tightly.

"You're an expert in subjects I did not even know existed. You hold a patent for a machine that performs human calculations." Papa lifted his brows. "And you doubt your ability to come to an understanding with your wife?"

"Fiona is far more complicated than an analytic engine," Hawk muttered.

Papa smiled slowly. "The ones worth having always are, lad."

That evening, Fi sat at her dressing table as Brigitte brushed out her hair. The knock on the door twisted her insides with anticipation and dread. Since the departure of their guests, she'd avoided her husband, taking supper alone in her bedchamber. She wasn't ready to speak to him...didn't know what she would do if he issued another ultimatum. While she appreciated Effie's advice, compromise was not her forte.

How am I supposed to choose between my independence and my heart?

"Fiona, I want to talk to you." Hawk's firm voice came through the door.

"Shall I let his lordship in?" Brigitte asked.

Fi sighed. "I will deal with it."

After the maid left, Fi went to the door. She inhaled deeply and opened it. Her heart fluttered at the sight of her husband filling the doorway. He looked stern and virile in his black dressing gown. His hair was damp from a recent bath, threads of silver gleaming in the dark waves.

"I will not give up the Angels," she blurted.

He drew his brows together ominously. "I am not asking you to."

"You...you're not?" Her heart jamming into her throat, she stared at his hard-set features. "But last night you said I had to stop my charity work."

"May I come in for this discussion?" he said curtly.

She moved aside, and he stalked into her chamber.

Wrapping her arms around herself, she said tightly, "I know I have disappointed you. That you wanted a different kind of wife. But I never lied about who I am."

Although I may have omitted a few details. She shoved aside the guilt. She'd obviously made the right choice given how he was reacting to the current situation.

"I told you before we were married about my work, what it means to me. And I cannot sacrifice my independence, change myself, to suit you," she declared. "To be the perfect lady Caroline was."

Hawk scowled. "As I've said, Caroline has nothing to do with this. And I don't want you to change. I just want you to be safe."

"And I want you to trust me." She hated the pleading in her

voice. "Life will always bear some risk, but I am stronger, more capable than you realize. I can take care of myself. Make my own decisions."

He inhaled through his nose. "I do trust you."

"Do you?" she asked warily.

He gave a terse nod. "Which is why I am not going to stop you from pursuing your passion."

"Oh, Hawk!" She threw herself at him.

His arms closed around her like steel bands, his heart thudding beneath her ear. "But I could not bear it if anything happened to you, sweetheart. You are too important to me."

"Nothing is going to happen to me," she promised giddily. "I will take every precaution—"

"You will. And I will ensure that you do."

His resolute tone made her ease away and tilt her head back.

"How, um, do you plan to do that?"

"I will begin by paying Lady Fayne a visit," he said. "To learn more about this charity of yours."

Thinking of Charlie's reaction, Fi said hastily, "I am certain that isn't necessary—"

"For my peace of mind, it is. I am offering a compromise, Fiona."

Rebellion warred with pragmatism. While she did not like Hawk's interference, his request was not unreasonable. She could concede to his wish...even if she did not like it.

"Fine. I will arrange a visit," she said ungraciously. "But you will find it boring."

Once I send word to Charlie, she will undoubtedly make it so.

"I can only hope."

"What if I wish to learn more about *your* work?" she asked meaningfully.

His smile was bland. "You are welcome to attend any of my meetings. The Society for Advanced Mathematics, for instance, is having a gathering next week."

The blasted man had an answer for everything.

"Sounds scintillating," she muttered.

"It is. Not nearly as scintillating as this, however."

The world spun as he scooped her into his arms.

Looping her arms around his neck, she said, "I'm not certain I am done being annoyed at you."

"You're done." His eyes gleamed. "Which means we get to move on to the best part of fighting."

"That being?"

"Making up."

Twenty-Eight

Seated in the well-appointed drawing room, Hawk accepted a cup of tea from Lady Fayne. He found the lapsang souchong tailored to his taste: no cream or sugar to detract from the smoky flavor. Odd that his hostess would know his precise preference...but perhaps Fiona had mentioned it.

God knew he needed the strong brew. His visit with the Society of Angels thus far had been soporific, to say the least. Upon their arrival, he and Fiona had been greeted by Lady Fayne and the other Angels: Lady Olivia, Lady Glory, and Pippa, the dowager Countess of Longmere and now Mrs. Timothy Cullen. Since Hawk had known Pippa since he was a lad, they'd exchanged friendly hellos. Then Lady Fayne had given him a tour of the house and described how the Angels spent their time.

Detail by excruciating detail.

At their mentor's behest, Lady Glory and Pippa had shown him their embroidery projects. Apparently, the ladies sold the decorated handkerchiefs to raise funds for the causes they supported. Lady Glory demonstrated the stitches she used—at least a dozen different kinds—until he fantasized about grabbing her needle and poking himself in the eye to end his misery.

That had been the first hour.

Then Lady Fayne had bade Lady Olivia to read the latest treatise they had been working on. Entitled *"A Vindication of Mary Wollstonecraft's Vindication: Further Thoughts on the Status of Women,"* the tome had looked as if it weighed more than its reader. With Pippa's help, Lady Olivia had managed to haul the volume onto a lectern. Then she'd proceeded to read.

As a man not unused to pontification, Hawk struggled to keep his eyelids from drooping as Lady Olivia droned on. Twice, he started when Fiona nudged him with her elbow. The reading seemed to go on for an eternity before Lady Fayne interrupted.

"Thank you for reading the Preface, Livy," she said. "Glory, my dear, will you take over for Chapter One? Unless, my lord, you would prefer some tea first?"

"*Yes.*" Hawk had grabbed onto the diversion like a drowning man to a piece of driftwood. "That is, tea sounds capital."

Now he found himself sharing a settee with his wife, who sipped tea and conversed with her friends. While he couldn't quite put his finger on it, something about the Society of Angels struck him as…off. Perhaps it was the excessive gentility. Or the mountain of a fellow who'd greeted them at the door.

Fi had introduced the butler to him. *"This is Hawker."*

"I hope you don't go by Hawk as well," Hawk had said in jest.

"Why would I ruin a perfectly good name?" The butler's unpatched eye had narrowed before he stalked off, barking, *"Right this way."*

"Don't worry," Fiona had whispered. *"Hawker warms up once you get to know him. He tends to be protective of the Angels."*

Hawk couldn't give a damn whether the butler warmed up to him. But he did wonder why the man felt a need to guard ladies engaged in a harmless altruistic hobby.

"What do you think of our society so far, my lord?" Lady Fayne inquired.

On the surface, Lady Fayne appeared to be a wealthy and

respectable widow. Yet Hawk sensed there was more behind those calm eyes and society-ready smile.

"Your organization is quite remarkable," he said.

Remarkably boring, that was. He found it difficult to believe that his spitfire countess was enthralled with such work. But who was he to question how she found fulfillment? She obviously enjoyed the company of her friends. It was a good thing, he told himself, that Fiona found meaning in charitable endeavors...as long as those endeavors posed no peril to her.

Lady Fayne smiled complacently. "A group is only as remarkable as its members. I am fortunate indeed to have recruited such talented young ladies to the cause."

"Speaking of which." Hawk set down his teacup. "I would like to have a word with you about my wife's recent activities." He slid a look at Fiona. "In private."

Glowering, Fiona said, "We agreed that you were not to pester Charlie—"

"That is quite all right, my dear. I would be glad to discuss the Society." Lady Fayne rose, the movement as smooth as her manner. "We'll talk in my study, my lord."

After Hawk's departure, Charlie reassured Fi that he had not seemed to suspect anything.

"I do not know how long you will be able to keep the wool over his eyes, however. For a man, he is quite intelligent," Charlie remarked. "And exceedingly protective of you."

She departed on an errand, leaving Fi with the other Angels.

"Even if we did not fool Hawk, at least we bored him to tears. He deserved it." Fi stabbed her fork into a slice of lemon cake. "I cannot believe how high-handed he is being."

"Now, dear," Pippa said. "You cannot blame Hawksmoor for being concerned."

"I told him I can take care of myself." Fi ate a bite, her eyes widening. "Heavens, this cake is delectable."

"The latest delivery from Fisher's Fine Foods." Glory polished off her slice. "For treats like this, I would help Mrs. Fisher with any problem she has."

"Back to the husband dilemma," Livy interjected. "I think Hawksmoor's overprotectiveness is to be expected. Hadleigh was the same way, as you recall. But he got over it. Eventually."

"How can I possibly tell Hawk about our work? Look at how he is reacting to one measly visit to Mrs. Swann's." Fi comforted herself with another lemony forkful. "He would never countenance my taking risks on an ongoing basis."

"You never know until you try," Pippa said. "And you haven't, not really. All you've told Hawksmoor are half-baked lies; how is he supposed to believe that you can take care of yourself? If you told him everything—about our training and experience—perhaps he would have a different view of things."

Fi felt a frisson of panic. "How can I risk the truth without knowing how he'll react?"

"That is how a relationship works. How *love* works." Pippa's smile was gentle and wise. "And you are falling in love with Hawksmoor, aren't you?"

Fi expelled a breath. "Is it that obvious?"

"Yes," her friends chorused.

It was a bit disconcerting to learn that her heart was apparently pinned on her sleeve. Yet these were her bosom chums. They knew her better than anyone.

"While I may have grown fond of Hawk," she admitted, "that doesn't mean I can just tell him everything. If he cannot accept me as I am..." Fear cinched her throat at the thought of losing Hawk's regard and tender affection. "Dash it all, I wish there was an easy way to tell him the truth."

"I have an idea," Livy said. "We can use the custard method."

Fi furrowed her brow. "Custard method?"

"Like tempering custard, you warm Hawksmoor up to the idea a bit at a time. That way, he doesn't curdle." Glory's grin was impish. "Livy did that with Hadleigh, remember?"

"And how, exactly, do I accomplish this with my husband?" Fi wanted to know. "I cannot just drop a hint here and there. *'Please pass the salt, Hawksmoor—and by the by, I retrieved my client's stolen letters from a blackmailer.'* Or *'My day was splendid, darling, thanks for asking. The Angels and I were tracking a missing woman down at a bawdy house.'*"

"I say just tell Hawksmoor the truth and be done with it," Pippa cut in.

"But Fi is afraid that he won't take the shock well," Glory said.

"He definitely won't." Fi chewed on her lip. "After losing his first wife, he is afraid of something happening to me."

"I have it," Livy announced. "*You* don't need to drop the hints, Fi. We'll have Hadleigh and Mr. Cullen do it."

Pippa lifted her brows. "We will?"

"Men are influenced by their peers," Livy said airily. "When Hawksmoor learns that our husbands support us, he'll fall in line. We shall coach Hadleigh and Mr. Cullen to emphasize our competence and ability to handle ourselves in any situation. By the time Fi is ready to tell Hawksmoor about our detection work, he'll already be convinced that she is a talented lady capable of taking on anything."

Pippa looked skeptical. "I don't know about this..."

"It will work," Livy said with enviable confidence. "We'll gather our husbands for a supper party at my place. On a night of Fi's choosing."

"But I don't have a husband." Glory's face fell. "Am I still invited?"

"Of course, silly," Livy said. "Hadleigh and I will be your chaperones, and I will invite Hadleigh's friend, Master Chen, to be your supper partner."

Glory's eyes lit up. "Jolly good. I can practice my Chinese."

"Well, Fi?" Livy asked.

Fi shrugged. "Might as well give it a go. It is not as if I have better options."

Hawker arrived, bearing a newly arrived note for Fi. Seeing the shape of a swan on the seal, she felt her heart speed up. She broke the wax and read the elegant copperplate.

Meet me at my shop in an hour. Come alone.

"Thank you for meeting with me, Mrs. Swann," Fi said.

They were back in the sitting room where they'd first met. Daylight shone through the drapes, softening the contrast between the proprietress's dark hair and light golden complexion. She wore another richly-hued dress, this one without the high neckline. Shock percolated through Fi as she saw the thin red line encircling the lady's throat, beads of scarred skin strung along it like a grotesque necklace.

Who did that to her? Fi felt a surge of helpless rage.

Knowing instinctively that this proud, self-made woman would not tolerate pity, she met Mrs. Swann's gaze squarely. She did not ignore the scar or allow herself to be distracted by it.

The businesswoman's mouth approximated a smile.

"As you were honest with me," she said calmly, "I will return the favor. The woman you seek was in my club on several occasions. The last time was three months ago. She went by the name Sarah Mallery."

"Lillian aspired to be as celebrated an actress as the great Sarah Siddons," Fi said quietly.

Mrs. Swann inclined her head. "Lillian, then, was brought here by her lover, a man who called himself Martin Wheatley. He wanted to play out his fantasies with her, and I was led to believe that she shared his predilections."

"Predilections?"

"He enjoyed pain. Specifically, inflicting it. It is not an uncommon fantasy, and at my club, patrons are not judged for their preferences. They have a right to pursue pleasure in whatever form it takes. With one caveat: what happens *must* be consensual. I make that very clear." Mrs. Swann's eyes were harder than blued steel. "Martin claimed that it was, and Lillian did too. They played in one of the dungeon rooms. I thought all was well until the time I heard her screaming, begging him to stop." The scar rippled on Mrs. Swann's throat. "My men broke down the door. He'd whipped her...badly. Not pain designed to pleasure but to indulge his cowardly and despicable need to feel powerful."

The bruise that Vera Engle saw on Lillian's face was no anomaly. The bounder hurt Lillian repeatedly. Enjoyed doing it.

Her chest tight, Fi asked, "What happened next?"

"I tried to get her to stay. So that I could tend to her injuries, perhaps help her in some way. But she insisted on leaving with that bastard." Mrs. Swann's hands balled in her lap. "He was controlling her, abusing her, and there was nothing mutual about it. I should have seen it. Should have never allowed him to hurt her in my domain."

"You can still help her now," Fi said urgently. "Do you know where I can find them?"

"I do not. What I can tell you is this. Martin Wheatley is approximately five foot ten, with a lean build, golden-brown hair, and green eyes. His accent is educated working class. He also has a natural, predatory charisma. I am certain Lillian is not his only victim. He struck me as having a roving eye; he purchased some of my trinkets in bulk—perfumes and such—probably to lure unsuspecting women."

"The description is very helpful, Mrs. Swann. Can you think of any other details? No matter how insignificant they may seem, they could be a clue to finding Lillian."

"There is something," Mrs. Swann said slowly. "His voice has a distinctive rasp to it. Due to his cough, perhaps."

"He was ill?" Fi asked alertly.

"He had a coughing fit here once; it had an odd, wheezing quality. When I asked him about it, he denied being sick. Said it was a chronic condition caused by his work."

Fi mentally rifled through trades known to affect respiration. "Was he a miner or sweep, perhaps? Or maybe he worked in a cotton mill?"

"He looked too spotless to be a miner or sweep: no sign of coal dust on his skin, clothes, or under his nails. A mill worker might be a possibility, but he did not have any of the usual loom-related injuries. No cuts or missing fingers. Although I did notice several small burns on the backs of his hands...old scars, by the looks of them." Mrs. Swann hitched her shoulders. "Given the rates I charge, men in those trades could not afford my establishment. Yet Wheatley seemed flush in the pocket. I am sorry, but that is all I know."

"Thank you," Fi said earnestly. "You've given me excellent leads to continue my search."

The proprietress dipped her chin. "Then our bargain is completed."

She rose, and Fi followed her to the door.

Mrs. Swann paused, pivoting to face her. "Would you mind answering a question?"

"It depends on what the question is."

"Does your husband know what you are up to?"

Pulse racing, Fi shook her head. "And I would like to keep it that way."

"You have nothing to fear on my part. As I've said, if my patrons are honest with me, I will guard their secrets with the utmost discretion. But I must confess that you provoke my professional curiosity, Mrs. Morgan."

Wariness tiptoed up Fi's spine. "Why is that?"

"You are a brave and enterprising woman. And yet I sense such fear in you."

"I...I don't know what you mean."

"Don't you?" Mrs. Swann's mouth quirked into a half-smile.

Panic swirled in Fi's chest. In the proprietress's bright eyes, she saw herself reflected. A girl who'd been a disappointment to her family, a debutante who'd pulled off a dazzling deception, a woman who was hiding so much from her husband.

"Fear keeps us from our heart's deepest desires." Mrs. Swann exited, her voice trailing behind her. "Vanquish yours, Mrs. Morgan, and you will become the woman you were meant to be."

Twenty-Nine

That evening, Hawk surveyed the streets of Covent Garden from a carriage. Given the premiere of a new ballet at the Theatre Royal as well as several other tony affairs in the vicinity, he'd calculated increased odds of an attack by the Sherwood Band. He had decided to go on patrol, but after von Essen's untimely demise, his gut had told him to keep his plan quiet. Securing Swinburne's permission, he'd tapped Trent to be his partner.

"We're searching for the proverbial needle," Trent muttered from the opposite bench.

"Our odds are higher." Hawk kept his gaze trained on the fog-filled maze. "We know the patterns of the Sherwood Band. We'll focus on back lanes and alleys where they carry out their heists. They use decoys and detours. Keep an eye out for overturned carts, 'injured' people or animals in the streets, and anything else that would make a carriage change its route."

"That logic o' yours might be more useful than I expected." Trent's craggy features held respect. "You've done good work, guv, organizing this and getting information from Mrs. Swann."

After the interminable visit at Lady Fayne's, Hawk had

returned to Swann's. He'd informed the assistant that Mrs. Swann could speak to him or the police. Within minutes, Mrs. Swann had appeared.

"Back so soon, my lord?" Her brows had formed thin arches.

His neck had heated at the memory of his prior night's visit. He'd let his desire for Fiona outweigh his good judgement, which was becoming a bad habit where his wife was concerned. He should have protected her; he *definitely* should not have tupped her in a pleasure house.

"Fret not, my lord." Above the high ruffle of her chemisette, the bawd's lips settled into what may have been a smile. "In my club, honest passion is rewarded with discretion. Now, what else may I do for you?"

Hawk had told her the truth: that he was on a covert mission to stop the Sherwood Band. He'd shown her Lizzy Farley's vinaigrette and described the man he was looking for. To his surprise, Mrs. Swann had been forthcoming. She'd told him that the man in question had called himself Martin Wheatley and had visited the club on several occasions with a woman named Sarah Mallery. The bawd had apparently ejected Wheatley for abusing the woman three months ago and did not know the location of either.

"At least we have the bastard's name to work with now," Trent said.

"Martin Wheatley is likely an alias."

"Wouldn't be the first time I tracked down a cove using his alias." Trent gave Hawk a considering look. "You didn't learn anything else at Mrs. Swann's?"

Feeling his face heat, Hawk was glad for the concealing darkness. He'd learned a great deal that he had no intention of sharing with Trent. About his wife's desires and his own and how hot they could burn together.

The thought of Fiona sent a warm pulse through him. Peace had been restored in his marriage. Given his current endeavor, he could not escort her to the ball she was attending this eve. His excuse was that an old friend was in town; in true Fiona fashion, she hadn't raised a fuss as they'd exchanged farewells in Lady Fayne's antechamber.

"However shall I entertain myself without you tonight?" she'd teased.

"Your hordes of admirers will keep you occupied, I'm certain. Just don't forget who your favorite dancing partner is."

She'd fluttered her lashes at him. *"Lord Sheffield, you mean?"*

The vixen had given him no choice but to kiss her until she couldn't recall any man's name but his. He recalled with satisfaction the dreamy expression he'd left her with. She hadn't even remembered to complain about his insistence that she take an escort to the ball. With the Sherwood Band lying in wait, Hawk wasn't taking any chances with his wife's safety. He'd asked Garrity to accompany Fiona; his father-in-law traveled with an armed retinue.

Fiona is safe. Nothing will happen to her. Concentrate on the assignment.

"I asked Mrs. Swann to show me the room Wheatley used at her club," Hawk said.

Trent raised his brows. "And?"

"It resembled a prison cell. Apparently, Wheatley requested a flogging box be installed," he said flatly. "Like the one used at Newgate. He derived pleasure from whipping his partner, and Mrs. Swann put an end to it when it became clear the enjoyment was not mutual."

"Sadistic bugger," Trent said in disgust. "What do we know about the woman he was with?"

"Sarah Mallery is petite, dark-haired, and young, probably not even twenty. Miss Mallery left with him even after he beat her," Hawk said grimly.

"Do you think she's involved in the robberies?" Trent's brow furrowed. "The last hold-up...didn't the driver report swerving into a back lane to avoid a woman who'd fallen in the street?"

"Aye. I would not put it past Wheatley to use her."

"Crikey." Trent ran a hand through his shaggy hair. "The bastard has a talent for manipulation, that's for certain. The public, Lizzy Farley, this Sarah Mallery. Nobody seems to see him for what he is: a thief after his own interests."

Before Hawk could agree, the driver's voice filtered into the cabin. "Guvs, got a costermonger's cart blocking the road ahead. What do you want me to do?"

Hawk looked out the window. They were on a narrow street flanked by shops, alleys branching off both sides. Through the drifting fog, he saw a man sitting atop a horse attached to an apple cart.

Hawk's senses went on high alert. "Stop the carriage."

As the vehicle slowed, he jumped out. He headed toward the rider on the horse, trying to see through the thick mist.

"You there," he called. "What is going on?"

The man twisted to look at him.

Hawk glimpsed a neckerchief-covered face, then the glint of the pistol in the man's hand. Hawk dove to the ground as the shot went off. Screams erupted, passersby running for cover. He rolled to his feet, drawing his own pistol and aiming in the direction of the enemy...but the man was no longer on the horse. People swarmed the street, shouting and moving in all directions. In the mayhem, Hawk strained to see where the bounder had gone.

"Bleeding hell." Trent ran up to him, pistol in hand. "Did you see where the bastard went?"

"Could have gone down any of the alleys," Hawk said. "Why don't we split up—"

Gunfire boomed. Shots exchanged.

"It came from this way." Trent sprinted off down the street.

Hawk followed him, pushing through the panicked mob. He and Trent turned down an alleyway. Two carriages were up ahead: one stopped, the second exiting the other end.

"Help!" A man's cry came from the parked conveyance. "Someone help!"

Hawk arrived first, saw the man in a groom's uniform slumped against the side of the carriage. He was clutching his shoulder, blood welling between his gloved hands. A pistol lay several feet away on the dirt.

"H-help me," he said weakly. "D-don't want to die."

"I've got him." Trent crouched beside the driver. "Check inside the carriage."

Hawk approached the cabin. The door was open. A white-haired man sat on the cushioned bench, holding a woman against him. Hawk recognized the elderly couple, who were friends of his parents. Lord and Lady Auberville...his gut clenched as he saw the stain spreading over the lady's bodice.

"H-Hawksmoor?" Auberville stammered.

"Let me take a look at her, sir," Hawk said.

Tearing off his cravat, Hawk knelt by Lady Auberville's side. He pressed it to the gaping hole in her chest; it was like using a twig to stop a broken dam. Fear drummed in his chest when she didn't flinch. Her gaze was focused on something far away, her breath rattling in her throat. He felt the life draining out of her, and he could do nothing to stop it.

For the second time, he witnessed death's power up close and was helpless to do anything. Helpless against the invisible hand that closed Lady Auberville's eyelids, that caused her body to go limp. Helpless as the last breath left her.

"Winnifred, wake up." Auberville's voice sharpened with panic.

"Sir." Hawk's throat thickened. "I...I'm sorry."

"No. *No*." Auberville's face froze with shock. "She's not gone, I tell you. We were just at the ballet. Left early...her rheumatism was acting up. Then the blackguards stopped us in the alley, but I'd read about them in the papers, and I was ready." He looked wildly at the discharged pistol on the bench beside him. "When the leader told us to hand over our valuables, I told him I'd see him hanged at Newgate first. And he laughed at me...the bastard *laughed*. Said he was never going back. So I pulled out my pistol and shot the bounder. But he got a shot off too—it was his accomplice's fault. She pushed his arm, and the bullet hit my Winnifred..."

The old man's face crumpled, and he broke into sobs.

Hawk placed a hand on Auberville's shaking shoulder. Wished he could do something—anything—to ease the other's pain. But there was naught he could do.

Except to say, "Allow me to escort you home, sir."

Fiona came to with a start. She was curled up in a wingchair in her room. Yawning, she peered at the ormolu clock: four in the morning. After returning from the ball, she'd decided to wait up for Hawk, even though he'd told her he would be out late with an old friend. She must have drifted off, for she hadn't heard him return.

Seeing the faint light beneath their adjoining door, she went over and pressed her ear against the wood. Hearing nothing, she turned the knob and entered stealthily in case Hawk was asleep. His bed was empty, the fire low in the hearth. She followed the faint sounds of sloshing to his bathing room.

Hawk was in the copper tub, the taps turned off. Eyes closed, he leaned his head back against the rim. His sinewy arms were draped along the edge, his taut shoulders gleaming in the lamplight. *He is magnificent*, she thought with pride. Steeped in sudsy water and surrounded by sandalwood-scented steam, he didn't seem to register her presence.

Then his eyes suddenly opened, and he twisted his head, his gaze colliding with hers. The ice in those grey depths made her breath catch with uncertainty. She hadn't seen him look this cold and remote since before their marriage.

He is alive. No longer sleepwalking through life...thanks to you.

Remembering what Effie had said gave Fi the courage to advance.

"I hope I am not interrupting. I wanted to see how your evening..." She trailed off as she spotted his clothes on the floor next to the tub. The bright-red stains on his shirt, his trousers. "Heavens! What happened—"

"I'm fine," Hawk said.

"There's *blood* on your clothes."

"It's not mine."

She rushed over, kneeling by the tub, needing to see for herself. She took his damp, stubbled jaw between her palms, turning his head this way and that. No signs of injury.

"You're welcome to examine the rest of me as well," he said.

His halfhearted attempt at levity alleviated some of her panic. Allowed her to breathe again.

"Whose blood is it?"

"Lady Auberville's," he said flatly.

"Winnifred Auberville?" The image of the kind, grandmotherly lady popped into Fi's head. She'd recently been introduced to them by the Hartefords. "Why would..."

"My friend and I were coming home, and we happened upon the Aubervilles. They had been attacked, their carriage held up by the Sherwood Band." Hawk's jaw tautened. "Auberville chose to resist. In the crossfire, his driver and Lady Auberville were shot. The driver's wound wasn't life-threatening, but the same could not be said of Lady Auberville's. I tried to help her...but it was too late."

Horror swamped Fi. "Oh, Hawk."

"I escorted Auberville home. They'd been married for fifty years, he said. Six children. I summoned his heir...didn't think he should be alone. He was in shock."

Hearing her husband's toneless words, the frozen look in his eyes, Fi realized that poor Lord Auberville wasn't the only one in a state.

"How awful it must have been," she said quietly. "To witness such a tragedy."

"It was a tragedy that could have been prevented." Hawk's jaw looked hard enough to slice diamonds. "I should have done something to prevent it. Should have stopped..."

"Stopped a gang of violent criminals?" Fi placed a hand on his damp shoulder, felt his quivering tension. "What could you have done? That is the police's job, not yours."

Hawk sent her a silent, brooding look.

"We will deal with this together in the morning," she said soothingly. "Let's get you out of the bath and into bed."

As she turned to fetch a towel, he grabbed her arm. His tight grip soaked through the sleeve of her robe.

"Hawk, you're getting me wet," she protested.

He pulled her closer, forcing her to lean over the tub.

"Do you know what my first thought was when I found the Aubervilles?"

Ensnared by his glittering gaze, she shook her head.

"What if it had been you?"

It took her a moment to register what he meant. And the howl of pain in his voice.

"Oh, darling. I'm here and perfectly safe—"

"After Caroline died, I vowed not to put myself through such pain again. Truth be told, I did not think I had anything left in me to give." Raw emotion tautened his features. "But then I met you. And you...you changed everything. You made me feel again, hope again, *live* again."

Her heart trembled at the intensity of his gaze. Of his words.

"Losing Caroline was hard. If I lost *you*?" His chest heaved, his voice low and ragged. "I would not bloody survive it."

His admission melted the protective shell around her heart.

"I love you, Hawk." The moment she said the words, she knew them to be true. "And you're not going to lose me."

Wonder blazed in his eyes. "God, I love you, Fiona. With everything that I am."

Joy expanded her chest. He yanked her to him, kissing her with a desperate passion that made her spirit soar. Then he rose, exiting the tub, and she squealed, instinctively retreating from the spray of water when he shook himself like a rain-soaked wolf.

Water sluiced from his sinewy frame, his pull upon her senses primal and undeniable. Desire pulsed through her as she took in the hair-whorled planes of his chest, the stack of muscles beneath. He was also fully, magnificently aroused. His cock swayed heavily between his corded thighs as he stalked toward her.

"Towel off first. You're wet," she said, giggling helplessly.

"Not as wet as you're going to be."

He moved with a predator's intent. She dodged him, racing into the bedchamber out of fun rather than a desire to escape. He caught up to her; in a casual movement, he grabbed the neckline of her night rail and ripped it off her. Then he hauled her, naked and laughing, over his shoulder.

"You're being a troglodyte," she accused playfully.

"You bring out my primitive instincts, wife."

He proved his words by tossing her onto his bed. She landed on her front, and before she could turn over, he was atop her. She trembled as he gnawed gently at the juncture of her neck and shoulder.

"I need you, sweetheart." His raw desperation heated her ear. "Let me have you."

Feeling the urgent weight of his desire against the small of her back, she stopped struggling. Twisting her head, she met her husband's passionate gaze.

She whispered the truth in her heart. "I'm yours."

A distant part of Hawk's brain knew that he was in no state to make love to his lady wife. But this was Fiona, the love of his life.

Who said she loved him back. And they were both alive and breathing, naked and tangled up.

The primal need to claim her raged through him. She was his wife, his mate, and if anything ever happened to her, he didn't know what the bloody hell he would do. But she was safe—*safe*. And she had offered herself up for the taking.

With a growl, he accepted her gift. Dark desire pounded in his blood; he did not have the capacity for gentle lovemaking, but Fiona did not seem to mind. She shivered and moaned as he kissed his way down the elegant ladder of her spine, his night beard abrading her tender skin. He kissed the red marks then bit them, and she squirmed with pleasure.

Reaching the sweet dip above her arse, he hauled her hips up and shoved a pillow beneath. He felt her tense at this new position, which elevated and exposed her pussy. He got behind her, pushing her thighs farther apart, his nostrils flaring at the perfection of his wife's glistening slit and the shy rosebud just above.

He cupped her, and her dew drenched his palm.

"This is mine," he growled. "And I'm going to have all of you tonight. Say it, love."

"You...you're going to have all of me..."

Her reply became gargled as he dove down, burying his face in her cunny. She cried out as he ate her from behind. He feasted on her succulence, leaving no part of her unsampled. He laved her pearl, then stabbed his tongue into her hot, clenching passage. He tongue-fucked her until she screamed her climax and then he continued upward, licking between the smooth curves of her bottom.

"*Hawk.*" She went rigid. "You shouldn't..."

"All of you," he bit out. "That's what I want."

He claimed her pucker with his tongue, and she groaned, her ladylike hands clenching the sheets by her head. His wild minx liked being licked here, liked the thrill of the forbidden...just as he'd known she would.

"Push against my tongue," he growled. "Show me how sweet and naughty you can be."

Whimpering, she wriggled obediently against his invading kiss, driving him out of his goddamned mind. He groaned, fucking the mattress as he tongued his wife's delicate rim. He delved deeper; feeling the squeeze of her untried ring, he shuddered, his cock weeping into the sheets.

Surging to his knees, he notched his dripping crown to her pussy and drove in. She encased him in hot, liquid velvet, and the beast in him took over. Molten pleasure trickled down his spine as he plowed his wife and watched himself doing it. His large hands clenched her silken hips, her bottom jiggling to his rhythmic pounding. When she convulsed again, he fought not to come. He wanted to prolong the ecstasy of their joining.

He ground his balls against her swollen folds. "I'm going to get so deep inside you, Fiona. So deep you'll never get me out."

"I want you there." Her pleasure-dazed eyes met his. "In my pussy, my heart, wherever you want to be. Because I want all of you too."

Christ, this woman.

Maddened with lust and love, he gave in to the need pulsing through his veins. He slammed into her harder and harder still, and she urged him on. The churning in his stones warned him he would not last, and he didn't want to go without having all of her. His vision darkening, he pressed a thumb against his wife's pucker.

"Say my name, love. My given name." He pushed deeper, feeling the decadent give of her ring. "I want to hear it from your lips when you come."

"Thomas," she cried.

Feeling her clench around his thumb and cock simultaneously shot him over the edge. He threw his head back and shouted as he erupted. As he emptied himself into his mate, the mysteries of the cosmos flashed before his eyes, and for a brief instant, he glimpsed the reason for everything.

THIRTY

Fiona surfaced from a deep, restful sleep. It took her a moment to register that she'd slept in her husband's bed last night. A smile tucked into her cheeks as she felt Hawk's warmth cocooning her. They were on their sides, fitted like a pair of spoons, his arm slung around her waist and his legs tangled with hers.

What a wonderful way to wake up.

Her dreamy thought gave way to another realization: he was up too. In the most delicious of ways. She gave an experimental wriggle and was rewarded by Hawk's muffled laugh.

"Christ, woman. Are you trying to kill me?"

"It is not my fault." She rolled over to face him. "You were already in a state when I awoke."

"In a state, am I?" His gaze was languid and amused. "It is your fault for having such a ravishing bottom. Waking pressed up against it is enough to give a dead man a cockstand."

She giggled. "That's terribly wicked."

"Lucky for me, you don't mind a bit of wicked, do you?" he murmured.

Guessing that he was referring to the depraved act she'd shamelessly enjoyed, her cheeks heated. Embarrassment slithered through her as she realized that passion had once again laid waste to her defenses.

Putting on a smile, she opted to divert the topic. "How are you feeling this morning?"

"Better, thanks to you." His expression sobering, he brushed his knuckles against her cheek. "But I wish to God I could have done something to help the Aubervilles."

"You did what you could. Poor Lord Auberville," she said tremulously. "I cannot imagine what he is going through right now. To lose one's spouse…"

She broke off, realizing that Hawk had known this kind of wrenching loss. Indeed, last night he'd mentioned Caroline. Had the attack triggered his own painful memories?

"I'm sorry," Fi said quietly.

"For what?"

"For, um, bringing up a topic I know you do not like to discuss."

"First of all, you didn't bring it up; we were already on the subject. And secondly…" Hawk's gaze was clear and intent. "Things have changed between us, sweetheart. I have fallen in love with you, and last night you gave me reason to believe my feelings are returned."

"They are," she said fervently.

"Then it follows logically that the terms of our marriage have changed too. I would like for us to share more of our lives…of ourselves. To share everything."

His earnest words elicited a thrill of anxiety. She wanted what he was describing, but she was also afraid of exposing her secrets. What if he didn't like how bold she was outside of the bedchamber? What if they clashed over her ambition and adventurous spirit? What if he tried to stop her from investigating…like he had once before?

Now that they were in love, the stakes were even greater.

He will never approve of who you really are, her inner voice whispered. *If you show your true self, he'll be disappointed. He might reject you...stop loving you.*

"What is going on in that head of yours, Fiona?"

She forced her lips to bend. "Nothing. I was woolgathering is all."

"Hmm." He leveled a stare at her. "Do you know you have a tell?"

She blinked. "How do you mean?"

"Whenever there is a subject you wish to avoid, you put on a certain smile. Then you proceed to charm and dazzle a man until he can't think straight, much less pin you down on the topic."

She'd felt less exposed when he'd ripped off her nightgown.

She managed an amused laugh. "I don't do that..."

"You're doing it now." He quirked a brow. "Shall I list other occasions when I've noticed you trying to divert my attention from whatever is bothering you?"

Drat. Why did I have to fall in love with such a blasted observant fellow?

"That is unnecessary." She huffed out a breath. "You've made your point."

She sat up against the headboard, and he did the same. His mouth crooked up when she tucked the sheet primly over her breasts.

"What if you don't like what I have to share?" she asked.

To his credit, he appeared to think it over. "Then I don't like it, and we will have a discussion."

"What if it changes how you feel about me? You may think you know me, but you don't."

"I think I know you rather well. Not just in the Biblical sense."

For some reason, his indulgent expression irked her. Here she was dipping her toe in the murky pool of intimacy, and he thought this was amusing? A part of her wanted to retreat, yet Mrs. Swann's words played in her head.

Fear keeps us from our heart's deepest desires. Vanquish yours, and you will become the woman you were meant to be.

"I may look like a lady on the outside," Fi blurted, "but on the inside, I...well, I'm not as good as you think."

"I'm aware that propriety isn't high on your list of virtues," he said solemnly. "But I am willing to live with your lack of decorum. Especially in bed."

"I'm being serious," she protested.

"So am I. I adore your naughty streak, darling. Always have."

She couldn't let him labor under his delusions any longer.

"I am not just naughty in bed. In real life, I am willful. Rebellious," she informed him. "You know I value my independence, but it goes deeper than that. I am not a good, well-behaved person like Caroline. I am ambitious and selfish, sometimes petty. I want what I want, and I cannot change who I am. I've managed to hide the truth from Society—mostly by working on my looks and charm—but it is all an act. A masquerade."

He drew his brows together. "Is that what you've been thinking? That you're not as good a *person* as my first wife?"

"Not just her." Fi squared her shoulders. "My mama and Max too. They are nice and giving, always putting the needs of others first. And my friends, they are all talented and brilliant. Compared to them, I...well, I am just me. Nothing special. Mainly I'm good at looking pretty and charming people."

"Christ, Fiona."

He looked...stunned? The knots inside her tightened. She'd known intimacy was a risk.

Yet you exposed yourself anyway, like the reckless fool you are. And now you are going to lose the one thing that matters most...

She pulled the sheets more tightly around her, fighting the appalling burn behind her eyes.

She felt her chin being tipped up. Then she was looking into Hawk's intense and tender gaze.

"Why would the Incomparable for two seasons running, the

debutante who is the envy of women and the desire of men, think so little of herself?"

His gentleness cracked open her heart.

"Because I know who I am." She blinked away a tear. "My so-called success isn't because I am special; I just work harder than the other debutantes. If you only knew all the hours I've spent memorizing Debrett's or practicing dance steps or learning all the fashion trends. It is just another one of my flaws. I am competitive, you see, and driven. While it hurts when others call me Miss Banks, there is a seed of truth in it," she acknowledged. "I am not blue-blooded or aristocratic, and because of that, I have had to fight my way to the top. To show them all I have what it takes to be a true lady. The irony of it is, I have somehow managed to fool everyone."

"Except yourself." Hawk's voice was deep with understanding. "You think you're an impostor, is that it? That you don't belong in rarefied circles?"

"Yes, precisely." Surprised by his acuity, she asked, "How did you know?"

"Because I have felt as you do."

She canted her head. "You have? But you were born into nobility."

"I haven't felt like an impostor in social circles," he amended. "But at university, I met some brilliant fellows and even though my achievements were equal to theirs, I had this feeling that I did not belong in their exalted group. That I wasn't as intelligent or talented as any of them. I thought that it was mere luck or hard work that got me there. At times, I even feared that my peers would discover that I did not belong."

"Why, that is exactly how *I* feel," she said, astonished.

"I think it is not uncommon amongst those of us who value achievement. Who hold ourselves to high—some might say, impossible—standards." Hawk gave her a wry look. "Mama has always said that I am my own worst critic. Perhaps you are your own as well."

Everything Hawk said made sense. The logic of it swept through her like a crisp breeze, clearing out some of the cobwebs of self-doubt. She would need time to mull things over, but for now she felt burgeoning relief. Despite her confession, her husband hadn't rejected her. He'd listened and empathized.

"You truly aren't disappointed?" she asked.

"Why do you think that I would be?"

Because I've been a disappointment before.

"I don't know." Confronted with Hawk's unyielding gaze, she mumbled, "Since I was a young girl, Papa has constantly lectured me to be less willful. Less driven by my own desires. He told me I should be more loving and good, like my brother and Mama."

Hawk's forehead creased. "Garrity said that to you?"

"Not in so many words," she was forced to admit. "But I know I've been a disappointment to him."

"I could not imagine how." Hawk lifted her chin. "Sweetheart, your papa is extremely proud of you. Of who you are and your accomplishments. When I offered for you, he told me he was entrusting me with the dearest thing he had to give to any man, his pride and joy."

"Papa said that?" she asked, startled.

"Yes. Then he made it clear that there would be consequences if I didn't take proper care of you."

That part *did* sound like her father. As Fiona struggled to absorb the new information, Hawk continued to shake the tree of her beliefs.

"But I didn't need your father to tell me how special you are," he said. "I know that what makes you beautiful isn't on the outside. It is your boldness and strength and, aye, even your willful streak. The way you aren't afraid to carve your own path. It is your loyalty to those you care about and how fiercely and passionately you care. It is even your insecurities, the way you have no idea how extraordinary you are."

"Oh, H-Hawk." Fi's voice hitched. "That is truly the n-nicest thing..."

For once, she couldn't control the tears that dripped down her face. Hawk cuddled her close, murmuring more devastating endearments. When she calmed, he took her hand, linking their fingers on the counterpane.

"I am glad you talked to me, sweetheart," he said.

She snuggled closer. "I am too."

"Perhaps you might talk to your papa as well. See what he truly thinks."

"Perhaps," she said cautiously.

Hawk squeezed her hand. "At any rate, this is what I meant about sharing our lives. We don't have to do it all at once, but little by little we can let each other in."

She slid him a look. "Do you have things you want to share with me?"

If I trust you with my secrets, will you return the favor?

"I suppose I do." He cleared his throat. "Not right now, for I have a morning appointment, but soon, love. There is no rush. We have a lifetime to get to know one another."

We have a lifetime together. I'll tell him about the Angels soon... and I'll test the waters tonight.

"Before you toddle off, don't forget we are promised to the Hadleighs this evening," she said.

"I wouldn't miss it." He kissed the top of her head. "I know how much your friends mean to you, and I would like to get to know them better."

Could any man be more perfect?

She looked at him with her heart in her eyes. "I love you so much."

"Devil and damn, sweetheart." His gaze heating, he reached for her, rolling her beneath him. "You're going to make me late for my appointment."

THIRTY-ONE

"You're late," Swinburne said by way of greeting when Hawk arrived at Garland's.

"Pardon." Hawk took his seat at the table, where the rest of the Quorum and Inspector Sterling were already gathered. "Couldn't be helped."

"Awful chipper for this time of day, aren't you?" Devlin leaned insouciantly back in his chair. "What has gotten into you?"

"Nothing." Hawk refused to take the bait.

Devlin smirked. "I know what it is. You've the look of a newlywed who has enjoyed a rather good morning."

"Devlin," Hawk growled, "I'm warning you—"

"Enough." Swinburne pushed to his feet. "Might I remind you gentlemen that we have urgent business to deal with?"

Devlin started it. Having no intention of sounding like a bloody schoolboy, Hawk bit back his retort. Christ, the bastard knew how to get under his skin. While he could take Devlin's underhanded jibes, he would not allow the other to dishonor Fiona in any fashion.

Protectiveness surged through him as he thought of his wife's aching vulnerability. He understood all too well those unfounded feelings of being a fraud; defying logic and facts, the beliefs caused anxiety and self-doubt. That Fiona had trusted him enough to share her inner workings gratified and humbled him.

So this is love, he thought with a ripple of awe.

Over their hurried breakfast, Fiona had also mentioned running into Melinda Ayles at the ball last night. She'd commented on Melinda's about-face, saying that Hawk's former mistress had not only complimented her on her looks but had made an effort to be friendly.

"Lady Ayles's face looked like it might crack from the force of her smile." Fiona had given him a suspicious look. *"Did you say something to her?"*

Knowing how proud and independent Fiona was, Hawk hadn't been sure how she would respond to his intervention. Warily, he had replied that he'd made clear to Lady Ayles that he would not countenance her bothering Fiona in the future. To his surprise, his wife had risen from her chair, thrown her arms around his neck, and kissed him soundly.

"I could have dealt with her myself." Fiona's face had been wreathed in smiles. *"But it was ever so lovely of you to take the initiative."*

She had acted as if he'd given her a priceless piece of jewelry instead of merely handling a problem for which he felt responsible. Damn, but she was more complex than an analytic engine...and he would gladly spend the rest of his life trying to understand the fascinating intricacies of who she was. To love and shield her from life's pain.

"Trent, Hawksmoor. Why don't you begin by giving us a summary of what you saw of the Auberville attack," Swinburne instructed.

Reality returned as Trent's succinct account blanketed the room with silence. Hawk saw his own sense of failure carved in the others' stony expressions. He relived the instant when Lady Auberville's last breath had left her, the heaviness of holding on as life slipped away. He flashed to the moment he'd found Caroline lying on her bed, the empty bottle of laudanum lolling on the ground where it'd fallen from her limp fingers. The clawing panic as he'd held her, tried to revive her, begged her to come back.

"I spoke with Auberville's heir, Lord Godfrey, this morning," Inspector Sterling said somberly. "He is enraged over what happened, of course. Against the advice of my superiors, he is issuing a five-hundred-pound reward for the capture of the Sherwood Band. In his words, 'breathing or not.'"

"Five hundred pounds?" Swinburne uttered an oath. "Every cutthroat in London will come out of the woodwork for that sum. They won't care whose heads they bring in as long as they get their money. This will fan the very flames of anarchy that we're trying to put out."

"That is what we told Lord Godfrey, but he won't listen," Sterling said. "He says if the police can't do something to stop the attacks, then he will."

"God save us from blue bloods with more money than sense," Trent muttered. "Can you buy us any time, Sterling? The attack last night may have turned the tide in our favor. The gang made a grievous mistake when they resorted to violence. While working-class folk may have supported a Robin Hood brand of justice, they won't condone the murder of a lady known for her charitable works and who was a grandmama, at that. Public opinion is turning against these criminals; once the streets are no longer a refuge, we'll be able to flush the bastards out."

"I will do my best." Sterling straightened his narrow shoulders, his tone apologetic. "My voice does not carry much weight, I'm afraid. Especially since we don't have much progress to share."

"As to that," Hawk cut in. "We do have a new lead. Two leads, in point of fact."

All eyes turned to him.

"Go on," Swinburne said.

"When I found Auberville in the carriage, he described the

exchange between him and the man we may presume to be Martin Wheatley. When told to hand over his valuables, Auberville said that he would see Wheatley hanged in Newgate first. And Wheatley apparently replied that he was never going back."

"Crikey." Trent sat up. "You think this Wheatley is an ex-convict?"

"The police have already considered that possibility." Sterling frowned. "As you know, I have personally gone through the files of ex-prisoners charged with robberies, and none matched the profile of the Sherwood leader. From what I recall, the name Wheatley was not amongst them."

"Wheatley is likely an alias," Hawk said. "And perhaps our man does not have a history of robbery. From what I've learned from Miss Farley and Mrs. Swann, I would say his greatest strength lies in manipulation. He is charming, particularly with the opposite sex. When the opportunity presents itself, he is also capable of violent behavior...indeed, according to Mrs. Swann, he may even enjoy it. She kicked him out of her club for abusing his lover, a woman named Sarah Mallery."

"Sick bastard," Pearson muttered.

"Auberville said that Wheatley had a female accomplice whose description matches that of Miss Mallery. After Auberville shot Wheatley in the arm, Wheatley returned fire, and Miss Mallery apparently tried to intervene. Unfortunately, Wheatley's shot hit Lady Auberville instead. And I found this in the carriage."

Reaching into his pocket, Hawk took out an old confectionary box and removed the lid. Inside was a scrap of cheap linen he'd found on the floor of the Aubervilles' carriage.

"Auberville said that after his wife was shot, the female accomplice took out this handkerchief, intending to stanch Lady Auberville's wound," he explained. "But the gang's leader dragged her away, and she dropped it."

"Handkerchiefs like those are two a penny." Devlin tilted his head. "Is there something on it that we can trace? A scent, perhaps."

As Devlin reached for the evidence, Hawk halted him.

"Careful," he said tersely. "The handkerchief contains traces of a white powder. I noticed it on my gloves last night, which is why I've kept it in a box."

Devlin's gaze slitted. "Poison, do you think?"

"I am not certain." To be safe, Hawk closed the box.

"I'll have a chemist try to identify this powder," Swinburne said. "In the meantime, we must split up and track the clues. Trent, go to Newgate and question the guards and prisoners. See if you can find any leads to this Wheatley fellow. Hawksmoor, help Trent while I work on gaining access to the Newgate prisoner files for the last five years; I'll want you to review them."

Hawk jerked his chin in assent.

"Pearson," Swinburne went on. "Auberville claims that he shot Wheatley in the arm. See if there are any sightings of an injured man near the attack. Check with physicians in the vicinity, too, in case Wheatley sought medical attention."

"Got it, sir," Pearson said.

"Devlin, dig up any information you can on this Sarah Mallery." Swinburne's keen gaze circled the room. "That's it for now, gentlemen. Let's get this bastard. Hawksmoor, I'd like a word."

After the door closed behind the others, the spymaster faced Hawk.

"I think your hunch was correct," Swinburne said grimly. "We have a leak."

Hawk nodded. He'd begun to suspect there was a mole after von Essen's untimely demise. The Sherwood Band always seemed a step ahead...as if they had inside information. Last night's breakthrough in the case confirmed Hawk's suspicions; when he had kept his plans concealed, they had made progress.

"Do you have any suspects in mind?" he asked.

"It could be any one of the men who just left. Or it could be a problem in the police force." Swinburne slammed a palm against the table. "Goddamnit, this is the last thing we need. We don't have the resources to go hunting for a mole. And we're close to wrapping up the case—I can feel it in my bones."

"What should we do, sir?"

Swinburne exhaled. "For now, nothing. We'll keep this between us...but keep your guard up. I want you to report directly to me and only to me."

Hawk nodded.

"Carry on, then."

"Actually, sir. I have something else to discuss." Hawk drew a breath. "As you know, I have recently wed. My marriage has led to a change in my circumstances."

"You are not resigning, are you?" Swinburne said with alarm.

"No. I cannot, however, continue to keep my work a secret from my wife. I request your permission to tell her the truth."

With crystal clarity, Hawk knew that he wanted to share everything with Fiona. He wanted the old, idealistic dream, the one he'd given up on until he found himself miraculously living it. He didn't know how his marriage of convenience had turned into the love of a lifetime, but he was done questioning it. He wanted to move forward. Wanted to remove all barriers between him and his love...which meant he could no longer work as a spy without her knowledge.

Swinburne studied him. "You did not have a problem with discretion before."

By "before," Hawk knew that his superior was referring to his prior marriage.

"As I said, things have changed." What had sufficed before would no longer satisfy him.

"I'll beg your pardon for asking this, but I must. Are you certain you can trust your lady?" Swinburne's expression was stark. "The security of our nation depends upon our work. One slip from Lady Hawksmoor, one indiscreet conversation, could compromise the welfare of our country."

"My wife can be trusted," Hawk said unequivocally. "You have my word."

Swinburne sighed. "Permission granted, then. With one caveat."

Hawk cocked his head.

"Given the possible leak, I don't want anything else to compromise our mission. Too much is at stake. Will you wait until we wrap up this business before telling your wife?"

It was a reasonable request. Hawk's instincts told him that they were on the cusp of apprehending Wheatley and his gang. Waiting a few days to tell Fiona the truth wouldn't hurt.

He inclined his head. "Yes, sir."

When Fi arrived at Charlie's that morning, she found the other Angels crowded around yet another basket of treats.

"Mrs. Fisher again?" Fi asked as she sat next to Glory.

Holding a pair of silver tongs, Glory gestured to a tray of prettily decorated teacakes. "You must try the almond ones. They are to *die* for. No wonder Mrs. Fisher is getting an appointment from the Queen; her bakers are royally good."

"Pass me a cake then. Make that two since I'm celebrating," Fi said casually.

"What is the occasion?" Glory asked.

"Hawk and I are officially in love," Fi declared.

When her friends squealed with excitement, Fi couldn't help but join them.

Pippa handed her a cup of tea. "Tell us everything."

Fi summarized the soul-baring conversations she'd had with Hawk, concluding giddily, "Hawk sees me in a way that no one else has before. He appreciates who I truly am."

"I should hope so." Glory paused to share a morsel of cake with her ferret. "He is lucky to be married to you."

"Hear, hear." Livy and Pippa held their teacups up in a toast.

"Thank you, dears." Taking a breath, Fi went on, "The talk with Hawk also helped me to realize that I've never felt deserving of my social success. I attributed my popularity to my dowry and the extra effort I put in. To my mind, I did not possess many merits, and all those years of being looked down upon for my origins didn't help. The truth is I felt like a fraud and not a true lady."

Her friends gawked at her.

"Why didn't you tell us you felt that way?" Livy sounded puzzled and a bit hurt. "We could have told you how very special you are. That you are more of a lady than many born with titles."

"I probably wouldn't have believed you," Fi admitted. "Because you are my bosom friends and have always been in my corner no matter what."

"If I had known that you felt insecure about your popularity, I would have *never* teased you about it." Glory's face creased with worry. "I'm so sorry, Fi. If I inadvertently poured salt into your wounds—"

"You didn't, dearest." Reaching over, Fi patted her friend's hand. "I knew you were being affectionate."

Glory gave a relieved nod.

"I am so glad that you trusted Hawksmoor with the truth," Pippa said.

"It was such a relief. In fact"—Fi inhaled deeply—"I want to tell him that I am an investigator soon. Are your husbands prepared to test the waters at supper tonight?"

"Hadleigh is ready and willing," Livy said.

"Cull, too," Pippa added.

"Thank you." Fi smiled. "Now that that's settled, let me catch you up on my meeting with Mrs. Swann yesterday."

Fi described what the proprietress had told her about Lillian and Martin Wheatley.

"The blackguard!" Glory said fiercely. "We must free Lillian from his dastardly clutches."

"Now that we have a name, description, and the cough..." Livy narrowed her eyes. "What trades might affect one's breathing and put burns on one's hands?"

"Blacksmithing?" Pippa suggested.

"Good thought," Fi said. "But Mrs. Swann said he didn't smell of coal, nor have visible traces of it on his skin or under his nails. Not easy when one is working at a forge all day."

"That rules out a miner as well. And you said Mrs. Swann didn't think Wheatley was a mill worker either." Glory twirled her cake-laden fork in the air, muttering, "What other occupation might result in burns, problems with the lungs..."

The realization struck Fi.

"*Baker,*" she exclaimed.

She and Livy grinned at each other; they'd spoken at the same time.

"When Max and I were little, Mama used to take us to her favorite bakeshop," Fi said. "The baker had a nagging cough, and I remember Mama offering to bring him her special tea. But he said he wasn't ill; his cough came from breathing in flour dust. *Baker's lung,* he called it."

"Assuming the name Wheatley is an alias," Livy said thoughtfully, "the choice would be apropos. Possibly a slip of the tongue."

"So how do we go about finding a baker?" Glory asked. "There must be dozens of bakeshops in London."

"Won't the Baker's Guild have a list of masters and apprentices?" Pippa suggested.

"Good thinking," Livy said. "Maybe someone there will recognize this Martin Wheatley from our description."

Pippa was needed back at home, leaving Fi, Glory, and Livy to visit the Hall of the Worshipful Company of Bakers located on Harp Lane. They were greeted by a lanky apprentice named Tom, whose straw-colored hair kept falling into his eyes.

"We would like to speak to someone about membership in your livery company," Livy said.

He swatted at his unruly front wave. "May I ask for what purpose?"

"We're looking for a baker, actually." Fi gave the story they'd prepared on the way over. "You see, my friends and I were at a ladies' tea and had the most divine baked goods. We were told the baker's name and would like to locate and hire him for our next charity event."

When she punctuated her request with a smile, Tom gave her a dazzled look.

"You'll be wanting to talk to Mr. Dobson, then. He keeps a registry of members." Tom tossed his hair back. "Follow me, ladies."

He led them through an airy hall paneled in rich oak and accented with stained-glass windows. They arrived at a small office at the back of the building. The fellow snoozing at the ledger-piled desk looked like he might have been around at the founding of the livery company—which, according to several plaques Fi had seen, had been in 1155.

Tom cleared his throat. Then did it again louder.

Mr. Dobson woke with a start.

"Eggs," he cried. "That's the secret."

"Sorry to disturb you, Mr. Dobson," Tom said with a respectful bow. "These ladies are looking for a baker, and I told them you were the one to talk to."

Mr. Dobson blinked. Then patted his chest until he found the spectacles dangling from his waistcoat. Putting them on, he peered at the Angels. In his heavily wrinkled face, his brown eyes were clear and sharp.

"I can take it from here, Tom," he said.

After the apprentice departed, Mr. Dobson tried to rise.

Hearing the painful creaking of bones, Fi said quickly, "If you don't mind, sir, my friends and I will join you in sitting."

"Yes, of course." Dobson lowered himself back into his chair with a sigh of relief while the Angels took the seats facing his desk. "Now, how may I assist?"

Fi repeated the story about looking for the talented baker.

"Never heard of Martin Wheatley," Mr. Dobson said, frowning. "But there was a fellow a few years back who matches your physical description."

With tingling excitement, Fi asked, "What was his name?"

"Oddly enough, he had the same initials. Michael Wilkes."

Fi thought this was no coincidence. When people chose aliases, they often stuck to the same initials. Easier to remember and no need to change monograms.

"But I don't think Wilkes is who you're looking for," Mr. Dobson went on.

"Why do you say that, sir?" Livy asked.

"Because as talented as Wilkes was, he was also a lazy sod," Mr. Dobson said dourly. "Never stayed long at any job. I doubt he'd put himself through the trouble of creating an exceptional product."

"Did you know him well?" Glory asked.

"Enough to know that he could make a pie crust as light as a feather. The trouble was that his morals were even less substantial. During his apprenticeship, he went through several masters. He always had complaints and problems, blaming others for his own shortcomings. Yet he had an astounding ability to charm his way into anyone's good graces, and it got him through apprenticeship and even landed him several plum positions. None of them lasted, however."

"Why not?" Fi asked.

"Because Wilkes had no interest in putting in a hard day's

work. He believed that he was simply entitled to wealth and success. Our guild's motto is *Praise God for All*, and Wilkes seemed to think of himself as the Almighty. Unfortunately, he had a way of making people around him believe the same thing. Masters, other apprentices, employers—you would be amazed at how Wilkes could wrap them around his finger." Mr. Dobson snorted, waving a gnarled hand. "Oh, and don't get me started on the females."

Fi sat up taller. "Females?"

"I've never seen anything like it. Women—milkmaids and ladies alike—would show up at the hall, looking for Wilkes. Many were slavish in their desperation to find him. My guess is that the blackguard strung them along until he had no further use for them."

A chill pervaded Fi. *What will happen to Lillian once she no longer serves Wilkes's purposes?*

The furrows deepened on Mr. Dobson's forehead. "I say, you ladies aren't looking for Wilkes for, ahem, personal reasons, are you?"

"Not for the kind you mean," Livy said. "The truth is that one of our friends, who is only nineteen, has gone missing, and we're trying to find her. We've discovered she was involved with an abusive fellow who we now believe to be this Michael Wilkes."

"The poor girl." Mr. Dobson sighed heavily. "I wouldn't wish that fate on anyone."

"Do you have any idea where we might find Mr. Wilkes?" Glory asked.

"Believe me, I would help if I could, but I haven't seen the scoundrel in years..." Mr. Dobson scratched his head, then began rummaging through the drawers of his desk, finally pulling out a worn ledger. "We do keep records of our members and their employment. Now this will be several years out of date..."

"Any information would be helpful," Fi said gratefully.

Mr. Dobson rifled through the record book. "Ah, here it is."

He tapped a blunt fingertip against a page. "According to my last entry on Michael Wilkes dated 21st of April 1845, he was...ah, yes. How could I have forgotten? That was a coveted job, that one. Many of our guild members would have given their eyeteeth for it. And they would have been right to do so, given the business's current success."

Fi's pulse accelerated. "Where was Mr. Wilkes employed?"

"Back then it was a small but promising bakeshop located in Soho. Now," Mr. Dobson said, "you may know the company as Fisher's Fine Foods."

THIRTY-TWO

That evening, Hawk found himself enjoying supper at the Hadleighs. After the delicious ten-course repast, the guests, who included the other Angels and their husbands, gathered in the drawing room for postprandial drinks and conversation. Lady Glory, the only unmarried miss, had been partnered with the Duke of Hadleigh's friend, Master Chen, for supper.

A healer, Chen apparently operated an innovative clinic in the East End that specialized in treating opium dependency. He was about Hawk's age, with chiseled, noble features and black hair clipped short. At present, he was having a lively conversation with Lady Glory in his native tongue while her pet ferret watched from her shoulder.

Hawk liked seeing Fiona with her fellow Angels, who were clearly birds of a rare and spirited feather. The ladies shared a propensity for mischief and fun. They chatted and teased their spouses, who did not seem to mind. Indeed, Hadleigh and Timothy Cullen, Pippa's husband, regarded their wives with amusement and obvious pride.

Hawk understood how they felt. Having a wife as special as

Fiona made him feel ten feet tall. As if sensing his thoughts, Fiona, seated beside him on the divan, gave him a flirty grin.

"Having a good evening, my lord?" she asked.

Kissing her hand, he murmured, "And I have hopes it will end even better."

Her delicious blush, which matched the color of her gown, made him want to haul her over his shoulder and to the nearest bed.

"Hadleigh," the duchess said to her husband, who stood with her by the fire. "Why don't you and the gentlemen enjoy some smelly cigars in the study?"

Her hint, Hawk thought with a flicker of humor, was not remotely subtle.

The duke obviously thought the same thing.

"How can we resist when you put it that way, little queen?" Hadleigh chucked his petite wife beneath the chin. "What will you ladies do without us, hmm?"

"I am sure we will think of something," Pippa said with a grin.

Cullen rolled his eyes. "That is what we are afraid of, sunshine."

Given the connection between Hawk and Pippa's families, Hawk had socialized with her new husband and liked the strapping, brown-haired fellow. Known in the streets as the "Prince of Larks," Timothy Cullen was the leader of the mudlarks, a gang of urchins who specialized in obtaining information. The larks were said to have eyes and ears everywhere...a fact that Pippa had confirmed over supper.

"This morning, when I opened my wardrobe, one of the larks popped out and shouted, 'Surprise!'" Chuckling, Pippa had clasped her hands to her bosom. *"I was surprised, all right. My heart nearly flew from my chest."*

"The larks adore Pippa and follow her around like she's the Pied Piper." The scar on the right side of Cullen's face had not diminished his fierce look of devotion.

As there probably weren't that many women—or men, for that matter—who'd welcome the task of housing, feeding, and schooling hundreds of street urchins, Hawk thought the Cullens were a brilliant match. And the newlyweds were clearly very much in love.

"All right, gentlemen," Hadleigh said easily. "Let us retreat to the study and give the ladies privacy to gossip about us to their hearts' content."

Lady Olivia wrinkled her nose. "What makes you think we don't have better things to discuss?"

Hadleigh gave her a smug look. "Call it a gut feeling."

"Well, I am sure our ears will be burning as well," the duchess said.

She gave her husband a pointed look that Hawk couldn't quite interpret. The duke, however, returned her stare with an amused one of his own and herded the men to his study.

Inside the bastion of male comfort, Hadleigh inquired, "What may I offer you to drink, old chaps?"

"I'll take that whisky that is older than the hills," Cullen said.

Hawk seconded the choice.

"Chen?"

"Tea for me."

Hadleigh also stuck with tea. Hawk had observed that the duke had abstained from spirits during supper as well. A few years ago, Hadleigh's reputation had been that of a hardened rake, but clearly marriage had changed him. Hawk understood the feeling. The men settled in the studded leather furnishings by the fire, a companionable silence blanketing the study.

Even though Hawk did not know the others well, he sensed a vein of similarity running through the group. Not necessarily in physical characteristics, backgrounds, or interests, but something that ran deeper. All were seasoned men upon whom experience had left a mark. That experience had likely made them better able to appreciate the uniqueness of the Angels.

As if reading his mind, Cullen raised his glass in a mock salute. "Welcome to the club, Hawksmoor."

"I am glad to be a part of it," Hawk replied.

"Spoken like a new bridegroom." Hadleigh's lips quirked above the rim of his teacup.

"You still talk that way," Cullen pointed out. "And you've been married for two years and have a daughter to boot."

"I have a strong constitution," Hadleigh said mildly. "A useful quality when wed to an Angel. Moreover, Esme takes after her mama, which means I get double the spirit for the price of one."

"Pippa says she wants our babe to be a girl," Cullen said with studied casualness. "That way, she and Esme can be bosom friends."

A grin split Hadleigh's face. "That is a devil of a thing to slip into the conversation. Congratulations, old boy."

The men rose and shook Cullen's hand.

"As the physician just confirmed it, I wasn't supposed to say anything yet." Cullen looked sheepish and proud at the same time. "But I reckon Pippa couldn't hold it in either and is telling her friends now."

Hadleigh passed around a box of cigars. "I've been saving these for a special occasion."

"I hope you have more." Lighting his cigar, Cullen blew out a puff and slid Hawk a sly look. "I have a feeling we'll have more good news to celebrate soon."

Imagining a daughter or son with Fiona's spirit warmed Hawk's chest.

"I am working on it," he said.

Hadleigh and Cullen guffawed. Chen looked like he was trying to fight a smile.

"A man married to an Angel has his work cut out for him." Hadleigh cleared his throat. "But the rewards far outweigh the challenges."

"What challenges do you mean?" Hawk queried.

"The Angels are dedicated to their cause, for one," the duke said seriously. "God forbid that I should try to interfere with Livy's work. Not that I would try; I admire her determination and drive. To, ahem, see justice done."

An interesting way to describe a charity, Hawk thought idly.

"Knowing that Pippa's, er, volunteerism has led to some risky situations has shaved years off my life," Cullen added. "But I've learned to live with it. To accept that my wife is quite capable of taking care of herself."

Hawk thought of Fiona's visit to Mrs. Swann. While the incident still didn't sit right with him, he'd told himself that it had been a one-time situation.

The way you rationalized her appearance at the Royal Arms, his inner voice reminded him.

Nape prickling, he asked, "What 'risky situations' are you referring to? And how often do they occur?"

The married men exchanged glances. Almost as if they were calibrating their responses.

"Occasional perils do present themselves," Hadleigh said. "But no matter how much Livy argues, I would never permit her to be exposed to danger she cannot handle. We have had to, shall we say, negotiate limits to ensure her safety. She says I am over-bearing; I tell her she is obstinate. We've had some battles but always work things out." A smile flickered in his dark-blue eyes, as if he were recalling some pleasant memory. "The important thing is that she is happy, which makes my own contentment possible."

"Compromise is the key." Cullen nodded sagely. "While Pippa isn't quite as, ahem, determined as Her Grace—no offense, Hadleigh..."

"None taken." The duke's mouth curved. "Having known Livy since she was thirteen, I knew what I was getting myself into."

"My wife has her moments as well," Cullen said with feeling. "Pippa has a reckless streak that will make me grey before my time.

Yet my job comes with dangers too, and if Pippa is willing to accept me as I am, then I want to do the same thing for her."

Like Cullen, Hawk's work involved perils. Having made the decision to tell Fiona about the Quorum, he had to be prepared for her reaction. Would she accept the dangers of espionage or demand that he stop his clandestine missions? And if it came down to a choice between his wife's wishes and his own, what would he do?

"Marriage is both less convenient and more fulfilling than I expected it to be," he mused.

"Love is not meant to be convenient. It simply is," Chen said.

Until now, the healer hadn't spoken much. Perhaps because he was the sole unmarried fellow in the group or simply quiet by nature. Chen seemed like a man who prided himself on self-discipline. His calm gaze conveyed that he'd seen too much of the world to be surprised by it.

Hadleigh raised a brow. "You are speaking from experience?"

"From the experience of observing others," Chen replied.

"No offense, man." Cullen snorted. "That is hardly the same thing."

Chen lifted his brows. "Does one have to fall off a cliff to know what the experience will be like?"

"From that comparison, I surmise that you *have* experienced love, Chen," Hadleigh quipped. "But I concur. Love has a way of making itself known, whether one is prepared for it or not. To me, the real question is how to ensure that love reaches its full potential."

"Trust," Cullen said promptly. "You must trust your better half to know what they're doing. Just as they trust you."

"Acceptance is vital as well," Hawk said.

Knowing Fiona's insecurities, he understood that she yearned to be loved for who she was. And he was determined to give her everything she needed.

"Undoubtedly." Hadleigh coughed in his fist. "Speaking as the husband of an Angel, I will admit that it has not always been easy to accept the gambles my duchess chooses to take. Even though I have the utmost respect for her abilities."

"If Fiona can accept my work, then I can do the same for her," Hawk said.

"You are a scholar, my lord." Hadleigh arched his brows. "While your work is unquestionably fascinating, I do not see many hazards involved."

Hawk took a swallow of whisky before saying wryly, "You would be surprised."

THIRTY-THREE

S nuggled under Hawk's arm as the carriage swayed along, Fi tilted her head up at him. "Did you enjoy yourself tonight, darling?"

"Indeed," Hawk said. "I like your friends."

"I knew you would. And they adore you, of course." Trying to sound casual, Fi asked, "What did you talk about in the study?"

Did Livy's plan work? Did the other husbands convince you that we Angels are capable of handling anything? That you have nothing to worry about and should support my passion?

"You know the rule of gentlemen. What is discussed in the study, stays in the study."

"Fine. Then I won't tell you what we ladies talked about."

Hawk gave her an amused look. "I already know what you discussed."

"I doubt that very much."

Especially since she and the others had talked about their case. Mrs. Fisher had just returned from a business trip and was scheduled to pay Charlie a visit tomorrow.

"You discussed the fact that Pippa is with child," Hawk said. "She is hoping for a girl who can start a society with the Hadleighs' daughter and continue the tradition of female friends wreaking havoc together."

"How did you..." Fi narrowed her eyes. "Mr. Cullen spilled the beans, didn't he? Pippa said it was supposed to be a secret for a few more weeks."

"She told you."

"That's different."

Hawk raised his brows.

Realizing she didn't have a leg to stand on, Fi muttered, "You gentlemen gossip far more than ladies do."

"If it makes you feel any better, the bulk of our conversation involved being the husband of an Angel."

Exactly as planned. In the drawing room, Fi had been on pins and needles, wondering how the men's talk was going. The others had tried to reassure her.

"Don't worry, dear. I coached Hadleigh on precisely what to say," Livy had said blithely. *"At this very moment, my husband is convincing yours that we are brilliant and capable and that he has nothing to worry about."*

"I just asked Cull to give his honest opinion." Pippa's tone had been dry. *"I thought it would be helpful for Hawksmoor to hear another husband's experience."*

"Was it useful to commiserate?" Fi joked.

Hawk smiled slowly. "Quite."

When he said nothing more, she said, "You didn't really commiserate, did you?"

"Why are you so curious about our conversation?"

Uh-oh. Retreat.

"No particular reason," she said.

"Hmm." Hawk's shrewd expression did not bode well.

Fi swiftly changed the subject. "I told my friends about our talk this morning. About my, well, insecurities."

"And?" Hawk asked gently.

"It felt good to talk about it. They were surprised," she mused.

"I suppose I'm rather good at bluffing."

Hawk tipped her chin up. "You never have to bluff with me."

The truth pounded in her heart, quivered upon her lips. *I am investigating a case of a missing woman. And I want to tell you all about it. But I'm afraid...so afraid you'll try to stop me from doing what I love. But as soon as this case is over, I am going to tell you and pray that you won't make me choose between my two greatest passions.*

"I hope you feel the same way," she said.

Longing and some other emotion she couldn't name flashed through his eyes.

"I am more myself with you than I have been with anyone," he said quietly.

"Including Caroline?"

Greeted by silence, she regretted her rash question. Regretted even more the flaw in her character that made her feel competitive with a ghost. Intellectually, she knew that his past marriage had no bearing on their present; it should be enough that Hawk was falling in love with her now. Yet she yearned to be the great love of his life. The way he was hers.

"I was a different man during my first marriage."

His somber reply heightened her embarrassment.

"I am sorry. I shouldn't have pried—"

"But you want to know. And I want you to have what you need," he said steadily. "Without compromising Caroline's privacy, I can say that I was an inexperienced lad when I first wed. I had a rather idealistic notion of love, and for a time I seemed to have found that in my marriage. But soon after we wed, Caroline developed...an ailment."

"She was ill?" Fi asked in surprise.

This was the first that she'd heard of Caroline being in frail health.

Hawk gave a curt nod. "She didn't like fuss and wanted it to be kept a private matter. Through no fault of her own, the illness worsened, making it difficult for her to participate in life and in our marriage. It frustrated both of us. I wanted badly to help, yet there was little either of us could do to change the situation. The so-called cures prescribed by physicians did nothing. Although I took care of her as best I could, her condition overwhelmed us both. When she died, I was ashamed of the relief I felt. The relief that her suffering was over. That...that my caretaking was over." He let out a harsh breath. "To this day, I bear guilt for not having done more for her."

"Knowing you, you did everything you could. You were a good husband to Caroline, and neither of you deserved the hand you were dealt." Hating the lingering pain in his eyes, Fi said wretchedly, "Forgive me. I should not have dredged up the past. It is small of me, I know, to make comparisons—"

"I understand." Hawk caressed her cheek, his easy acceptance of her faults making her eyes sting. "To answer the question I think you're truly asking: what I felt for Caroline was a different kind of love than what I feel for you. It was a young man's love, tempered by disappointment and guilt. After the experience, I did not want to open my heart again."

Fi nodded, understanding now why he'd agreed to a marriage of convenience. Knowing Hawk—how protective he was—it must have killed him to be powerless to stop his wife's suffering, which sounded like it had gone on for years. No wonder he'd wanted to avoid intimacy again.

"But you came along." His features were fierce with emotion. "With your courage and boldness and saucy proposition of marriage. I did not think I had anything left to give—especially not to a spirited young chit pursued by every bachelor in town—but you showed me otherwise. Showed me what it is like to have a partner in passion and in life. I did not think I would love again; I never thought I would find the love of my life."

"Oh, Hawk." Emotion clogged her throat. "You are everything to me."

He bent his head and kissed her. A joining that went beyond lips and tongues, that melded souls. When they broke apart, they were both panting.

"About your earlier suggestion that I enjoy myself this eve." His gaze molten, he wound one of her ringlets around his finger. "I realize that I haven't yet made love to you in a carriage. An oversight I intend to rectify."

With a flush of embarrassment and regret, she said, "I'm afraid I can't tonight."

At Hawk's quirked brow, she clarified, "That is, um, I *want* to, but my, um, monthly visitor has arrived."

"I see." His manner turned solicitous. "Are you having any discomfort, my dear?"

"No." She fiddled with a button on his waistcoat. "I feel fine. In fact, I was thinking..."

"Yes, love?"

"That perhaps I could, um, pleasure you?" Peering up at him, she slid her gloved palm downward. Heady arousal filled her when she encountered his hard, pulsing length. "Help you with this?"

"Now?" he asked in a low voice.

"No time like the present."

Feeling very bold, she slipped off the bench and knelt between his legs. Her skirts rustled against the bouncing floor of the carriage. His eyes gleaming, Hawk cupped her jaw, and she gloried in his strong touch.

"What a naughty minx you are," he murmured. "Offering to perform fellatio on your husband. In a carriage, no less."

Her tummy flipped at his wicked words. "You don't mind, do you?"

He rolled his eyes, eliciting a giggle from her.

Then he unfastened his trousers and the sight of his rampant erection stoppered her laughter. Her pussy clenched in longing as he fisted his huge shaft, drawing forth a milky droplet on the engorged head.

"Have a taste," he said.

His husky command, the way he held his cock out to her like an offering flooded her with desire. Eagerly, she dipped her head and swirled her tongue over the fat, swollen crown. Hawk's growl of approval and his salty essence set fire to her senses. Hungrily, she took more of him, drawing him into her mouth.

"That's it, sweeting," he said thickly. "You suck my cock so well. Take more."

Relaxing her jaw, she managed to fit more of his length inside. Stretching her lips around his thick girth, she bobbed her head, aroused by the feel of him inside her this way. His harsh pants and the way he clutched her hair filled her with a sense of feminine power. Wild with the need to pleasure her lover, she dove deeper, gagging when he lodged too deep in her throat.

She came up gasping.

Hawk rubbed his thumbs over the wetness at the corners of her eyes. Even in the dimness, his face radiated savage wonder.

"So goddamned beautiful," he rasped. "And you're mine, aren't you?"

"Just as you're mine," she said in a sultry whisper.

"Possessive chit." His mouth crooked into a brief grin. Tracing her lips with a blunt fingertip, he said, "I want to have your mouth in a different way."

Shivering with anticipation, she nodded.

He stood and turned her around so that she was kneeling with her back against the bench. His turgid cock bobbing with the vehicle's movements, he grabbed hold of the carriage strap to keep his balance.

His legs planted firmly, he said, "Put your hands on my thighs and keep them there, love."

She did as she was told, feeling his corded strength beneath her palms. With his free hand, he cupped the back of her head, threading his fingers through her hair and bringing her lips to his erection. The glossy tip, ripe as a plum, made her mouth pool. She wanted to pleasure him the way he'd so often pleasured her. To explore their love without limits.

Until his dying breath, Hawk would remember this carriage ride. Never had he imagined a marriage like this, in which he would possess the heart of his sweet lady and burn in the fires of their wicked passion. He'd never felt this close to a woman...never wanted to do such hot, filthy things to one.

"Open for me," he said huskily. "Let me have that sweet mouth of yours."

Fiona parted her lips like an acolyte ready to worship at his altar. With one hand, he held on to the leather strap. With the other, he steadied her head and pushed into her mouth, groaning as her velvety warmth engulfed him. *By Jove*, that was fine. Better yet was the way she looked up at him: the beguiling sparkle in her eyes told him she was enjoying herself nearly as much as he was. Nearly.

He'd always admired Fiona's achievement-oriented spirit. She excelled at everything she did, and fellatio was no exception. With just a little practice, she was learning to drive him out of his mind. She kept her jaw loose, letting him thrust freely into her lush opening. His knees weakened when her tongue flicked friskily at his plunging head. When she hollowed her cheeks, adding suction, he bit out an oath.

"You are getting too bloody good at this," he said between ragged breaths.

She released him with a ball-tautening *pop*.

"Practice makes perfect," she said.

Her demure reply was undoubtedly designed to make him wild. And it worked.

"In that case."

Clenching his hand in her hair, he drove deeper and deeper,

watching her face for any discomfort. He saw only a loving acceptance that made his heart thud as if he'd been running for miles. Running his entire life...to find this.

This woman, his love. His mate.

Feeling the sensual clinch of her throat, he grunted with bliss. She made a gagging sound but kept sucking. Her eyes, tearing with effort, beseeched him to take her gift. Mesmerized, he lost himself in his wife's sweet, wanton generosity. Her tongue teased a groove that made his hips buck. Crazed for her, he gripped her head and fucked her lovely mouth. When her lips kissed his stones, he knew he was done for.

"Love, I have to pull out—*Christ*," he bit out.

Her reply had been to shift her hands from his thighs to his arse. Her fingers dug into the flexing muscles of his buttocks, urging him on. Giving him permission to do what he'd never done before. With a howl of need, he let go. White-hot ecstasy forked through him as he gave himself over to her keeping. Shuddering, he spilled over and again, her soft gurgles vibrating against his pulsing flesh. In his goddamned soul.

He sprawled onto the bench, pulling Fiona onto his lap.

"Thank you, sweetheart," he said when he could speak again. "You are bloody magnificent."

"You're welcome, but this is just my second go." Her smile was saucy, and she looked adorably pleased with herself. "Wait until I really get the hang of it."

THIRTY-FOUR

The next morning, Fiona, Livy, and Pippa watched from the viewing hole as Charlie led their former client into her study.

"Thank you for coming today, Mrs. Fisher," Charlie said.

"As your note said the matter was urgent, I made the time." Mrs. Fisher swept into the office, a vision of female authority in a cerise pelisse and walking dress with black frogging. A matching chapeau perched at a rakish angle atop her ash-blonde curls. "I haven't long, however. I have a meeting at the office."

"I shall cut to the chase." Charlie waved the other to a divan, taking the adjacent chair. "I wish to ask you about a man named Michael Wilkes."

Fi sensed Mrs. Fisher's formidable self-control at play as the lady regarded Charlie. The lines bracketing her mouth were her only sign of distress.

"Why?" Mrs. Fisher asked bluntly.

"I am assisting a mother to find her missing daughter. I believe Wilkes is involved—that he is abusing the young woman and using her for nefarious purposes." Charlie was equally direct. "In my search for Wilkes, I have uncovered clues that suggest he was the man you were addressing in the letters we retrieved from Count von Essen."

"Dreadful what happened to von Essen." Mrs. Fisher's mouth formed a thin slash. "Even if he was a blackmailing bastard."

"My sentiments exactly. Now back to my request. Anything you can tell us about Wilkes may help us find our client's daughter."

Mrs. Fisher studied Charlie. "If I tell you what I know, do I have your assurance of anonymity? Your word of honor that my name will not be involved in any way?"

"You do," Charlie said gravely. "You will also have my gratitude and that of a very worried mama."

After a pause, Mrs. Fisher gave a brisk nod. "You are correct in that Michael Wilkes was the man I had an affair with. It was a foolish decision on my part, and one I have come to regret. In my defense, I can only say that I was lonely after my husband's death... lonely, in truth, for a long time before that. My marriage had been a practical but not passionate union, and there was a part of me that had always longed for something more. Which made me ripe for the plucking where Wilkes was concerned."

"How did you meet him?" Charlie asked.

"He was an employee at the shop. A junior baker," Mrs. Fisher said tightly. "He was charming, seductive, and over twenty years my junior. I had never met anyone like him. He had a way of making me feel special and desirable, neither of which I had felt before. I fell under his thrall. I thought I was in love for the first time but, in retrospect, what I felt was..."

"Physical in nature?" Charlie's tone held no judgement.

"Precisely." Mrs. Fisher folded her gloved hands on her lap. "Strange, isn't it, how difficult that is to admit? I own a company that has become a household name. I employ dozens and am about to receive the patronage of Her Majesty. Yet despite my success"— she shook her head bitterly—"when it comes to my own needs, I feel like an embarrassed child."

"You are not alone. As women, we are taught to feel shame over the pleasure our bodies can give us. We are trained to be daughters and wives, roles convenient to men," Charlie said matter-of-factly. "A passionate woman, one who embraces her own needs and power, represents a dangerous threat to the patriarchal establishment."

Mrs. Fisher tilted her head. "I have never thought of it that way."

"Most women don't. That is what makes us easy prey for men like Wilkes. He knows a woman's desires perhaps better than she does. And he uses them to manipulate and control her to his own ends."

"What you described is what happened to me," Mrs. Fisher admitted in a low voice. "Michael drew forth my darkest fantasies, things that shocked me just to think of them. At first, it was titillating and exhilarating to explore such passions, to embrace my basest needs. I became infatuated with him, adored him for being my guide down that sensual path. Then things took a turn for the worse."

"How?"

"He became controlling and possessive," Mrs. Fisher said flatly. "In sexual matters, I...I enjoyed relinquishing control. I was managing so many things with the business, and it felt, well, freeing to let go. But that was only in the bedroom and only a fantasy. In reality, I had no desire to give up my autonomy.

"Michael, however, started taking over more of my life. At first, I thought he was trying to be helpful with his suggestions for my company, but then it became clear that he expected his presence in my bedchamber to give him a say in how I ran my bakeries. We began to fight. And his personality changed overnight. He went from showering me with trinkets and affection to being demeaning and cruel. One night, we had an argument, and the bounder...he struck me." Mrs. Fisher's voice trembled. "I realized then what a monster I had let into my life. The next time I saw him, I brought along armed footmen. I ended things and told him that I would make him pay if he tried to hurt me again."

Fi was impressed by Mrs. Fisher's wherewithal.

"And you didn't hear from him again?" Charlie asked.

"Surprisingly, no. I lived in fear that he would come back and try to extort me over our affair. Instead, he disappeared. It wasn't until von Essen began blackmailing me with those letters that I began to wonder if Wilkes might turn up again like a bad penny. I don't know how von Essen got his hands on those letters, but my intuition tells me that Wilkes was involved."

"If Wilkes was involved, why wouldn't he just blackmail you himself?" Charlie asked.

"I wondered the same thing. Perhaps he feared that, with the resources at my disposal, I would make good on my threat to retaliate. Von Essen had less to fear from me, given his wealth and status." Mrs. Fisher paused. "Wilkes is also a proud bastard who believes he is God's gift to womankind. He thrives on adulation and knows how to manipulate women to get what he wants. It would gall him to have to resort to blackmail. He would be far more likely to give von Essen the letters out of spite, a desire to retaliate, and he would not be above taking a cut."

"Do you know where we might find Wilkes now?"

"Back then, he practically lived at a public house. A seedy place in St. Giles called the Lyon's Den. The owner, Mrs. Lyon, fawned over Wilkes, and treated him like royalty." Mrs. Fisher's fingers interlinked in a tight ball. "He and I played a game where I would go there, disguised as a trollop, and he would pretend to hire me for the eve. I cannot tell you how ashamed I am for participating in such degradation."

"You had the opportunity to explore a fantasy that hurt no one, and you took it," Charlie said. "The problem was that you gave your trust to the wrong man. But you survived and now you have the power to free someone else caught in his snare."

"I was lucky—I had resources to protect me from that predator. If I hadn't..." Mrs. Fisher exhaled. "Whoever this young woman is, I hope you find her and free her from the bastard's clutches."

The Lyon's Den was located in the heart of the Seven Dials. Squished between two equally ramshackle buildings, the pub looked like a drunk being held up by other drunks. Inside, the place was smoky and spacious, with a central stairwell that led up to a ring of rooms on the upper floor. The Angels snagged a table in the corner, ordering drinks and food from a surly barmaid.

"You were right about Vera's artistry, Fi." Livy spoke under her breath as she surveyed the rowdy crowd. "No one is giving us a second glance."

Vera Engle, Lillian's friend and fellow actress, had shown up at Charlie's that afternoon, looking for work. As a demonstration of her skills, she'd helped Livy, Pippa, Fiona, and Glory with their disguises this eve. She'd transformed them into male dock workers, and Charlie had hired her on the spot.

"Thank goodness." Pretending to take a swig from a greasy tankard, Fi said in hushed tones, "The last thing we want is to attract attention from this crowd."

"Public house is a rather polite term for the establishment," Glory agreed.

The place was a flash-house populated by the criminal underclass. On their way in, Fi had observed that the patrons were armed to the teeth...those who had teeth, anyway. Mrs. Lyon, the owner, was a brassy-haired mort with mean eyes. She screeched at the scrawny, terrified children who darted between the scarred tables, picking up empty cups and plates. As she was unlikely to give up Wilkes, the Angels had opted to surveil the premises incognito.

"No sign of Lillian and Wilkes in the crowd, but they could be staying up there." Beneath her cap, Pippa's eyes were trained on the closed doors along the perimeter of the upper floor. "It won't be easy getting up there without being seen."

The only way up was the stairwell in the middle of the room. Once upstairs, there was no cover; the Angels' activities would be exposed to anyone watching from the ground floor. The openness of the flash-house, Fi realized, served as a security measure.

"If we cannot go up," Livy murmured, "then we need whoever is up there to come down. Glory, are the devices ready?"

"Ready and waiting." In her dirt-smudged face, Glory's eyes lit with glee as she gave her battered leather satchel a discreet pat.

"We need to cover the exits to see everyone who leaves the building." Fi scanned the room. "There are doors front and back. And probably less obvious escape routes...underground tunnels and such."

"We'll assign the main exits to Hawker and Mrs. Peabody," Livy said. "The rest of us can split into pairs to monitor the street in case there are exits through the adjacent buildings. Fi and I can take the street in front, Glory and Pippa the back lane."

"Can I set up the diversion now?" Glory asked eagerly.

"I'll go with you," Pippa volunteered. "To, um, make sure everything goes smoothly."

Thank heavens, Fi thought.

When it came to hazardous equipment, Glory could be a bit reckless.

"I accidentally set off a canon that *one time*." Glory scowled. "I know what I am doing."

When she turned to check the smoke-emitting devices, the rest of them exchanged wide-eyed looks.

"Give us ten minutes to set things up with Hawker and Mrs. Peabody," Livy said.

Glory and Pippa bobbed their heads in agreement.

Then all of them leaned in and whispered their motto for luck. "*Sisters first.*"

Fiona headed out with Livy to the carriage, where Hawker and

Mrs. Peabody were waiting. The tension between the butler and housekeeper was thicker than the fog. When Livy explained the plan, the pair left to take their separate posts without exchanging a word.

"What was that all about?" Livy mused.

"What do you think?" Fi rolled her eyes. "At this rate, they'll be married by Christmas."

She and Livy took up their patrol. Fi kept careful watch on the buildings flanking the Lyon's Den. To the left, occupying a corner lot, was a boarding house, with weary-faced men coming and going. A pawn shop sat to the right, lights out for the night. Next to that was an establishment with shuttered windows and no identifying sign. The pair of painted, scantily dressed women lounging in the entryway conveyed the nature of the wares.

"Looking for company, gents?" one of the prostitutes cooed at Fi. "Me and me sister 'ere are free for the eve. Or the hour."

"Already spent me week's wages, dove," Fi replied.

The light-skirt lost interest. Fi and Livy circled back toward the pub.

Shouts punctured the night. "Fire! Fire!"

Smoke and people began pouring out of the Lyon's Den. Knowing that Hawker was posted out front, Fi swept her gaze over the adjacent buildings.

"Come on, Lillian," she murmured. "I know you're here somewhere..."

As the raucous crowd filled the street, Fi craned her neck to keep watch on the entrances. Then she saw them: Mrs. Lyon, along with a man with a bandaged arm and a slight, dark-haired woman. They were not pushing their way out of the Lyon's Den like the others but exiting from the boarding house.

Glimpsing the young woman's face, Fi felt her heart thump with recognition.

"I see Lillian," Fi whispered excitedly. "The boarding house."

Livy whipped her head in that direction. "Good work. Let's go."

They dashed toward their target, grabbing Hawker along the way. They pushed through the throng of people, which wasn't easy since most were drunk and some still drinking from the tankards they'd brought with them.

"Hurry." Fi saw Lillian and her companions veer into an alleyway. "We're going to lose them."

Like Moses, Hawker created a path through the sea of people. They broke free of the horde and headed down the dark vein between buildings. The scent of rot enveloped them. Her breath loud in her ears, Fi led the charge as the alley drained into a large moonlit courtyard with a coach house at the far end.

Livy shouted, "Watch out!"

Fi dove to the ground as a bullet whooshed overhead. Shouts followed, and she rolled to her feet, running to take cover behind a nearby barrel. Pulse racing, she scanned the environs. Livy and Hawker were both unharmed, sheltered behind bales of hay.

With a shock of confusion, Fi saw that a melee was underway in the courtyard. A dozen or so men were brawling with fists and other weapons. She had no idea who they were or why they were fighting.

"Lillian is in the coach house." Livy's shout broke through Fi's paralysis; the former had her pistol drawn. "You're closest; we'll cover you."

With a nod, Fi eyed the building, only several yards away. Taking a breath, she made a run for it, keeping low to avoid gunfire. She sprinted through the open doorway, seeing stalls and a bay that contained a carriage. A woman was madly harnessing horses to the vehicle.

Fi said softly, "Lillian O'Malley."

The woman spun to face Fi, pulling out a gun.

"Don't come any closer," she warned. "I will shoot."

"I'm not here to hurt you." Fi slowly held up her hands,

showing that she had no weapon. "Your mama sent me to find you."

"M-mama?" Lillian whispered. "I-I don't understand."

"My name is Fiona." With her raised hand, she yanked off her cap and wig, letting her hair tumble free. "I work with a female investigative society. Mrs. O'Malley hired us to look for you. She is very worried and wants you to come home."

Lillian's bottom lip trembled.

The lip, Fi saw with a surge of anger, was swollen and cut. It was accompanied by a large bruise on the girl's cheek.

"I can't," Lillian said, her voice cracking. "The things I've done —I'm too ashamed. I thought I was helping ordinary folk like me. Thought I was doing something noble. I never wanted to hurt anyone... But now it is too late."

"It isn't too late," Fi said firmly. "Whatever Wilkes has done to you or made you do, you are safe now. Come with me."

The gun wavered in Lillian's hand.

"I will never be safe. Nor will Mama." A tear trickled down Lillian's cheek; she tightened her grip on the weapon. "Tell her... tell her I'm sorry. You have to go now."

"I am not leaving without you—"

A door behind Lillian opened, and Wilkes stormed in.

"I told you to get the carriage ready, you useless bitch..."

Wilkes froze, spotting Fiona.

At the same time, a deep, familiar voice shouted, "Fiona, watch out!"

Hawk?

She pivoted and saw her husband running toward her. He tackled her to the ground just as a shot exploded. Splinters of wood rained over them. Fi had an instant to glimpse Hawk's stormy expression before he rolled off her and onto his feet.

"Stay down," he roared.

Before she could respond, he whipped out his pistol, aiming at the carriage as it barreled past. Lillian was handling the reins, Wilkes yelling at her to drive faster as he reloaded his weapon.

"No," Fi gasped. "You'll hit her."

She jumped up, grabbing Hawk's arm just as he fired. The shot went wide. The carriage sped through the courtyard, racing away. When her husband turned to face her, the rage on his face caused her to stumble back.

"I can explain," she said weakly.

"It had better be a bloody good explanation," he said with menacing calm.

THIRTY-FIVE

Bridling his emotions, Hawk tried to focus on the meeting taking place in Swinburne's carriage. He shared a bench with Trent, facing Swinburne and Sterling. Hawk's famed powers of concentration were compromised by Fiona's presence in his own carriage several yards away. His blood simmered; he had to shut down his emotions. To let numbness take over so that he would not lose his godforsaken mind.

"We finally have the bastards," Sterling said with satisfaction.

Four members of the Sherwood gang had been captured and carted away by the police.

"Not all of them," Hawk said grimly. "Wilkes and several of his accomplices escaped."

The image flashed of Wilkes aiming a pistol at Fiona. Of Fiona interfering when Hawk tried to shoot the escaping villains. In the moments afterward, she'd given him a brief and crazed explanation: the Society of Angels was, in reality, a secret investigative society. She and the other Angels had been hired to find Wilkes's lightskirt, who Fiona claimed was a "victim" of abuse.

The pressure shot up in Hawk's veins; his temples pounded.

You will deal with her, he told himself. *As soon as you wrap up this damned business.*

"Now that we have some of the gang, Wilkes and the others won't get far." Sterling paused. "I am curious how you discovered the villain's identity and his foxhole."

"The credit goes to Hawksmoor," Trent said. "My interviews at Newgate yielded nothing, even though I suspected a few of the prisoners knew Wilkes but were keeping mum in support of the Sherwood Band's purported cause. Hawksmoor suggested looking up the register of guards to see if there were others we could talk to —men no longer at their posts but who might know of Wilkes. We started going down the list of former prison keepers; the second fellow we spoke to, Alvin Camden, recalled a prisoner who fit the description of Martin Wheatley. Camden told us the prisoner's name was Michael Wilkes.

"According to Camden, Wilkes was a baker convicted for stealing from his employer, although he, like every other inmate, professed his innocence. The difference was that people believed Wilkes. Camden described him as charismatic and manipulative, popular with the other prisoners and guards alike. Wilkes was swarmed by visitors, especially females. Some of Camden's own colleagues vouched for Wilkes's 'good character,' allowing for his early release over a year ago."

"Well done," Sterling said. "How did you track Wilkes down to the Lyon's Den?"

"I went through the Newgate visitor's logs," Hawk said curtly. "Mrs. Lyon, owner of the Lyon's Den, paid frequent visits to Wilkes. The pub seemed like a prime location for Wilkes to hide and carry out his operations. When we searched the vicinity and found the stables and the carriage, which had bloodstains on the interior, we knew we just had to wait for Wilkes to show himself."

"How did Wilkes manage to escape the trap we laid?" Swinburne's brows formed a foreboding line. "And what in God's name is your wife doing here, Hawksmoor?"

Frustrated rage rattled at Hawk's cage of control. Despite Fiona's foolish and reckless actions, he had to protect her. If her addlepated plan to help Wilkes's accomplice came to light...Hawk clenched his jaw. He could not let Fiona bear the consequences of her behavior.

"She followed me, sir." He hated lying—hated that he was sacrificing his honor to cover up his wife's perfidy. "Apparently, she has suspected for some time that I've been up to something and trailed me here. My surprise at seeing her compromised my ability to capture Wilkes. I bear the responsibility for his escape."

"I see." Frowning, Swinburne said, "In the future, my lord, you will have to keep a firm rein on your lady. She cannot be allowed to run amok. You did say that she can be trusted?"

That was before I knew the bloody secrets she was keeping from me.

Gut twisting, Hawk realized that he probably didn't know the half of what Fiona was up to. How often had she risked her neck as part of her damned society? What shady places had she been, what dodgy people had she consorted with?

How close have I come to losing her without even knowing it?

A vise clamping around his temples, he gritted out, "I will make sure of it, sir."

Swinburne gave him a meaningful look. "See that you do."

Sterling cleared his throat. "Now, I've never been married, but I do have a cat. She doesn't listen to me either."

"My wife will do as I say," Hawk snarled.

From now on, I will monitor Fiona. I will protect her—from her own damned self.

"Easy there, guv," Trent murmured.

"I was jesting. Didn't mean anything by it," Sterling said hurriedly.

The inspector's apologetic expression made Hawk feel like even more of a fool. More out of control. He tried to call upon his numbness, to shield the parts of himself that felt like raw nerve endings.

"It's late," Swinburne cut in. "We all need rest. Let's reconvene in the morning to plan Wilkes's capture."

Hawk's stoic expression, the icy detachment in his eyes when he entered the carriage, spiked fear in Fiona's chest. He positioned himself across from her. It was as if the weeks of passion and intimacy had never happened, and he'd reverted to being a judgmental stranger. The clip-clop of the horses counted out the seconds. As her apprehension surged, so did her defiance.

Taking a breath, Fi plunged in. "I told you from the start that I had my own interests."

A muscle leapt in Hawk's jaw. "You led me to believe that you were part of a bloody charity. You and your friends put on quite a show at Lady Fayne's. Did you enjoy having fun at my expense?"

"We weren't making fun of you," she protested. "The reason I couldn't tell you the truth was because I feared you would react the way you are reacting now."

"How am I supposed to react when my wife suddenly tells me she and her friends have a harebrained notion that they are investigators?" His voice vibrated with barely repressed anger. "When she nearly gets shot because of her foolish and reckless behavior?"

"I had everything in hand until you distracted me." She straightened her shoulders. "And if I've been assigned the role of the pot, then you are clearly the kettle. I fail to recall you informing me of your clandestine activities."

Discovering that Hawk was a spy had been shocking. Yet it also made sense and explained his presence in von Essen's study that night. Knowing the adventurous, hot-blooded man beneath Hawk's staid surface, she could see why the work appealed to him. Why he would be good at it.

"This is not about me. This is about you," he said coldly.

"That is dashed unfair!"

"Do not talk to me about *fair*. To save your reputation and your neck, I had to lie to the police and my colleagues about your interference this eve. You botched a months-long operation and helped criminals to escape."

His voice rose to a bellow. She supposed she preferred his rage served hot rather than cold. And the truth was, she could understand his anger. She'd heard the police talking before Hawk had banished her to the carriage; putting two and two together, she'd come to the shocking conclusion that Lillian had gotten herself mixed up with the Sherwood Band.

"While Wilkes is a criminal, Lillian O'Malley is not." Fi tried to appeal to Hawk's sense of logic. "She is a victim of his manipulation and abuse. When I spoke to her, it was clear that she not only repented the wrongs she'd committed, but she was terrified of Wilkes. Of what he might do to her and her mother. That is why she is staying with him."

"Miss O'Malley is an active participant in the Sherwood Band. She was there when Lady Auberville was murdered," Hawk clipped out. "When she is apprehended—and I will see to it that she is—she will spend the rest of her life in prison."

Fi stared at him in dismay. "You cannot mean that."

"By now, you must know I do not say things I don't mean."

"I will not let you do that to Lillian."

Fury flashed in Hawk's eyes. "You have no say in this. Tomorrow, I will be informing Lady Fayne that you are no longer a part of her society. If she continues to encourage your unacceptable behavior, I will expose her and her supposed charity."

Fi's jaw slackened. "You *wouldn't*."

"Your investigating days are over," he stated.

Rage overwhelmed despair.

"You do not get to tell me what to do," she said in a trembling voice. "We had an agreement. You promised to respect me and my autonomy."

"Our agreement did not include you courting death and danger at every turn," he roared back. "If you had a bloody ounce of sense, you would see the madness of your actions. Clearly, you do not. Therefore, as your husband, it is my duty to protect you—from your goddamned self."

"I am an *adult*. I am fully capable of making my own decisions!"

"Your behavior indicates otherwise."

A slap would have hurt less. Her greatest fear about marriage was unfolding, and she felt powerless to stop it. Powerless to make her husband understand that when he rejected her independence, he was rejecting the very heart of her.

"If you loved me, you would understand." She hated the pleading in her voice. "Don't do this, Hawk. Don't destroy our love just because you are afraid. Of losing me...the way you did Caroline."

Raw anguish scored his features. "You know nothing about that."

"Caroline's death caused you great pain; it is only natural that you would fear history repeating itself. But the situations are different—"

"Caroline overdosed on laudanum."

It took a moment for his words to sink in.

"I-I'm sorry," she stammered. "I didn't realize her death was an accident—"

"It wasn't. She took the entire bottle on purpose. Because the burden of her illness—her melancholia—had become too great," he said tonelessly. "At least, that was what she said in her note."

Fi's throat clogged; she didn't know what to say.

"In that same note, she apologized for failing me—failing our marriage. And her last request was that I protect her honor by not revealing the true cause of her death."

Understanding percolated through Fiona, leaving her chilled.

"I am breaking my vow to Caroline," he continued in that same detached voice, "because I need you to understand something. Caroline's illness robbed her of everything. She fought it the best she could and lost. In the end, her illness forced that bottle to her lips, poured the poison down her throat, and took her life. I failed to help her. But I will not fail you.

"Unlike Caroline, you, Fiona, have a choice." Hawk's blade-sharp gaze pierced her to the quick. "You can make the decision to act like the lady and countess you are. You can give up this selfish and asinine notion of being an investigator."

In her husband's expression, Fi saw unyielding fury and scorn. His rejection hurt more than anything because he was the one man to whom she'd exposed her innermost desires. The one man she'd trusted with her heart. The heart that he now judged as wanting.

You should have known better than to trust love. The familiar agony wrapped like thorny vines around her heart. *To believe that anyone could understand and accept you for who you are. Now what are you left with?*

Pride lifted her chin. "What is my other option?"

"You can defy me and continue to pursue this death wish of yours. If that is your decision, then I will wash my hands of you." His eyes were grim and resolute. "You will have the marriage you initially proposed: one in which I do not give a damn about you or what you do."

THIRTY-SIX

Fiona woke up in a groggy, despondent state. Arriving home last night, she and Hawk had retreated to their separate bedchambers. She'd managed to dismiss Brigitte before climbing into bed and succumbing to tears. She hated crying, not only because it wreaked havoc on one's eyes, but because it made her feel out of control.

Yet she couldn't stop the momentum of her sorrow. She'd wept over the unfairness of Hawk's ultimatum, of being forced to choose between her independence and her heart. She'd wept for their passion and intimacy and broken promises. Mostly, she'd wept for herself: she'd exposed her true self to the man she loved... and he had rejected her.

Papa was right, she thought morosely. *I am a handful. Too much trouble for anyone to love.*

As a woman used to knowing her mind, Fi found herself at a crossroads. Lillian needed her help, and she couldn't give up the Angels—didn't want to. Yet she also didn't want to lose the man she loved. Last night, she'd been furious at Hawk, hurt by his callous disregard of the things that mattered to her and defined who she was. It was especially galling since his own work as a spy should have made him more understanding of her situation.

This morning, however, she found herself mulling over their argument, in particular his revelation about Caroline. Her own pain subsided a little as she contemplated his: the burden he'd been carrying all these years. He'd taken care of his wife and protected her with fierce loyalty. He'd cut himself off from family and friends and kept that awful secret to himself all these years.

I failed to help her. But I will not fail you.

While Hawk did not blame Caroline for the illness that had wreaked havoc upon their lives, he clearly held himself responsible. It was just like him to be protective of others while denying his own needs. Fi ached for his suffering; more of her anger drained away, clearing her head. While she did not know the solution to her marital problems, she did know one thing: she and Hawk needed to talk.

With renewed resolve, she went to check her reflection...and winced at the sight of her swollen eyes. Heavens, she could not have the most important conversation of her life looking like *this*. She rang for Brigitte, who arrived promptly.

She pointed at her puffy face. "I have an emergency."

"Not to worry, my lady." Brigitte held up her tray, which contained a cup of ice with silver spoons and a dish of sliced cucumbers. "I'll fix you up in no time."

Apparently, Fi's emotional state last evening had not escaped her maid's notice.

"You're a treasure," Fi said gratefully. "Have you seen my husband?"

"My lord left early this morning."

"Oh." Hawk's abandonment punctured Fi's optimism.

Brigitte cleared her throat. "He, ahem, requested that you stay home today."

Fi drew her brows together. "Requested or decreed?"

"He said to tell you that if you left the house, he would know your decision."

Hawk's high-handedness vexed Fi. If she stayed home, she would be kowtowing to him. If she left, she might do irreparable harm to her marriage.

Her will battled with her heart. *What should I do?*

By the time Fi finished getting ready, she still hadn't come to a decision. Luckily, the Angels arrived, trooping into her bedchamber.

"We thought you could use company," Livy said.

"And cake." Glory held up a large box. "We brought a selection of Gunter's best."

"Nothing like cake for breakfast to drown one's sorrows," Pippa added.

"I'm so glad you came," Fi blurted. "I don't know what to do!"

Between forkfuls of vanilla sponge, raspberry jam, and chocolate ganache, Fi confided what had happened between her and Hawk. She told her friends everything, except the specifics of Caroline's illness, which wasn't her secret to share.

"If you were me, what would you do?" she concluded. "Leave or stay home today?"

"Stay," Pippa said.

"Leave," Glory said simultaneously.

Fi looked at Livy. "What do you think?"

"I think you should do what feels right to you," Livy replied. "What do your instincts say?"

As Fi tried to listen to her intuition, Hawk's voice surfaced instead.

I know that what makes you truly beautiful isn't on the outside. It is your boldness and strength and even your willful streak. The way you aren't afraid to carve your own path... It is even your insecurities, the way you have no idea how extraordinary you are.

She blinked. How could she have forgotten? Hawk *had* seen who she was...and loved her for it. For most of her life, she'd fought to prove her worth. But Hawk had made her realize that she didn't have to fight. His love had made her feel accepted and special.

The dreadful ultimatum he'd given her had been the product of fear. He'd lost Caroline due to brutal circumstances beyond his control; with aching remorse, Fi realized that she must have triggered those same feelings of powerlessness with her behavior which, admittedly, did involve danger and risk. Hawk's concern was not unfounded. And while *she* knew she was a well-trained investigator who could handle anything, he would not have that same confidence in her abilities...because she'd never been fully honest with him. She had been too afraid of his rejection to tell him the truth.

How can I expect him to accept me when I've been hiding from him?

"I have to find Hawk," she said with sudden clarity. "I won't give up the Angels, but I cannot sneak around any longer. I have to be honest with my husband, tell him everything, and explain things from my point of view."

"What if he doesn't understand?" Glory asked.

"We'll come to a compromise, if necessary," Fi said.

She realized now that her heart and will did not have to fight one another because they were aligned. They wanted the same thing: Hawk.

Livy's smile was knowing. "Your husband will come around."

Fi would do everything in her power to make that happen. To fix her marriage and win back her husband's love.

"I know what I need to do," she said determinedly. "Now, what are the plans for finding Lillian?"

"Because of the urgent situation, Charlie has enlisted Cull's assistance," Pippa said. "The mudlarks are helping us look for Lillian and Wilkes. For Lillian's safety, we need to get to her before the police do."

"Once we locate the pair, we will extract Lillian for her safety," Livy declared. "Then we'll leave Wilkes to the police."

"Separating Lillian from Wilkes may be more difficult than you think." Fi chewed on her lip. "She is afraid of him. Of what he might do to her and her mama."

"Charlie sent word to Mrs. O'Malley, alerting her to the situation," Glory said. "She is asking Mrs. O'Malley to stay put in Yorkshire until the business is concluded. Charlie thinks Wilkes is full of hot air, but better safe than sorry."

"We'll be aiding in the search as well," Pippa added. "We're organizing our shifts from Charlie's."

"I'll join you there," Fi promised. "As soon as I've spoken with Hawk."

After her friends left, Fi took out her trollop's earrings and put them on—a reminder that she was no longer going to hide anything from Hawk. Then she tackled the task of finding her husband. She had no idea where he might be. Marriages of convenience turned out to be highly inconvenient when one needed to track down one's spouse. She wasn't an investigator for nothing, however.

She began by questioning Weatherby and Livingston. All they could tell her was that Hawk had left before eight o'clock this morning and hadn't said when he would return. The groom and carriage were still out, so no help there. Desperate times called for desperate measures. Fiona entered Hawk's study to search for clues.

His woodsy scent lingered in his private domain, stirring her longing. Going to his cluttered desk, she sifted through the rubble with wifely exasperation and located his appointment book. He had nothing scheduled for today; then again, no spy worth his salt would record his covert missions. She contemplated contacting Sir Charles Swinburne, whom she recognized from Society affairs and had seen Hawk conferring with last night. She'd also observed policemen taking Wilkes's gang into custody. Might Hawk be questioning Wilkes's accomplices right now? Would he be at Scotland Yard?

As if on cue, Weatherby came in to tell her that a policeman had arrived.

Fiona hurried to the drawing room. She was greeted by a lanky, sandy-haired man whose clothes looked as if he'd slept in them. She recalled seeing him with Hawk last eve.

"My lady." The fellow bowed. "I am Inspector Sterling. We have not been introduced, but I am an associate of Lord Hawksmoor."

At the other's grim expression, Fi's heart knocked against her ribs. "Has...has something happened to my husband?"

"I'm afraid so, my lady," Sterling said in somber tones. "We tracked down the Sherwood villains, and in the ensuing battle, his lordship was injured."

Seized by terror, Fi could barely get the words past the cinched ring of her throat.

"H-how badly is he hurt?"

"The wound is quite serious. I was told to bring you to him as quickly as possible."

Fi felt the ground crack and crumble beneath her feet. In the tumult, she clung to one certainty: her and Hawk's love could overcome anything...if they had the chance to make things right.

"Ma'am?" Sterling said. "Are you ready to go?"

"Yes." She willed her composure into place. "Please take me to my husband."

THIRTY-SEVEN

"You're certain we're not wasting our time?" Trent grumbled as he sifted through rolls of parchment. "Maybe we'd be better off searching for Wilkes."

"The police are combing the city for him. We're of more use here." Hawk rifled through a ledger. "We found Wilkes last time by learning more about him. And that is what we are doing now."

Hawk and the other members of the Quorum had been at the Old Bailey since early this morning. Swinburne had gained them access to the records room. Seated at a table piled with boxes, they were combing through court proceedings, looking for documentation on Wilkes's case.

The work was a welcome distraction. Nearly losing Fiona haunted Hawk. He hadn't slept; he kept reliving the moment Wilkes had pointed a gun at her. That instant of gut-shredding terror. Fiona was everything to Hawk. If he lost her...he couldn't even contemplate it.

He knew he'd let his anger and fear get the best of him; he'd managed Fiona with the delicacy of a sledgehammer. He told himself that once he had Wilkes behind bars, he would find some way to make amends. Find a way to negotiate her need for independence with his need to protect her. He wouldn't fail Fiona—would do everything in his power to make their marriage work.

If Fiona still loves you enough to try, his inner voice said starkly.

"I agree with Trent." Devlin sounded exasperated. "Going through paperwork like a damned clerk is Hawksmoor's idea of a good time, not mine."

Devlin's tone lacked bite, and he did not appear like his usual debonair self. Last night, he'd fought heroically to capture two of Wilkes's men and had an ugly shiner and cut on his cheek to show for it. He also appeared to be limping.

Hawk felt a prick of guilt. On his list of possible moles, Devlin had occupied the top spot.

"My idea of a good time is wrapping up this mission. Which we're close to, thanks to everyone's efforts." Hawk paused. "Including yours, Devlin."

Devlin blinked. "Was that a compliment?"

"I am giving credit where it is due. You took down two of the Sherwood bastards." Hawk shrugged. "That was no small feat."

Devlin gave him a strange look. Almost one of...guilt.

"Hawksmoor." Devlin took a breath. "I have something—*oof.*"

He lurched forward; Pearson had come up behind him, giving him a friendly slap between the shoulder blades.

"Too bad you had to sacrifice your pretty face for it," Pearson chortled.

"Watch it, you brute," Devlin snapped, straightening his lapels.

Grinning, Pearson returned to perusing papers. "Now 'ow do you spell 'Wilkes' again?"

Devlin groaned. "We're going to be here forever."

"Actually, I think I've found something." Trent stabbed his finger at the parchment in front of him. "It's the record of the proceedings against Wilkes."

Hawk strode over, reading aloud over Trent's shoulder.

"On this day of our Lord the 17th of March, 1847, Mr. Michael Anthony Wilkes stands accused of fraud by Mr. Robert

Dolan, owner of Dolan's Bakeshop on Roupell Street. Mr. Wilkes is an employee at the bakeshop. According to Mr. Dolan, Wilkes convinced Mr. Dolan's wife, Betty Dolan, to give him the Dolans' life savings, which he promised to invest in a shipping scheme. According to the plaintiff, the accused made no such investment, instead keeping the money for himself.

"Witnesses present today include bakery employee Herbert Smith, scullery maid Mary Lipton, arresting constable..."

Hawk's blood turned to ice as Trent swore.

Devlin cocked his head. "What is it?"

"Sterling," Hawk said grimly. "He was the one who arrested Wilkes."

"Why didn't he mention it?" Pearson looked confused.

"I'll give you three guesses," Devlin said.

Hawk headed for the door, the others at his heels.

THIRTY-EIGHT

"Wake up, Fiona. Please don't die."

Fi felt herself being shaken. She blinked, disoriented by the blurry face in front of her. As her vision adjusted, the face settled into familiar lines.

"Lillian?" Her voice scratched her throat.

"Yes. Here, have some water."

Lillian held a cup to Fi's lips, and she drank greedily. When she tried to move, however, she realized with a shock that her hands were manacled and chained to the wall. Everything returned to her. Sterling's sneak attack in the carriage, the chloroform-soaked handkerchief he'd used to smother her and render her unconscious.

"Are you all right?" Lillian asked anxiously.

"I'm fine." Fi took a deep breath, her wooziness fading. "How long have I been here?"

"A few hours. It's dusk now. I'm so sorry."

Remorse creased Lillian's brow. Fi felt anger spark at the fresh bruise on the other's cheek—Wilkes's nefarious handiwork, no doubt. Even with the injury, an untidy topknot, and ragged clothes, Lillian's ethereal beauty shone through.

"Sterling kept you sedated," Lillian said in a low voice. "I begged him not to, but he said you would be trouble otherwise."

He doesn't know the half of it, Fi thought darkly.

The blackguard had tricked her. Used her love for Hawk to bait the trap. And he was going to *pay.* Rage cleared her head. She assessed her surroundings: the room was Spartan, cold. It was unnaturally quiet, removed from the usual sounds of London. Listening intently, she thought she heard flowing water... *The Thames?*

"Where are we?" she asked.

"In an abandoned flour mill in Battersea."

That explained the sounds of water. Mills had cropped up along the south bank of the Thames, harnessing the power of water to run the machinery.

How long will it take for Hawk and the Angels to find me here?

Fiona had no doubt that her husband and friends were out searching for her; she had the utmost confidence in their abilities. She did not, however, trust Sterling. The devious bounder had obviously kidnapped her to use as a bargaining chip...which meant he knew that the jig was up.

He was cornered; desperate men were dangerous men.

I will not allow Sterling to use me, she thought with fierce resolve.

Fi looked at Lillian. "Where are Sterling and Wilkes now?"

"They left to arrange passage to France, but they won't be gone long." Lillian bit her trembling lip. "This is my fault. You're in danger because of me—"

"Listen to me carefully. We haven't time to waste," Fi said firmly. "I know what happened. How Wilkes caught you in his snare, enticing you with love, then keeping you trapped with shame and fear."

Lillian's eyes filled.

"None of it matters," Fi stated. "The only thing we care about now is escaping. Getting to safety. Do you understand?"

"I cannot leave." Lillian hung her head. "After what I've done..."

"You've made some bad choices. Choices for which you will have to face consequences. But you never intended to hurt anyone, did you?"

Lillian shook her head vehemently. "At first, I thought I was doing something noble. Joining a worthwhile cause. Michael said that we were like Robin Hood and his merry band, taking money from the rich who didn't need it to feed the poor. To give working-class folk a chance to survive. He has a way of...of convincing people. Of making them believe what he wants to. I thought I was in love with him and did what he asked.

"But I started to notice that he wasn't giving away all the money we stole. When I confronted him, he said it was to cover our expenses, but I suspected the truth. Knew it for certain when I overheard him talking to that policeman Sterling about splitting the profits between the two of them. Turns out, Sterling was the true mastermind behind the plan. He said he was tired of working for a policeman's pay and got the idea for the Sherwood Band after witnessing the popularity of the Chartists. Only he wasn't trying to improve the conditions of the working class; he was using the desperation of good, ordinary folk for his own gain. I should have left then—should have done something. But I was a coward."

"You are no coward," Fiona insisted.

Lillian's voice had a remote quality to it. "By then, Michael had started...hurting me. And he threatened to harm Mama. One day, he gave me her address in Yorkshire, told me the times of day when she was alone. He s-said that he could have her k-killed if he wanted to. He is powerful. He has friends everywhere..."

"His power is based only in fear. That is how he is controlling you," Fi said. "We've alerted Mrs. O'Malley to the danger. She is safe. She knows about Wilkes, about everything that has happened. All she wants is for you to come home."

"Mama is safe?" Lillian whispered.

"Yes. And I know that beneath your fear, there is so much strength inside you." Fi appealed to the girl whose spirit felt like a twin to her own. "I've read your letters to your mama. I know you are strong—strong and bold enough to go after your dreams. Even if you haven't achieved those dreams yet, you had the courage to try. That courage is what you need to call upon now. To get us both free and back to the people we love."

Lillian drew a shuddering breath. "Tell me what to do."

Fiona held out her manacled hands. "First, you need to free me."

From the deck of the lighter, Hawk surveyed the old mill through a telescope. Against the dusk-splattered sky, the three-story brick building stood like Gothic ruins. Sections were crumbling, smashed windows resembling a line of broken teeth. Hawk fought the panic that threatened to consume him as he thought of Fiona being held hostage inside.

Knowing that Hawk was about to uncover his nefarious deeds, Sterling had struck first. He'd kidnapped Fiona and sent a note: call off the search for him and the Sherwood Band, or Fiona's dead body would be deposited on Hawk's doorstep. Sterling claimed that he would know if the police continued to hunt him. Fiona would be returned to Hawk after, and only after, Sterling and his gang made their escape.

Now Fiona's life hung in the balance. Hawk clenched the telescope, the metal crumpling in his grip. With force of will, he summoned the cool head he would need to get his wife back. He exhaled, turning to the others. The Angels, their husbands, Lady Fayne, Hawker, and Mrs. Peabody had accompanied him on the rescue mission. The members of the Quorum were arriving on another boat. Given the situation, the two organizations had traded notes and agreed to work together. They had left the police out of it, couldn't risk their plan being exposed if Sterling had accomplices on the force.

"You are certain they are in there?" Hawk said tersely.

"My larks sighted Wilkes headed south over the river," Cullen said. "They lost him in Battersea. But when you told me about the handkerchief, I knew where they had to be."

Swinburne's chemist colleague had run a series of tests on the handkerchief Hawk had found. The scientist had ruled out several kinds of poisons to arrive at a surprisingly mundane conclusion: the white powder was milled wheat. Flour.

"The larks found fresh tracks around the mill," Cullen went on. "The place has been abandoned for years, which makes it the perfect hiding place."

"And Wilkes, as a baker, would know about the mill," Lady Olivia said.

"That also explains Wilkes's persistent cough," Lady Glory put in. "According to Master Chen, who has had patients with baker's lung, the cough can improve if the afflicted person stays away from flour, but it is often triggered by the slightest exposure."

"And there's plenty of flour dust in that old mill." Cullen's scarred face was somber. "Which means we cannot go in there with our guns blazing. Watch where you shoot, and don't miss. Flour is highly flammable. We do not want a repeat of what happened at the Albion Mills or, God forbid, on Pudding Lane."

In both instances, flour had fueled the massive conflagrations.

"What is the layout of the building?" This came from Lady Fayne.

Like the Angels, she was outfitted for the mission in a dark ensemble that included trousers. Her hair was hidden beneath a cap, her gaze calm and steady. Hawk felt a surge of resentment: the woman had filled Fiona's head with dangerous ideas about being an investigator. She bore some responsibility for the peril that his wife now faced.

As if catching wind of his thoughts, the lady raised her brows slightly.

"The larks scouted two exits at the north and south ends of the building," Cullen was saying. "Between our group and Hawksmoor's colleagues, we have those covered. We'll also have to cut off a third escape route: a waterway that was used for transporting flour runs beneath the building. We'll have to post boats where that waterway connects to the Thames. Hawksmoor, what is your best estimate of Sterling and Wilkes's forces?"

"At the fight last night, my group counted thirteen enemies in the fray," Hawk replied. "We have four in custody. Which leaves at least nine, plus any other cutthroats Sterling may have on retainer. With the Quorum, we should be an even match. We'll split into teams and go in when it's dark."

For some reason, Cullen shot a look at his wife.

"See, sunshine?" he muttered. "It is as I said. We have more hands than we need. In your condition—"

"I am going." Pippa wore a determined expression that Hawk was all too familiar with. "*Sisters first.* I am not abandoning Fiona in her time of need."

As Cullen pulled his wife into the cabin to continue their discussion in private, Hawk went to the railing, raising the telescope again. Was that a flicker of light in one of the windows or a mere reflection? His chest knotted; he wished it was dark and time to go in. Waiting, knowing that Fiona was inside, was driving him mad.

"She will be all right." Lady Fayne came to stand beside him.

"No thanks to you and your damned society," he muttered.

"On the contrary, it is because of the Society of Angels that Fiona has the skills to take care of herself," Lady Fayne said coolly. "Let us not forget that Sterling kidnapped her to get to *you,* my lord. Because of your work with *your* organization."

Hawk clenched his jaw, unable to argue because her logic was sound. He *was* responsible for Fiona's plight. He'd failed the woman he loved...again. Only this time the pain ran deeper. Straight into his soul, which he would trade for another moment with his beloved.

"At first, I was not certain you were a good choice for a spirited young woman like Fiona," Lady Fayne said conversationally.

You were right. Gritting his teeth, Hawk said nothing.

"But there is more to you than meets the eye. I understand now what Fiona sees in you. Once we have her back, I do believe the two of you can have a successful match. If you remember something important, my lord."

"And what is that?" Hawk asked broodingly.

"You must allow Fiona to make her own choices. Determining her destiny is her right, not yours. The only way you can fail her is by failing to love the woman she truly is." Lady Fayne arched her brows. "And I think deep inside you do know what Fiona is capable of."

"I know she's capable. Clever and bold as well. But when all is told, she is still a *lady*, not a bloody agent," he growled.

"It would take a skilled agent to pull the wool over your eyes, I'm certain." Lady Fayne tilted her head. "The lady would have to be able to masquerade as a light-skirt, break into a count's study to retrieve stolen goods, and make a daring escape from a balcony. All without giving away the fact that she is London's most celebrated debutante."

The realization struck Hawk like a thunderclap; the sudden clarity left him stunned. The light-skirt...*his wife.* Why hadn't he bloody seen it? Two women who represented his deepest fantasies, who affected him like no one else had because...because they were one and the same.

"Devil take it." Even though he knew the answer, he had to ask, "That was Fiona?"

Lady Fayne merely smiled and walked away.

Gripping the railing, Hawk stared into the dark, churning waves.

THIRTY-NINE

"You almost have it," Fi said encouragingly. "Use the bottom hairpin as a lever and wriggle the upper one. Listen for the click."

Lillian was bent over the manacles that bound Fi's hands. Following Fi's instructions, she was using a pair of Fi's hairpins to pick the lock. As Lillian worked, Fi kept her senses on alert for the arrival of guards. According to Lillian, Wilkes and Sterling hadn't bothered posting men outside Fi's door, presuming that a lady would not attempt to escape.

Click. Fi felt the manacles loosen.

"I did it." Lillian blinked as if she couldn't believe it.

"So you did." Beaming at her, Fi set the heavy bonds aside and rubbed her wrists. "Now to get out of here. Do you have any weapons?"

Lillian shook her head.

"No matter. Our best weapon is stealth." Fi headed to the door. "Where are the exits?"

"There are two, at the north and south ends of the mill. We're closest to the north exit. There is also a waterway beneath the building, but that is heavily guarded and where Wilkes and Sterling will be returning."

"Let's go to the north exit," Fi decided. "You'll have to take the lead."

Lillian drew back her shoulders. "I'll do my best."

Opening the door, Lillian peered out, gesturing for Fi to follow. The corridor was dark and narrow, lit by the occasional lantern. They passed what looked like former offices, Fi wincing whenever a floorboard creaked beneath their steps. Vermin scurried in the shadows.

"The exit is just around the corner," Lillian whispered.

Fi took the lead, crouching and sneaking a peek around the wall. The corridor opened into the milling area, which contained a half-dozen millstones used for grinding wheat. The apparatus stood some five feet tall and would provide some cover. Two armed men patrolled the open entryway, which framed the moonlit river just beyond. Fi spied a dock with two bobbing rowboats.

"I can get us past the guards," Fi murmured. "But I need you to distract them, so they don't see me coming. Once we're outside, we'll make a run for the boats."

Lillian gave a nervous nod. Smoothing her skirts, she visibly composed herself before rounding the corner and approaching the guards. She greeted the men, her manner disarming; Fi had to admire the other's acting skills. As Lillian managed to make the men laugh, Fi dashed to one of the millstones, taking cover behind it. To her delight, she found a shovel propped up against the equipment. She grabbed the makeshift weapon, moving stealthily between the millstones until she was mere yards from the guards.

Fi sized them up: large and muscular, pistols in their belts. She would need the element of surprise to best them. Seeing that they were both preoccupied with Lillian, she sprung her attack. She ran toward the nearest brute, whose back was turned to her. Before his partner could shout out a warning, she swung the shovel, hitting him in the head. He groaned, crumpling to the ground.

"You're going to pay for that, bitch," the other guard snarled.

He came at her. Fi swung the shovel again; he dodged. The weight of the shovel threw her off-balance. Before she could regain her momentum, he barreled toward her, yanking the shovel from her grip, throwing it aside with a loud clang. He tackled her to the ground, pinning her beneath his weight.

"Hoity-toity slut like you needs a lesson." Leering, he shoved up her skirts, groping her thigh. "I've never swived a countess before. Think I'll 'ave me some fun—"

Fi drew up her knee, hard. He bellowed, his face contorting in agony; his grip on her loosened. They tussled, but she gained the top position. Grabbing him by the shoulders, she slammed his head against the ground. Repeatedly, until he moaned and went limp. She patted him down for weapons, shoving his dagger into the pocket of her skirts and seizing his pistol. She went to Lillian, who'd remained frozen in place, her eyes wide.

Fi grabbed her hand. "Let's go."

"I'm afraid you're not going anywhere, my lady," Sterling said.

Fiona backed away, pushing Lillian behind her. Sterling blocked their exit; beside him was Wilkes. The villains had a team of ruffians with them. Dash it, her battle with the guards had made too much noise, alerting the entire gang. There was no way she could take on all of them.

Bluff your way through.

She gripped the pistol, leveling it at Sterling.

"My friends will be here soon," she said calmly. "Cut your losses and let us pass."

"And be deprived of your charming company?" Wilkes drawled. "I think not. You will make a lovely addition to our band, my lady. I've grown tired of Lillian and could use a new friend."

Wilkes's predatory smirk sent a revulsed slither up Fi's spine. Behind her, Lillian let out a sobbed breath. When Wilkes advanced toward them, Fi cocked her pistol.

"Stay back," she commanded.

"Come, darling. You're not going to shoot me," he said confidently.

Would you care to wager on that? Fi's finger trembled on the trigger. Her hesitation wasn't over whether to shoot the bounder but her plan afterward. She counted a dozen men; after she used the pistol, she would have only a single dagger to protect Lillian and herself.

"She's not going to shoot you," a familiar voice said.

Fi's gaze flew beyond the gang of villains.

"Hawk," she breathed.

Her husband stood there, pistol in hand. His gaze seared into hers for a heart-stopping instant before he directed his attention back at Wilkes.

"But I am," he said calmly.

He pulled the trigger.

FORTY

Hawk shot Wilkes in his injured arm. The bastard dropped to his knees, howling with pain.

As chaos erupted, Hawk had only one goal in mind: get to Fiona.

With the Quorum and Angels behind him, Hawk led the charge. He discharged the second chamber of his pistol, taking down one of the brutes. When another came at him with a knife, he dodged, catching the man's weapon arm, twisting it until the blade clattered to the ground. He plowed his fist into his foe's gut; while the other doubled over, he landed a right hook. His enemy slid to the ground, unconscious.

"Look out," Devlin shouted.

Hawk whirled around: a ruffian a few yards away aimed a gun at him. Devlin barreled into him as the shot went off. Hawk staggered back while Devlin cursed. As Pearson grabbed the shooter and began pounding the latter into a fare-thee-well, Hawk turned his attention to Devlin, whose sleeve was torn and soaked with blood.

"Your arm," Hawk said tersely.

"Flesh wound." Devlin gritted his teeth. "Consider it an apology. Go get your lady."

Now was not the time to ask Devlin what he meant. With a gruff nod of thanks, Hawk continued fighting his way to his beloved. Seeing a bearded brute charging toward her, he shoved at the foe he was grappling with.

"Fiona, watch out," he roared.

Her gaze turned to the oncoming danger. A blade appeared in her hand. In a balletic movement, she let the dagger fly. The brute screamed, dropping to his knees, clutching the knife embedded in his shoulder.

Damn and blast. Hawk blinked.

He knocked out his opponent with a jaw-cracking punch. Then he sprinted over to Fiona, who was facing off another attacker. She stomped on the bastard's foot. As he yelped, she brought her knee up so hard that Hawk instinctively winced. Christ, his wife fought dirty. Her feminine ruthlessness cheered him immensely. Not that she needed the help, but he finished the job for her, punching the bastard's lights out.

Then Hawk stared into his countess's beautiful eyes, his heart thundering.

"My love," he said. "Are you all right? Did Sterling hurt—"

"I'm fine, darling," she said tremulously. "I knew you would come for me."

She shifted her gaze behind him. In the next instant, she whipped out a pistol, letting off a shot. Another brute hit the ground.

"Maybe I should have saved myself the trip." Hawk smiled slowly. "You seem to be holding your own."

Wariness entered her gaze. "I told you that I can take care of myself."

"Thank bloody Christ for that," he said with feeling. "I love you, Fiona—all that you are. Now, shall we wrap this business up...together?"

Her eyes sparkled, her dimple peeking out. "That is a brilliant idea."

They scanned the milling room together. Hawk saw that the Angels and the Quorum had everything well in hand. Except...

"Lillian is missing," Fi said alertly. "Wilkes as well."

"And Sterling," Hawk said. "We have the building surrounded, so they couldn't have escaped through the main exits. They're probably headed for the underground waterway."

"We have to save Lillian," Fiona said. "She helped me to escape. Wilkes must have forced her to go with them."

"We'll find them. Ready, love?"

Hawk held out his hand. He frowned when, instead of taking it, his lady dashed off. She bent over a fallen brute, yanking her dagger from his shoulder, wiping it off on the moaning fellow's shirt. Tucking the weapon neatly into her skirts, she pranced back to Hawk, her hair a wild, fiery mass over her shoulders, her eyes shining with passionate resolve.

To Hawk, his Sól had never looked more beautiful.

"Now I'm ready," she said.

Fi and Hawk entered the storage room. Lanterns on the wall sent flickering shadows over the low-ceilinged room, the perimeter heaped with old flour sacks. As she advanced, Fi felt the grit of milled wheat beneath her shoes. At the back of the room was a pair of wooden chutes that led to the underground boats; Sterling and Wilkes were trying to shove Lillian down a chute.

The trio spun around at Fi and Hawk's approach.

With his uninjured arm, Wilkes held a knife to Lillian's throat.

"Let her go," Fi demanded.

"I don't think so."

It was Sterling who spoke. All signs of the genial policeman were gone. His eyes were cruel and pitiless.

He leveled his pistol at Hawk; Hawk mirrored the stance.

"We are making our exit now, and if you try to stop us," Sterling said with deadly calm, "Wilkes will slit Miss O'Malley's throat."

To prove his partner's point, Wilkes pressed his blade against Lillian's neck. She whimpered as a thin red line appeared, a ruby droplet trickling down her neck.

Fi met the other girl's gaze, sending her a silent message. *You are strong, Lillian. Don't let him rule you with fear. He's injured—look for the opportunity to escape.*

Was it her imagination, or did Lillian's eyes widen a fraction?

"You will not get far, Sterling," Hawk stated. "We have the place surrounded. You cannot escape with an injured partner and a hostage."

"No need to concern yourself on my account," Sterling sneered. His gaze on Hawk, he issued an order to Wilkes. "I will go first down this chute. Once I am off, take Lillian down the other chute."

"Right," Wilkes said through clenched teeth.

Fi noticed that Wilkes looked waxen, likely due to the blood dripping down his arm.

He is weakened. Now is the time to strike. To divide and conquer.

"Do you actually believe that Sterling is going to wait for you and Lillian?" Fi addressed Wilkes in conversational tones. "With your arm bleeding and Lillian of no value to him whatsoever?"

"Don't listen to that bitch," Sterling snapped.

"You know she is right, Wilkes." Hawk backed her up with the cool voice of reason. "Sterling was the one who had von Essen killed, wasn't he? Because he couldn't trust your pawn not to give up the operation."

"Wait. You killed von Essen?" Wilkes swung his gaze to his partner, his voice wavering. "I thought you said his death was an accident."

"It *was* an accident," Sterling said shortly. "Cove got hit by a carriage. Happens all the time."

"And if you believe that," Fi said, "I have a bridge to sell you in London."

"*Shut your gob*, you nosy wench."

When Sterling swung his pistol in her direction, Hawk made a low warning sound in his throat, his fist tightening around his own gun. Fi knew he would not hesitate to shoot, and she loved him for it. Loved that primal streak she'd always sensed below his proper surface. When needed, her husband could be ruthless and wicked... her perfect match in every way.

"The only reason for Sterling to shoot me," she said to Wilkes, "is because he's afraid that I am telling the truth. Think about it: why is he choosing to take one boat and directing you to the other? You have a stash of stolen goods that you haven't been able to pawn yet, don't you?" She knew her deduction was correct when Wilkes's gaze narrowed. "Where are those goods now? In your boat...or Sterling's?"

Forehead wrinkling, Wilkes turned to his partner. "Where did you put the jewelry?"

"For God's sake, man," Sterling bit out. "Don't be a fool. She's manipulating you—"

"You insisted on overseeing the goods. *Where are they?*" Wilkes yelled.

In that instant, his focus was entirely on his partner. Fiona looked at Lillian, willing the girl to believe in herself. *You can do this, Lillian. I know you can.*

Lillian grabbed Wilkes's weapon hand. Bit it.

"Bleeding hell!" he exploded.

He dropped his blade, grappling with Lillian.

Taking the opportunity, Hawk sprang at Sterling, tackling the bounder to the ground. He plowed his fist into the policeman's face. Seeing that Hawk had things covered, Fi dashed over to help Lillian...who was more than holding her own. Evading Wilkes's backhand, Lillian seized his injured arm, pressing her fingers into his wound as he screamed.

Dagger in hand, Fi lifted her brows and waited for Lillian to get her due.

"You are never laying hands on me again!" Lillian shouted.

She kicked him in the knee. He fell to the ground, groaning. Lillian went over, kicked him again, and at that moment, Fi saw him grab his dropped knife.

"Watch out, Lillian!" Fi called.

Wilkes grabbed Lillian's leg, yanking her off-balance. Fi gripped her dagger, ready to wade in, yet afraid of hurting Lillian while she wrestled with Wilkes on the ground. The pair rolled, trying to get control of the dagger. They came to a sudden halt with Lillian on top, Wilkes beneath her...Wilkes's eyes widening as he looked down at the knife embedded in his chest.

Fi helped Lillian up. Wilkes remained unmoving, his last expression one of utter disbelief. As if he couldn't fathom that he had been bested...by a woman.

"D-did I...is h-he...?" Lillian's cheeks were blood-splattered, her pupils dilated. As her fury wore off, shock rapidly took its place.

"You defended yourself. Did what you had to." Fi was tracking Hawk, saw that he had dragged Sterling up against the wall and was continuing to work out the rage of betrayal. "Now you must go down this chute. I'll join you once I've helped my husband—"

"If I'm not leaving with my money, then neither are you," Sterling suddenly snarled.

He reached up and grabbed a lantern from its hook on the wall, a crazed look in his eyes.

"*Don't*—" Hawk roared.

Sterling smashed the lantern onto the ground.

Hawk jumped back, a wall of flame springing up where he'd been a heartbeat ago.

Sterling screamed as the fire leapt onto his flour-speckled clothes.

"Go." Fi shoved Lillian toward the closest chute. "The whole place is going to burn!"

With a frightened nod, Lillian climbed into the chute and vanished from sight.

Fi ran to Hawk, pulling him back as he tried to get through the barrier of flame to his shrieking former colleague, now engulfed in flames. She grabbed his jaw with both hands, staring into his storm-filled eyes.

"You can't help him," she said. "We have to get out of here."

Hawk's gaze cleared. He grabbed her hand, and they raced to the chute. The flames chased them, swallowing the floorboards behind their pounding steps. Smoke billowed through the room, stinging Fi's eyes and filling her lungs. Coughing, she stumbled, but Hawk dragged her to the chute. She went first, sliding into darkness. She landed with a thump, the world wobbling; she was on a small boat roped to a dock. At the end of the waterway, she could see a foggy moonlit sky...the Thames.

An instant later, Hawk slid onto the boat, landing beside her. Cupping the back of her neck, he pulled her in for a hard kiss.

"Let's go," he said.

Wordlessly, they worked together. She unanchored the boat; he found the oar. Within moments, they were gliding through the passageway as explosions sounded overhead.

"I hope our friends got out," she said worriedly.

"They did, love," he said with calm assurance.

They made it out from under the building into the openness of the Thames. The fog shifted, revealing a sky studded with stars. Lanterns twinkled on the nearby bank where the Angels were helping Lillian ashore. Hawk's colleagues were there as well.

Fi exhaled with relief. "You were right."

"I usually am." Hawk set down the oar, taking her hands in his own. "Except about you. Can you forgive me, Fiona, for not supporting your dreams? For failing to see who you are? It is no excuse, but you were right—I *was* afraid of losing you, the love of my life that I'd given up hope of finding, and because of that I acted like a fool."

"I am equally at fault," she said tremulously. "When we started falling in love, I should have told you the truth about the Angels. About what I want and who I am. But I was scared of disappointing you, of losing you, and fear prevented me from being honest."

"You have nothing to fear," he said ardently. "I love you, Fiona. Your ambition, passion, and boldness."

"You can truly accept that I am an investigator?" she whispered.

"I am *proud* of you. Of your derring-do and genteel accomplishments and everything that makes you who you are." He cupped her cheek. "My beautiful wife who is my perfect match in every way."

Joy flared inside her.

"You have stolen my heart," she said. "And something else, apparently. Remember this?"

Tossing back her hair, she tapped one of her golden earrings.

Hawk's mouth curved in that slow smile she adored.

"The earring, which you promptly stole back." He raised his brows. "At the Royal Arms?"

She nodded.

"I wondered where it had gone," he said wryly. "On the boat ride over tonight, Lady Fayne told me you were the light-skirt in von Essen's study. But I should have figured it out on my own. After all, you and the trollop are the only two women who have affected my senses in this way."

Fi gave him a saucy look. "And what way is that, *monsieur*?"

"Tell me this first, *madame*. Are you good at keeping secrets?" he asked tenderly.

"Keeping secrets is my job."

He swept her into his arms, pressing her down to the bottom of the boat and out of sight of their friends cheering on the shore.

She gazed up into her husband's eyes, which blazed with love brighter than the stars overhead.

"Then allow me to demonstrate your effect on me, my love," he murmured.

To her everlasting delight, he did.

FORTY-ONE

iona took a short respite with her mama in a secluded alcove. Surveying the packed ballroom, she saw with satisfaction that her first ball as a hostess was a success. Guests *ooh*ed and *aah*ed over the refreshment tables, and footmen were in constant motion, refilling the champagne fountains. She spotted her friends twirling with their husbands to the strains of the Viennese orchestra she'd hired for the occasion. She also saw her brother Max by a row of potted palms. He was being nudged by Henry, Hawk's youngest brother, toward a shy debutante.

"Your ball is a triumph, Fiona." Mama beamed with pride.

"Because of you," Fi said fondly. "You taught me everything I know about being a hostess."

"No, my dear." Mama's tone was gentle yet firm. "You must take credit where it is due. You've refurbished your home beautifully, and you made the arrangements that the guests are raving about."

At Hawk's urging, Fi had confided in her mother about her insecurities. To her surprise, Mama had understood completely, sharing that she, too, had struggled with self-doubts. Fi had been shocked that a lady as sweet and good as her mother could have ever questioned her worth. The heart-to-heart chat had cleared up other things as well, and Fi felt closer than ever to her mother.

Papa joined them, placing an arm around Mama's waist.

"What are the guests raving about, my dear?" he inquired.

Mama smiled up at him. "Our daughter's skills as a hostess, of course."

"You have outdone yourself, Fiona," Papa said. "This affair is a crush."

"Oh, there is Max," Mama blurted. "I need to, um, remind him about something. Please excuse me."

Mama rushed off, leaving Fi alone with her father.

"Your mama has many virtues." Papa's mouth curved. "Subtlety, however, is not one of them."

Fi chuckled. "Artlessness is part of Mama's charm."

"It is. Just as self-possession is one of yours." Papa slid her a look. "Mama told me about the talk you had."

This came as no surprise. Her parents shared everything.

Papa drew his brows together. "If I have given you cause to doubt my regard for you—"

"You haven't, Papa," Fi said earnestly.

Her talk with her mother had helped her to see her misperceptions. While she'd attributed her father's sternness to disapproval, Mama had told her that it stemmed from a different place altogether.

"Papa was stricter with you than Max because that was what you needed," Mama had explained. *"Papa has always loved you, but before his injury, he was too indulgent. To be frank, he spoiled you, dearest. After his recovery, he was determined to be a better father... and he was. He always acted with your best interests in mind."*

In her heart, Fi had always felt her father's love, and the talk with Mama had lifted a weight from her chest. It also allowed her to speak the truth.

"I wanted to apologize, Papa. For being, well, difficult at times," she said in a small voice. "And for not always being honest."

"Regardless, I am proud of you, Fiona," Papa said gravely. "Of the girl you were and the woman you've become. You have, and always will have, my love."

"I love you too." Fi sniffled. "But please, *please* don't make me cry. I don't want my eyes to get puffy and ugly."

"You have your mama's looks; you could never be anything but beautiful." Papa clasped her shoulder. "But you also have my ambition and drive, which means you are capable of doing whatever you set your heart upon. As I've learned, that is both a blessing and a curse. I did not want you to make the same mistakes I did—wanted to make sure you knew what truly matters in life."

His words came back to her.

"The people you love and who love you in return," she said softly.

"Love is the true key to happiness." Papa's eyes glinted. "And you are happy, my dear?"

"Yes," Fi said tremulously. "Very."

"Good. Because that, my dearest girl, is all I have ever wanted for you." He kissed her cheek. "Now, I will leave you in good hands."

Turning, Fi saw that her husband was waiting. Hawk and Papa exchanged polite greetings before the latter went to find Mama for a dance.

"Had a good chat?" Hawk asked.

"The best." Fi sighed happily. "You were right. I should have talked to my parents ages ago."

"I am rather good at giving advice I don't follow."

"Your situation is different." Knowing that he was referring to the secret he kept for Caroline's sake, Fi felt compelled to defend him. "You gave your word, and you are a man of honor. I only hope that you no longer carry the burden of guilt."

"I don't."

The love in Hawk's gaze warmed her to the tips of her dancing slippers.

He brought her hand to his lips. "Because of you."

Over the past three weeks, she and Hawk had shared their deepest selves. It had been scary and wondrous and the opposite of their initial agreement. And they could not be happier.

As for work, Hawk and the Quorum had wrapped up the Sherwood Band matter, and Fiona and the Angels had fulfilled their quest to find Lillian O'Malley. At present, Lillian was in prison. The judge had been lenient in sentencing, based on Sir Swinburne's testimony that Lillian had, herself, been a victim of Wilkes and assisted in his defeat.

Mrs. O'Malley had visited Lillian frequently, as had the Angels.

"Six months will be over before you know it. You will be all right," Fiona had said.

"I already am." While small, Lillian's smile had been real; her bruises had begun to fade. *"I am free of Wilkes. And I have Mama and friends who care about me. After I serve my debt to society, I shall have a chance to start afresh. To show you that your faith in me was not in vain."*

"Show yourself, if you must." Fiona had squeezed Lillian's hand. *"I already know how deserving you are."*

Since closing their cases, Hawk and Fiona had both decided to take a brief hiatus from work. They'd wanted the freedom to enjoy newlywed life...which they had. Rather abundantly. Indeed, beneath her tiered, sky-blue skirts, Fiona could feel the aftermath of her husband's pre-ball passion trickling down her thigh.

It made her feel naughty, excited, and, most of all, loved.

For their bonding hadn't just been physical in nature. They'd spent long, lazy hours talking in bed and taking companionable strolls through the park. Sometimes they said nothing at all, just cuddled while they read. They also spent time with their friends and family, weaving their lives seamlessly together.

Fiona fell more in love with her husband every day. His acceptance melted away her insecurities; for the first time, she felt no pressure to do or prove anything. She didn't have to be the perfect lady, daughter, wife, or even investigator.

All she had to do was be *herself*.

Feeling comfortable in her own skin allowed her to let down her guard and relax. She played, laughed, and enjoyed being alive. Of all the gifts Hawk had given her—and he'd developed a delightful habit of showering her with jewelry—the best one was the knowledge that she wasn't an impostor.

She was Fiona Garrity Morgan, the Countess of Hawksmoor, and she was the genuine article.

Fi aimed a flirty smile at her earl. "Is it terribly rude for me to say that I cannot wait for our guests to leave?"

"Greedy chit." Lines fanned around his warm grey eyes. "You had your way with me before the ball and now you're ready for another round."

"You like that about me," she said confidently.

"I adore everything about you and your insatiability especially. Shall I kick the guests out?"

"Don't tempt me." She leaned closer. "By the by, I saw you talking to Lord Devlin."

Devlin had confessed that he'd been behind Hawk's beating at the Royal Arms. Admitting that he'd acted out of immature spite —out of envy that Hawk was outshining him as a spy, the only role he took any pride in—he had asked for forgiveness. Hawk, being Hawk, had shaken the other's hand. Devlin had resigned from the Quorum and, from the looks of it, was giving up some of his rake-hell ways as well. He looked unusually sober this evening.

"Devlin apologized. Again," Hawk muttered. "As if I would hold anything against a man who took a bullet on my behalf."

"We do owe him," Fi said thoughtfully. "Which is why I promised him a dance."

"We don't owe him that much. And that dance had better not be a waltz."

Fi chuckled. "And you're calling *me* greedy?"

"Speaking of which." Hawk held out his arm as the opening bars of the waltz they'd first danced to floated into the room. "They are playing our song, my lady. Will you do me the honor?"

"You remembered, my lord." Placing her hand on his sleeve, Fi teased, "And you claim you are not a romantic."

"As it turns out, I am a selective romantic." Hawk's smile made her heart flutter. "Exclusively when it comes to you, my love."

EPILOGUE

With practiced stealth, Hawk entered the study.

He locked the door behind him. Through his mask, he took note of the room. By the blazing hearth sat a small table set *à deux*. Upon it, a vase of hothouse roses perfumed the air. There was a cart piled with silver-domed dishes; champagne rested in a bucket of ice, the bottle beaded with condensation.

Signs of a celebration yet to come.

His heart thudding with anticipation, he prowled toward his target. The desk was large, the blotter strangely devoid of clutter. Crouching, he looked beneath it.

"What have we here?" he murmured.

Framed by a golden demi-mask, blue eyes stared playfully back at him.

"Oh, sir! You gave me a fright," the trollop said in a breathy voice.

He helped her up, his throat going dry as he got his first full look at her.

Devil and damn.

The woman dazzled in everything from ballgowns to negligees, but she had managed to outdo herself with the present ensemble. The naughty black satin corset cinched her waist and pushed up her delectable breasts. Her berry-ripe nipples played peek-a-boo through the black lace trim. Below the corset, she wore black silk stockings and garters...and nothing else. The triangle between her thighs was as bright and bold as the tresses flowing over her shoulders.

Beneath his dressing gown, he went instantly hard. Yet this game was too much fun to be rushed.

Firming his voice, he gave her a stern look. "You ought to be frightened. I have caught you in the act of stealing, haven't I?"

"I wasn't stealing, sir." Her eyes widened with feigned innocence. "I was, um, looking for this."

She tapped one of her earrings. Made of real gold and studded with costly gems, the jewelry was inspired by an Ancient Egyptian design. It was fit for a queen...or, in this case, a countess. He planned to surprise her with the matching necklace after he enjoyed her delightful gift.

"Likely story." He played his part. "I have caught you in the act, and you shall face the consequences."

"Please, I beg of you. Don't tell anyone." She sank gracefully to her knees, saying in sultry tones, "I'll do *anything* you say."

Even as she spoke those cock-hardening words, the naughty minx directed her gaze to the bulging front of his dressing gown and wetted her lips.

His pulse racing, he quirked a brow. "Anything?"

He untied his belt. He was naked beneath, his erection jutting out like a lance.

"Anything," she breathed.

"Please me with your mouth then, wench."

"Yes, sir."

His abdominal muscles tautened as she took him in her lady-soft hands, brushing her lips lovingly over his burgeoned crown. She lapped at his dripping desire like it was a delicacy to be savored.

He twined his fingers in her hair, luxuriating in the sensations she bestowed upon him. In the way she teased his slit, running her tongue along his throbbing vein, covering his balls in honeyed kisses. Then she took his cock into her mouth, smoothly, deeply, with a skill that made his breath hiss through his teeth.

Christ, she was good at this. An expert at driving him wild.

"You suck my prick so well, vixen," he growled. "Does it feel good between your lips? Does it make you hungry to have it in another sweet hole?"

Although her reply was muffled by his shaft, the way she squeezed her thighs together conveyed her excitement and made him burn.

"Take me deeper," he ordered.

She surrounded him with her lush kiss. Her glowing eyes enticed him to take more—to enjoy her generous giving. Holding her gaze, he fucked her lovely mouth, losing himself in their connection, wanting it to last forever.

Alas, he was only a man, and she a goddess beyond compare.

"I'm close, love," he gritted out.

Her fingers digging into the rock-hard muscles of his arse, she performed her divine magic and swallowed him whole. Lodged in that special place in her throat, he shouted out as flames consumed him, every cell of his being exploding with bliss. She took all of him, coaxing out every drop of his essence and replenishing him with ecstasy.

Panting, he pulled out. He was still hard. Still hungry for her.

He hoisted her onto the conveniently bare desk with a haste that made her giggle. Unlacing her corset, he tossed it aside and pushed her back against the hard surface. He manacled her wrists above her head and claimed her mouth, his blood rushing at the forbidden flavor. At the proof of how hot they burned for one another. Their tongues danced, stroked, played.

Then he feasted his way down her body. He took his time with her nipples, sucking and nibbling on those pretty buds. By the time he pushed her thighs apart, she was shaking. A kiss away from coming apart. Exactly how he wanted her.

"Ask me for it, my wicked girl," he murmured.

She bit her lip, wanton and sweet. His fantasy come true.

"Please eat my pussy," she whispered.

Bloody hell, yes. He ate her cunny until she forgot the game and chanted his name through her climaxes. Her luscious cream on his lips, he dragged her to her feet, spun her around, and bent her over the desk. He drove into her pussy, and they both groaned at the perfect fit.

"Christ, I'll never get enough of you," he said hoarsely.

"Take me," she gasped. "Please, darling, I need you."

He obliged, gripping her soft hips as he rammed into her. Her moans escalated as he drilled his cock into her hole, harder and harder still. He held nothing back from his beloved, his match in passion and life. He smacked his balls against her sopping cunny, and she pushed back against him, taking him even deeper.

Their loving was too good. It always was.

His stones swelled, his seed climbing. Determined to have his lady go first, he swiped a finger through her lushness, bringing it to her shy pucker. He pushed, feeling her tremor of resistance before her body sucked him in. As she moaned, he pumped his digit and his cock in wild unison, glorying in how fully she accepted him. She cried out, her spasms dragging him over the edge, and with a roar of joy, he fell with her.

His wife's giggle was muffled by the blotter. "Happy anniversary, Thomas."

He nuzzled the curve between her neck and shoulder. "Undoubtedly." Helping her up, he removed their masks and kissed her soundly. "Thank you for the splendid celebration, my love."

She gave him a coquettish look as she pulled on a frilly wrapper. "It was my pleasure."

"I do have a question, however."

"Do not fret, darling." Rolling her eyes, she proved she knew him all too well. "I didn't throw anything away. The papers that were on your desk are now neatly stored in a box in the corner."

His lips twitching, he fastened his dressing gown. "Men don't fret."

"And they don't gossip either." She straightened his lapels in a wifely manner. "How was your day?"

"I worked on a cipher. Almost cracked it. What did you do, sweetheart?"

"I've started on an intriguing new case. I'll tell you about it over supper." Linking her arm through his, she canted her head. "Should we check on the children first?"

"I visited the nursery before I came down. Miracle of miracles, they are all asleep." Hawk led his wife to the table, pulling out a chair for her. "We can relax and enjoy the rest of the evening. Champagne?"

"Yes, please."

Popping the cork, he poured two glasses and sat next to her.

"To my darling light-skirt and wife." He held up his flute, his voice husky with pride and adoration. "The love of my life."

"To my dashing thief and husband." Her eyes outsparkling the champagne, she tapped her glass to his. "Who has shown me the joys of a complicated marriage."

They drank to their toast. Then he pulled her close to steal another kiss.

Author's Note

The writing of every book is, for a me, a personal journey, and this was especially true for *Fiona and the Enigmatic Earl*. While I have never been a debutante with a secret life as an investigator—I only wish!—I am familiar with some of Fiona's insecurities around being "an impostor." As a young graduate student many, *many* years ago, I remember thinking that my peers were brilliant and that I must have been admitted to that select class by accident.

To don my psychologist's hat for a moment, "the Impostor Phenomenon," a term first coined by Clance and Imes (1978)[1], refers to an internal feeling of being an intellectual fraud, even when there is ample external evidence to indicate otherwise. The participants in Clance and Imes's original study were all high-achieving women: women who had earned Ph.D.s, were considered experts in their fields, and/or had been recognized for their academic excellence. Yet they had persistent beliefs that externalized their achievement: somehow their success was an accident or a mistake and that they were not intelligent but simply worked hard. Many had a fear that they would be exposed for being a fraud.

In recent years, much has been written about the Impostor Syndrome, with many famous and accomplished people—men and women—reporting that they have experienced such feelings. The phenomenon may be accompanied by stress, anxiety, and depression. Psychotherapy may offer effective tools to manage this issue.

On a historical note, readers may be curious about Hawk's "computation engine." I modeled it after Swedish inventor Pehr Georg Scheutz's[2] calculation engine, which was a mechanical calculator capable of calculating series with 5-digit numbers and, eventually, third-order differences. The Scheutzian calculation machine was completed in 1843, and an improved model was shown at the World's Fair in Paris in 1855. Scheutz's machine was based on the work of Charles Babbage, an English polymath whose ideas and inventions have led him to be considered "the father of the computer."

1. Clance, P.R., and Imes, S.A. (1978). The impostor phenomenon in high achieving women: Dynamics and Therapeutic interventions. Psychotherapy: Theory Research and Practice, 15, 241-247.
2. Copeland, B. Jack. (18 December 2000). "The Modern History of Computing". *The Modern History of Computing (Stanford Encyclopedia of Philosophy). Stanford Encyclopedia of Philosophy*. Metaphysics Research Lab, Stanford University.

ACKNOWLEDGMENTS

Writing this book took me back to the beginning of my journey, when, for fun and stress relief, I wrote a story called *Her Husband's Harlot*. I was stunned and humbled by the readers who cheered on Helena and Nicholas's unconventional romance, and I continue to feel that way when readers support my stories. This is a round-about way of saying thank you: to all of you who have read my books, told a friend about them, shown your love on social media, wrote me a personal note about how my stories have affected you... you're the reason why I love doing what I do.

Much appreciation also goes out to my editing team: Ronnie, whose insights make my books shine; Alyssa, Faith, and Judy, my proofreaders extraordinaire.

To my Friday backyard writing group and retreat pals: thank you for keeping the creative spirit alive through thick and thin.

To my family: the harder the times, the greater our love.

ABOUT THE AUTHOR

USA Today & International Bestselling Author Grace Callaway writes hot and heart-melting historical romance filled with mystery and adventure. Her debut novel was a Romance Writers of America Golden Heart® Finalist and a #1 National Regency Best-seller, and her subsequent novels have topped national and international bestselling lists. She has won the Daphne du Maurier Award for Excellence in Mystery and Suspense, the Maggie Award for Excellence, the Golden Leaf, and the Passionate Plume Award, and her books have been shortlisted for numerous other honors. She holds a doctorate in clinical psychology from the University of Michigan and lives with her family in a valley by the ocean. When she's not writing, she enjoys dancing, dining in hole-in-the-wall restaurants, and going on adapted adventures with her special son.

Keep up with Grace's latest news!

Newsletter: gracecallaway.com/newsletter

facebook.com/GraceCallawayBooks

bookbub.com/authors/grace-callaway

instagram.com/gracecallawaybooks

amazon.com/author/gracecallaway

Made in the USA
Las Vegas, NV
12 November 2022

59315112R00217